3319 9844

WITHDRAWN

# Whispers
# in the Wind

*Also by Al and JoAnna Lacy
in Large Print:*


The Little Sparrows
All My Tomorrows
A Measure of Grace
So Little Time
A Prince Among Them
Undying Love
Let Freedom Ring
The Secret Place

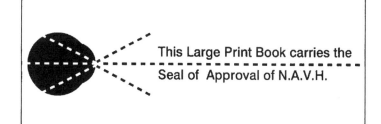

This Large Print Book carries the
Seal of Approval of N.A.V.H.

The Orphan Trains Trilogy
Book Three

# Whispers in the Wind

## Al & JoAnna Lacy

Thorndike Press • Waterville, Maine

Published in 2005 by arrangement with
Multnomah Publishers, Inc.

Thorndike Press® Large Print Christian Historical Fiction.

The tree indicium is a trademark of Thorndike Press.

The text of this Large Print edition is unabridged.
Other aspects of the book may vary from the original edition.

Set in 16 pt. Plantin by Liana M. Walker.

Printed in the United States on permanent paper.

**Library of Congress Cataloging-in-Publication Data**

Lacy, Al.
    Whispers in the wind : the orphan trains trilogy, book three / by Al & JoAnna Lacy.
        p. cm.
    ISBN 0-7862-7981-8 (lg. print : hc : alk. paper)
    1. Homeless children — Fiction.   2. Orphan trains — Fiction.   3. Orphans — Fiction.   4. Large type books.
I. Lacy, JoAnna. II. Title.
PS3562.A256W47 2005
    813′.54—dc22                                        2005016204

This book is dedicated to our dear friend,
neighbor, and faithful fan,
Rosella Halsey.
God bless you, Rosella.
We love you.

2 Timothy 4:22

As the Founder/CEO of NAVH, the only national health agency solely devoted to those who, although not totally blind, have an eye disease which could lead to serious visual impairment, I am pleased to recognize Thorndike Press★ as one of the leading publishers in the large print field.

Founded in 1954 in San Francisco to prepare large print textbooks for partially seeing children, NAVH became the pioneer and standard setting agency in the preparation of large type.

Today, those publishers who meet our standards carry the prestigious "Seal of Approval" indicating high quality large print. We are delighted that Thorndike Press is one of the publishers whose titles meet these standards. We are also pleased to recognize the significant contribution Thorndike Press is making in this important and growing field.

Lorraine H. Marchi, L.H.D.
Founder/CEO
NAVH

★ Thorndike Press encompasses the following imprints: Thorndike, Wheeler, Walker and Large Print Press.

# Prologue

In midnineteenth century New York City, which had grown by leaps and bounds with immigrants from all over Europe coming by the thousands into the city, the streets were filled with destitute, vagrant children. For the most part, they were anywhere from two years of age up to fifteen or sixteen.

The city's politicians termed them "orphans," though a great number had living parents, or at least one living parent. The city's newspapers called them orphans, half-orphans, foundlings, street Arabs, waifs, and street urchins.

Many of these children resorted to begging or stealing while a few found jobs selling newspapers; sweeping stores, restaurants, and sidewalks; and peddling apples, oranges, and flowers on the street corners. Others sold matches and toothpicks. Still others shined shoes. A few rummaged through trash cans for rags, boxes, or refuse paper to sell.

In 1852, New York City's mayor said there were some 30,000 of these orphans on the city's streets. Most of those thousands who wandered the streets were ill-clad, unwashed, and half starved. Some actually died of starvation or froze to death. The orphans slept in boxes and trash bins in the alleys during the winter, and in warm weather, some slept on park benches or on the grass in Central Park.

Some of the children still had both parents, but were merely turned loose by the parents because the family had grown too large and they could not care for all their children. Many of the street waifs were runaways from parental abuse, parental immorality, and parental drunkenness.

In 1848, a young man named Charles Loring Brace, a native of Hartford, Connecticut, and graduate of Yale University, came to New York to study for the ministry at Union Theological Seminary. He was also an author and spent a great deal of time working on his books, which slowed his work at the seminary. He still had not graduated by the spring of 1852 but something else was beginning to occupy his mind. He was horrified both by the hordes of vagrant children he saw on the streets daily, and by the way the civil authorities treated them. The city's solution for years had been to sweep the wayfaring children into jails or run-down almshouses.

Brace believed the children should not be punished for their predicament, but should be given a positive environment in which to live and grow up. In January 1853, after finishing the manuscript for a new book and submitting it to his New York publisher, Brace dropped out of seminary and met with a group of pastors, bankers, businessmen, and lawyers — all who professed to be born-again Christians — and began the groundwork to establish an organization that would do something in a positive way to help New York City's poor, homeless children.

Because Brace was clearly a brilliant and dedicated young man — all of twenty-seven — and because he was a rapidly rising literary figure on the New York scene, these men backed him in his desire, and by March 1853, the Children's Aid Society was established. Brace was its leader, and the men helped raise funds from many kinds of businesses and people of wealth who believed in what they were doing.

Sufficient funds were coming in from contributors, allowing Brace to take over the former Italian Opera House at the corner of Astor Place and Lafayette Street in downtown Manhattan.

From the beginning, Brace and his colleagues attempted to find homes for individual children, but it was soon evident that the growing number of street waifs would have to be placed elsewhere. Brace came upon the idea of taking groups of these orphans in wagons to the rural areas in upstate New York and allowing farmers to simply pick out the ones they wanted for themselves and become their foster parents.

This plan indeed provided some homes for the street waifs, but not enough to meet the demand. By June 1854, Brace came to the conclusion that the children would have to be taken westward where there were larger rural areas. One of his colleagues in the Children's Aid Society had friends in Dowagiac, Michigan, who had learned of the Society's work and wrote to tell him they thought people of their area would be interested in taking some of the children into their homes under the foster plan.

Hence came the first "orphan train." In mid-September 1854, under Charles Brace's instructions, Dowagiac's local newspaper carried an ad every day for two weeks, announcing that forty-five homeless boys and girls from the streets of New York City would arrive by train on October 1 and on the morning of October 2 could be seen at the town's meetinghouse. Bills were posted at the general store, cafés, restaurants, and the railroad station, asking families to provide foster homes for these orphans.

One of Brace's paid associates, E. P. Smith, was assigned to take the children on the train to Dowagiac, which is located in southwestern Michigan. Smith's wife accompanied him to chaperone the girls.

The meetinghouse was fairly packed as the children stood behind Smith on the platform while he spoke to the crowd. He explained the program, saying these unfortunate children were Christ's little ones who needed a chance in life. He told the crowd that kind men and women who opened their homes to one or more of this ragged regiment would be expected to raise them as they would their own children, providing them with decent food and clothing, and a good education.

There would be no loss in their charity, Smith assured his audience. The boys would do whatever farm work or other work that was expected of them, and the girls would do all types of housework.

As the children stood in line to be inspected, the applicants moved past them slowly, looking them over and engaging them in conversation. At the same time, E. P. Smith and his wife looked at the quality and cleanliness of the prospective foster parents and asked them about their financial condition, property, vocation, and church attendance. If they were satisfied with what they heard, and saw no evidence that the prospective parents were lying, they let them choose the child or children they desired.

When the applicants had chosen the children they wanted, thirty-seven had homes. The remaining eight were taken back to New York and placed in already overcrowded orphanages. Charles Brace was so encouraged by the high percentage of the children who had been taken into the homes, that he soon launched into a campaign to take children both from off the streets and from the orphanages, put them on trains, and take them west where there were farms and ranches aplenty.

When the railroad companies saw what Brace's Children's Aid Society was doing, they contacted him and offered generous discounts on tickets, and each railroad company offered special coaches, which would carry only the orphans and their chaperones.

For the next seventy-five years — until the last orphan train carried the waifs to Texas in 1929 — the Children's Aid Society placed some 250,000 children in homes in every western state and territory except Arizona. Upon Brace's death in 1890, his son, Charles Loring Brace Jr., took over the Society.

In 1910, a survey concluded that 87 percent of the children shipped to the West had grown into credible members of western society. Eight percent had been returned to New York City, and 5 percent had either disappeared, were imprisoned for crimes, or had died.

It is to the credit of Charles Loring Brace's dream, labor, and leadership in the orphan train system that two of the orphans grew up to become state governors, several became mayors, one became a Supreme Court justice, two became congressmen, thirty-five became lawyers, and nineteen became physicians. Others became successful gospel preachers, lawmen, farmers, ranchers, businessmen, wives, and mothers — those who made up a great part of society in the West.

Until well into the twentieth century, Brace's influence was felt by virtually every program established to help homeless and needy children. Even today, the philosophical foundations he forged have left him — in the minds of many — the preeminent figure in American child welfare history.

# Chapter One

Lightning spread its thin white branches across the cloudy sky and sent its jagged roots down toward New York City on an evening in mid-April 1871. Crashes of thunder rocked the air like giant cannons venting their wrath on some unseen enemy.

A shrill wind pelted the pedestrians who were hurrying along the streets, threatening to upend the sea of umbrellas in the hands of the teeming crowds as they made their separate ways toward home and shelter.

Inside Chadwick's Bookstore in downtown Manhattan, the patrons were aware of the slanting rain drumming on the windows, the flashes of light in the dark sky, and the rumble of the thunder.

Ceiling lanterns cast a soft glow over the crowded bookshelves, and a small fire burned in the black potbellied stove at the center of the store. A coziness was laying over the few customers who were doing some last minute browsing, hoping the downpour would stop before closing time came and they were forced back onto the street.

Craig and Fay Weston watched their two youngest children, twelve-year-old Diane and nine-year-old Ronnie, draw up to the shelves in the children's section and begin looking at books. Craig and Fay moved on toward the historical section. As they drew near, Craig smiled and looked at Fay. "There it is."

He reached up and took a thick book from the top shelf with the bold title printed on the spine: *The History of Medicine.* Fay watched as he thumbed his way through it and looked at the last page. "Just as the ad in the newspaper said, honey — seven hundred and forty-three pages."

Then he flipped back to the front of the book and looked at the first page. "Mmhmm. Just as the paper said, the contributing authors went back and began in 200 B.C. and have brought it up to today."

At that point, Fay noted the price where it was penciled on the inside of the cover. She looked up at her husband, a small frown marring her pretty face. "Twelve dollars, honey," she said in an undertone. "The newspaper didn't tell us the price. I — I've only got seven dollars saved up. Can we afford twelve dollars?"

Craig smiled. "Yes, sweetheart. I've been saving up, too. Let's use my nine dollars, and three of yours. This is going to be the best birthday surprise Dane has ever had. He's going to love it."

"He sure will!" said Fay, her eyes sparkling as she reached into her coat pocket, drew out a worn envelope, and handed it to him. "We want to do all we can to encourage and support him. Let's go buy it."

Craig opened the envelope and extracted three one-dollar bills.

"We can use all of my savings, honey," she said softly.

Craig shook his head and handed the envelope back. "That's all right. You keep the rest of it." A wide grin split his face and he added, "You have really been cutting some corners from your household and grocery money, love, to save this much!"

She giggled. "Well, you'd be surprised at what can be done when a woman sets her heart and mind to it!"

Craig reached into his pocket and brought out his own tattered envelope. He took out the nine one-dollar bills and placed her three with them.

Fay's dark eyes shone with happy tears. "Oh, Dane's going to be so thrilled with this book! He will probably have his head buried in it for weeks and months to come. What a very special birthday he is going to have!"

Craig smiled. "That's for sure!"

Fay gave him an impish look.

He looked at her skeptically. "Yes, honey?"

"You know what I'd like to do with some of this money I have left?"

"What?"

"Well, we don't get to eat out very often. And since Dane's eating with the Baxters this evening, how about we walk the half-block down to the Twenty-Third Street Café and have supper when we leave here?"

"Well, why not?" He shook his head and frowned.

"What's wrong?"

"Oh, nothing. I just have to marvel at how you were able to save such an amount of money on the small bit I can give you each week."

Fay smiled and wrinkled her nose. "Oh, you know the old saying: 'Where there's a will, there's a way.' "

Craig tweaked her nose, grinning. "Well, my love, let's go pay for this book and head for the café."

She took hold of his arm, and as they headed for the front of the store, Fay called to Diane and Ronnie, who were still at the children's book section. "Come on, children. We found the book. Let's go."

Diane and Ronnie hurried and caught up with their parents, both happy to hear that their parents had found the book they wanted to give their big brother for his birthday.

When they drew up to the counter, Frank Chadwick was just finishing with his last customer, except for the Westons. When the man walked away, clutching a paper bag, Chadwick smiled. "Hello, Weston family. Where's Dane?"

"He's spending the evening with one of his friends in the neighborhood," Craig advised him. "We worked this out so we could come in here and buy this book for him. His birthday is next Tuesday, April 25."

Chadwick eyed the thick book as Craig laid it on the counter. "Ah, yes. *The His-*

*tory of Medicine.* He will love it. I've sold you several books on medicine for him, but this is the best yet. It will give him insight on medicine all the way back to 200 B.C."

Craig nodded. "When we saw the advertisement on this book in the *New York Times* a few weeks ago, and that it covered such a tremendous span of time, Fay and I agreed that no matter what it cost, we would find a way to buy it for Dane and give it to him for his birthday."

Chadwick smiled. "You two should be very proud of that boy."

"We are indeed very proud of him, Mr. Chadwick."

"Yes," put in Fay. "Ever since Dane had scarlet fever when he was ten and had to be hospitalized with it, he has been fascinated with medicine, doctors, nurses, and hospitals. From that time on, he has had one ambition: to become a medical doctor and a surgeon."

"We have no idea how we're going to pay for his medical education," said Craig, "but since he's just turning fifteen, we still have time to figure it out. We'll work something out, I can tell you that for sure."

"I have no doubt of that," said Chadwick as he placed the book into a paper bag.

Craig paid him, and as he picked up the

paper bag, Chadwick said, "I'd like to know how Dane likes the book."

Fay smiled. "We'll have Dane come in and tell you himself."

"Good!"

Chadwick followed the Westons to the door, and since it was closing time, when they moved outside, he locked the door behind them and put the *closed* sign in the window.

The cold rain was still coming down as the happy foursome made their way down the street, with both Craig and Fay carrying umbrellas. Ronnie was walking close to his mother, and Diane was under her father's umbrella.

"I'm so excited!" said Diane. "Dane is going to love that book!"

"Yeah!" said Ronnie. "I can't wait to see his face at his birthday party when he opens that present!"

Suddenly it dawned on Diane that they were going the opposite direction than they would in order to go home. "Papa, how come we're going this way?"

Ronnie's eyes widened. "Oh. Yeah! How come?"

"We're going to eat supper down here at the café!" said Fay.

Both children let out a squeal, and soon

21

they had covered the half-block, and turned into the Twenty-Third Street Café, their spirits high.

Warm air and delicious aromas greeted them, and immediately everybody in the family was hungry. They chose a table in the corner next to the large rain-streaked window that overlooked the street. A waitress approached them and took their orders.

While they were waiting for their food, they talked about Dane's upcoming birthday party. Fay told the others that she had been able to secretly contact Dane's five closest friends from school: Todd Baxter, Henry Wilson, Willie Thornton, Becky Simpson, and Matilda Andrews. They all planned to be at the party.

"That's great!" exclaimed Diane. "Dane's going to be so surprised. I'm so glad that he and Todd are best friends. Todd is such a nice boy."

Ronnie giggled and looked at his sister. "Todd's a nice boy, all right, and you're in love with him!"

Diane blushed. "Oh, Ronnie, I'm not in love with him. I just think he's a nice boy."

Fay smiled. "Ronnie, Diane is too young to be in love."

"That's for sure." A sly grin curved

Craig's lips as he looked at his daughter. "She won't be old enough to fall in love and get married until she's forty-five. Until then, she will stay home with her papa!"

They all had a good laugh, and at that moment the waitress arrived with their food.

At the Baxter home, where there were four children, including Dane Weston's friend, Todd, everyone was enjoying the meal prepared by Mona Baxter and her daughters, Letha, Angie, and Tippy, who were twelve, ten, and eight.

While they were eating, Dane and Todd were talking about school things. Todd snickered and gave his friend a teasing look. "If you don't keep your grades up for the next three years, ol' pal, you'll never qualify to enter medical school."

Dane knew his friend was teasing him. He set his dark-brown eyes on him and made a face.

Mona said, "Todd, wouldn't it be marvelous if you had such good grades? I happen to know that Dane is a straight-A student. His mother told me so."

Todd laughed. "I know it, Mama. I was just giving my pal a hard time."

Dolph Baxter frowned playfully at his

23

son. "Tell you what, Todd. If you don't get your grades to look more like Dane's, I'm going to give *you* a hard time!"

"Yes, sir," said Todd. "I promise to do better, Papa."

Dolph chuckled. "I'm not really complaining, son. Sure, I'd like to see you getting A's, but at least you're not giving your mother and me the kind of heartaches that these boys in the teenage gangs are giving *their* parents. We're thankful for that."

"That's for sure," said Mona. "You said something about the gangs when you were reading the newspaper this afternoon, dear, but I was passing by your chair on my way to answer the door when that salesman was here, and didn't get to ask you what was in the paper about them."

Dolph shook his head in disgust. "The front page of the *New York Herald* was loaded with it, as well as two articles inside. Those gangs are getting bolder and meaner all the time. They are robbing, beating, and killing people in the five New York boroughs every day. The front-page article declared that the mayors in all five boroughs are working with the police chiefs on a plan to crack down on the gangs, as well as other criminals, and make the streets of New York safer. Governor

Halstead has offered his complete backing of the plan."

"So what is the plan?"

Dolph had everyone's attention. "The plan is to hire more policemen in all five boroughs so that those officers who walk beats or ride the streets on horseback will each have a partner. There will be no more officers walking or riding by themselves. In the past month just here in Manhattan, three officers working alone have been killed and seven have been seriously injured. The other boroughs have had similar incidents."

"So when are they going to put the plan into action, Mr. Baxter?" asked Dane.

"It already is. The police departments of all five boroughs already have hundreds of new men in training. They will be ready for duty in a matter of weeks, and then the streets will be safer."

Dolph, Mona, and the boys discussed the citizens who had been beaten and robbed in their own neighborhood in the past few weeks, and stories they had heard about the orphans who lived in the alleys and on the streets of downtown Manhattan who had been attacked and beaten by the teenage gangs. Dolph pointed out that Governor Merle Halstead had announced there were going to be stiffer penalties for the gang members and any other criminals who were caught and sentenced.

Mona sighed. "It's bad enough to have this kind of crime on New York's streets to endanger its citizens, but at least most of them have homes where they can go at night and lock their doors. But I so often think of those poor orphan children who live in the alleys and on the streets who have no such protection. Not only are many orphans starving to death year-round and freezing to death in the winter months, but they are vulnerable to the gangs at all times."

"Yes," said Dolph. "It's a pitiful shame. I wish there were more orphanages in this city. Every one of them is already over-crowded. Craig Weston and I have talked about it. We both wish we had a giant-sized orphanage where we could give all of the orphans homes. But with what little money we make being janitors, it is all we can do to keep a roof over the heads of our families, clothes on their bodies, and food on the tables."

Mona drained her coffee cup and set it down. "Fay and I have talked about this orphan problem several times. We have the same wish. That's why I so much appreciate the Children's Aid Society. They send so many of those poor orphans out West on the orphan trains. This orphan problem would be much greater than it is if it wasn't for Charles Loring Brace and his staff."

"Right. Brace has done a marvelous thing with those orphan trains. At least those children who have been transported out West are off the dangerous streets of New York and for the most part, according to the newspapers, in good foster homes on farms and ranches." Dolph paused and chuckled. "Come to think of it, I wouldn't mind being one of those fortunate orphans myself. I've always wanted to go out West and see the great wide open country where the air is fresh and clean — not like the smelly, putrid air here in the big city."

Mona touched fingertips to her temple. "That reminds me. Dolph, did you see that article in the *Herald* last week about the orphan trains and the song the orphans sing while they're on the trains, heading west?"

"No. I missed that one."

"I'd like you to hear the words of that little song. That copy of the *Herald* is still in the cupboard, waiting to be used as shelf paper. I'll go get it. I'd like for all of you to hear it."

As Mona spoke, she pushed her chair back, but before she could rise, Todd jumped up. "I'll get it for you, Mama. What's the date on it?"

Mona eased back on the chair. "It was exactly a week ago. Thursday, April 6. You know where the stack of papers is — in the left section of the cupboard, bottom shelf."

"Uh-huh."

Todd dashed to the cupboard, and after sifting through the newspapers briefly, he returned with the previous Thursday's edition of the paper. He handed it to his mother.

Mona thanked him and began flipping pages. "Yes. Here it is. The article says the song was made up by one of the ladies who travels as a sponsor with the girls in their coaches on the orphan trains. Both the boys and the girls learn the song while they are on the train and sing it often while traveling west. Talk about the difference between the big city and the wide open spaces. Listen to this:

From city's gloom to country's bloom,
Where fragrant breezes sigh;
From city's blight to greenwood bright

28

Like the birds of summer fly.
O children, dear children,
So blessed are you and I!

Dane chuckled. "Hey, Mrs. Baxter, I really like that! If I didn't have such a good home with my wonderful parents and sister and brother, I wouldn't mind going out there on the western frontier where the fragrant breezes sigh myself! When those fragrant breezes sigh to the orphans out there, maybe each one hears whispers in the wind, welcoming them to a new and wonderful life."

Mona smiled. "Whispers in the wind welcoming them. That's good. Yes, from what I've read, I think they do, Dane. I think they do."

At the Twenty-Third Street Café, Craig and Fay Weston lingered over steaming cups of coffee. Fay ran her soft gaze over the faces of her two younger children and sighed contentedly. "This has been such a treat. I can't even remember the last time we ate out." She looked at her husband and smiled. "Not that I'm complaining, honey. I'm always grateful that we have food for me to cook, but it's nice for a change to eat someone else's cooking."

Craig smiled back at her. "I'm sure it is, sweetheart, but I'm very partial to your cooking. It's the best in the world."

"Thank you, honey. You always know how to make me feel special."

Diane and Ronnie were busy scraping up the last crumbs of chocolate cake and frosting from their plates. Fay and Craig noted it and exchanged satisfied looks, glad that they could give them this special evening.

When the children had gleaned the last crumb from their plates, Craig looked out the steamed-up window. "Well, family, I think it's time we head for home. It's been great fun, but tomorrow's another day, and morning comes all too soon at best."

A bit reluctantly, Diane and Ronnie nodded their agreement. All four rose from the table, put on their coats, and the parents picked up their umbrellas. Craig went to the counter with the others following and paid the bill. They opened the umbrellas, and as the foursome stepped out onto the rain-drenched, ill-lighted street, Craig said, "The rain is letting up some. Well, let's head for 218 Thirty-third Street."

Craig shared his umbrella with Diane and Fay shared hers with Ronnie as the

Westons headed back up the street. They passed Chadwick's Bookstore, and when they reached the corner, they turned northward on Third Avenue and headed for Thirty-third Street. The book they had purchased for Dane's birthday was in the paper bag, tucked under Craig's arm.

As they approached the dark mouth of an alley with the rain splattering on the street and sidewalk all around them, they saw several shadowed figures emerge from the alley in the dim light, and block the path in front of them.

Fay gasped, stopped, and took a deep, shuddering breath.

Craig steeled himself, his own heart pounding.

# Chapter Two

At the Baxter flat, which was located down the block from the Weston apartment building at 284 Thirty-third Street, supper was almost over.

Dane Weston finished his bowl of vanilla pudding, placed the spoon in the bowl, and smiled as he looked at the Baxter family. "Thank you so much for the delicious supper. I always enjoy coming to this home. It's so much like my own home, and I feel so comfortable here. One reason, of course, is because Todd is my best friend. Another reason is because I always enjoy talking to all of you about the things that are happening here in our city. Another reason is because all of you support my wanting to become a doctor."

Dolph wiped his mouth with a cloth napkin. "Dane, we are glad that our son is best friends with you, and we most certainly are proud of you in your desire to become a doctor."

"We sure are," said Mona.

Letha, Angie, and Tippy all nodded, smiling at him.

Todd grinned and clipped Dane's chin playfully. "Hey, who knows? Maybe someday you'll be the family doctor for all us kids when we grow up and get married."

Dane chuckled. "That would be all right with me." He paused, then said, "Well, I'd better be going. Papa and Mama and my little sister and brother are probably finishing supper right now and will be expecting me to be home real soon. Thank you again for the good supper."

As he spoke, Dane pushed his chair back and stood up.

Todd rose from his chair. "I'll walk you downstairs to the front door, Dane."

"All right." Dane bid the others goodnight, and the two boys went to the door, where Dane's coat hung on a clothes tree. He slipped into the coat, and they moved out into the hall.

While they were descending the stairs,

Dane said, "It's your turn to eat at our place next, ol' pal. How about next Friday? We can just come to our flat straight from school together."

"Sounds good to me," responded Todd. "If it's all right with your parents."

Dane laughed. "What are you talking about? Mama and Papa have both told you that you're welcome anytime. I'll tell them you're coming next Friday."

"Okay. I'll ask my parents. I'm sure they'll let me."

They reached the first floor and both saw that the rain was still coming down, though it was less heavy than when they started supper.

Dane picked up a newspaper from a small table by the vestibule door, unfolded it, and held it over his head. "Good night, Todd. See you tomorrow."

"Sure enough," replied Todd, and pulled the door open for his friend.

Dane moved out into the falling rain and headed down the block toward his own apartment building. As he hurried along, he saw a group of teenage boys standing under a street lamp across the street. They were watching him, but made no move to cross the street. He thought of the discussion at the Baxter table about the teenage gangs, and a chill slithered down his spine. He wondered if those boys were one of the gangs, and if they were to start after him could he outrun them to his apartment building?

He picked up his pace, keeping the newspaper above his head, but the rain was still putting its spray on his face and in his hair. Twice, he glanced over his shoulder to see if the teenage boys were following him, but they were still grouped beneath the street lamp.

Soon he drew up to 218 Thirty-third Street and bounded up the wet steps to the vestibule door. He used his key to unlock it, and plunged inside.

A few blocks away on Third Avenue, near an alley, four policemen bent over the crumpled bodies of a man, woman, girl, and small boy.

One of the officers picked up a wallet that lay on the wet pavement and opened it. "Man's name is Craig Weston, Captain. No money in the wallet. Lived over on Thirty-third Street. These are no doubt his wife and children. Dirty gang beat every one of them to death."

"Wait a minute, Captain!" said an officer who was bending over the girl. "This little gal is still alive! She's breathing!"

The captain stood up and moved over beside him. "Sure enough. No time to wait for an ambulance. Sergeant Bickford and I will take her to the hospital. You men use the paddy wagon and take the bodies of the others to the morgue. Pick up the woman's purse and that paper bag. Take them to the station after you've been to the morgue. We'll get back to you later."

At the apartment building, Dane Weston placed the wet newspaper in a wastebasket by the vestibule door and hurried up the stairs. He was unaware that a man moved into the vestibule from outside, glanced up at him, then shook the rain off his umbrella and entered the combination office and landlord's apartment.

When Dane reached the second floor, he quickly moved down the hall and drew up to apartment number 42. He grasped the knob and turned it, but was surprised when the door did not budge. Frowning, he knocked on the door. When there was no sound of footsteps inside the apartment, he knocked again, wondering why somebody hadn't come to let him in.

When there was still no sign of life inside the apartment, Dane took out his skeleton key, unlocked the door, and moved inside. Except for the light coming through the windows from the windows of the next apartment building, the flat was dark. An uneasy feeling came over him, akin to the one he had experienced a few minutes earlier when he saw the group of teenage boys watching him from across the street.

He closed the door and looked toward the bedrooms. "Mama! Papa! You back there?"

Silence.

Dane shook his head, wondering why his family was not home yet.

He removed his coat, hung it on a wall peg near the closet door, and made his way into the small parlor. While lighting two lanterns, he told himself his family would be arriving at any minute.

His next move was down the narrow hall, through the kitchen to the washroom. In the dim light that was coming from the windows of the adjacent apartment building, he dried his face and hair with a towel, then returned to the parlor.

His family was still not home.

He sat down on the sofa and watched the raindrops running down the window. He was only able to do that for ten minutes. Unable to sit still, he left the sofa and began pacing the floor. Every few seconds for the next hour and a half, he went to the rain-spattered window and looked toward the street for some sign of his family. Since the window was on the side of the building, his view of the street was limited.

He went back to the sofa and plopped down on it with a heavy sigh. He thought of the discussion at the Baxter table that evening about the teenage gangs and their attacks on people who were on the streets. He shook his head, telling himself nothing like that had happened to his family.

He glanced at the clock on the parlor wall.

Nine-twenty.

Worry gripped him. They told him they were going to do a little shopping before supper, but certainly it wouldn't take this long. Where could his family be?

Again, he went to the window and looked out. He could tell that the rain had almost stopped. Only a few windows in the adjacent apartment building were still showing lantern light.

The strange feeling from earlier washed over him again. He took a deep breath and hurried into the hall. He took his coat off the hook, put it on, and went out the door.

Dane made his way down the stairs and

out on to the street. He looked both ways for some sign of his family, but there was only a buggy on the street, moving away from him with the clatter of the horse's hooves echoing among the buildings. There was no one on the sidewalks. Clenching his teeth, he let out a moan and returned to the flat.

Once again in the parlor, he found himself pacing the floor. The worry inside Dane Weston was growing stronger as he ran shaky fingers through his black, curly hair.

Suddenly he heard male voices in the hall, along with heavy footsteps. He stopped and looked toward the door. He jumped when there was a sudden knock. His mouth went dry as he opened the door to find two uniformed policemen. The one who had captain's bars on his shirt collar said, "Are you Dane Weston, son?"

"Y-yes, sir." Dane's mouth went even drier.

"I'm Captain J. D. Slater and this is Officer Calvin Bickford. We just talked to the landlord downstairs, and he told us he had seen you come home a while ago, so he figured you would still be here in the apartment."

Fear gripped Dane's heart.

"May we come in and talk to you, son?" asked Slater.

Dane ran his tongue over equally dry lips. He backed up a step. "Yes, sir."

When the policemen had entered, Dane closed the door and led them into the parlor. There was an ever-tightening knot in the pit of his stomach as he told them to sit on the sofa, then sat down on the chair that faced them and waited for them to speak.

"Dane," said the captain, "we hate to have to tell you this, but your parents and sister and brother were assaulted by a teenage gang on Third Avenue near Twenty-third Street at about seven-thirty."

A frown creased the boy's brow. "Are — are they all right, sir?"

Slater looked at Bickford, ran a palm over his mouth, then looked back at Dane. "No, they're not. All — all but your sister, Diane, are dead."

Dane felt as if the blood was running from his heart. He began to shake like a man in a palsy. His strength seemed to drain away. He sat, mouth gaping and breathless, with wide-open horror-struck eyes. "P-Papa and Mama and Ronnie are — are dead?"

The captain rose to his feet and laid a

steady hand on the boy's shoulder. "Yes, son."

"And — and Diane is s-still alive?"

"Yes. Officer Bickford and I took her to Good Samaritan Hospital. She was unconscious when we picked her up off the ground. She regained consciousness shortly after we got her to the hospital and talked to us. Though she was battered and somewhat in shock, she spoke slowly and told us what happened. She's in bad shape, son, but we're hoping she'll make it."

Officer Bickford rose and laid a hand on the other shoulder. "Would you like us to take you to her?"

"Oh, y-yes, sir."

"We have a paddy wagon. Let's go."

Dane put on his coat and the officers took him to the paddy wagon, which was parked in front of the building. The landlord and his wife were watching through their front window as Dane climbed up onto the seat. He was sitting between the officers as the paddy wagon pulled away and moved down the street.

On the seat, Dane felt like he was in a nightmare. He was numb with grief, and overcome with the enormity of it all. His tortured mind kept telling him it wasn't really happening. But it was all too real. It wasn't raining any longer.

Only a few hours ago, they were a happy, loving family, and now these men in uniform had told him that all but Diane were dead.

As the paddy wagon made its way along the dark streets, Captain J. D. Slater said, "Dane, when we talked to your sister at the hospital, she told us there were eight gang members who approached them from the alley there on Third Avenue when they were headed for home. They dragged all four of them into the alley and demanded her father's wallet and her mother's purse. When her father told them he had only a few dollars in the wallet, and her mother only had two dollars, he asked them to have mercy and not take their money. She said one of them slapped her father across the face and demanded his wallet."

Dane winced and his head bobbed.

Slater went on. "At that moment, Diane said her mother begged the gang members not to take her husband's wallet, and one of them slapped her face while another one snatched her purse from her hand. This stirred your father's anger. He punched the one who had hit your mother, and suddenly the whole gang was beating all four of them."

Dane drew in a shuddering breath and shook his head. Tears were in his eyes.

Officer Calvin Bickford put an arm around his shoulder and squeezed him tight.

The captain proceeded. "Diane said that after the gang members had emptied what little money was in her father's wallet, they threw it and her mother's purse on the ground and ran away, cursing because they hadn't gotten more money. Diane told us that she felt herself passing out as she lay on the ground with her parents and her little brother lying around her. Some people on the street had seen the family dragged into the alley, and one of them ran to find a policeman. By the time the nearest policeman was located, the gang members were nowhere to be found. I'm so sorry, son."

Dane looked up at him through a wall of tears. "Th-thank you, sir."

"The bodies of your parents and Ronnie have been taken to the city morgue, Dane. It was your father's identification in his wallet that told us who he was and where the family lived. Diane told us you would be at the flat. This is how we found you."

Bickford said, "Oh. And with your father's wallet and your mother's purse, we

43

found a book that was wrapped in a paper bag. We left them at the nurse's station just outside the emergency room where the hospital attendants took Diane."

The wagon continued to move through the wet streets.

Staring straight ahead with his tear-dimmed eyes fixed on nothing in particular, Dane tried to make his mind grasp and accept all of this dreadful information.

Completely unprepared for such an horrific event, he felt his stomach heave with nausea. He quickly put both hands over his mouth.

Officer Bickford still had his arm around the boy's shoulders. He looked at Slater, who was driving. "Captain, you'd better stop."

Slater noted Dane and pulled rein quickly.

Bickford jumped out and helped Dane to the ground. He laid a hand on his shoulder and bent his head down so he could look into Dane's eyes. "Is it coming up?"

Dane closed his eyes and removed his hands from his mouth enough to say, "I'm not sure."

"Take some deep breaths, son. I know all of this has been such a shock to you."

Dane drew one deep breath after another, and after a few minutes, he looked at Bickford and said in a ragged voice, "I think — I think I'll be all right, now."

"Good. Just breathe easy, now. You'll be okay."

Dane did as the officer said, still keeping his hands close to his mouth and his head bent forward. After taking several gulps of the rain-dampened air, he straightened up, swallowed hard, and said haltingly, "We — we can go on now. I need to get — to my sister. She must be frantic with all that's happened tonight." His features pinched. "How awful for her to have to watch our parents and little brother beaten to death! I must get to her. Please. Let's hurry!"

Officer Bickford hoisted Dane on to the wagon seat and climbed up behind him. "Let's go, Captain."

In his sick heart, Dane kept pleading with Diane not to die, but the same feeling of doom that he had experienced earlier claimed him. When the paddy wagon came to a halt in front of the Good Samaritan Hospital, Dane surprised Officer Calvin Bickford by squeezing past him and hopping to the ground.

He ran into the hospital while Slater and Bickford were alighting from the wagon.

They called to him. He spotted the receptionist's desk and darted toward it. He was skidding to a halt at the desk while the officers were hurrying through the door.

There was a portly, gray-haired nurse standing over the receptionist and talking to her. The older woman glanced at the two officers coming toward the desk, then looked at the teenage boy, whose eyes were wide. Her face turned pale. She moved around the desk. "You must be Dane Weston. I'm Nurse Martha Simpson. I work in the emergency room. Captain Slater and Officer Bickford said they were going to bring you here."

"Yes, ma'am. I want to see my sister! Please take me to her. She needs me."

The officers drew up, having heard Dane's words.

Slater noted the pale look on Nurse Simpson's face. "Can he see her?"

Martha blinked painfully, looked at Dane, then at Slater.

"Oh no!" gasped Dane. "Not Diane, too!"

Martha laid a hand on Dane's shoulder. Tears brimmed in her eyes. "I'm sorry, son. Diane died about twenty minutes ago."

Dane was stunned. He drew a sharp

breath and burst into tears. Martha's heart went out to the boy. He was an inch or two taller than her, but she took him into her arms and held him tightly as if he were a small child.

Not even aware of what he was doing, Dane wrapped his strong young arms around her ample body and gave way to the despair that was tearing him apart. Clinging to her, he sobbed incoherently. Other people passing through the lobby looked on with pinched faces as they heard the heartrending sobs of the teenage boy.

The officers stood observing the pitiful scene, both glad for the motherly instinct of Nurse Martha Simpson. They knew that she was of more help to him than both of them could give him together.

Finally, Dane gained control, eased back from Martha's tender grasp, and wiped tears from his cheeks with trembling hands. He looked into her sympathetic eyes, sniffed, and said, "Th-thank you, ma'am. I'm sorry I broke down. All of this just seems like an impossible nightmare. I don't know what to do about having a funeral for my family, or how to have them buried."

Tears once again filled his red-rimmed eyes.

Captain Bickford moved up close. "Dane, do you have someone you can stay with? You know, some relatives?"

"No, sir. I have no relatives at all. My school friends all have brothers and sisters, so there would be no room for me in any of their homes, even if their parents wanted to take me in. For right now, I'll just have to live at our apartment."

Slater nodded silently. "On the subject of a funeral and burial for your family, Dane, the coroner at the morgue will take care of it. I'll take you to him as soon as I can. As chief of police, I want to talk to the coroner myself. We'll take you home now."

"Captain," said Bickford, "I'll go get the wallet, purse, and book at the nurse's station. Be right back."

Nurse Martha Simpson tried to comfort Dane while Bickford was gone. Dane hugged her and thanked her for caring.

Bickford returned, and with the wallet, purse, and paper sack containing the book in his hand, he said, "All right, son, let's take you to your apartment."

While the paddy wagon was moving along the streets, Dane felt like the weight of the world had settled on his shoulders. He took a deep breath and told himself that somehow he would make it alone, and a determination to do so filled his aching heart.

Captain Slater interrupted Dane's thoughts. "Son, when is the rent on the apartment due?"

Dane looked up at him. "Papa paid the rent every Saturday for the following week. This is Tuesday, so the rent is paid through next Saturday."

"I'm concerned about where you're going then."

Dane shrugged his shoulders. "Well, sir, I guess I'll just have to take to the streets like so many orphans have to do."

"I hate that, Captain," said Officer Bickford. "I wish there were more orphanages in this city."

"I do, too," said Slater, "but there's nothing either one of us can do about it."

"Yeah. I know."

When they arrived at 218 Thirty-third Street, Captain Slater said, "Dane, we've got to get back to headquarters. I'll come back and take you to the morgue as soon as I can."

Dane moved past Officer Bickford and hopped down. "All right, Captain. I appreciate all the help you and Officer Bickford have been to me."

Bickford leaned down and handed him

the purse, wallet, and paper bag. "See you later, son."

Dane tried to smile. "Yes, sir. See you later."

"Keep your chin up, Dane," said Slater. "If you ever need help of the kind that takes a policeman to handle, don't hesitate to come and see me."

"Yes, sir."

"It'll probably be day after tomorrow before I can take you to the morgue. See you then."

"Yes, sir. See you then."

Slater rubbed his chin. "In fact, tell you what — I'll go by the morgue tomorrow and just tell the coroner to come to the apartment and let you know when the funeral will be. It'll probably be three or four days from now. Going by myself will save time, since the morgue is only a block and a half from precinct headquarters. I won't have to come all the way over here and pick you up."

"All right, Captain. That will be fine."

The wagon pulled away. Dane stood and watched until it turned the corner and disappeared, then headed for the front door of the apartment building.

# Chapter Three

Upon entering the apartment building, a heavy-hearted Dane Weston knocked on the door of the landlord's apartment. When Mitchell Bendrick — who was in his midfifties — opened the door, he smiled. "Hello, Dane. I saw you go in the paddy wagon with Chief Slater and the other officer. Is everything all right?"

"They told me they had talked to you. Didn't they tell you what happened?"

"No. Come in and tell me what has happened."

As Dane stepped in and Mitchell closed the door, Sylvia Bendrick appeared, curiosity showing on her face. To her husband, she said, "Did you find out why the police wanted to see Dane?"

"Not yet, honey, but Dane is about to tell us."

Sylvia focused on the purse, wallet, and paper bag in Dane's hand, then on his ashen face. "It's something bad, isn't it? Is that your mother's purse? Is that your father's wallet?"

Dane looked at her with tears welling up in his eyes. "Could we sit down? I'll tell you all about it."

When they were seated in the parlor, the brokenhearted boy told the Bendricks the story, and when he finished, tears were flowing.

Mitchell and Sylvia were stunned, and together left their chairs and wrapped their arms around the sobbing boy, telling him how sorry they were that this awful tragedy had happened.

When Dane's emotions had settled down and the Bendricks had let go of him and returned to their chairs, he set his gaze on them. "Will I be able to stay in the apartment until Saturday since Papa already paid you for this week's rent?"

"You most certainly can," replied Mitchell. "Where are you going to live after Saturday?"

Dane took a deep breath. "I'll have to live on the streets like so many orphans do."

"Oh, honey, I'm sorry," said Sylvia. "I wish we could afford to let you just keep on living in the apartment, but we have to have the rent money from it."

"We'd sure do it if we could," Mitchell assured him.

Dane managed a thin smile. "I know you would. But I understand. Thank you, though."

Sylvia looked at him compassionately. "Dane, you can take your meals with us until you move out on Saturday."

His face brightened a bit. "Okay. I'd like that. Thank you very much."

Mitchell stood up and laid a hand on the boy's shoulder. "Since we only have one bedroom in this apartment, we can't offer you a bed, but would you like for me to stay in your apartment with you tonight so you will have some company? I'll be glad to do it."

"I appreciate your offer, Mr. Bendrick, but I'll be all right. I — I sort of need some time alone. I hope you understand."

"Certainly. But if you should need us for anything, all you have to do is knock on our door."

Dane rose from his chair and picked up the purse, wallet, and paper bag. "Thank you. I appreciate that. Well, I'd better go."

Sylvia stood up. "Are you hungry, dear?"

"Not really, ma'am. Right now my stomach is sort of tied in knots."

"Of course. Well, we'll plan on you eating breakfast with us in the morning. Maybe you'll feel better by then."

The landlord and his wife walked Dane to the door, and as he started up the stairs, they reminded him that if he needed them, he was to let them know.

When Dane stepped into the apartment, it was pitch black. But knowing every nook and cranny, he made his way to the small table in the parlor that stood at one end of the couch, and laid the purse, wallet, and paper bag on it. He then moved to a larger table in the center of the room, and his fingers found the matches and the lantern that lay on it. Striking a match on the disk, he lit the wick. At first it gave off a feeble glow, then the flame brightened as he turned up the wick.

Standing there in the center of the room, he let his weary eyes roam over the shabby furnishings. Memories of happy family times in the parlor flooded his mind. Fighting his upsurge of emotions, he picked up the flickering lantern and made his way to the small kitchen. Faint odors of his mother's cooking still remained in the room.

He swallowed hard as a hot lump rose up in his throat. "Oh, Mama, I will miss you so. I can't even imagine never seeing your smiling face again, or feeling the comfort of your arms around me. You — you had a special knack for making every day seem like a happy event."

Blinking at the tears that were surfacing, Dane went to the cupboard, set the lantern down, and picked up a pitcher of water and a cup. He filled the cup with water and drank it slowly while letting his eyes roam around the room, which was once filled with laughter and joy.

Now it lay in total silence.

Listening carefully, he thought he could almost hear that sound again. Scalding tears were now on his cheeks. He shook his head, set the empty cup down, picked up the lantern, and left the kitchen.

Slowly, Dane made his way down the narrow hall. When he came to Diane's room, he paused and held the lantern so he could see inside. Sniffling, he moved to the next room, which was the one he and Ronnie had shared. After a few seconds, he moved to the back bedroom, which had belonged to his parents.

He swallowed with difficulty and took a step inside. Memories quickly flooded his troubled mind. He remembered himself as a small child seeking the security of his parents' loving arms in that big feather bed many a time when he had woken up from a nightmare.

Dane wiped tears with the back of his hand. "Papa, where are you? You have always been here. You have always protected me and cared for me when I needed you. I need you now! What will I do without your strength and your guidance in my life?"

A shudder consumed his spent body. He turned away from the memories the room stirred within him and ran up the hall to the parlor. He set the lantern back on the table in the center of the room, and overwhelmed with grief, he dropped onto the worn-out sofa, gave in to the bereavement that was tearing at his heart, and sobbed uncontrollably for over an hour.

It was one o'clock in the morning when finally, from exhaustion, he fell into a fitful sleep.

When dawn's light touched Dane's eyes through the parlor window, he awakened and the grief hit him afresh. He wept for several minutes, calling to his parents and his siblings, telling them he missed them. When he gained control of his emotions, he sat up on the sofa and his eyes fell on the paper bag that lay on the small table with his parents' wallet and purse.

Curious as to what kind of book his parents had bought, he arose from the sofa and took it out of the bag. When he saw the title, his features pinched. He held the book reverently in his hands and let his fingers run over the title. "This was for my birthday, wasn't it? But how will I ever become a doctor now? I've dreamed of becoming a doctor almost as long as I remember. But now I'll be forced to live on the streets. How will I ever have the money to pay for medical school?"

While he was fighting off another wave of despair, his mother's soft voice came to him: *"Anything worth having is worth working for, son. Where there's a will, there's a way."*

His mother had proven the old adages to be true in her everyday life.

Dane held the big thick book against his chest.

"You're right, Mama. I have absolutely no idea how, but someday I will realize my dream. It's certainly worth having, and I'll find a way to work for it and make it happen. Where there's a will, there's a way. Dr. Dane Weston will make his mama and papa proud of him."

A fresh wave of grief washed over him. Clutching the book to his chest, he fell on the sofa and wept again.

When he finally stopped weeping, he went to the wash room next to the kitchen, washed his face and hands, and went downstairs to the Bendrick apartment for breakfast.

That same morning, at 10:00, Manhattan's mayor, Raymond Fachinello, stood on the platform in the auditorium at city hall before some three hundred uniformed police officers, nearly two hundred of whom had just finished their training and were ready to go on duty.

Fachinello explained that after Manhattan's chief of police, Rex Tilman, addressed them, many of the new recruits would be paired off with the experienced men who were present. The rest of the new men would be paired off with officers who were presently on duty at a meeting this evening when the shift changed. He spoke of how pleased he was that there were some two hundred more recruits in training at the moment.

The mayor went on to give statistics of Manhattan's citizens who had been robbed, beaten, and killed on the streets by gangs and other criminals in the past six months. He also gave statistics on stores, banks, and street vendors that had been robbed. He then called for Chief Tilman to come and speak to the men.

When Chief Rex Tilman stepped to the platform, it was obvious to the crowd of officers that he was deeply concerned about the crime statistics that had just been given by the mayor. It showed on his face as he explained that many of the muggings, robberies, and killings in Manhattan had been in the middle class and well-to-do areas. It wasn't just the ghettos and poorer sections of the city that were feeling the impact of the growing crime rate.

Tilman went on to say that all of New York City was bursting at the seams with people coming in from Europe, as well as from the Orient, Cuba, and the Caribbean Islands. Most of them thought they were coming to a promised land of milk and honey, and when it became obvious that they were misled, many of them turned to crime in rebellion, and now the entire population was suffering.

The uniformed men before him were nodding their agreement to what Tilman was saying.

He scrubbed a palm over his mouth and

went on. "Men, I have been thinking of all the reasons people come to live in New York City, and I can't even remember what my own reason was. A friend once said to me about this city, 'People don't pull up in covered wagons to the center of Longacre Square and say, "Here it is — a good land, a strong land, a decent land where our children can grow strong and free." Yes, that happens out West in the wide open spaces, but not here. I hate to have to say it, but New York City is not a good land or a strong land. It certainly is not a place to bring children. Yet they have come here by the thousands, and a good many of the orphans that live in the streets and alleys were made orphans by the killers who have stalked the streets and murdered their parents."

Tilman then challenged the new officers, as well as the experienced ones, to do everything they could to make the streets of Manhattan safe for its citizens, even as the officers — experienced and inexperienced — were seeking to do so in the other four boroughs.

He charged the men as they were assigned to their partners to guard each other's lives as if they were brothers. He thanked them for being willing to pin on a badge and strap on a gun in the war against crime, then began reading off the names of the new men and assigning them to their partners.

That afternoon, when Dane Weston knew his friend Todd Baxter would be home from school, he went to the Baxter apartment. The girls were playing hop-scotch on the sidewalk farther down the street. When he was invited in, tears streamed down his face as he told Todd and his parents about his family being killed by the gang.

Dane's words shocked them totally. They were sitting around the kitchen table, and both Dolph and Mona wept as they showed their sympathy for Dane in his loss. Todd wrapped his arms around his best friend and wept, saying how sorry he was that Dane had to suffer like this.

Dolph set his gaze on Dane as Todd held him in his arms. "Dane, what are you going to do? Where will you live?"

Dane sniffed and wiped tears. "I will simply live on the streets as so many or-phans do, Mr. Baxter. I'll have to find a job of some kind to provide for my food and other needs. My plan is to get a night job so I can go to school in the daytime as usual."

Dolph gave him a solemn look and shook his head. "No, Dane. You will not be allowed in school as a street waif. You can only go to public school if you have at least one parent or guardian, and you live in their home."

Dane frowned. "Really?"

"Yes. I'm sorry, but that's the law."

A finger of disappointment stabbed Dane's raw heart, but instantly his mother's words came to mind: *"Where there's a will, there's a way."* A new resolve filled him. He would still one day become a doctor, no matter what he had to do to accomplish it.

Dolph and Mona exchanged glances, each knowing what the other was thinking, but both knew there was no way they could take Dane into their home. Dolph's income as a janitor just wouldn't cover the cost of another mouth to feed, let alone clothes and shoes and other expenses that come with raising a child. It was all they could do to care for Todd, Letha, Angie, and Tippy.

Dolph set soft eyes on the boy. "Dane, Mona and I wish we could take you into our home, but this apartment is already too small for the family we have."

Dane smiled thinly. "I understand, Mr.

Baxter. Thank both of you for wanting to do that, but I don't expect you to provide a home for me. I'll be okay. Other orphans make it, living on the streets. I will, too." He paused, then said, "Since Todd is my best friend, I'd still like to come and visit now and then, if that would be all right."

Relieved that Dane understood, Mona said quickly, "Of course. You are welcome here anytime."

Todd had released Dane from his arms, but patted his shoulder and said with a smile, "You sure are!"

"And please stop by often, Dane," said Mona. "I'll be happy to see that you get a good meal whenever you're here. It may not be anything fancy, but I can always stretch it enough to feed another mouth."

Dane's smile spread wide this time. "Thank you, Mrs. Baxter. You are very kind. I promise I won't make a pest of myself, but I want to keep my close friendship with Todd and everyone else in this family, too. You're all I have left of what was once a happy life."

Mona gave Dane a hug. At the same time, Dolph patted him on the back. "Don't be a stranger, son. We want you to come by often."

"Thank you, sir. I appreciate it more

than I could ever tell you." Dane felt as though a small part of his crushing burden had been lifted.

Todd said, "Dane, I'll tell our friends at school about what happened to your family, and that you won't be back to school, at least until you find someone in this school district to adopt you and give you a home."

Dane smiled again. "That would be something, wouldn't it? Well, I guess I'd better head for the apartment. I want to thank all of you for being my friends."

As Dane pushed his chair back and rose to his feet, Mona asked, "Can you stay for supper?"

A low grumble in his stomach reminded Dane that he hadn't eaten anything since that morning. "I sure can!"

That evening when Dane arrived at 218 Thirty-third Street and turned off the sidewalk to enter the building, he saw Mitchell Bendrick looking at him from his office window. The landlord motioned that he would meet him in the vestibule, and before Dane could put his key in the door, Bendrick swung it open. "Have you had anything to eat, son?"

As he moved inside, Dane said, "Yes, sir.

I had supper with my friend Todd Baxter and his family."

"Good. I have a message for you from the coroner."

"Oh?"

"Mm-hmm. He came by to see you late this afternoon. He said Captain J. D. Slater had come to him about the funeral for your family, and wanted to let you know that your parents and Diane and Ronnie will be buried at eleven o'clock Friday morning at the 116th Street Cemetery. A minister has been engaged by the coroner to preside over the burial. I told the coroner I would pass the message on to you when you came home."

Dane's features went grim. He sucked in his breath so hard it hollowed his cheeks. "All right, sir. Thank you."

Bendrick took hold of the boy's upper arm. "Dane, Sylvia and I are going to take you to the graveside service."

Dane's eyes brightened a bit. "Oh, thank you, Mr. Bendrick. You and Mrs. Bendrick have been so kind to me."

"We couldn't let you face it alone. And I want to tell you something else: you can stay in the apartment another week at no charge."

"Really?"

"Really. I wish we could afford to let you stay in the apartment indefinitely, but we'll have to rent it out after next week."

"I understand, Mr. Bendrick. Thank you for the extra week."

When Dane entered the apartment, its utter silence overpowered him. The place had always been filled with sound. Mama would hum happily as she did her household chores. Dane, Diane, and Ronnie were usually involved in some activity or game that kept the apartment filled with chatter and laughter, and Papa's voice would boom joyfully over all the rest when he returned home at the end of the day from work.

In the evenings, Mama often read aloud to the family from one of the few books they possessed, and often Ronnie would fall asleep on the couch while listening to the soft sound of her voice.

Now as Dane stood just inside the door, the only sound was his labored breathing. He took a deep breath and said aloud, "Someday I'll have my own family, and I'll make sure that our house is filled with laughter and music and other sounds that make a house a home."

These thoughts gave him a measure of comfort and hope. His mother would sometimes say, *"Without hope, there is nothing to live for."* The thoughts of his mother brought another rush of tears.

The next day, Dane went back to the Baxter apartment to let them know that his family was being buried on Friday morning.

When Friday came, dark rain clouds hung low, making the day even more somber. Dane was pleased to find the entire Baxter family at the cemetery when he and the Bendricks arrived. Having the Baxters there meant a lot to him. It was especially comforting to have Todd standing beside him during the service.

The rain slanted down on the little group as they huddled beneath their umbrellas.

When it came time for the four coffins to be lowered into the cold, unfeeling earth, Dane broke down and sobbed. The Bendricks and the Baxters encircled him, giving all the comfort they could.

That evening, after eating supper with Mitchell and Sylvia, a weary Dane Weston climbed the stairs and entered the apartment. It was still raining outside. He was glad he had left a lantern burning low when he went down to supper. A shiver washed over him, and he decided to build a fire in the stove.

The little stove looked cold and forlorn, too, he thought as he wadded up a portion of the *New York Times* and stuffed it with the paper. He placed several pieces of kindling on top of the paper, then struck a match and lit the paper. He closed the heavy door, and the flames flickered brightly through the small window, sending out its warm glow and dispelling some of the gloom in the parlor.

Dane went to the shabby sofa, sat down, and let his mind run back over the sad day. Soon his thoughts settled on the scene at the grave site when the grave diggers lowered the four plain pine coffins in the ground while the rain continued to fall. It had been the worst moment of all in the devastating loss of his family.

The thoughts that had filtered through his mind while the coffins were being lowered into the ground came to him anew. He recalled how the only thing that kept him from totally giving in to the despair that was trying to claim him was his dream of becoming a doctor and helping the sick, injured, and wounded of this world. Holding tight to this determination had enabled him to survive the horrific day.

He adjusted his position on the sofa, sighed, and whispered, "Mama, Papa, someday I'll make you proud of me. I'll find a way to get my education and be the doctor that you always wanted me to be."

On the following Tuesday, the Bendricks had a little birthday party for Dane at suppertime. Later that evening in the apartment, he picked up *The History of Medicine* that his parents had bought for his birthday and wept as he thumbed through its pages.

Once again he vowed that somehow, some way, he would one day become a medical doctor and surgeon.

# Chapter Four

On the following Saturday morning —
April 29 — the New York sun beamed
down from a clear sky and the children who
lived in the apartments in the 200 block on
Thirty-third Street were playing games on
the sidewalks. Happy chatter and joyful
laughter were heard on both sides of the
street.

At 218 Thirty-third Street, Sylvia
Bendrick held the door of the office-apart-
ment open while her husband and Dane
Weston reached the bottom of the stairs
and carried in Dane's belongings. Dane
was carrying his several medical books,
and Mitchell bore the boy's winter
clothing. Strapped on Dane's back was a
knapsack that held his summer clothing.

When they stepped into the parlor, Mitchell laid the clothing on the couch. "Just put the books here on this end table, Dane. I'll put them all away in a little while."

The boy placed the books on the table with *The History of Medicine* on top and patted it. "I'll come for these books someday when I can concentrate on becoming a doctor."

Sylvia smiled. "We'll take care of them for you, dear. And your winter clothes, too."

"I appreciate this," said Dane, running his gaze to the faces of both people. "I'll come for my winter clothes when cold weather is on its way."

Mitchell smiled and clipped his chin playfully. "You come and see us before fall, Dane. We want to know how you're doing."

"I will, sir. And thank you both for being so kind to me."

The fifteen-year-old hugged both people and headed for the door. They followed, and when he reached it, he turned and said, "You wouldn't mind, would you, if I went up and just spent a few minutes in the apartment? I . . . I mean, since it will be the last time I can ever go inside."

Mitchell smiled down at him. "Take your time. I'll be going up tomorrow morning to make it ready to show to prospective renters. I'll lock the door later."

Dane thanked them again and hurried up the stairs.

His heart felt like it was made out of lead as he opened the door and stepped into the apartment. This was the only home he had ever known. And now he must leave it. Knowing he was taking his last look at the apartment, he moved slowly from room to room, mentally picturing each member of his family in happy times.

When Dane had gone into each room, his parents' bedroom being the last, he made his way back to the parlor, carrying so many memories deep in his heart. He opened the door, turned around for one last look, swallowed hard, and stepped into the hall, closing the door behind him. He thumbed tears from his eyes, but with determination to realize his goal in life spurring him on, he hurried down the stairs and stepped out into the beauty of the bright spring day.

Adjusting the knapsack on his back, he headed for downtown with the laughter of the children at play in his ears.

When Dane reached Manhattan's gigantic business district, he entered the first store he came to, which was Milford's Clothiers. The man behind the counter was waiting on a female customer, but smiled at him. "I'll be with you in a moment, young man."

Dane smiled and nodded, then stood where he was and ran his gaze around the store. There were racks of clothing along the walls and down the center of the store. Men's clothing was in the section along the wall to his left, and women's clothing was in the section along the other wall. Children's clothing, from infants to teenagers, was on the rack down the center, as well as the long, narrow tables in between.

The woman left, and the man came from behind the counter. "May I help, you young man?"

Dane smiled again. "I — I'm not here to buy anything, sir, but I'm looking for a job. Are you the proprietor?"

"Yes. I'm Thomas Milford. But I have no job openings."

"I'd do anything, Mr. Milford. Sweep the floor, wash the windows, clean the sidewalk out front, and . . . and anything else that needs doing."

"I'm sorry, son, but I already have a janitor." He frowned. "How old are you?"

"Fifteen."

"Why aren't you in school?"

"I'm an orphan, sir. My parents and my little sister and little brother were killed by a gang over on Third Avenue a few days ago."

Milford's hand went to his cheek. "Oh yes. I read about that in the newspaper. The name is Weston, isn't it?"

"Yes, sir. I'm Dane Weston. I wasn't with them that night, or I'd have been killed, too."

Thomas Milford's features pinched. "Oh, I'm so sorry, son." His hand went into his pants pocket. He pulled out two silver dollars and handed them to Dane. "I really don't have any work for you to do, but take this money. It'll buy you some food."

Disappointment showed on Dane's face, but he managed a smile. "Thank you, Mr. Milford. This will help, for sure."

The proprietor looked on with compassion as the boy walked out of the store and headed on down the street.

By the time the sun was setting, Dane had been into twenty-two stores, and had been told twenty-two times by store

74

owners and managers that they had no work for him. Thomas Milford was the only one who had given him money.

Dejected, but determined to start job hunting again in the morning, he began looking for a place to call home. Moving along the sidewalks, he glanced into one alley after another as he passed them, looking for what he knew was a colony of orphans and street waifs that he might join.

Soon he spotted a group of teenage boys in an alley, who were sitting in a circle, eating. He turned into the alley and headed toward them. As he drew close, one of the boys spotted him and said something in a low voice to the others. There were seven of them, and every one of them looked at him in an unfriendly manner.

The one who looked to be the oldest fixed him with a stony glare. "Whatta you want?"

"I just became an orphan a few days ago. My parents and little sister and little brother were murdered. I'm looking for a colony here on the streets to live with. Could I join up with you?"

"No, you can't. You're not welcome. We don't want anyone else in our group."

Dane bit down on his lower lip, wheeled, and walked back to the street. Less than a block from where he had just stopped, he came upon an alley where he saw a colony which was made up of boys and girls from their teens down to about eight or nine years of age. They were eating, too. As he made his way toward them, a boy about sixteen rose to his feet. "If you're lookin' for a group to join, it ain't us. We get our food from the garbage cans of that café over there, and there ain't enough to feed another mouth. That answer the question you were about to ask?"

Dane couldn't reply. His tongue was too heavy to form words. A flicker of emotion skittered across his disconcerted face as he turned and walked away.

The last rays of the setting sun were lighting up the western sky as Dane reached the street and headed toward the next alley. As he drew near it, suddenly he heard a girl screaming. He dashed to the alley, turned in, and saw a group of frightened street waifs looking on as two husky teenage boys had a smaller boy on the ground, beating on him with their fists.

The one girl was screaming for them to stop.

Dane was infuriated at seeing the small

boy, who was no more than six or seven years old, being pounded by the bigger boys. He ran toward them, shouting, "Hey! Cut that out, you two! Stop hitting him! Get away from him!"

The children in the group — which included some teenage boys — looked up and saw Dane running toward them. The little boy's mouth and nose were bleeding.

The assailants paid him no mind, and this infuriated Dane.

He grabbed one of them by the shirt collar, yanked him off the boy, and sent him rolling. He then barked at the other assailant, "Get off him, right now!"

The assailant looked up and glowered at him with fire in his eyes. "Mind your own business, kid!"

"I said get off him!" Dane exploded with rage, grabbing him and throwing him off the bleeding child.

While the assailant rolled in the dirt from the force of Dane's strong hands, the girl who had been screaming clapped her hands. "Atta boy, whoever you are! You did good!"

The other children began cheering him.

At the same time the second assailant was rolling on the ground, the first one lunged at Dane, tackling him.

Dane quickly freed himself and jumped to his feet. The husky teenager also leaped to his feet and took a swing at Dane, who dodged the punch and countered with a stinging left that smashed his nose. Right behind it came a powerful right cross that rocked him and sent him stumbling backward. He tripped over his own feet and fell, stunned by the punch. Blood was running from his nose.

The small group was cheering Dane on.

By this time, the other one was closing in, swinging both fists, eyes wild.

Dane met him head-on, ducking a punch and dodging another. He retaliated with a stiff, whistling blow to the nose, followed by a series of powerful, rapid punches to the jaw that put him down.

By this time, the other one's senses had cleared. He bent over his friend and said in a wheezing voice, "Let's get outta here!"

His friend staggered to his feet, wiped blood from his nose, and nodded. He flicked a fearful glance toward Dane. "Yeah. Let's go."

"Make it fast!" hissed Dane, his shoulders thrust forward and his fists still clenched.

As the two bleeding teenagers ran from the alley, the group jeered them. When they vanished from sight, the group turned to Dane, who was kneeling beside the battered boy, and they patted him on the back and shoulders, lauding him for what he had just done.

One teenage boy knelt beside Dane. "My name's Russell Mims. I want you to know that those two bullies you just beat up are not part of our colony. They came in here, planning to steal what food we might have. Little Billy Johnson was the first to resist them, so they started pounding on him."

While examining Billy's nose and mouth, Dane took a moment to look up at Russell and the other teenage boys and said in a kindly tone, "How come you guys didn't go to Billy's rescue?"

The girls looked on, waiting for the boys to answer.

They ducked their heads ashamedly, and Russell Mims said, " 'Cause those two are supposed to be really tough, and we — well, we were afraid to take them on."

Dane nodded. "Thanks for being honest. I guess they were both bigger than any one of you."

He then turned his attention back to the bleeding little boy, who was sniffling. "Billy, my name is Dane Weston. I want to help you if I can. How old are you?"

Billy choked on a sob, then replied, "Seven."

The small group was gathered in a tight circle around Billy and Dane. Bending low over him, Dane noted that his nose was still bleeding, as was a deep cut in the center of his lower lip. Billy could hardly open his right eye for the dirt that had gotten into it.

Dane looked up at the group. "Do you have any water?"

The girl whose screams had first gotten Dane's attention moved close. "We have some water in a jug. Mr. Powell, the man who owns the grocery store on the corner, fills it for us whenever we need it."

One of the boys hurried to a small cardboard box next to the rear of the nearest building, pulled the jug from it, and hurried back. He handed it to Dane, who thanked him.

Removing the lid from the jug, Dane looked at the group again. "Do any of you have a clean piece of cloth? I'm going to use the water to wash the dirt out of Billy's eye, but I'm going to need a piece of cloth to help stop the bleeding from the cut on his lip."

At first no one answered, then the same

girl said, "I'll go ask Mr. Powell for some cloth."

Dane smiled at her. "What's your name, little lady?"

"Bessie Evans."

"And how old are you?"

"Eleven. How old are you, Dane?"

"Fifteen."

"Do you know how to fix Billy's cut and stop his nosebleed?"

"I'm sure going to try. Hurry, will you?"

"Sure will," said Bessie, and with that, she turned and ran toward the closest end of the alley.

Dane held the jug ready. "Billy, I'm going to pour some water in your eye and get the dirt washed out. Hold as still as you can, okay?"

Billy nodded.

Dane leaned close and focused on the boy's nostrils. "It looks like your nose has quit bleeding, Billy. I'm glad for that."

Billy sniffed and put fingertips to his nose. "Me too."

Dane went to work on the eye, and after a few minutes, had the dirt washed away. Billy blinked his eyes. "That's better. Thank you, Dane."

"You're welcome, little pal," he said, focusing now on the cut lip. "Your lip is still bleeding pretty bad."

At that moment, one of the girls said, "Here comes Bessie!"

All eyes turned to the girl who was running down the alley waving a worn but clean piece of toweling like a banner. She drew up, panting, and handed it to Dane. "This . . . is . . . all I could . . . come up with, but . . . it's clean. Will it . . . do the job?"

Dane looked at the cloth, then the expectant look on the girl's face, which was red from running. "It will do just fine, Bessie. You're a good girl. Thank you."

Bessie smiled at his words of praise and shyly dipped her head.

Dane poured water on the cloth and put compassionate eyes on the little boy. This opportunity was giving him a hint at what it would be like to be a doctor, and he was reveling in it. "Billy, I'm going to have to press on the cut to try to stop the bleeding. It may hurt, but the bleeding has to be stopped."

Still panting, Bessie spoke up. "Billy's a brave . . . boy, Dane. He'll be . . . all right."

Billy set appreciative eyes on the pretty girl, then looked at Dane. "Go ahead. I'll be all right."

The look in Billy's eyes showed Dane

that he trusted him.

While the group looked on, Dane dabbed the wet cloth on the cut lip carefully, trying not to hurt the boy any more than was necessary. Billy winced, but did not cry out.

After several minutes, Dane held the wet cloth against the lip and looked around at the group in the gathering darkness. "The cut is really deep. I've got the bleeding slowed down, but Billy will need a doctor to stitch it up. Any of you know where the nearest doctor might be?"

Russell was about to speak up when Bessie said, "There is a very kind doctor who has an office a few blocks away, Dane. His name is Dr. Lee Harris. He and his wife and daughter live in the apartment above his office. Dr. Harris has a concern for the children who live on the streets. One afternoon a week — usually on Saturdays — he goes into some of the alleys to see if there are any sick or injured street waifs like us who need his help. We've heard that he helps so many poor families in this part of the city, that he doesn't make a lot of money. They can't pay him, but he helps them, anyhow. He's really a wonderful man. Dr. Harris was here just about three hours ago, so he won't be back for another week."

Dane rubbed his chin. "Billy needs his lip stitched up immediately. It can't wait a week. I'll take him to Dr. Harris right now if you will tell me how to find his office. Since he lives in the apartment above the office, he'll probably be home."

"I'll take you there, Dane," said Russell.

"All right," said Dane, sliding his hands underneath Billy's small body. He picked him up and rose to his feet, cradling him in his arms while holding the cloth against the cut lip to stay the flow of blood as much as possible.

Bessie smiled at Dane. "Thank you for being so kind, and for caring about Billy." She frowned and cocked her head to one side. "You don't live in this neighborhood, do you?"

"Actually, I don't live anywhere right now. I used to live in the two hundred block over on Thirty-third Street, but I became an orphan a few days ago when gang members murdered my parents and my little sister and brother. I came down here to live on the streets with orphans like you. I tried to get into two other colonies today, but they didn't want me."

"Well, you're welcome to live with us," spoke up Russell.

All the others joined in chorus to show their agreement with Russell, including Billy Johnson.

Bessie stepped up to Dane and laid a hand on his arm. "I'm so sorry about your family. I know we can't take their place, but we'll try."

Dane smiled at them. "Thank you. I feel at home with you already."

Russell's eyes sparkled, matching his smile. "We're very glad to have you."

One of the other boys said, "Dane, we have an extra cardboard box. You can sleep in it, just like we sleep in ours. It's big enough for you." He was pointing at the number of cardboard boxes that were grouped near the rear of the closest store.

Dane took a cursory glance at the boxes, then around the alley. "I want to thank all of you, again, for taking me in. I'll do my part to provide food. I'm trying to find a job of some kind. And I'll do what I can to provide safety for all of you, too."

"You're plenty good at that!" said Russell. "Believe me, we'll get the word around about how you handled those two bullies. Nobody will want to bother us once they know you're living here." He paused. "Could I ask you something?"

"Sure."

"Where'd you learn to fight like that? Both of those guys outweigh you ten pounds, if not more."

"I learned to take care of myself in school and in our neighborhood. Plenty of toughs to put up with. When you fight enough of them, you learn real quick."

"Well, you sure did all right with those two."

Dane's face tinted. "We'd better get going. Billy's lip is still bleeding." He looked at the others. "We'll be back later."

The small group of street waifs watched with appreciative eyes as Dane and Russell headed for the street with Billy cradled in Dane's arms.

When the boys reached the street, twilight was on Manhattan and the lamplighters were busy doing their job.

Russell pointed Dane in the proper direction, and they headed that way, walking fast. As they moved along the street, they saw a pair of policemen on a corner across the street, walking their beat together.

Russell focused on them. "That's different."

"What's different?"

"Two policemen on a beat together. It's always one officer by himself."

"Not anymore. I have a close friend who

lives in the same block where I used to live, and his father told me that all five boroughs are putting two officers together on a beat as partners. Too many police officers have been killed and wounded by the gangs because they were alone on their beats, and the criminals on the streets are braver when a police officer is by himself."

Keeping his eyes on the two officers as they walked, Russell said, "I'm sure that'll make the streets safer. Some of the officers in our area check on us street kids once in a while. It's good to know they're around, and it'll be even better with them working in pairs."

"Um-hmm," said Dane as he checked Billy's lip and picked up the pace.

It was dark by the time they drew up in front of the doctor's office, but there was a street lamp right in front of the building. There were no lights in the office — as they had expected — but there was a light in the apartment window above. A sign on the office door gave Dr. Harris's office hours, but added that in emergencies, if the doctor was home, he could be reached upstairs. An arrow pointed to the door that led up to the apartment.

Russell opened the door, allowing Dane to pass through with Billy in his arms. Together, they mounted the stairs. When they were almost to the top, Russell moved ahead and knocked on the door.

Footsteps were heard inside and the door opened. A tall, slender, gray-haired man appeared. His shoulders were stooped. He looked at Billy and the bloody cloth Dane was holding over his mouth. "Come in, boys. What have we here?"

"Some bullies beat Billy up, Dr. Harris," said Russell. "They cut his lip real bad. Our new friend did what he could to stop the bleeding, but he said Billy needed to have the cut stitched up."

Harris's bushy gray eyebrows arched. "Oh, now I know you boys. Your colony is in the alley behind Powell's Grocery."

"Yes, sir. My name's Russell Mims. Billy's last name is Johnson, and our friend's name is Dane Weston."

The doctor moved up close to the boy in Dane's arms, lifted the hand that held the bloody cloth, and studied the cut lip.

While he was doing so, Dane noticed an elderly silver-haired woman sitting on a sofa in the parlor behind the doctor, with a woman he judged to be about forty-five or so. He recalled that Bessie said the Harrises' daughter lived with them in the apartment. Dane had not expected the doctor and his wife to be that old, nor their daughter to be in her forties, either. He noted that the daughter was looking at him with her mouth hanging open. There was a blank stare in her eyes.

Wondering how a boy Dane's age would know whether or not the cut on Billy's lip would need stitches, and how he knew what to do to slow the bleeding, Dr. Harris said with a hint of admiration in his eyes, "You're right, Dane. The cut definitely needs to be sewn up. Not only for the bleeding's sake, but otherwise it will leave a nasty scar, and it could cause him a problem with his speech. You did the right thing by bringing him here. We'll go down to the office, and I'll get it stitched up."

Dane felt a thrill of satisfaction run through him. Guess I diagnosed my first case correctly, he thought. Too bad I didn't have the equipment or the capability to tend to him. Someday . . . Yes, someday.

Maude Harris drew up beside her husband. "Do you need my help, dear?"

"I don't think so, honey. Thank you, but I can handle this one by myself."

Maude ran her bespectacled eyes over Billy, noting the dried blood on his shirt. "Looks like this boy has lost quite a bit of blood."

Billy put fingers to his nose again. "My nose isn't bleeding anymore, though."

"That's good, dear," she said, patting his arm.

"He has lost a lot of blood," agreed Dr. Harris, "but this young man, here, did a good job of staying its flow."

Maude smiled at him. "Good for you, son."

Dane felt a warmth flow through his body. As he was turning toward the door, he noticed the Harrises' daughter standing in the center of the parlor. Fear showed in her vacant eyes, her hands were trembling, and her mouth still hung open.

The doctor said in a low voice, "Honey, you'd better take Lawanda back to the sofa."

Maude turned and took Lawanda's hand. "Come, sweetie. Let's sit down. These boys won't hurt you, I promise."

Lawanda gave her mother a blank stare, working her lips and making a low mumbling sound, then obediently followed with faltering steps as Maude took her by the hand and guided her back to the sofa.

Dr. Harris led the boys downstairs to his office, guided them into the examining room, and when he had lit three lanterns and placed them on small tables to give sufficient light for his task, he pointed to the table. "Lay him right here, Dane."

Dane laid him down gently. "Here you go, Billy. Dr. Harris is going to make everything better."

While the doctor was gathering materials at the medicine cabinet, Billy's eyes showed fear. His small shoulders twitched with an involuntary shiver. In a tremulous whisper, he said to Dane, "It's gonna hurt, isn't it?"

"Maybe a little bit, Billy," Dane said softly, "but you're tough, aren't you?"

Billy swallowed hard. "I try to be."

"You'll be fine," said Russell, patting his hand.

There was nothing wrong with Dr. Harris's hearing. With the necessary tools and supplies in his hands, he stepped up to the table and laid them on the cart next to it. "Don't be afraid, Billy. I'll do my best to make this as painless as possible."

The little boy met the kindly doctor's gaze and nodded.

Dr. Harris looked at Russell and Dane. "You boys can sit down over there on those chairs."

"Yes, sir," said Dane, moving toward the chairs. "C'mon, Russell."

When the boys were seated, Dr. Harris went to work.

While the split lip was being sutured, Russell sat quietly, his eyes on the doctor and his patient.

Billy made no sound.

Dane let his gaze roam around the room. He studied the medicine cabinet, the other examining table, and the cart that sat next to it.

There was a counter by the medicine cabinet where a large pitcher of water sat next to a metal wash pan. There were towels on a rack, and a bottle of lye soap sat next to the wash pan.

With his eyes still roaming about the room, Dane's attention was drawn to a picture frame on the wall closest to him that contained a Scripture verse printed on white paper. It read:

For the wages of sin is death; but the gift of God is eternal life through Jesus Christ our Lord. — Romans 6:23

Dane recalled hearing that verse somewhere one time, but could not think of where it was. His line of sight went to another wall where a similar frame had another Scripture verse. This one read:

Jesus answered and said unto him,

Verily, verily, I say unto thee, Except a man be born again, he cannot see the kingdom of God. — John 3:3

As soon as Dane read this one, he saw another frame on a third wall. The inscription read:

Jesus saith unto him, I am the way, the truth, and the life: no man cometh unto the Father, but by me. — John 14:6

Dane licked his lips and read all three again, twice.

# Chapter Five

Russell Mims was still keeping his eyes on the doctor and Billy Johnson while the stitching was being done on the little boy's lip.

Dane Weston glanced at the doctor and his patient periodically, but his eyes kept going back to the picture frames and the Scripture verses that were printed on the white paper. He was pondering their messages.

He kept trying to think of where he had heard the verse that spoke of the wages of sin being death and the gift of God being eternal life.

He scratched at an ear. Was it that Christmas program at school that time when that famous preacher was in town preaching at that big church on Forty-seventh Street? Yeah, that was it. What was his name? Oh yes. Charles Spurgeon. He was from England and was preaching in churches in three of the boroughs and in New Jersey. Principal Bateman belonged to that church on Forty-seventh Street, and invited Mr. Spurgeon to come and speak at the school's Christmas program. That was . . . let's see . . . four years ago last Christmas.

Dane recalled how the preacher had explained the Christmas story better than he had ever heard. He talked about Jesus Christ being born into this world to save sinners and that if people died without opening their hearts to Him, they would reap the wages of sin — eternal death, which was the lake of fire. Mr. Spurgeon emphasized that the opposite of eternal death was eternal life, and that eternal life was only found in Jesus Christ.

He also recalled how that sermon stayed with him a long time. In time, it finally drifted from his mind, and he hadn't thought of it since.

His eyes strayed to the picture frame on the far wall. The one which quoted Jesus as saying He is the way, the truth, and the life, and that no one could come to the Father but by Him. Dane thought of prayers he had heard people pray which began: *"Our Father which art in heaven . . ."*

He pondered that a moment. Since the Father is in heaven, Jesus was saying that no man could go to heaven but by Him. *Hmm,* he thought. *That means there is only one way to heaven, and that is Jesus.*

While these words were passing through his mind, he looked again at the framed message that intrigued him the most. Jesus said unless a man be born again, he cannot see the kingdom of God. Dane's brow furrowed. *How could a person be born another time? And how would that make it possible for him to go to heaven?*

Suddenly his attention was drawn to Dr. Harris. "Okay, boys, Billy's all stitched up."

Dane and Russell hurried to the examining table and looked down at their little friend.

"Did it hurt much, Billy?" asked Russell.

Billy did not try to speak. He only shook his head. "Hmmp-mm."

"I'm glad of that."

"Me too," said Dane.

The doctor smiled at Dane. "Russell called you his *new* friend. I don't recall seeing you before in the alley."

"Right, sir. I only showed up there this afternoon."

"But you're an orphan? I mean . . . you live on the streets?"

"As of today, sir. My parents and little sister and little brother were murdered by one of the street gangs a few days ago."

The doctor's face blanched. "Oh, I'm so sorry, Dane. So you have nowhere else to go but the streets?"

"That's right. I have no other relatives. The owner of our apartment building let me stay in our flat until today. He needs to rent it out again."

Dr. Harris nodded, compassion showing in his eyes. He looked down at Billy, then back at Dane. "You're to be commended for your quick thinking. Billy's going to be fine, thanks to you."

Dane's features tinted. "I'm glad I was there in the alley so I could look after him."

"You did a good job of getting the blood flow down to a minimum. Most boys your age wouldn't know what to do."

Dane took a short breath. "Well, Dr. Harris, let me explain something to you. My lifetime dream and goal is to someday be a doctor . . . a physician *and* a surgeon.

My parents have bought me some medical books, and I've just about memorized all but the one they bought me on the very evening they were killed. The police found it and gave it to me. It's a big one called *The History of Medicine*."

"Oh yes. I saw it advertised in the newspaper a short while back. Looked like a good one."

"It is. Goes all the way back to 200 B.C. and brings it right up to today."

A serious look came into the doctor's eyes. "Dane, I hope you're able to realize this dream someday. In your situation, it isn't going to be easy."

"I know, sir, but I'm not giving up. I'm concerned that I won't be able to attend school unless I have a guardian and live in the guardian's home."

"Yes, I know that law."

"Somehow, I'm going to get my high school education, then my medical education, which I know is going to cost a great deal of money. The main thing now is to get a job. I tried to find a job today. I went into over twenty stores, asking for work, and got turned down every time. It was late afternoon when I began looking for a colony of children to join in an alley. After being turned away by two groups, I was walking down Broadway and heard a girl screaming in an alley. I ran into the alley and found two teenage boys beating up on Billy. The girl was screaming for them to stop. They didn't. So I —"

"He plowed into them with both fists flying, Doctor," cut in Russell. "You should have been there to see him handle those bullies! He bloodied their noses and they took off running!"

Harris smiled at Dane, who was obviously embarrassed by Russell's praises.

Dane hunched his shoulders. "I only did what had to be done."

"Well, you did right, son. Now back to your situation. You're right about looking for a job. Right now, that has to be your first priority. I want to compliment you for the goal you have set for yourself. There's an old saying, and it's true. 'Where there's a will there's a way.' "

Hearing those words come from the doctor brought a melancholy smile to Dane's lips. "My mother used to quote that same saying often, Dr. Harris. And I'm trying my best to hang on to it and live by it. Today was discouraging job-wise, but I did find a home of sorts, and some new friends. Tomorrow's another day. I'll be out there bright and early, looking for a job. I need to find a good one and stay with it for the sake of food and other needs I'll have until the solution for my education presents itself."

"I appreciate your attitude. You stick with it. You did a good job taking care of Billy. I really believe you have the heart and mind for being a doctor. You're going to make a good one."

"Thank you for the encouragement, Doctor."

Harris smiled. "You're going to get some more valuable experience. I need you to take care of Billy's lip during this next week."

"I'll be glad to do it, sir."

The doctor turned and went to the medicine cabinet. He opened a glass door and took out a small jar of ointment. Moving back to the examining table where Billy lay, he handed the jar to Dane. "Wash the cut with clean water every morning, then apply the ointment. He has enough on the cut now to last till morning."

Dane nodded as he noted the shiny substance on Billy's lip.

"Another thing, Dane."

"Yes, sir?"

"Billy won't be able to eat solid food until I take the stitches out. Chewing will cause him pain. He will have to have liquids only. That means broth for breakfast and soup for his other meals."

"I'll explain this to the others in the colony, Doctor," said Russell. "We get food quite often at the café near our alley. They give us what they have left over at the end of the day. Sometimes they don't have any, and other times it isn't very much, but we'll explain this to the people at the café and I'm sure they'll see that Billy has broth and soup to eat. We may have to pay for it sometimes out of the money we bring in by begging on the street, but one way or another, we'll see that Billy gets his broth and soup."

"Good. Also, this boy needs to drink a lot of water." The doctor looked down at his patient. "Do you hear me, Billy? Lots of water. I know it will hurt some to put a cup to your mouth, but it's important that you drink plenty of water. It will ward off infection. Understand?"

Billy met his gaze and nodded.

"Good. And try not to touch your lip with your hands. Any germs that might be on them could get into the cut and that would be bad. Okay?"

Billy nodded again.

"I'll do my best to take care of him, Dr.

Harris," said Dane, "even though I'll have to be away from the alley to look for a job."

"The girls and I will take care of him when you're not there, Dane," said Russell.

Dane smiled at him.

"I'll come to the alley next Saturday to check on Billy's lip and make sure it is healing all right," said the doctor.

"We'll be looking for you, Doctor," said Dane. He reached into his pocket and took out the two silver dollars that Thomas Milford had given him and extended them to Dr. Harris. "Will this cover your bill for taking care of Billy?"

Harris shook his head. "There is no charge, Dane. I take care of the street children for free."

"But Bessie Evans told me you help lots of poor families who can't pay you, sir. Bessie is the girl who was screaming when I drew near the alley. She said you don't make a lot of money and even though many people can't pay you, you help them anyhow. I want you to take this money."

Dr. Harris shook his head. "No, Dane. I can't take money for caring for the alley children. Besides, I have a feeling that's all the money you have in the world. Right?"

Dane's eyes dropped to the ground, then he raised them and met the doctor's gaze. "Yes, sir. But I —"

"You keep it, son. Use it to buy food for yourself and your friends there in the alley."

Dane dropped the coins back in his pocket. "All right, sir. Thank you." Then he looked down at Billy. "Well, little buddy, are you ready to go?"

Billy nodded. "Mm-hmm."

As Dane was picking the boy up off the table, Dr. Harris said, "I'll see you next Saturday, Billy. And remember — drink lots of water."

Billy nodded as Dane cradled him in his arms.

Dr. Harris led them to the front door of the office and opened it. "Good night, boys. May the Lord keep His hand on you."

Dane and Russell thanked him once again for taking care of their little friend and headed down the dimly lit street.

As they walked toward the alley, Dane looked at Russell. "How old are you?"

"Fourteen."

"That's what I figured. Do you mind telling me how you became an orphan?"

"Of course not. My parents both died of illnesses in 1862. Papa died of pneumonia in February, and Mama died of diphtheria in March. I was four at the time. I turned five in April. My grand-mother Mims lived just a few blocks from us and took care of my parents when they became sick, and of course, took care of me, too. After Papa and Mama died, Grandma took me into her apartment. I lived with her until I was eight, then she died. It was then that I had no choice but to live on the streets."

"So you've been a street waif for six years."

"Yeah. Seems like sixty years."

"I can imagine."

The moon was up and spraying the city with its silvery light as the boys entered the alley to find the group of seven children sitting on the ground, leaning against the rear wall of the store. They all jumped to their feet and ran to meet Dane, Billy, and Russell.

Between Dane and Russell, they learned about Dr. Lee Harris's treatment of Billy's cut lip and were glad to hear that with proper care, the cut would heal up in time and Billy would be all right.

Bessie spoke up. "Billy, are you hungry?"

The little boy nodded from Dane's arms. "Uh-huh."

"Well, I went to the café and got you

some soup. I figured it would hurt you to chew food."

Dane chuckled. "That's exactly what Dr. Harris told us, Bessie. He said we'd have to see that Billy gets broth for breakfast and soup for his other meals until he takes the stitches out. He's also supposed to drink lots and lots of water."

"Well, water we have plenty of. The people at the café are good to give us food they have left over and would have to throw out, but to get broth and soup from them each day, we'll probably have to pay them. In our begging today, we took in a dollar and five cents. If we have to buy some broth and soup tomorrow, we'll have to pay for it out of that. It won't leave much for the rest of us, but we'll get by."

Dane took the two silver dollars out of his pocket and handed them to Bessie. "Put these two dollars with it. One of the store owners I asked for a job today gave them to me."

Bessie's eyes widened as did those of the rest of the group. "Wow! This will really help, Dane. Thank you." Then Bessie said, "We saved some supper for both of you, too. While you're eating, I'll feed Billy his soup."

When Dane and Russell sat down, Dane

was grateful to eat from the meager portions of leftover spaghetti that were on the tin plates. He ate slowly, making the portion last as long as possible.

While they ate, Russell told the rest of the group that he found out while they were at Dr. Harris's office that Dane was planning to be a doctor someday. He added that he thought Dane would make a good doctor, and they all agreed.

Finishing up with a long drink of water from a tin cup, Dane said to the others, "Thank you for sharing this food with me." He yawned and covered his mouth. "Mmm. Excuse me. It must be bedtime. It's been a long day."

Everyone agreed, and began preparing to go to bed in their cardboard boxes, which Russell explained to Dane, had come from a furniture store at the other end of the block. Each child had a couple of tattered blankets to cover them. Dane was given two such blankets by Bessie, and the boys led Dane to his cardboard box. Dane slid his box up next to Billy's box. "Billy, if you need me anytime during the night, wake me up, okay?"

Lying in the box, Billy nodded and reached his arms up. Dane bent down, and the little boy hugged his neck. When he let go, Dane smiled. "I'll wash your cut in the morning and put some fresh ointment on it."

The children told each other good-night, then got into their cardboard boxes and covered up with their blankets.

Dane's stomach was growling with hunger as he covered himself with his blankets. He rubbed a hand over it and told himself that his body would get used to living on less food than it had in the past. His mother didn't always prepare food that he liked, but the meals were filling, and the love shared around the table more than made up for it.

When he had made himself as comfortable as possible in the box, he thought about the events of the day. This was a whole new world for him. He wondered how long it would take him to get used to it. He told himself the winters would have to be difficult.

His mind went to his dead family. Tears surfaced, and speaking in a low whisper, he spoke to each one, telling them that he loved them.

While wiping tears, Dane thought of the picture frames in Dr. Harris's office containing the Bible verses. He tried to recall the exact words of each one and came reasonably close. The one he remembered best was what Jesus said about being born again: *"Except a man be born again, he cannot see the kingdom of God."*

He told himself the kingdom of God Jesus spoke of had to be heaven, but he couldn't imagine what it meant to be born two times.

He fell asleep with these words on his mind.

Dane awakened the next morning to see the sky brightening and knew that the sun was rising, though the tall buildings blocked his view of it. He was surprised that he had slept so well in his cardboard bed with only the hard ground beneath.

Rubbing his eyes, he stretched his cramped legs and crawled out of the box. He bent down to look into Billy's quarters and found him awake. "Did you sleep all right, little buddy?"

Billy started to move his lips to speak, winced slightly, and simply nodded.

"Good. Come on out here into the light and let me have a good look at you." As he spoke, Dane reached down into the box and helped him out. Carefully taking the boy's chin in his hand, he eyed the stitched lip and turned his head from side to side.

"It looks pretty sore yet, and is still swollen some. After you have your broth, I'll wash the cut and put some more ointment on it. We'll have it feeling better in a few days."

After a meager breakfast of yesterday's biscuits and gravy donated by the café owner — along with broth for Billy — Dane washed the cut and applied a fresh coat of ointment. Bessie announced that she would stay with Billy while the others went out on the street to beg and Dane went job hunting. She and two of the other girls would go to the local market and buy some food late in the afternoon when the begging was done for the day. The two dollars Dane had put in the kitty would supply more food than they had been able to purchase in a long time.

It was just past 4:30 in the afternoon when seven of the orphans on the street corner saw Dane coming down the street toward them. His countenance told them he still had not found a job.

As Dane drew up, Russell said, "Guess it didn't go so good."

Dane shook his head. "No, but I'll be back out on the streets tomorrow. I've got to find a job. How'd it go here?"

"Well, we just pooled our money and

were about to head back to the alley," said Russell. "We got ninety-seven cents today."

At that moment, one of the girls — Melinda Scott, who was twelve years old — pointed to a buggy passing by. "Oh, look! It's Mr. and Mrs. Charles Loring Brace."

Dane eyed the couple in the buggy. "You mean the Charles Loring Brace who's the director of the Children's Aid Society?"

Melinda nodded. "Mm-hmm. So you know about the Society and that they send orphans out West."

"Sure do. I've heard about the orphan trains many times. Just recently I was eating supper at my best friend's apartment. His mother was talking about Mr. Brace and the orphan trains. She read some things to us at the table from a newspaper about the orphan trains."

A tear formed in the corner of Melinda's left eye as she watched the Braces' buggy turn the corner and vanish from sight. She looked at Dane as she wiped away the tear. "I used to live in another alley a few blocks from here. I watched Mr. and Mrs. Brace pick up some of the children in that alley and take them away to put them on orphan trains. I — I always hoped I would be chosen, but it never happened. Of course, I realize they can only take so many children off the streets to send them out West. I just wasn't one of the fortunate ones."

"Well, maybe one of these days you will be," said Russell. "Let's get on back to the alley. Bessie wants to go get some groceries."

As they headed for the alley, Dane's thoughts went back to Mona Baxter, and what he had said when she read aloud the words of the orphans' song from the newspaper: *"Hey, Mrs. Baxter, I really like that! If I didn't have such a good home with my wonderful parents and sister and brother, I wouldn't mind going out there on the western frontier where the fragrant breezes sigh myself! When those fragrant breezes sigh to the orphans out there, maybe each one hears whispers in the wind, welcoming them to a new and wonderful life."*

Quickly, Mrs. Baxter's comment came back to him: "Whispers in the wind welcoming them. That's good. Yes, from what I've read, I think they do, Dane. I think they do."

Dane thought again about his words: "such a good home." His heart felt like cold lead. He had no such home now. His family was gone. It would be the streets for him until someday he could find a way to finish high school and go to medical school.

But first, he must find a job.

When they turned into their alley, they saw Bessie sitting on the ground next to the rear wall of the store with Billy beside her. Both jumped to their feet, and as the group drew up, Bessie looked at Dane expectantly. "Did you find a job?"

Dane shook his head. "Nothing so far. I'll be back at it in the morning."

Bessie said, "Maybe you should just beg on the street corner like the rest of us do."

Dane shook his head. "I'll keep trying to find a job. I have to."

Russell gave Bessie the ninety-seven cents from the day's begging, and with the two dollars Dane had contributed, she and two of the girls headed for the market.

As the days passed, Dane returned to the alley each afternoon, still with no job. On Thursday morning, he went out job-hunting again. When he returned that afternoon, he sadly told his friends that he was still jobless.

Russell said, "Dane, I know you want a job real bad, but maybe Bessie's right. Maybe you should start begging with the rest of us. You might only come up with a nickel or a dime a day, but at least it would be more than you're bringing in now."

"Maybe it *would* be best if I beg for a few days, then when I have some money in my pocket to pay for my part of the food, I can go back to looking for a job. If I don't have some money saved up by the time I work out how to finish high school, I won't be able to enter medical school. I've just got to find a job."

"We all understand that, Dane," said Melinda, "but Russell and Bessie are right. You need to bring in some money by begging, like the rest of us do."

Dane smiled at her. "I agree. Tomorrow morning I'll be on the corner out there with you."

On Friday, Dane begged with the others and ended up with a whopping forty cents. He pooled it with the money the others had taken in so they could have a meager supper of day-old bread and celery.

When Saturday morning came, the children had their small portions of breakfast provided by the café, which included broth for Billy Johnson.

Five-year-old Nettie Olson had a stomachache and did not eat.

Dane placed a palm on Nettie's brow

113

and told the others she didn't seem to have a fever. When he suggested that he carry her to Dr. Harris's office, Bessie reminded him that Dr. Harris would be coming today to check on Billy's lip. He could examine Nettie at the same time. Dane said since Nettie wasn't vomiting, it would be all right to wait for Dr. Harris.

After breakfast, Dane washed Billy's lip and applied the ointment as usual. Bessie told the others she would stay with Billy and Nettie.

The other seven were about to head for the street corner for their day of begging when they saw the physician enter the alley, carrying his black medical bag. One of the boys commented that he had never come in the morning before. It was always in the afternoon. One of the girls said, "I'm glad he's here, now. I'm worried about Nettie."

As Dr. Lee Harris drew up, he said, "Good morning, children. I've come to check on Billy's lip. Everybody else all right?"

"All but little Nettie Olson, Doctor," said Dane. "She's over here in her cardboard box. She has a stomachache. She doesn't seem to have a fever."

Harris smiled. "So you checked for

that already, did you?"

"Yes, sir. She hasn't been vomiting, or I would have brought her to your office."

"Good thinking, son," said the doctor as he moved up to the cardboard box that held the little girl. He looked at Billy, who stood close by. "Billy, I'll check you in a minute, but I want to examine Nettie first."

Billy nodded and tried to smile, but when he felt a stinging in the cut, he let the smile die on his lips.

Dr. Harris knelt down beside Nettie's box with some difficulty, and as he felt her brow, Dane Weston knelt down beside him. The doctor said, "I think you're right, Dane. She doesn't feel like she has a fever, but I'm going to take her temperature just to be sure."

Harris opened his black bag and took out a tongue depressor. "I need to check your throat, honey," he said to Nettie. "Open wide for me, will you?"

Nettie complied, and after a few seconds, the doctor laid the depressor aside and took a thermometer out of his bag. He told Nettie he was going to place it under her tongue and asked her to press her lips tight around it. When it was in place, he said, "It will take a minute to get the

115

reading, Nettie. Hold it right there, won't you?"

She nodded, tightening her lips around it.

Dane observed as the doctor carefully and methodically pressed experienced fingers on her stomach, covering every inch. When he finished, he slipped the thermometer out of her mouth and read it. "You were exactly right, Dane. No fever. Nettie, you just worked yourself up a tummy ache. Nothing serious at all." He turned to the others. "I need some water and a cup."

"Coming right up," said Bessie. She hurried to a box where they kept their tin cups and the jug of water, and was back in a matter of seconds.

Dr. Harris examined the cup to make sure it was clean. Satisfied that it was, he poured the cup half full, then took a dark-colored bottle from his bag. He poured a portion of the clear liquid from it into the cup, then took an eyedropper from his bag and used it to stir the mixture.

He filled the eyedropper. "Nettie, I'm giving you oil of peppermint mixed with water. Open your mouth a little bit for me."

Nettie did so and the children watched

as he gave her several droppers of the liquid.

When he had finished, he took a stick of peppermint candy from the bag. "Nettie, I've given you a sufficient amount of oil of peppermint to do you until noon. At that time, I want you to suck on this peppermint candy until it is all gone. You should start feeling better in about half an hour. You'll feel even better when you've consumed the candy."

Nettie smiled up at him. "Thank you, Dr. Harris."

"My pleasure, sweetheart. Now I need to tend to Billy."

The aging physician had difficulty rising to his feet.

Dane moved to the spot where Dr. Harris had Billy sit down on a wooden crate near the back door of the store and observed as the cut was examined. The others pressed up close.

After making a close examination, Dr. Harris looked at Dane. "You've done an excellent job on this cut, Dr. Weston."

Dane grinned. "Thank you, sir, but I'm a long way from being Dr. Weston."

Harris chuckled. "Yes, but at least you are headed in the right direction. I called you that because I see the potential in you to be an excellent physician. Keep doing the same as you've done with Billy's lip. I'll take the stitches out next Saturday."

In spite of his injured lip, Billy grinned — enduring the pain — and said, "Dane really is a good doctor."

"He sure is!" Russell said with a lilt in his voice.

Dane's features crimsoned.

Dr. Harris closed his medical bag and looked at Dane. "Dr. Weston, keep a close eye on Nettie. If her stomachache isn't gone by sundown, come to my office and let me know."

Dane was eyeing the medical bag in Harris's hand. He looked up and said, "I'll do that, Doctor. In fact, Russell and I will bring her to you just like we did Billy."

"That will be fine."

When Dane looked back at the bag, Harris grinned. "You'll have one of these someday, son."

Dane grinned back. "I sure am planning on it, sir."

"Have you found a job, yet?"

"No, sir. So far, I can't find anybody who wants me."

"Good!"

The children eyed Dr. Harris curiously.

Dane's dark eyebrows arched as his brow furrowed. "Good?"

"Yes. I have found you a job. If you want it, that is."

Dane swallowed hard, eyes widened. "Sure I do! What is it?"

# Chapter Six

The rest of the children looked on with interest as Dr. Lee Harris laid a wrinkled hand on Dane Weston's shoulder. "Dane, I have a close friend whose name is Bryce Clarkson. Bryce is a pharmacist. He owns the Clarkson Pharmacy on Broadway just four blocks south of here. I do all my medicine business with him, and —" Noticing the strange look that had come into Dane's eyes, Harris said, "What is it?"

Dane grinned crookedly. "I went into the Clarkson Pharmacy on Monday. Mr. Clarkson said he didn't have any work for me."

"Oh, really?"

"Yes, sir."

"Well, that's changed. Just yesterday, I

was in the pharmacy, picking up some various kinds of medicine I had ordered for my office, and Bryce told me that the young man who did the sweeping and cleaning and sometimes delivered prescriptions to his customers' homes, had quit on Thursday without notice, saying he was moving to Brooklyn immediately. He asked me if I knew a reliable young man anywhere in the area who might want the job."

Dane's eyes brightened. "And — and you told him about me?"

"Yes, I did. I explained that you were fifteen years old and were living among other orphans in a nearby alley and that I would be seeing you today. I told him that you have been looking for a job, and that if you hadn't found one yet — or even if you had — and the job at the pharmacy sounded better to you, I would bring you to him today so the two of you could talk."

Bessie Evans said joyfully, "Oh, Dane, I think that's wonderful!"

Dane smiled at her. "Thanks, Bessie."

"So do the rest of us," spoke up Russell.

"Yeah!" chimed in Billy Johnson. He winced and his hand went quickly to his cut lip.

The rest of them joined in, saying they hoped it worked out.

Dr. Harris said, "Dane, I asked Bryce for some particulars about the job. It pays twenty cents an hour. You would work three hours each morning, six days a week. Your job would be to sweep and mop the floors, wash the windows, keep the store dusted, and any other cleaning job Mr. Clarkson might give you. When it was needed, you would also deliver prescriptions to his customers, and you would sweep the sidewalk in front of the store periodically, and shovel snow off the walk in the wintertime."

Excitement built inside of Dane with each word Dr. Harris was saying. Eyes dancing, he said, "How soon can we go so I can talk to Mr. Clarkson, Dr. Harris?"

The doctor chuckled. "Well, right now, if you want to. My first appointment today isn't until one o'clock this afternoon."

"Yes, sir! I want to!"

"Yes, Dane!" said Melinda Scott, jumping up and down and clapping her hands. "Hurry, so you can come back and tell us you got the job!"

Dane looked up at the silver-haired physician. "Thank you for thinking of me, Dr. Harris. This sounds like a golden opportunity. Being around medicine will connect me with the medical profession, even though I'm only cleaning the pharmacy and making a delivery now and then. I'm sure I'll learn things that will help me in my goal to be a doctor."

"I had the same thing in mind, son. Let's go."

The children in the colony — except for Nettie Olson — stood together in a tight circle and watched as Dr. Lee Harris and Dane Weston walked to the street, made a right turn, and disappeared from view.

Pharmacist Bryce Clarkson had just finished waiting on a customer when Dane opened the door, allowed Dr. Harris to move in ahead of him, then held the door open so the lady could step out on to the sidewalk. She smiled. "Thank you, young man."

Dane gave her a grin. "You're welcome, ma'am."

When Dane stepped inside, Dr. Harris had already moved up to the counter and spoken to the pharmacist, who looked at the boy as he hurried up beside the doctor.

Clarkson fixed his eyes on Dane's face. "This is the boy you told me about, Doc?"

"Yes. His name is Dane Weston."

Clarkson frowned. "Weren't you in here a few days ago, looking for a job?"

"Yes, sir. It was last Monday. I still need a job, sir. Dr. Harris explained what my duties would be, the working hours, and the pay. I sure would like to have the job."

The pharmacist looked at Dr. Harris. "You can recommend Dane without reservation, Doc?"

"Totally without reservation. I'm sure he will do you a very good job."

Clarkson extended his hand across the counter. "All right, Dane. You're hired."

Dane grasped his hand and shook it vigorously. "Thank you, Mr. Clarkson! When do you want me to go to work?"

"I want you to start Monday morning at eight o'clock."

"I'll be here a few minutes earlier than that, sir."

Dr. Harris said, "Dane, as long as there's no one else here in the pharmacy at the moment, I think you should tell Mr. Clarkson your story — where you lived up until recently and how you became an orphan."

Clarkson listened intently as Dane told him he had lived in an apartment building in the two hundred block on Thirty-third Street with his family until several days ago when his parents and siblings were murdered by the street gang.

The pharmacist's features pinched and sadness filled his eyes. He moved around the counter and put an arm around Dane's shoulders. "Dane, I'm so sorry about your loss. That's a lot for a boy your age to handle. It has to be hard enough to have your family taken from you so suddenly, but then to have to take to the streets in addition to this . . . I know it has to be overwhelming."

Tears misted the boy's eyes. "Yes, sir. It's been very hard, but knowing I have a job now really helps. I can put some money aside so I can finish my education."

Clarkson smiled. "Well, that's an admirable objective. If a man's going to get anywhere in this world today, he must have a good education."

Dr. Harris smiled. "Tell him what your ultimate goal is, Dane."

"I want to become a physician and surgeon, Mr. Clarkson."

"Wonderful! That indeed is an illustrious ambition. And it can't hurt you to be working in a pharmacy around medicine, either."

Dane laughed. "You're right about that, sir."

Dr. Harris said, "Thank you for giving my young friend the job, Bryce. I appreciate it very much."

"Well, Doc, I appreciate your telling me about him. He'll do fine, I'm sure of it."

At that moment, a pair of customers entered the store. Dr. Harris told Clarkson he would see him later, and Dane said he would see him Monday morning.

The two headed down the street in the direction of Dane's alley home, which would take them past Harris's office.

As they moved along, Harris said, "Dane, how would you like to come to our apartment this evening for supper?"

Dane's eyes lit up. "I sure would!" Suddenly, his countenance changed and the light left his eyes.

Dr. Harris asked, "Is something wrong, son?"

"Well-l-l . . ."

"What is it?"

Dane cleared his throat. "Well, sir, it's just that — that I'll feel guilty eating what I'm sure will be a delicious meal while my friends in the alley will be having only scraps and stale food. Please don't misunderstand. I'm very grateful for the invitation."

Dr. Harris smiled and a twinkle appeared in his eyes. "You are quite a lad, my young friend. You're going to make an excellent doctor. You have that selflessness that is so vital to being a caring physician. Too many that choose a medical career, unfortunately, are only looking for monetary gain. It saddens me when I think of these men that God has blessed with the ability to do great things for humanity, and instead they use it only to build up their bank accounts."

Dane looked up at the elderly physician with admiration. "Dr. Harris, I happen to know that you care for people because you love them, and it makes no difference whether they can pay you for your services or not. I'm sure your bank account is not a fat one."

"Well, I —"

"And sir, I want to be the kind of physician that you are. I want to serve my fellow man and make a positive difference in people's lives."

Dr. Harris's face crimsoned. "Dane, I can't say that I'm the shining example for you to follow, but —"

"Oh yes, you are!"

The crimson in the doctor's features deepened. "Thank you, Dane." He took a deep breath. "What you just said about wanting to serve your fellow man and make a positive difference in people's lives . . . good for you. Don't ever lose sight of that goal. Now, back to the subject of coming to supper. When I told my wife that I was going to take you to see Bryce Clarkson about the job, she told me to invite you to supper this evening."

"Really?"

They were drawing up to the office.

"Really. You see, I've told her your whole story, and she wants to get to know you better."

"Oh. I see."

"And let me say this. Mrs. Harris always makes sure there is plenty of food on the table, so whatever is left after we eat supper, you can take to your alley family."

A smile curved the boy's lips. "Oh! Well, in that case, I would be very happy to eat supper with you!"

As Dr. Harris stepped up and inserted the key into the lock, he said, "We'll look forward to it. And I want you to come into the office for a minute. I have something I would like to give you."

Curious, Dane followed him in, and this time he noticed picture frames on the walls like those in the examining room — each with a Scripture verse on the subject of salvation. His mind flashed back to the one in the examining room about being born again. He wanted to ask Dr. Harris to explain that verse to him, but he didn't have the nerve to do so.

The doctor went to his desk, opened a drawer, and took out a small glass jar with money inside. He pulled three crisp one-dollar bills from the jar, along with a fifty-cent piece and a dime. Holding the money so Dane could see it, he said, "At twenty cents an hour, Dr. Weston, you will make sixty cents a day. That's three dollars and sixty cents a week, right?"

Dane grinned. "Mm-hmm. I already figured it out."

Dr. Harris handed him the money. "I'm giving you a week's pay. This will carry you until you get your first week's pay from the pharmacy next Saturday."

Dane shook his head. "Oh no, sir. I can't let you do this. I'm sure you need it for yourself and your family. I'll get along all right until I have a pay day. I wouldn't feel right taking your money. Like I said, I'm sure your bank account is not a fat one."

The kindly man laid a blue-veined hand on the boy's shoulder. "Dane, someone helped me out when I was a young man trying to find a way to fund my medical education so I could become a doctor. I tried later to pay him back, and his words to me were, 'You don't need to pay me back, but whenever you see a sincere young man who is struggling like you were to become a physician, then you help him.' Dane, what I've just put in your hand is nowhere near the amount he gave to me, but please let me do this much to help you. In a small way over the years I've been able to help some other young men who were working toward becoming doctors. Please accept this money. And someday after you've become a successful physician, maybe you'll find some aspiring young doctor-to-be that you can help."

Humbled by the dear man's generosity, Dane nodded. His voice was tight with emotion as he slipped the money into his pocket. "All right, sir. Thank you. I appreciate it more than I can ever tell you. And I promise you that one day when the opportunity arises, I will do the same for someone else."

Harris smiled. "That's all I ask, son."

"And Dr. Harris . . ."

"Yes?"

"Thank you for getting me the job with Mr. Clarkson."

Harris squeezed the boy's shoulder. "You're very welcome, Dr. Weston."

Dane blushed. "One day, sir, I will indeed be Dr. Weston. Whatever it takes, I am going to make it."

"I have no doubt of that. Supper is at 6:30."

"I'll be here, sir!"

"Mrs. Harris will be glad to hear it. And, Dane, since it will be getting dark by the time supper is over, I'll take you back to the alley in my buggy. It's at the stable in this same block on the next street behind the office."

"All right. Thank you. I'll be back in time for supper."

When Dane reached the alley, his new family members were eager to hear if he got the job for sure, and when he told them he did, they wanted to know all about it.

After he had given them the details, he reached into his pocket, showed them the money, and explained that Dr. Harris had given it to him to get him by till he got paid next Saturday by Mr. Clarkson. He told them of his invitation to eat supper with the Harrises that evening, and said, "Russell, how about you and I go to the grocery market and buy some real good food for all of us? And some of this money can be used to buy a real nice meal from the café so the rest of you can have a good supper too."

Bessie Evans had tears in her eyes. "Dane, thank you for being so generous."

He grinned at her. "Hey, friends should share with friends, and I'm glad I can do it."

Dane then turned his attention to Nettie Olson, who was now sitting up. "How are you feeling, Nettie?"

"My stomach is much better, Dane. I think by tonight, I can eat some of that supper you were talking about."

"I'm glad to hear that. But if you should get worse, we'll take you to Dr. Harris."

Melinda Scott moved up beside Dane and chuckled as she elbowed him in the ribs. "Who needs Dr. Harris? We've got our own doctor now. We'll just call you 'Doc'!"

They all laughed, and Dane laughed with them. "Okay, Russell, let's go get some food for this bunch."

Russell grinned. "Doc, I think we'd better take at least one of the girls with us. They know more about buying groceries than we fellas do."

Bessie laughed. "Russell, you're going to make some woman a good husband someday."

Everybody laughed.

Bessie said, "I'll go with you two. We'll make that money stretch real far. And when it's time to go to the café this evening, I'll go along with Russell and see that we get our money's worth."

"I'll vote for that!" piped up Melinda, and everybody laughed again.

That evening at 6:20, Dane knocked on the door of the small apartment above the doctor's office. Dr. Harris opened the door and smiled. "Come in, Dane!"

As he stepped into the parlor, Dane sniffed. "Smells mighty good, Dr. Harris. One whiff of that sweet aroma has my stomach growling already!"

"Good! Let's go to the kitchen."

As they moved through the parlor and entered the narrow hall that led to the kitchen, Dane noticed how clean the apartment was, and what a homey atmosphere pervaded the place.

When they entered the kitchen, Maude smiled and left the cupboard where she was cutting hot bread. "Welcome, Dane. I'm so glad you came."

"Me too, ma'am," said Dane. He looked around the room and noticed there were only three places set at the table. He frowned.

Harris noticed Dane's frown. "Something wrong, son?"

"Uh . . . no, sir. I thought your daughter would be eating with us. I saw her when we were here the other day."

The Harrises exchanged glances, then the doctor said, "Dane, we need to explain about our daughter."

"Yes, sir?"

"Lawanda . . . well, she's mentally deficient, Dane. She was born that way forty-four years ago. She has the mind of a two-year-old."

"Oh."

Maude said, "Dane, Lawanda has great fear of other people. If we brought you into the room and she was here, she would be terrified. She is in the bedroom, lying down. I fed her already."

"She should really be in a home for the mentally deficient, Dane," said Harris, "but we can't afford to put her in one. We love her with all of our hearts and want to take the best care of her possible. Maude and I can't go to church together, because one of us has to stay home with Lawanda. So we alternate. One of us goes to church on a Sunday morning while the other one stays home with our little girl, then the other one goes on that Sunday night while the other stays home with her. We switch off who goes Sunday mornings and nights each week. When Maude goes to church, there is a family who are members of the church who come by and pick her up. When I go, I drive my buggy."

Dane was not sure what to say, so he commented, "I can see that you are wonderful parents. Do you have any other children?"

"Yes. We have a son who lives in Roanoke, Virginia. He has a lovely wife, and they have given us three grandchildren. Two of those grandchildren are now married and have families of their own. They all live in Roanoke."

"I see. Do you get to visit them often?"

"Usually once a year we go to Roanoke, and they come here a couple of times a year."

The room went silent.

Maude broke the silence. "Well! You men sit down at the table, and as soon as I finish cutting the bread, we'll eat."

As Dane sat down at the place designated by Dr. Harris, he noticed a Bible lying on a small table near the window. He also noticed a picture frame on one wall with a Scripture verse on it, like those in the office and examining room downstairs. This one read:

> The name of Jesus Christ . . . Neither is there salvation in any other: for there is none other name under heaven given among men, whereby we must be saved. Acts 4:10, 12

The doctor sat down at his place, and as Maude placed the plate of hot bread on the table, Dane took in the array of food. The hot bread was in huge slices, with a butter plate and a jelly dish to go with it. There was succulent glazed ham, sugared sweet potatoes, and green peas with tiny onion chips. Dane had already spied a yellow cake with chocolate frosting sitting on the cupboard. He had to keep swallowing the saliva that filled his mouth in anticipation of what he was about to enjoy.

When Maude sat down at her place, Dr. Harris ran his gaze over both faces and said, "Let's pray."

Dane saw the Harrises bow their heads and close their eyes, and he did the same.

The doctor led in prayer, thanking the Lord for allowing Dane to come into their lives; he then thanked Him for the food and closed in Jesus' name. When the amen was said, Dane raised his head and opened his eyes to see both people smiling at him. The food was passed around, and the doctor and his wife smiled at each other as Dane wolfed everything down.

While they were eating, Dr. Harris looked at the boy, swallowed a mouthful of sweet potato, and said, "Dane did your family attend church anywhere?"

Dane shook his head. "No, sir. We didn't go to church."

Approaching the subject carefully, Harris asked, "Do you believe God exists?"

"Oh, yes, sir. I sure do."

"Do you believe the Bible is God's written Word to mankind?"

"Yes, sir. I have heard enough about it to know that it is God's Word. There was a family who lived in our tenement who went to church regularly. Several times I heard the man and his wife talking to my parents about what God says in the Bible concerning many different subjects."

"I see. Was there ever any discussion about heaven and hell, and sin and salvation?"

Dane swallowed a mouthful of green peas. "I remember the neighbors bringing those subjects up sometimes, yes. They told my parents that God's Son, Jesus

Christ, was the only one who could cleanse and forgive their sins and take them to heaven."

He pointed to the picture frame on the wall that he had looked at earlier. "That Scripture up there . . ."

"Yes?"

"I remember hearing our neighbors say something very much like that."

The doctor went on to question Dane along these lines to see just how much he understood about sin and its consequences. He was pleased to learn that the boy had some of it right, but quickly saw that he needed further instruction in several areas. He realized he must be as wise as a serpent and as gentle as a dove in dealing with the boy, so he explained a few things for him to think about and quoted Scriptures to plant the seed of the Word firmly in his heart.

Both Harrises were pleased at the way Dane accepted what he was being told as the absolute truth.

Maude said, "Dane, tomorrow morning it's my husband's turn to go to church while I stay home with Lawanda. Would you like to go to Sunday school and church with him?"

Dane had just swallowed a piece of the

yellow cake. "I really would like to go with Dr. Harris, ma'am, but I really don't have any church-going clothes. I have three more shirts that I brought with me when I left the tenement flat, two more pair of trousers, three pair of socks, and two pair of long johns. My shirts and trousers are much like the ones I have on right now. They're just not dress-up clothes."

Dr. Harris smiled at him. "You will be welcome at our church dressed as you are."

"Really?"

"Yes."

"Then I will go with you in the morning, sir."

"Good! I'll be by your alley at about 9:15. Just wait right there on the street for me."

"I will, sir. I can check the big clock on the front of the bank on the corner, so I'll know what time it is."

After supper the doctor took Dane back to the alley in his buggy.

The next morning, Dane was picked up by Dr. Harris and taken to Sunday school and church services.

In the preaching service, Dr. Harris was pleased to see the boy keeping his eyes on the pastor as he was preaching. The sermon was on the subject of hell, and Dane was amazed to see the preacher wiping tears with a handkerchief as he warned of the consequences of dying without Jesus Christ.

Dane was strongly impressed by the sermon, and the doctor could see conviction on his young face during the invitation. As others were walking the aisle to receive Jesus into their hearts as their personal Saviour, Dane gripped the back of the pew in front of him but did not move.

# Chapter Seven

When Dr. Lee Harris and Dane Weston climbed in the buggy after the church service, Dr. Harris said, "I didn't tell you this yet, Dane, but Mrs. Harris told me to ask you if you would come home with me and eat Sunday dinner with us. How about it?"

Dane grinned at him. "I'd love to, sir. My family in the alley have probably already eaten their lunch."

Harris snapped the reins and put the horse into motion. "Good! Whatever she's got cooked for dinner will be tasty, I assure you."

"I don't doubt that," said Dane. "That supper last night was really a treat."

As the buggy moved down the street, Dr.

Harris noticed that Dane was unusually quiet. He sat very still, looking straight ahead as if his thoughts had him a million miles away. Harris was sure it was because the sermon on hell had a powerful effect on him.

When they arrived at the apartment, Maude was just ushering Lawanda from the kitchen toward the bedroom. Lawanda heard the door open and looked back past her mother, fixing her eyes on Dane. She stopped and a fearful frown surfaced on what had been the placid pool of her round face.

Both Dane and the doctor heard Maude say in a low voice, "Come on, honey. Your tummy is full now. It's time for you to lie down and take your nap."

The frown deepened as Maude urged her forward; she kept her head turned back, her dull eyes fixed on Dane.

"Lawanda," said the mother, "that boy would never hurt you."

Lawanda mumbled something indistinguishable, and Maude hurried her into the bedroom.

The doctor and his young guest were standing near the kitchen table when Maude returned. She set her eyes on Dane and smiled. "I'm glad you are here to eat with us again. How did you like Sunday school and church?"

It took the boy a few seconds to say, "Fine, ma'am."

Maude noted the delay in his response. She moved toward the cupboard, and when her face was out of Dane's line of sight, she looked at her husband questioningly. Dr. Harris nodded and gave her one of his looks that told her she was right. Dane had shown conviction upon hearing the sermon. She gave him a secret smile. "Well, gentlemen, take your seats. Dinner's on the table and ready to be devoured."

Dr. Harris led in prayer. He thanked the Lord for those who had walked the aisle at the invitation and opened their hearts to Jesus — then gave thanks for the food and closed as usual.

The food was passed around. Dr. Harris said, "Okay, Dane. Dig in!"

As the meal progressed, the Harrises noticed a definite difference in Dane over the way he had devoured his meal the night before. He seemed to be toying with his food rather than eating it.

The Harrises glanced at each other surreptitiously across the table. Maude finally asked her husband, "So what was Pastor's sermon about? It must have been good, as usual, for those people to have gone forward to be saved."

"He preached a scorcher on hell," replied the doctor. "It was really good."

Dane kept his face turned down toward his plate.

The Harrises exchanged glances again.

*Must have really gotten to him,* mouthed Maude.

The doctor nodded.

Maude changed the subject. She and her husband talked about the orphans on the streets, trying to get Dane to open up to them, but when they addressed him on the subject, they received only perfunctory remarks. He definitely was lost in his own thoughts.

Finally, Maude asked, "Is the food not to your liking, Dane?"

Dane's head came up. "Wh-what did you say, Mrs. Harris?"

She smiled at him. "I asked if the food was not to your liking."

Embarrassed, Dane replied, "Oh, it's good, ma'am. Really good."

"You don't seem to be eating it."

Quickly, the boy picked up a fork full of mashed potato, put it in his mouth, and smiled while he chewed.

The Harrises picked up the conversation about New York's orphans once again, and soon the boy was pushing the food around on his plate, a small frown on his brow.

The doctor and his wife quietly finished their own meals, and Maude collected the dishes and placed them on the counter at the cupboard. She looked at Dane's plate and shook her head. *Lord,* she said in her heart, *the sermon must have really disturbed him. Give us wisdom. We both want to handle it in the right way.*

Maude returned to the table with three plates, each containing a generous slice of cherry pie. Dane glanced up at her when she placed one of them in front of him. Rather absentmindedly and with a ghost of a smile, he said, "Thank you."

The doctor looked into his wife's questioning eyes and nodded. "Dane, something's bothering you. Want to talk about it?"

Dane laid his fork down and took a deep breath. He met Dr. Harris's steady gaze, then looked down at his plate.

"Is it what you heard preached today? Is that what's bothering you?"

Dane's eyes came up and he met the doctor's unchanging gaze. "Yes, sir."

Harris glanced at Maude again, then

looked at the boy. "What did the pastor say that bothers you?"

Dane swallowed hard. "Well, sir, I have never heard most of the things the pastor said about hell before."

"Like what?"

"The — the unquenchable fire. The torment of burning forever. The weeping and wailing and gnashing of teeth. I heard a preacher only one time, years ago. He talked about hell in his sermon, but I guess I'd forgotten what he said. Since then, I've heard people talk about hell, and from what I could pick up, they figure it's just a place where the bad people go when they die . . . but not a place of burning and torment."

"Well, since the pastor was reading it to us right out of the Bible, it has to be true, doesn't it?"

"Yes, sir."

"Let me ask you, Dane — if you were to die right this moment, could you say that you would go to heaven?"

Dane moved his head back and forth slowly. "No, sir."

"As you saw this morning, the Bible makes it clear that there is no other place to go than hell if a person dies without being saved."

The boy did not comment. "Dr. Harris, I really need to be going. If I don't show up at the alley pretty soon, my friends will be worrying about me."

The Harrises exchanged glances again, and being wise in these matters, they would not attempt to push salvation on their young friend.

The doctor said, "Sure, Dane. We understand. Will you go to church with me next Sunday morning? I'm sure Mrs. Harris won't mind letting me go two Sunday mornings in a row."

"Of course not," said Maude. "And how about coming to supper next Saturday evening, Dane?"

A smile broke across the boy's face. "Sure. Supper on Saturday and church on Sunday."

Moments later, when the Harrises watched Dane move down the stairs and go out the door, Maude said, "Honey, we've got to pray hard for him, that the Lord will do His work in his heart, and that by next Sunday, he will come to Jesus."

"Yes, sweetheart. By next Sunday."

When a disturbed Dane Weston arrived at the alley, he was greeted by all, and found Nettie Olson looking even better. Standing over her as she sat on a small wooden crate with one of the other girls, he said, "Nettie, you're getting your color back. You were pretty pale before."

"I'm feeling lots better, Doc," she said with a sparkle in her eyes. "Thank you for caring about me."

Billy Johnson piped up. "Thanks for caring about me too. You did a good job on my lip. It hardly hurts anymore. I'm sure glad you came along and ran those bullies off then fixed me up." He paused. Then with a teasing twinkle in his eye and a lopsided grin, he added, "Of course Dr. Harris did help a little bit."

Everybody laughed.

On Monday morning, Dane awakened at sunrise and crawled out of his cardboard box. Some of the girls were up, and Bessie and Melinda were busy pouring cold oatmeal — which they had gotten from the café the day before — into tin cups. Billy Johnson would get his regular helping of broth.

When breakfast was finished and the rest of the group was preparing to go to the street corner for their day of begging, Dane left for work. As he walked along the street, he told himself he was one fortunate boy. *He had a job! With regular pay!*

He whistled a cheery, nameless tune as he hurried in the direction of the pharmacy, a new look of determination on his face and a lilt in his step.

Along the way, Dane observed orphan children begging on the street corners, while others were milling about in the alleys they called home.

Later that morning, after enjoying his three hours of work at the pharmacy, Dane was heading for his alley when he saw the couple identified several days earlier by Melinda Scott as Mr. and Mrs. Charles Loring Brace of the Children's Aid Society putting four orphans in their buggy. He knew those children would be put on an orphan train and sent out West to find homes on farms and ranches and in towns much smaller than New York City.

The song Mrs. Baxter had read to him from the newspaper came back to mind. He smiled as he walked past the buggy, looked at the happy faces of the four orphans who were settling on the back seat, and said, "I hope those fragrant breezes come to them with whispers in the wind when they get out West, welcoming them to a new and wonderful life."

The rest of the week went good for Dane on his job. During the daytime he stayed busy enough at the pharmacy, and later on the street corner he begged with his friends, so the sermon he heard on Sunday didn't bother him. However, when lying in his cardboard box he couldn't get the sermon out of his mind, until finally sleep came to relieve him.

After work on Friday, he begged with the others on the street corner until three o'clock in the afternoon. At that time, he went to the Baxter home to see Todd and explained to him and his mother about his job at the pharmacy. They were happy to see him making a go out of his hard lot in life. Todd said he would pass the word on to Dane's old friends at school. Mona made sure Dane understood that he was welcome to come and have a meal with them whenever he could. He assured her he would be back.

On Saturday, Dr. Harris came to the alley late in the afternoon to check on Nettie and to take the stitches out of Billy's lip. He was glad to see Nettie feeling completely well again. After he had re-moved Billy's stitches, he commended

Dane for doing such a good job of keeping the cut clean and administering the ointment as directed.

It was late enough when Dr. Harris was through with Billy that he took Dane home for supper.

When they entered the apartment, the aroma was tantalizing. Dane said, "Sure smells good, Doctor. Mrs. Harris is an excellent cook."

"Can't argue with that, son," said the doctor. "Her cooking has kept me satisfied and healthy for fifty-six years."

At that moment, they heard Maude's voice coming from the bedroom. She was trying to soothe Lawanda about Dane's presence in the apartment.

"Dr. Harris, maybe it would be better if I didn't come here. I sure don't want to upset your daughter."

Harris shook his head. "No, no, Dane. Lawanda has been this way since she was very small. We've had to learn that we must go on with our lives in spite of her problem and live as normally as possible. She'll settle down in a minute or two. Whenever we have other guests the same thing happens, but it only takes Maude a few minutes to calm her down and get her on the bed for a nap."

Dane nodded. "All right, sir. I just don't want to be a problem."

Harris laid a hand on his shoulder as they saw Maude coming toward them. "A problem you could never be, my boy."

Maude welcomed Dane, and when the three of them sat down at the kitchen table, Dane looked at the fried chicken and all that went with it. "Wow, Mrs. Harris! That sure looks good."

While they were eating, Dane surprised the Harrises by saying, "This week, when I've been in my cardboard bed at night, I've thought a lot about last Sunday's sermon. I have some questions I'd like to ask you."

Pleased at this obvious answer to prayer, the Harrises smiled at each other, and the doctor said, "Of course. You enjoy your meal right now and after supper, we'll answer your questions."

When supper was finished, Maude left the dishes till later and sat down with her husband and Dane in the small parlor. The doctor and the boy sat on the sofa together, and Maude sat in an overstuffed chair, facing them.

The Bible Dane had seen on the small table next to the sofa was still there, within the doctor's reach.

Dr. Harris said, "Dane, are your questions about hell?"

"No, sir. Though I was shocked to learn some of the things the pastor preached about, I have it straight in my mind. I believe hell is exactly what the Bible says it is. My questions are about being saved."

The Harrises exchanged smiles, then the doctor said, "Ask away, son."

Dane brought up the picture frames with Scripture verses that hung on the walls of the office and the examining room downstairs, and the one right there in the kitchen. "I've thought a lot about them, sir, especially the one in the examining room about being born again. I can quote it for you. 'Jesus answered and said unto him, Verily, verily, I say unto thee, Except a man be born again, he cannot see the kingdom of God.' Dr. Harris, I don't understand. How can a person be born a second time? Since this is what it takes to go to heaven, how can I be born again?"

Dr. Harris smiled as he picked his Bible up off the table next to the sofa. "Let me show you first, Dane, *why* you have to be born again. Then we'll deal with *how*."

"All right, sir."

Maude was in silent prayer as she watched her husband open his Bible.

Dr. Harris took Dane to Genesis chapter 1 and showed him God's great work of creation, having the boy read certain verses aloud. After all the animal kingdom had been created according to verse 25, Harris had Dane look at verse 26, and showed him that the triune God said, "Let us make man in our image, after our likeness." He pointed out the use of the plural words "us" and "our," making sure the boy understood that the Godhead is triune: Father, Son, and Spirit.

When he was satisfied that Dane had grasped this, he showed him verse 27, which states that God created man in his own image — a triune being of body, soul, and spirit. He pointed out that the body is the house a human being lives in here on earth, the soul is the person, and that the spirit is the God-contact. He used John 4:23–24 to show him that in order to truly worship God, man must have a spirit because God is a Spirit, and they that worship Him must worship Him in *spirit* and in truth.

Dr. Harris then took Dane to Genesis chapter 2, where God took Adam into the Garden of Eden and showed him all the trees, saying he could freely eat of every tree in the garden but one, that being the tree of the knowledge of good and evil. The doctor showed him God's warning in verse 17 that "in the day that thou eatest thereof thou shalt surely die." He emphasized the fact that *the very day* he ate of that tree, Adam would surely die.

The doctor went on to show the boy in Genesis chapter 3 that the serpent (Satan) caused Adam and Eve to disobey God's command. They ate of the fruit of the forbidden tree. He then asked Dane if God held their funeral and buried them that day.

When Dane said He did not, Harris pointed out that the death that day was spiritual death. Adam and Eve became depraved beings of only body and soul, but were dead spiritually. They later died physically, but on the very day they ate the forbidden fruit they died spiritually.

Harris then took him to Ephesians chapter 2 and pointed out that the Apostle Paul was addressing born-again people: "And you hath he quickened, who were dead in trespasses and sins." He explained that to "quicken" is to *give life to*. These people had been dead spiritually — which they inherited from our father Adam — but God had given them spiritual life when they were born again. He then showed him

Romans 5:12, pointing out that sin and death entered the world by Adam.

"You see, Dane," said the doctor, "we have to be born again because we were born wrong the first time. We must have a *spiritual* birth."

He then took him to 1 Thessalonians 5:23. Paul was writing to people who had been born again and showed him that those people had spirit, soul, and body. The new birth made them complete beings in the image of God.

When Dane understood this, Harris took him to John 3:3 where Jesus said, "Except a man be born again, he cannot see the kingdom of God." He then showed him that Nicodemus had asked a question similar to Dane's: "How can a man be born when he is old? Can he enter the second time into his mother's womb, and be born?"

Dane smiled at the similarity to his own question. "I understand why I need to be born again, Doctor. I am dead spiritually. Now show me *how* to be born again."

Harris then showed him John 1:12, where it speaks of Jesus Christ and says, "But as many as received him, to them gave he power to become the sons of God, even to them that believe on his name."

He then took him to Ephesians 3:17 and showed him that he must receive Jesus into his heart.

Once Dane had grasped this, Harris showed him that Jesus said in Mark 1:15, "Repent ye, and believe the gospel." He explained that he must repent of his sin, believe that Jesus died for his sins and shed His blood on the cross, was buried, and rose again the third day. He explained that repentance is a change of mind that results in a change of direction. He must turn the opposite direction from the path that he was walking toward hell as a lost sinner, put his faith totally and only in Jesus to save him, then do as Romans 10:13 says: "For whosoever shall call upon the name of the Lord shall be saved."

When Dane said he understood all of this, the doctor took the time to go over the verses that were in his picture frames. Dane now totally grasped their message. "Dr. Harris, I am ready to repent of my sin and receive the Lord Jesus into my heart as my Saviour."

Harris smiled. "Then call on Him right now, Dane, and ask Him to come into your heart and save you. I'll help you."

The doctor put his arm around Dane's shoulders as they bowed their heads, and

Maude wiped tears while her husband had the joy of leading young Dane Weston to the Lord.

All three were wiping tears. Dane thanked the doctor for answering his questions and for leading him to the Lord. "You and Mrs. Harris have been so good to me. I can see that the Lord brought you into my life."

Maude dabbed at her eyes with a napkin. "Dane, the Lord brought you into our lives too and made you very special to us. Lee and I talked about it late last night. We both wish we could just take you into our home and be your foster parents, but the way things are, it just is not possible. We have only one bedroom. It's our bed that Lawanda takes her naps on while you're here. At night, she sleeps here on the sofa. We would have nowhere for you to sleep."

"And even if you would agree to sleep on the floor," said the doctor, "there is still the problem with Lawanda being afraid of other people. The only other people she isn't afraid of are her brother and his family. So there isn't any way we can take you into our home."

Dane smiled thinly. "Dr. and Mrs. Harris, you don't know what it means to me that you would even want to be my foster parents. I understand your situation completely. But anyhow, thank you for wanting me."

"And thank *you* for understanding, son," said Harris. "There's one other thing I need to show you in the Bible, now that you're saved."

Opening his Bible again, Dr. Harris showed Dane that his next step of obedience to the Lord was to be baptized. Dane understood it immediately and said he wanted to be baptized as soon as possible.

The next morning in the invitation at the close of the sermon, Dane walked the aisle, gave his testimony of salvation, and told the pastor he wanted to be baptized. The whole congregation rejoiced to see him go into the baptismal waters. Dr. Harris was wishing that Maude could be there to see it.

When Lawanda had been fed and was lying down on her parents' bed, the Harrises and Dane sat down at the kitchen table for Sunday dinner. When the doctor said his amen at the close of his prayer over the food, Dane added his own amen.

This time, with his sins forgiven and washed away in Jesus' blood, Dane found himself ravenous. He ate everything on his plate and reached for seconds.

With a twinkle in his kindly eyes, Dr. Harris smiled "My, honey, doesn't it make a difference in one's appetite when you're a new creature in Christ Jesus and know you're going to heaven?"

Maude nodded, her own eyes shining. "It sure does, dear. He's not just picking at his food now."

Dane swallowed a mouthful of corn-bread. He grinned. "It sure does make a difference, Dr. Harris. It sure does!"

The Harrises laughed, and Dane quickly returned to eating again.

When the meal was over, Dr. Harris left the room for a moment, and when he returned, he had a Bible in his hand. Dane could tell it was not the same Bible that the doctor had used to lead him to the Lord. It was a bit smaller.

Harris laid the Bible in front of Dane. "This is a spare Bible we've had around the apartment for a while. We want you to have it."

Dane's eyes brightened as he picked up the Bible and looked at it. "Oh, boy! A Bible all my own! I'll read it every day!

Thank you, thank you, thank you!"

On Saturday morning May 6, Dane arrived at the Clarkson Pharmacy at five minutes before eight and began his work by mopping the floor. Bryce Clarkson was behind the counter filling prescriptions that his customers had brought in and left with him late in the afternoon the day before.

Soon Dane was behind the counter wiping dust off the shelves and the medicine bottles with a damp cloth.

Almost reverently, Dane picked up each bottle of medicine and carefully wiped away every speck of dust. While doing so, he read each label and tried to pronounce the name of the medication aloud.

Still filling prescriptions, Bryce heard his attempts to wrap his tongue around some of the words and chuckled.

Dane heard him and turned around with a perplexed look on his earnest face. "Mr. Clarkson, why do they use such big words that are so hard to pronounce?"

"Most of them come from the Latin, Dane. At first it seems like an impossible task to ever keep them straight and pronounce any of them correctly, but believe me, with a lot of practice it gets easier and

161

simply becomes a part of your vocabulary."

Dane was holding a bottle in his hand. He nodded. "Okay, sir. If you say so." He looked at the label on the bottle in hand, studied it a moment, then shook his head. Wiping it clear of dust, he set it back on the shelf, picked up another one, glanced at the label trying to figure it out, and went on with his work.

When Dane had finished dusting the shelves and bottles, he turned to the pharmacist, who was just finishing his last prescription. "Mr. Clarkson, I hope you don't mind me talking to you about medicine and all."

"Of course not. Since you're going to be a doctor, it will help you to understand all you can about medicine and pharmacies."

"Pharmacies. That's exactly what I wanted to talk to you about."

"Sure."

"If memory serves me right, one of my medical books said that until late in the eighteenth century, medication was prepared and dispensed by the physicians themselves. In about 1790, the practice of pharmacy began to be separated from the practice of medicine. Am I remembering correctly?"

"You sure are. In late 1790, a group of

physicians in Philadelphia, Pennsylvania, took it on themselves to train men as pharmacists so the task of preparing and dispensing of medication could be done by someone else. This would give the doctors more time to devote to their practices."

"That makes sense."

"Yes. This meant that physicians would have to authorize the dispensing of medication to their patients by giving them written authority. Thus was born the prescription, which the patient would carry to the pharmacist."

Dane nodded. "Okay. I recall reading about this in that same medical book."

"Well," proceeded Clarkson, "this procedure worked so well that the Philadelphia College of Pharmacy and Science was founded in 1821. The concept spread over the eastern half of the country, and soon there were other such colleges being established — some on their own — and others being incorporated into established universities; especially those that already had medical colleges.

"Physicians everywhere in the eastern half of the country started writing prescriptions for their patients to carry to pharmacies in their cities and towns. All five New York City boroughs had plenty of pharmacies by 1835."

"How about out West? When did the prescription idea take hold out there?"

"Well, as early as 1852, a pharmacy was opened up in San Francisco. One was established in Portland, Oregon, in 1860, and one was established in Seattle, Washington, in 1868."

"That's interesting, Mr. Clarkson. My medical book didn't give this much detail. Thank you for the information. I'm glad to have learned about it."

Bryce Clarkson's attention was drawn to the front window, where he saw a woman and a girl standing near the door, waiting. He glanced at the clock on the wall. It was five minutes until nine o'clock. "Tell you what, Dane, I'm going to open a few minutes early for Mrs. Myers and her daughter, who are waiting at the door. Mr. and Mrs. Myers are good customers."

"Gotta take care of those good customers, Mr. Clarkson."

"That's for sure," Clarkson said over his shoulder as he headed for the door.

# Chapter Eight

Dane Weston stepped around in front of the counter and watched as his boss opened the door. "Good morning, ladies! As of this moment, we are officially open. Please come in."

As mother and daughter moved inside, they looked at Dane and smiled.

He smiled back, thinking how strongly the girl resembled her mother. She had long auburn hair and sky blue eyes. He estimated that she would be a couple of years younger than himself.

This was confirmed immediately as Bryce Clarkson looked at her and said jokingly, "I haven't seen you since the day before your birthday in March, Tharyn. How does it feel to be an old lady of thirteen?"

Tharyn giggled. "It feels real good, Mr. Clarkson."

Mrs. Meyers said, "I appreciate your opening a few minutes early for us, Bryce."

"No problem. As I told my new hired man, Mr. and Mrs. Myers are good customers, and I didn't want to keep mother and daughter waiting."

Mrs. Meyers smiled and looked at Dane again. "New hired man, you say. What happened to Leon?"

"He moved to Brooklyn on very short notice. Come, I'll introduce you."

As the pharmacist and the two ladies moved toward him, Dane's gaze went to the girl, and she warmed him with another smile.

"Ladies," said Clarkson, "I want you to meet Dane Weston. Dane, this is Erline Myers and her daughter Tharyn."

Erline offered her hand first, and as Dane grasped it, he said, "I'm happy to meet you, ma'am."

"Same here," said Erline.

Tharyn then offered her hand.

"And I'm happy to meet you, Tharyn. That's a very pretty name. I've never heard it before. Do you mind if I ask how it is spelled?"

Thinking how handsome he was, the girl

batted her eyelids. "Of course not. It's T-H-A-R-Y-N."

Dane grinned. "Oh. It's even spelled pretty."

Tharyn giggled. "You are so kind, Dane."

Erline set her gaze on the boy. "I don't recall ever seeing you around here, Dane. Do you live in the neighborhood?"

Before Dane could answer, Clarkson said, "I need to explain that Dane is an orphan. His parents and little sister and brother were murdered recently by a street gang."

Both females were stunned at Clarkson's information. While Tharyn's hand went to her mouth and her eyes widened, Erline looked at Dane with sympathy. "Oh my. I'm so sorry, Dane."

"Me too." Tharyn brushed her hair from her cheek. "Are you living with relatives now?"

Dane shook his head. "No. I don't have any relatives. We used to live in the two hundred block on Thirty-third Street in a tenement. The landlord let me live there a few extra days, but I had to go then because he needed to rent out the flat to someone else."

Erline's brow furrowed. She handed two

prescriptions to Bryce Clarkson, then set her soft eyes on Dane. "And where do you live, now?"

Dane licked his lips. "I — I live among the thousands of other orphans on the streets."

"Near here?"

"Not too far, ma'am. My street home is in an alley with nine other orphans in the twelve hundred block on Broadway. They took me in and offered me a cardboard box for a bed like they sleep in."

"Cardboard box?" gasped Tharyn. "You sleep in an alley in a cardboard box?"

"Better than some of the street urchins have, Tharyn. Lots of them sleep in filthy trash bins or on doorsteps of commercial buildings. At least the cardboard boxes are clean and they protect you from the wind better than a doorstep."

Erline's heart went out to the boy. She was fully aware of children who lived that way on the streets. Often when seeing the street waifs, she had wished there was something she could do for them, but there was nothing she could do. Her mind went to the twelve hundred block on Broadway. "Which side of Broadway is your alley, Dane?"

"On the east side, ma'am."

"Then you're in the alley behind Powell's Grocery. Goldstein's Taylor Shop is in that block on the east side, too."

Dane nodded. "Yes, ma'am. Mr. Powell is very kind to us. He always makes sure we have plenty of water."

"That's nice of him."

"Yes, ma'am."

Tharyn said, "Isn't the Bluebird Café in that block, too?"

"Sure is. Sometimes when we have money, we buy food from them. And sometimes they even give us food they have left over after a day's business."

Erline's face pinched. "Sometimes, Dane? You mean sometimes you and the others in your colony don't have money to buy food? You beg on the streets, don't you?"

"Yes, ma'am, but there are days when no one gives us any money."

"You said sometimes the people at the café give you leftover food. What happens when you don't have money to buy food, and they don't have any food left over to give you?"

Dane swallowed hard. "Well, Mrs. Myers, when that happens we pick up food that has been thrown into the café's garbage cans. You know, food that people don't finish on their plates."

Tharyn's stomach lurched. She put a hand over it. "Oh, you poor boy. You have to eat garbage and sleep in a cardboard box! That's awful!"

Bryce Clarkson looked at the prescriptions Erline had handed him. "Erline, I can fill your prescription, but I'm out of the medicine for Ron's prescription. My supplier is due this morning, though. I'm sure I can have Ron's medicine ready by eleven o'clock."

"That's fine, Bryce. I'll send Tharyn and a neighbor girl to pick it up just before noon. The family is going to Grand Central Station to meet Ron's sister, who is coming from Boston to spend a few days with us. We should be back by eleven forty-five. I'll go ahead and pay you for both prescriptions, then Tharyn won't have to carry any money."

Clarkson nodded. "That'll be fine."

Dane turned to his boss. "Mr. Clarkson?"

"Yes?"

"If it's all right with you, sir, I will deliver the medicine to the Myerses' home and save Tharyn from having to come and pick it up."

"Sure, Dane," said Clarkson. "You can do that."

"Thank you, Dane," Tharyn said warmly.

Erline nodded. "Yes, Dane. Thank you."

"My pleasure, ma'am."

Clarkson turned and took the medicine for Erline's prescription from a shelf, and as he turned back to the counter to prepare it, he said, "Dane is only fifteen years old, but he already has set a goal for himself, and that is to become a physician and surgeon."

"Oh, Dane," said Tharyn, "that's wonderful! You're going to be a doctor!"

"I sure am," he said in a determined voice. "I've had that goal since I was very young."

A faint look of skepticism filled Erline's eyes for a brief moment, but when she saw the look of sheer tenacity in Dane's eyes and recognized the resolution in his voice, she said, "That's very commendable, Dane."

Dane had seen the skeptical look in Erline's eyes. He ran his gaze first to Tharyn, then to her mother. "I know you may be wondering how I will ever be able to get my medical education, but believe me . . . somehow I will."

Tharyn fixed her eyes on the good-looking boy. *If anyone can do it, Dane, I believe you can.* At that instant, he became her hero. "I know you will, Dane. I just know it."

A smile spread from ear to ear. "Thank you, Tharyn."

"Don't ever lose sight of your goal," said Erline.

"I won't, ma'am."

Erline paid the pharmacist for both prescriptions, and as he handed her the medicine for her prescription, she thanked him, then turned to her daughter. "Come, Tharyn. We must hurry."

As mother and daughter headed for the door, Erline glanced back. "We'll look forward to seeing you at the apartment about noon, Dane."

Dane smiled and nodded.

Tharyn waved. "See you then."

An elderly couple were just coming in. The silver-haired man held the door open for Erline and Tharyn. They thanked him and moved on down the street. As they hurried toward home, Tharyn talked about what a nice boy Dane was and how proud she was that in spite of being a street orphan, he had set such a marvelous goal for himself.

Erline agreed. "I have to admire him for the way he is going on in spite of the loss of his family. You know it had to have been a horrible blow to have both parents and both his sister and brother taken from him at the same time. And if it had been some kind of accident that took them, it would have been easier on him than to have them murdered. Bless his heart. It had to have been devastating."

The tenement where Ron and Erline Myers and their daughter lived was less than three blocks from the pharmacy, down a side street in the residential section.

As Erline and Tharyn moved into their block, they noticed two construction workers who were adding a balcony across the front of a tenement four buildings down. All of the tenements in their block had five floors. The balcony being added to this building was on the fifth floor, and they had been told that when the project was done on that particular building, each floor would have a balcony.

A team of horses was hitched to a wagon that was loaded with building materials, which was parked directly in front of the building.

The two construction workers were carrying materials toward a scaffold at the front of the tenement, which at the moment was resting on the ground.

Erline said, "Honey, wouldn't it be nice to have balconies on our tenement, especially since we live on the fifth floor?"

"It sure would, Mommy. Be a nice place to go out and sit on summer evenings and enjoy the cool air." At that instant, Tharyn pointed at the hired buggy that was parked in front of their tenement with her father and the driver standing beside it. "Look! The buggy's here already."

"Sure enough," said Erline, picking up pace. "We'd better shake a leg."

Keeping up with her mother, Tharyn noticed her father look their way and waved. "Hi, Daddy!"

Ron Myers smiled and waved in return.

As they drew up, Erline said, "I'm sorry, honey. I didn't realize we were late. We got to talking to Bryce and the new teenage boy he just hired to take Leon's place, and the time got away from us."

Ron smiled. "It's okay, sweetheart. I wasn't aware that Leon wasn't with him anymore."

"I wasn't either. He said Leon quit suddenly and moved to Brooklyn."

"So what's the new boy's name?"

"Dane Weston. He's fifteen years old."

"He's a real nice boy, Daddy," said

Tharyn. "You'll like him."

Ron nodded and noted the paper bag in his wife's hand. "I'll run the prescriptions up to the apartment, then we need to head for Grand Central. You know Althea Corbin. She's the ultrapunctual type, and she'll expect us to be there when she gets off the train."

Erline smiled. "Well, your sister may be the ultrapunctual type, but I doubt she would be upset at us if we were a few minutes late."

Ron shrugged. "Maybe not, but let's not find out."

Erline handed him the paper bag. "There's only one medicine bottle in here. Bryce was out of the medicine for your prescription, but he's going to send Dane Weston over here with it about noon."

"Fine," said Ron. "I'll help you into the buggy, then I'll run your medicine up to the apartment."

"I'll help the ladies in, Mr. Myers," said the driver. "You go ahead."

Ron nodded and hurried toward the apartment building.

Moments later, Ron returned and climbed into the buggy next to Tharyn, who was now positioned between her parents on the seat.

The driver put the horse to a trot, and as the buggy pulled away from the curb, Ron turned to his wife and daughter. "I guess you noticed that the tenement down the street is getting the balcony on its fifth floor first."

"Uh-huh," said Erline. "I figured they'd put the balcony on the second floor first, then work their way up."

Ron shook his head. "It's much easier to start at the top and work down. The other balconies would be in the way if they did that."

"Oh. Of course. I hadn't thought about that."

"Well, building construction isn't something women think about."

Tharyn giggled. "Daddy, there are plenty of things we women think about and know about that men don't."

Ron tweaked her nose. "I'm sure that's true, baby. Just don't remind me how much smarter you females are than us males."

Tharyn giggled again. "Sure won't. I wouldn't want to embarrass you!"

The Myerses laughed together, and having heard the conversation, the driver laughed with them.

After a brief silence, Ron said, "Back to

our conversation about the balconies on that tenement . . ."

"Yes?" said Erline.

"I heard some of the neighbors in our tenement talking on the sidewalk yesterday morning when I was leaving for work. Wally Dodd said he had talked to our landlord about the possibility of having balconies put on the front of our building. Wally said the landlord didn't seem very enthusiastic about it."

Tharyn said, "Oh well, Daddy, at least we have a home. That's more than I can say for poor Dane Weston."

Ron looked at her and frowned. "Poor Dane Weston? Bryce's new hired man?"

"Uh-huh."

"What do you mean?"

"Dane is an orphan, Daddy. His parents and little sister and little brother were murdered by a street gang recently."

"I'm sorry to hear that."

"He lives with other street urchins in an alley a few blocks from the pharmacy. But you know what?"

"What?"

"Mr. Clarkson told Mommy and me that Dane has set a goal for himself. He wants to become a physician and surgeon. He had made that plan for his life when he was very young."

Ron's eyebrows arched. "Well, that's admirable."

"We certainly think so," said Erline.

"It will be impossible for a boy who lives on the streets to even get a high school education, let alone to go to a medical school, which is very expensive."

"That's true, Daddy, but Dane has something special about him. Even though we only spent a few minutes with him, Mommy and I were impressed, weren't we, Mommy?"

"We sure were."

"And Daddy, just getting to know him that little bit, I have a feeling that Dane will realize his dream in spite of the obstacles he's facing. He just impressed me as being that kind of person. You know — the Abraham Lincoln type. Mr. Lincoln rose from poverty and became president of this country because he set a goal for himself and had the intestinal fortitude and drive to realize his dream."

Ron caught Erline's eye over Tharyn's head with a questioning look on his face. Erline shrugged and glanced lovingly at her daughter, who was saying, "I just know Dane will overcome every hurdle and become a doctor."

Ron smiled and elbowed his daughter lovingly. "It's so sad that such a horrible thing happened to this nice boy, honey. And I hope you're right about Dane. I hope he is able to realize his dream."

Tharyn smiled up at him. "Oh, Daddy," she said with enthusiasm, "if anyone can do it, I'm sure Dane can. I wish I had a brother just like him!"

"Well, little missy, I wish you did too, but that's out of the question, now, isn't it?"

Tharyn nodded. "I know, Daddy. My little brother died at birth and Mommy had to have an operation so she couldn't have any more children. But that doesn't keep me from wishing."

Erline patted her daughter's hand. "Me either, sweet baby."

Ron cast a loving glance in his wife's direction, but she was staring straight ahead, lost in her own thoughts of dreams long past, of things that were never to be.

After half an hour of traversing Manhattan's busy streets, they finally arrived at Grand Central Station and found themselves about twenty minutes early for the scheduled arrival of Althea's train.

Ron helped his wife and daughter from the buggy, and the driver said, "Mr. Myers,

I'll be waiting right here for you when you come out."

Ron nodded and led Erline and Tharyn inside the terminal. They made their way to the platforms where the trains came in, and went to the one where Althea's train was to stop. A small crowd was already waiting.

Tharyn looked across the tracks to the next platform where passengers were boarding a train. She noticed a large group of children — all dressed nicely and well-groomed — being led by four adults as they boarded the last two coaches, just ahead of the caboose. The boys were boarding one and the girls the other. A couple of small girls were crying as they were led aboard with one of the women holding them each by the hand.

"Mommy, Daddy," said Tharyn, "look at all those children. I wonder where they're going."

Ron was looking up the tracks to see any sign of his sister's train coming in. Erline looked at the children. "That must be one of those orphan trains, honey. You've heard about them, haven't you?"

"Oh. Yes." Tharyn's gaze was fixed on the boys and girls as they were boarding the coaches. "They take them out West, don't they?"

There was no indication that an approaching train was on the track beside the platform as yet. Ron glanced at the children. "That's right, honey. They take those poor orphans out there and help them to find homes on ranches and farms or in the towns on the frontier."

"They sure are dressed nice."

"Mm-hmm," said Ron. "I've heard that the Children's Aid Society always dresses them like that."

"Me too," said Erline. "And notice that the boys have nice haircuts, and all the girls have nice hair-dos."

Looking up at her parents, Tharyn asked, "Have all the children who are put on the orphan trains been living on the streets?"

"Most of them have," replied Erline, "but the Children's Aid Society also takes them out of orphanages that are overcrowded."

Tharyn studied the boarding children a moment. "Maybe Dane Weston will get a chance to ride out West on an orphan train someday. He could find a family to adopt him who would put him through medical school."

Ron smiled down at her. "That would be a wonderful thing, wouldn't it? I hope it happens for him just like that."

At that moment, the sound of a train's bell clanging met their ears, and Tharyn pointed toward it. "Here comes Aunt Althea's train."

The Myers family huddled together as the train chugged to a halt. The big engine hissed clouds of steam from its bowels, and the bell stopped clanging. The conductor stepped out of the first coach, and seconds later, passengers began to alight.

Soon Erline pointed at the third coach. "There she is!"

The three of them hurried to meet Althea Corbin, and Tharyn was the first one to hug her.

After Althea's brother and sister-in-law had embraced her, Ron picked up Althea's one piece of luggage from the baggage handlers. The four of them headed out to the parking lot with Tharyn holding her aunt's hand.

The driver took the piece of luggage from Ron and placed it in the small luggage compartment at the rear of the buggy while Ron helped the women climb aboard. There was happy chatter as the Myerses and their guest headed toward home.

At 11:50, Dane Weston entered the

block where the Myerses' tenement was located, as directed by Bryce Clarkson. The paper bag containing Ron's medicine was in his hand.

In his heart, Dane was excited about seeing Tharyn again. He told himself he had never met a nicer girl, or a prettier one.

As he drew nearer the Myerses' tenement, his attention was drawn to the location where the two construction workers were standing on the scaffold, pulling ropes through pulleys which were anchored at the top of the building. They were slowly nearing the fifth floor balcony, which was partially in place.

As Dane was moving past the building, he glanced at the wagon parked in the street, which was loaded with building materials. His attention then went to the two husky horses that were hitched to the wagon.

Just as Dane passed the team and wagon, he heard hoofbeats coming up behind him, along with the sound of buggy wheels spinning on the surface of the street.

Seconds later, he saw that the oncoming vehicle was a hired buggy, and as it passed him, he saw Tharyn Myers sticking her head out the window. She called, "Hello, Dane!" and waved to him.

Dane waved back and quickened his pace.

The buggy rolled to a stop in front of the Myerses' tenement. Ron jumped out and helped Tharyn from the buggy first. She backed up a couple of steps from the sidewalk while her father was helping her mother out, and turned her attention to Dane, who was now in front of the second building from their tenement.

Suddenly two wild cries were heard from behind him, and Dane paused to look back over his shoulder. What he saw chilled his blood. The two construction workers who had been on the scaffold at the building's fifth floor were helplessly falling toward the ground, arms swinging and legs kicking. The scaffold was also falling.

The two men hit the ground not more than two seconds before the scaffold hit it a few feet away, with a loud bang and clattering noise.

The piercing noise startled the team of horses hitched to the wagon loaded with building materials. They both reared, whinnying shrilly. Eyes bulging, they pawed the air, then bolted in blind terror.

# Chapter Nine

For an instant, Dane Weston's legs seemed to have turned to stone. As the wild-eyed team thundered down the street in his direction, his chest shuddered with a convulsive breath. Inhaling raggedly, he turned and looked at Tharyn, who was frozen in place, terror on her face.

Erline was now looking at the oncoming team, her features suddenly void of color.

At the same time, Ron Myers was helping his sister out of the buggy. Suddenly the horse hitched to the buggy bolted, throwing the surprised driver back against the seat. The abrupt lurch of the buggy sent Althea flying. She fell on top of her brother, knocking him down, and they both rolled against Erline's legs, toppling her.

The team was bearing down on them at full speed with the heavily-loaded wagon fishtailing behind them.

People along the street were dashing to safety.

Abruptly the feeling came back into Dane's legs. Tharyn and her family were in grave danger. He dropped the paper bag containing the medicine and dashed toward Tharyn. He could hear the rumble of the oncoming team and wagon on his heels. When he reached Tharyn, who was fixed in terror like a statue, he grasped her by the shoulders and used his body weight to knock her out of the path of danger. The impact caused both of them to roll on the sidewalk and collide with the steps of the tenement.

The charging horses and wagon slammed into Ron, Erline, and Althea, then headed on down the street, leaving them a battered, bloody heap.

On the sidewalk, both Dane and Tharyn lay against the bottom step with the wind knocked out of them. With the sound of people shouting in his ears, along with the fading, thunderous sound of the team and wagon, Dane struggled to his feet and leaned over Tharyn. He glanced at the three people who lay in crumpled heaps on the street as people began to gather around, looking at the scene. Two men were kneeling down and looking at the victims, and Dane heard one of the men speak to another standing over him and tell him to go for the police and an ambulance.

Tharyn's eyes were closed as she gasped and wheezed, trying desperately to draw some air into her lungs. Her mind was in a whirl as she looked up and saw Dane reaching down for her. She couldn't make her arms reach toward him.

Observing the look of stunned panic on Tharyn's features, Dane knelt beside her and took hold of her hand. Keeping his voice as calm as possible, he said, "Just lie there for a minute and breathe slowly."

She relaxed a bit, made herself breathe slowly, and after a brief moment, put her dazed eyes on him. "Wh-what happened?"

He knew it would all come back to her shortly. "Just lie still and breathe easy, Tharyn."

She closed her eyes and concentrated on her breathing. The crowd on the street was growing, but people were keeping their voices to a hush as they saw Tharyn being tended to by the teenage boy.

When Dane saw some color coming back into Tharyn's face, he said, "Breathe deeper now."

She opened her eyes, looked up at him, and nodded. Again she did his bidding and soon was breathing normally, although she was trembling and a couple of bruises were starting to appear on the left side of her face.

She focused on him. "Dane, what happened? Tell me what hap—" Suddenly her eyes bulged and she sat up. "Mommy! Daddy! They — they — the horses! Aunt Althea!" Her head turned toward the spot where the victims lay, but she could not see them for the crowd of people who stood around them. She put a hand to her forehead. "My . . . my head is all fuzzy inside. Help me up. I've got to find them."

Dane was trying to control his own emotions. Tharyn was about to see the crumpled heaps in the street. His voice trembled as he gently helped her to her feet. "Tharyn, what you're about to see —"

"Mommy! Daddy! Where are they? Aunt Althea! Where is she?" Tharyn's knees buckled slightly and she staggered toward the street.

Dane put an arm around her, pulling her to a halt. "Easy does it. Take a few more deep breaths, Tharyn. It'll help clear the fuzzy feeling in your head."

She gripped his arm and drew in one breath after another. "D-Dane, I've g-got to f-find them. Please help m-me."

Dane knew he could not prolong the inevitable any longer. Tightening the arm around her, he said, "All right. They're right over here."

Some of the people who were gathered around the victims saw the teenage boy guiding Tharyn their way, and with grief-stricken faces, they moved aside, making a path for them to the bloody scene.

Dane noted that the driver of the hired buggy had returned and was looking on with a chalky face.

When Tharyn's eyes fell on her fallen family, she recognized the men who were kneeling beside them as neighbors who lived in the tenement next door. One of them looked at her. "Tharyn, your father and this other woman are dead. Your mother is unconscious, but she's still alive. The police have been summoned, and an ambulance is on its way."

"The other woman is her aunt, sir," said Dane. "They just picked her up at Grand Central Station."

The man nodded. "Oh. I see."

Tharyn looked at the lifeless bodies of her father and her aunt. Cold sweat chilled her body. She made a tiny mewing sound, then said breathlessly, "Mommy-y-y . . ."

She knelt beside her mother. She made another mewing sound, burst into sobs, and gathered her unconscious mother in her arms.

As she continued sobbing, Dane laid a firm but gentle hand on her shoulder. Two men threaded their way through the crowd and announced that both the construction workers who had fallen from the scaffold were dead.

While rocking her mother back and forth in her arms, Tharyn sobbed out, "This can't be happening! It just can't be! Only moments ago, we were a happy family. How can this be?" Then her voice turned into a wail, and she shrieked loudly, "No-o-o! No! It can't be happening!"

Keeping his hand on her shoulder, Dane knelt down beside her.

"Tharyn. Tharyn, listen to me. If your mother comes to and hears you crying like this, it will frighten her. Please try to get a grip on yourself."

She looked at him through red-rimmed eyes and nodded.

"Y-you're right, Dane," she whispered,

gulping down a fresh onslaught of tears. "I'll try. But — but this is so . . . so awful!"

Dane's heart went out to her. He knew exactly how she was feeling. He heard someone in the crowd say that a police wagon and an ambulance were arriving. He would stay close to Tharyn through this entire ordeal.

The two vehicles came to a halt and both teams of horses were panting hard.

When the men who had been with the victims explained the situation to the police, one of the officers moved up to Tharyn, who was weeping silently. "Young lady, I'm Officer James Hankins. We have an ambulance here. The attendants will take you along to the hospital with your mother."

Tharyn sniffed, wiped tears from her eyes, and looked at Dane. "You'll come with me, Dane, won't you? I don't have anyone. My only living relative besides my parents was Aunt Althea. And now she's dead. Please stay with me."

A wail was beginning to form in her voice.

Dane patted her cheek. "I won't leave you, Tharyn," he said softly, trying to keep her from becoming frantic. "You can count on me." He turned to Officer Hankins. "It *is* all right if I go in the ambulance with her, isn't it?"

Hankins nodded. "Of course. Are you a neighbor?"

"No, sir. I'm a friend, though."

"Well, you stick with her. She's going to need all the strength and comfort you can give her."

"I'll do everything I can, sir."

Tharyn sniffed again and wiped away more tears. She focused on his face and squinted. "Dane, you've got a big bruise on your cheek. Does it hurt?"

Abruptly, he was aware of a stinging sensation on his right cheek. He touched it lightly with his fingers. "Oh. Must have happened when we slammed into the stairs in front of your tenement. You've got a couple of bruises on your face, too."

As she put a hand to the left side of her face, she looked at his clothing. "Your shirt is torn, Dane, and there is dirt on your pants."

He looked at the front of his shirt, touched the rip in the cloth, and looked down at his pants. "Yeah. Your dress is smudged with dirt too. We must have hit the ground pretty hard."

She examined the place where the dirt was evident in the fabric, then met his gaze. "What will I do with Mommy like this, Dane? I've never even been inside a hospital."

"I'll be right beside you," Dane said in a steady, reassuring voice. "Once we get her to the hospital, the doctors will examine her and do what they have to in order to make her regain consciousness. They'll tell us exactly how she is once they've had a chance to work on her."

His voice had a calming effect on her. Dane could see it in her eyes.

The two ambulance attendants came with a stretcher, and when they had taken Erline from Tharyn's arms, Dane gently helped her to her feet.

Officer James Hankins came up to Tharyn and Dane. "Miss Myers, the police wagon will take the bodies of your father and your aunt to the morgue, along with the two construction workers who were killed when they fell from the scaffold."

Tharyn nodded slowly, the agony showing on her drawn features. She seemed to be looking right through him.

Hankins looked at Dane. "I'm not sure she's comprehending it. Will you see that she understands where the bodies have been taken?"

"Yes, sir."

"All right. Well, the ambulance attendants are waiting for you."

Dane took Tharyn's arm and ushered her to the ambulance. He helped her to climb in the back so she could be close to her mother, then climbed in behind her.

The driver put the ambulance in motion, and while the medical attendant kept watch over the unconscious Erline, Dane held Tharyn in his arms. He spoke in a low tone, trying to encourage her about her mother. She clung to him with all her might, sobbing and saying that her father and her aunt were dead and that she was afraid her mother would die, too.

Dane continued to do his best to assure her that her mother would be all right.

When they reached Manhattan's Mercy Hospital, Dane and Tharyn were led to a waiting room while Erline was wheeled into surgery on a gurney.

At the moment, the waiting room had no other occupants. Dane continued to do his best to comfort Tharyn in the loss of her father and her aunt, and to encourage her about her mother. He made sure she understood where the bodies of her father and her aunt had been taken.

Tharyn clung to Dane, gripping him tightly. "Oh, Dane, what will I do if

Mommy dies? I'll have nowhere to live and no one to take care of me."

"Your mother's going to be all right." But in his heart, he wondered if it was so. From the looks of Mrs. Myers when he last saw her, he secretly wondered if she would make it.

When Tharyn's emotions had settled down some, she choked out in wide-eyed wonder, "Dane, you . . . saved . . . my life. I would have been trampled to death too, if you hadn't moved me out of the way. As fast as those horses were coming, you could easily have been trampled, yourself. Thank you for risking your life to save mine."

Dane squeezed her hand. "Tharyn, my own safety wasn't even in my thoughts. I just knew I had to get you out of the way so you wouldn't be struck by the charging horses and the wagon."

"I'll . . . never forget . . . what you did."

"I think you need some water. Stay right here. I'll be back shortly."

Dane returned with a cup of water he had obtained at the nurses' station. Sitting down beside her once again, he raised the cup toward her face. "Here. Take a few sips. It'll relieve the dryness in your throat."

She looked at the cup. "I . . . I don't think I can swallow anything."

"Sure you can. Come on now. You can do it. Just two or three swallows, okay? You really need to get some moisture into your system, so —"

His voice trailed off as he followed her eyes to the door of the waiting room, and he saw a man in a white smock coming in. His face was gray and solemn.

Tharyn gripped Dane's arms, knowing in her heart the news was not good.

As the doctor stepped into the waiting room, he noted that there was no one there besides the two teenagers. As he drew up, he looked at Tharyn. "You're Miss Tharyn Myers, aren't you?"

She tried to speak, but nothing would come out.

"She is," said Dane.

"I'm Dr. Walter Lynch," he said, bending low to look Tharyn in the eye. "I'm sorry to — to have to tell you this, Miss Myers, but your mother died of a cerebral hemorrhage from the blow she received to her head when the horses and wagon struck her."

Tharyn's face contorted. "No! No! No-o-o-o!"

Dane wrapped both arms around her as

she broke into sobs. The doctor knelt down in front of her, trying to comfort her in a soft voice.

She went quiet for a moment, then looked at Dane, eyes wide, and opened her mouth again to scream. Suddenly, her eyes rolled back in their sockets and she collapsed in a faint.

Dr. Lynch bent over, raised her eyelids, and looked into her eyes. "The emotional disturbance she has been through today was just too much for her. I've got to take her into the examining room. You wait here. I'll be back as soon as I can."

With that, Dr. Lynch took the unconscious Tharyn up into his arms and hurried into the hall.

On his heels, Dane went as far as the door and watched until the doctor passed from view through the door of the examining room. He sighed, went to one of the chairs, and sat down. Dane Weston was young in his salvation, but he had learned enough already in church and Sunday school to know that as a child of God, he could call on the Lord concerning any matter. He prayed for Tharyn, that God would help her through this horrible ordeal, and that He would give him the wisdom he needed to be a pillar of strength to her.

Almost half an hour had passed when Dane looked up to see Dr. Walter Lynch enter the room. He jumped to his feet. "How is she, Doctor?"

"Well, she's conscious, but she's in shock. I gave her a strong sedative, which will help her to rest. I'm going to keep her here in the hospital at least overnight so she can remain under observation."

Dane nodded. "I don't have much money, Doctor. I'm an orphan, and I live on the streets. But I do have a job. I work at the Clarkson Pharmacy. Mr. Clarkson just paid me my week's wages today. Three dollars and sixty cents. I'll pay that much on Tharyn's hospital bill."

"No need to worry about that now. The bill can be settled later. The main thing right now is to give Tharyn proper care." He studied the dark-haired boy for a moment. "Are you a friend of the family?"

"Not really, sir. I only met Tharyn and her mother this morning at the pharmacy. I was delivering a prescription to the Myerses' home when — when the awful thing happened."

"I see. Well, I'll say this. You're a mighty fine young man to take her under your wing like you've done. What's your name?"

"Dane Weston, sir."

"Well, Dane, can you come back tomorrow?"

"Yes, sir. And I will . . . but I will also come back this evening to check on her."

Lynch smiled. "Fine. She'll be in a room of her own by then. Just stop at the receptionist's desk when you come in. She'll tell you what room Tharyn is in."

Dane left the hospital and went to the pharmacy. Not expecting to see him until Monday, Bryce Clarkson was surprised when his hired man came in. Dane told his boss that he wanted him to know what had happened to the Myers family.

When the pharmacist heard the story he was stunned, but told Dane he was glad that Tharyn was not struck by the runaway horses and wagon.

Though Dane had made little of his having saved Tharyn's life, Clarkson commended him for his courage and quick thinking.

From there, Dane went to Dr. Lee Harris's office. He found the Closed sign in the window, so he climbed the stairs to the apartment and knocked on the door.

When Dr. Harris opened the door, Dane could see Maude rushing with Lawanda toward the bedroom.

Dr. Harris looked over the rims of his half-moon spectacles and frowned. The bruise on Dane's face was deep purple. "Dane, what's wrong? You're pale as a ghost. Come in."

As the boy stepped in, Dr. Harris noted the dirt on his pants and the rip in his shirt. He reached a hand toward him and placed it on his shoulder. "Have you been in a fight, laddie?"

Dane shook his head. "No, sir, I —" Suddenly the emotion of the day overwhelmed him, and he started to cry.

Maude was now coming from the bedroom and observed as her husband put an arm around the boy and led him to the sofa in the parlor.

As Dane sat on the sofa, Maude drew up, noting his bruised face, torn shirt, and dirty trousers. "Dane, honey, what on earth has happened?"

"Please tell us," said the doctor, looking down at the boy with compassion.

Dane looked up into the kind eyes of the loving couple, his eyes awash with tears. He tried to blink them away, but instead, they trickled in a stream down his face. He tried to speak, but could only weep.

Dr. Harris patted his arm. "It's okay, son. Go ahead and cry. Whatever has happened, tears are good for healing any kind of emotional hurt."

Maude sat down beside the boy and put her arm around his shoulder, pulling him close to her. "Go ahead, honey. Cry it out. Then you can tell us what's happened."

Dr. Harris sat down in a chair, facing them.

The Harrises remained quiet, just looking at each other periodically as the boy wept. Finally, with a valiant effort, Dane gained control of himself and wiped a sleeve over his eyes and down his wet face. Taking a deep breath, he looked from one to the other. "My heart is so torn for a thirteen-year-old girl I just met this morning at the pharmacy."

With this established, Dane related the entire story to his elderly friends.

"Oh, the poor dear," said Maude, shaking her head. "The poor dear."

Ever the physician, Lee Harris said, "What can I do to help, Dane? Would you like for me to go see the poor girl? I still have hospital privileges at Mercy, even though most of my patients go to Manhattan Hospital because it is closer to this neighborhood."

A look of hope came into Dane's red-rimmed eyes. "Oh, Dr. Harris, would you

201

do that? I'm sure Dr. Lynch is a fine doctor, but I would feel so much better if you would examine her. He would understand, wouldn't he?"

"Of course. Dr. Lynch and I know each other. It wouldn't disturb him if I simply went in and checked on her — especially since he knows you are her friend and asked me to."

Dane smiled. "Oh, thank you."

"Now, you said since they are keeping Tharyn in the hospital at least overnight, you are going back to see her this evening."

"Right. I just want to make sure there are no other problems from the shock and grief she has experienced today."

Harris nodded. "And you said you're going from here to your alley to let your friends know what has happened."

"Yes, sir. They are no doubt concerned about where I am by now."

"Okay. How about since Mercy Hospital is quite a few blocks from your alley, that I pick you up with my buggy at seven o'clock? You've already covered a lot of ground today."

"That will be fine, sir."

Maude's arm was still around Dane's shoulder. She squeezed him tight. "You're such a good boy."

Dane grinned at her. Then he said to both of them, "When Tharyn gets out of the hospital she has nowhere to go, and no one to take care of her. The only living relative she had outside of her immediate family was her Aunt Althea. From what I've heard many times, all the New York City orphanages are already overcrowded."

Dr. Harris nodded. "That's true."

"Well, I'm going to offer to let Tharyn join my orphan colony in the alley so I can look after her. I'm sure when I tell my friends her story, they will agree to let her become a part of the colony."

Dr. Harris smiled. "I commend you for this, son."

"Yes," said Maude. "I wish we could take her into our home, but you already know why we can't do that. Given the circumstances in Tharyn's life, your plan to take her into your colony is the right thing to do."

"Well, it's the very least I can do," said Dane. "I know how hard it was for me after my family was killed. The streets and alleys of this city are not friendly places for children . . . especially for a girl. I feel an obligation to take care of Tharyn. Since I guess I pretty much saved her life, it's up to me to be responsible for her, since she has no one else to do it."

Dr. Harris smiled. "You are quite the boy. I'm sure Tharyn will be grateful to have you looking after her. And don't forget that Maude and I are here to help you in any way we can."

"I appreciate that, more than I could ever tell you. Well, I'd better get to the alley."

Dr. Harris reconfirmed that he would pick him up at the alley at seven o'clock, and thanking both of them once more for being such good friends to him, Dane left the Harris home and hurried to his "home."

The other nine children in the alley were very glad to see Dane when he arrived. When they asked where he had been, he told them the story. Their hearts went out to the thirteen-year-old girl, who had been suddenly orphaned.

Knowing that the street colonies had an unwritten code of their own, Dane explained his desire to take Tharyn into their colony. He made sure they knew he was taking full responsibility for her.

"Hey, we'll help her, Dane," piped up Russell Mims. "Any friend of yours is a friend of ours. She's welcome here."

"She certainly is," spoke up Bessie

Evans. "Right, everybody?"

The rest of the group spoke up in unison, rallying around Dane.

"I want to thank all of you," said Dane, running his appreciative gaze around the ragtag group. "I'm not sure right now just when they'll let her out of the hospital, but it's important that she has a 'home' to come to. Tharyn is full of raw heartache and pain right now, and we all know what that feels like."

They all spoke their agreement. Dane thanked them for being willing to take in his new friend, Tharyn Myers.

# Chapter Ten

At Mercy Hospital, Tharyn Myers awakened from the effect of the sedative to find a nurse in white dress and cap sitting in a chair beside the bed. She was reading Tharyn's medical chart and did not notice that her patient's eyes were open.

Totally disoriented, Tharyn blinked and ran her gaze around the room, then turned her head to face the nurse. The movement caught the nurse's attention. She laid the chart down, rose to her feet, and moved up beside the bed. "Hello, Tharyn," she said softly, smiling down at her. "I'm Donna Yetter. I'm your nurse for this shift."

Tharyn blinked again and frowned. "Wh-where am I?"

"You're at Mercy Hospital. Don't you remember?"

"No. What happened to me?"

"Well, honey, you were brought in here to —"

"To see my mother!" she gasped as her mind suddenly cleared. A fresh wave of grief overwhelmed her. "Oh-h-h! Mommy's dead. I remember. Why — why am I in this bed?"

"The ordeal of losing your parents and your aunt this morning was too much for you, Tharyn. You passed out."

Her hand went to her forehead. "I — I was in the waiting room, and a doctor came and told me Mommy had died." She burst into tears. Miss Yetter took hold of both her hands, and talked to her in a soothing manner, but Tharyn wailed, "Mommy is dead! Daddy is dead! Aunt Althea is dead! I'm all alo— Wait! Where's Dane?"

Nurse Yetter was confused. "Who's Dane? Is he a relative?"

"No. He's not a relative. I have no relatives. Dane's the best friend I ever had. He saved my life — ah — did you say this is still the same day?"

"Yes."

Tharyn bit her lower lip. "Dane saved

my life when the horses and the wagon were charging at us. He . . . he moved me out of the way. If he hadn't, I would have been killed like the rest of my family was."

"I see. What's Dane's last name?"

Tharyn closed her eyes and concentrated. "Ah . . . Weston. His name's Dane Weston."

"How can he be contacted?"

"Well, he's an orphan. He's fifteen years old. He lives in an alley — ah . . . I'm trying to remember where."

At that moment Dr. Walter Lynch entered the room. A smile broke across his face as he drew up to the bed beside the nurse. "Well, Tharyn, you're awake! Do you remember me?"

She studied his face. "No, sir."

"Well, no surprise. I'm Dr. Walter Lynch."

"He's the doctor who came into the waiting room to tell you that your mother had died, Tharyn."

Tharyn fixed her gaze on him. "Oh yes. Now I remember you."

"You were in the waiting room with Dane Weston, and I'm the one who took care of you after you passed out."

"Dane?"

"Yes."

Tharyn looked toward the door. "Is Dane somewhere in the hospital?"

Dr. Lynch shook his head. "Not now. He left after I went back to the waiting room and told him about you."

Tharyn's body stiffened and her brow furrowed. A cold ball formed in her stomach. A note of concern seeped into her voice as she raised her head from the pillow. "He's gone?"

The doctor smiled and patted her arm. "He said he would be back this evening to see you."

Relief showed in her eyes. She relaxed and eased her head back on the pillow. "Oh, thank you, Doctor, for telling me that. I was afraid maybe he had left for good." She closed her eyes, swallowed hard, and opened them again. "How silly of me. He did promise that he would see me through this. Without him I would be all alone."

"Tharyn, don't be tough on yourself. You've been through a horrible ordeal. But that young man impressed me. I'm sure he meant it when he said he would see you through this. He'll be back this evening."

Tharyn made a tiny smile. "Of course he will. I can't wait to see him again."

Nurse Yetter turned to the doctor. "How

209

soon do you want her to have another sedative?"

He looked down at his patient. "Wait a couple of hours."

"All right."

Tharyn frowned again. "Doctor, could we wait till after Dane has come to see me? I want to be fully awake when he's here."

Lynch looked at the nurse, then at Tharyn. "All right. I won't order another sedative between now and then as long as you can remain in a quiet state."

"I will, Doctor. Promise."

"All right. Well, I have other patients to tend to. I'll see you in the morning."

"Thank you, Doctor."

Nurse Yetter said, "I have some things to do, Tharyn. You lie here and rest. I'll be back in a little while."

Tharyn nodded.

The nurse picked up a small bell from the table beside the bed. "See this?"

"Yes, ma'am."

"If you need anything while I'm gone, just ring it. Someone will be here in a hurry."

"Yes, ma'am."

Tharyn watched doctor and nurse leave the room, then laid her head back and closed her eyes. Suddenly a huge wave of grief and loneliness engulfed her as she faced the fact that her parents and aunt were dead. Tears coursed down her cheeks as she gave in to her anguish.

After giving free rein to her sorrow for several minutes, she slowly began to feel some healing from the tears. She sat up in the bed, and using a corner of the sheet, she mopped her face and dried her tears while looking out the window at the buggies and carriages moving past the hospital down on the street.

A cold chill came over her when she spied a team of horses pulling a wagon similar to the one that had killed her parents and her aunt. She buried her face in the pillow, closed her red-rimmed eyes, and wept once more. When the weeping subsided, she laid her head back on the pillow, closed her eyes again, and pictured her mother and father.

She let her wounded mind drift back over her brief thirteen years as their daughter. "Oh, Mommy, Daddy, how will I ever live without you? Why did you have to die?"

Tears once again threatened to overwhelm her, and she forced her mind away from the death of her parents, trying to think of something else. Instantly Dane

Weston came to mind. She thought of the impact of his body against hers when he came on the run and removed her from harm's way, and how they rolled on the sidewalk and slammed into the stairs of the tenement.

Her hand went to the bruises on her cheek. "Because of you, Dane," she said in a whisper, "all I have are these bruises. If you hadn't been willing to risk your life to save mine, my body would also be lying in the morgue."

She took a deep, shuddering breath. "Dane, you are the best friend I've ever had. You're the nicest boy I've ever met. If I had a brother, I'd want him to be just like you."

That evening, Tharyn was sitting up in her bed with another nurse at her side when they heard footsteps in the hall, and Dane entered the room with Dr. Lee Harris at his side.

A smile spread over Dane's face when he saw Tharyn awake and sitting up. The nurse looked on with pleasure when she saw tears mist Tharyn's blue eyes as she opened her arms and reached for him, speaking his name.

Dane wrapped his arms around her as

she clung to him, then for a moment, they just held on to each other.

When they eased back in each other's arms, Dane looked into her eyes. "Are you all right, Tharyn?"

She managed a sweet smile. "Much better, now that you're here."

He held her gaze briefly. "Tharyn, I want you to meet Dr. Lee Harris. He's a friend of mine. He takes care of the children in the alleys in our neighborhood. That's how I met him. He and his wife have been very good to me. They take me to church with them."

Tharyn extended her hand to the doctor. He took it gently in his own. "I'm very glad to meet you, little lady. Dane has told me all about what happened today. I'm so sorry about your loss, but I'm glad that you are still alive."

Tharyn managed another smile. "Thank you, sir. If it weren't for Dane, I would have been killed, too." She turned her eyes on Dane. "He risked his own life to save mine."

Dane's features tinted. "I only did what anybody would have done."

"I disagree," said Dr. Harris. "Not everyone has that much courage."

"Tharyn told me the story, Dane," said

the nurse. "I agree with Dr. Harris."

Dane's face tinted deeper.

"Oh!" said Tharyn. "Where are my manners? Dane, Dr. Harris, this is my nurse for this shift. Her name is Betty Thaxter."

Betty shook hands with Dane, then the doctor. "Dr. Harris, we have never met, but I have heard about you. I can say that you are well-respected for the work you do in your part of the city, helping poor families who would not otherwise be able to afford medical care and helping those poor little waifs who live on the streets. You are to be commended."

It was Dr. Harris's turn to have a tinted face. "Thank you, ma'am."

Dane had discussed Tharyn's plight with Dr. Harris on their way to the hospital, saying he hoped she would accept his offer to come live in the alley with his colony. Not quite sure how to broach the subject, he prayed in his heart, asking the Lord to help him.

Dr. Harris knew the boy was about to talk to her about it. He nodded as if to say, *"It'll be all right, son. Go ahead."*

Dane took in a small gulp of air and said softly, "Tharyn, Dr. Harris came with me at my request. I wanted him to check on you and see if all is well. We'll talk about that in a moment, but there's something else I need to talk to you about."

She looked into his dark brown eyes and found another smile to give him. "Yes, Dane?"

"Well, I know you haven't had much time to think about all that is involved in what has happened, and I'm sure you are still in shock to some degree. But some decisions must be made right away."

She looked at him with a puzzled frown creasing her flawless brow. "What are you talking about, Dane?"

"Tharyn, your family has been taken from you, and you told me that you have no other relatives."

"Yes."

"Do you have any friends or neighbors who might take you into their home?"

The puzzled look altered into one of confused despair. In a tiny voice, she said, "No, Dane. There are some friends and neighbors, but there aren't any who would want to take me into their home and finish raising me. There are none who would want that expense or that responsibility. I have no one. I'm as alone in this world as you are. If Aunt Althea had lived, I know she would have taken me, but she's gone, and there's no one."

Silent tears pooled in Tharyn's eyes and slowly slid down her cheeks. The pain of her grief and the weight of the world reflected in her eyes as they sought Dane's.

Wanting to calm her fears the best he could, Dane took her hand in his. Tears splashed on their joined hands as Tharyn tried to stem their flow.

Dane squeezed her hand. "Tharyn, don't you worry. I've got it all worked out."

She sniffed. "You do?"

"Well, it's not the Ritz Hotel, nor anything near what you're used to, but I've talked to the kids in my colony, and they are willing to take you in. I . . . I wish I could offer you more, but as you know, my situation is much the same as yours. How about it? Would you like to join our colony?"

Tharyn's eyes took on a distant look as her mind flashed back to the humble tenement where she had lived with her parents. *We didn't have much, but Mommy kept it shiny clean and it always smelled of pine soap and delicious aromas. We were happy there. Oh, Daddy, Mommy . . . I miss you so!*

A sigh escaped her lips, then she lifted her gaze up to meet Dane's.

He smiled. "Well, how about it?"

She smiled back. "I'd love to join your colony, Dane."

Their tear-stained hands were still joined. "Good! As soon as they let you out of here, I'll take you home."

Dr. Harris smiled and winked at Dane.

Tharyn's eyes misted. "Thank you so much, Dane. I don't know what would have become of me if it weren't for you."

"I'm glad to be able to help you, Tharyn. Living on the streets is no picnic, but when you have other friends there with you, it isn't so bad. I well remember how hard it was for me until I found my little group in the alley. You'll love them as I do, and I'll do everything I can to help you."

Tharyn smiled through her tears. "That means more to me than I can tell you." She used a corner of the sheet to dry the tears that had fallen on Dane's hand. She then twined her fingers with his. "Thank you again, Dane, for coming to my rescue and saving my life."

"I'm just glad I was there when those horses bolted, Tharyn. And if I'm ever called upon to rescue you again, I'll do it gladly."

She dipped her head shyly, then looked up at him. "Dane, I've always wanted a big brother. Would you be that for me? Can I call you *my* big brother?"

At first, Dane was stunned by the request, but the idea slowly brought a smile to his face. "Being your big brother would make me very happy, Tharyn, as long as I can call you my little sis."

Tharyn's smile was from ear to ear. Her face lit up and there was a sparkle in her eyes. She slipped her fingers from his, then extended her hand. "It's a deal, big brother!"

Dane gripped the small hand extended to him, and a pact was sealed between the two homeless children.

Dr. Harris looked on with pleasure, then said to the nurse, "Dane told me that Dr. Walter Lynch is Tharyn's doctor. He and I know each other. Since he works the day shift, he's gone home by now, but would it be all right if I check her over?"

"Of course, Doctor," said Betty. "Even though we haven't met before, I know you have privileges here at Mercy Hospital. However, it just so happens that Dr. Lynch is still here. He was about to leave for home just as this shift started. An ambulance came in with an elderly woman who had fallen from a second story balcony at her apartment house, and emergency surgery was necessary. Dr. Lynch was called upon to do it. I was out of the room briefly a half hour ago. One of the nurses told me he was still in surgery, and from what she said, he would be for another hour or so. You go ahead and examine Tharyn. I'll go see how close he might be to finishing up."

Harris nodded. "All right."

As soon as Nurse Thaxter was out of the room, Dr. Harris checked Tharyn over, asking questions to ascertain her emotional stability. When he had listened to her heart, examined her eyes with a light reflector, and taken her temperature, he told her and Dane that she was fine. He was sure if she did not take a turn for the worse with her emotions during the night, she would probably be released tomorrow.

While they were waiting for Nurse Thaxter to return, Dane said, "Tharyn, you know that the street waifs beg for money on the street corners, don't you?"

"Yes. I've seen them many times."

"Do you think it will bother you to beg?"

"No. If they can do it, so can I."

"Good. I beg with my friends in the afternoons, too. And most of the money I make from my job at the pharmacy goes into the food fund. I keep a dollar or two in my pocket for emergencies. And then, of course, some days we don't do so well in the begging department. When the food fund is empty, we sometimes get leftover food from the Blue Jay Café. And there are times when the only food we can get our hands on is in the garbage cans behind the café."

Tharyn nodded. "I know about that."

"Does this bother you?"

"Dane, if you and the others can eat it, I can, too."

At that moment, Nurse Thaxter entered the room with Dr. Walter Lynch on her heels. The doctors smiled at each other and shook hands.

Looking toward Tharyn, Dr. Harris said, "I checked her over."

"Yes," said Lynch. "Mrs. Thaxter told me. What do you think?"

"She looks all right to me. I think the initial shock has worn off now."

"That's my opinion, too. She's doing much better."

"So when will you release her?"

"If she's still doing as well tomorrow morning, I'll release her by noon."

"Good. Dane and I will be in church services in the morning, but we'll come to the hospital to pick her up right after the morning service. We'll be here about twelve-thirty."

"That will be fine, Dr. Harris. I'm fully optimistic about being able to release her at that time."

"Dr. Lynch, has anything been said to you about when the funeral for Tharyn's parents will be held?"

"No. I haven't heard any word on that. You probably should check with the police department."

"I will."

Dane was standing next to Tharyn's bed, and as the funeral was mentioned, he felt her tense up. He took hold of her hand and gave it a good squeeze. She looked into his eyes, showing gratitude in her expression.

Betty Thaxter moved to the head of the bed. "Well, Tharyn, it's time for your sedative. We want you to sleep well tonight."

Dr. Harris said, "Dane, we need to be going."

"Dr. Harris, it was good to see you again," said Dr. Lynch. "Any date set on your retirement?"

Dane's head came around at Lynch's question.

"Sometime in the next six months," said Harris. "This old body is demanding it."

"I understand," said Lynch, who was barely in his fifties. "This city's going to lose one of its very finest doctors when that happens."

Harris smiled. "Thank you, Doctor."

The two physicians shook hands, and Dr. Lynch hurried away.

Tharyn looked up at Dr. Harris. "Thank you for coming."

"My pleasure, Tharyn. See you to-morrow."

She turned her eyes on Dane. "Thank you for caring enough to take me into your colony."

Dane patted her arm. "Hey, a big brother should care about his little sister."

Tears filmed her eyes. "Thank you for being my big brother."

"I always kissed my little sister, Diane, good night, so now I will do that with you." He bent down and planted a tender kiss on her forehead.

Tharyn's tears began spilling down her cheeks as she watched Dane and the elderly Dr. Harris go out the door.

As Dr. Harris was driving Dane toward the neighborhood where his colony lived, Dane turned on the seat and looked at him by the light of the lamps along the way. "Dr. Harris, I didn't know you were making plans to retire."

The doctor guided the horse around a corner, then met Dane's gaze.

"It's just about time, son. Like I told Dr. Lynch, this old body is demanding it."

Dane nodded. "Yes, sir," he said with a sad tone in his voice. "You said you were planning to retire sometime in the next six months."

"Uh-huh."

"Then what?"

"It looks like we'll be moving to Roanoke, Virginia, so we can live close to our son and his family."

"I see. Well . . . ah . . . it would be nice if you could live close to them." He paused briefly, then asked, "How will you get Lawanda to Virginia, since she's afraid of people? I mean, how could you get her on a train?"

"We won't be able to do that. We'll have to buy a covered wagon and drive down."

"Oh. Sure. That would work. Six months, huh?"

"Well, that all depends on how soon I can find a young doctor to take over my practice. Shouldn't be too hard. The hospitals in the five boroughs have a great number of young medical school graduates doing their internship, and they're chomping at the bit to finish that so they can get into their own practices."

"Guess I don't have to tell you, sir, but I'm going to miss you. I . . . I sure hope whatever doctor takes over your practice will look after my little colony like you do."

Dr. Harris chuckled. "That will have to be part of the agreement when the sale is made, Dane. I promise."

Soon the doctor pulled the buggy up to the end of the alley where Dane's friends were watching for him. Dr. Harris told him he would pick him up at the usual time in the morning, and Dane jumped out of the buggy and hurried to his friends. They quickly gathered around him, wanting to know how Tharyn was doing and if she was going to join them.

They were glad when Dane told them she was doing well and was indeed going to join them.

Later, in his cardboard box, Dane fell asleep praying for Tharyn.

After church the next day, Dr. Harris and Dane drove to the hospital. They entered the lobby and approached the front desk.

The receptionist smiled at the doctor as they drew up. "Hello, Dr. Harris. Nice to see you."

"You too, Isabel. My young friend and I are here to pick up a thirteen-year-old girl named Tharyn Myers. She's in room 123. Has Dr. Lynch released her?"

Isabel looked down at a sheet of paper before her. "Yes, he has, Doctor. You will need to pay the bill at the cashier's desk."

"All right. Thank you."

As Harris and the boy drew up to the cashier's desk, the cashier had a sour look on her face as she was reading a book that she had laid before her on the desk. She looked up. "Yes?"

"I'm Dr. Lee Harris, ma'am. I don't believe we've ever met."

"I'm new here, Doctor."

"Oh." He noted the name plate on the desk corner. "Hazel Callahan."

"Yes. What can I do for you?"

"My young friend and I are here to pick up Tharyn Myers, room 123. Dr. Lynch has released her."

Hazel glanced at a sheet of paper to her left and studied it a moment. "Yes, he has. The bill is twelve dollars."

Dane was a bit surprised that the bill was that much. Reaching into his pocket, he said, "I'm sort of Tharyn's brother, ma'am. It's up to me to pay the bill, but I only have two dollars right now. I have a

225

job, and I'll pay the rest as soon as I can."

As he spoke, Dane pulled two crumpled one-dollar bills from his pocket and handed them to her.

She laid them on top of the desk, smoothed them out, then looked at Dane. "I don't know how you can be 'sort of' someone's brother. Anyhow, I must have the full amount before the patient can be released."

"But that's all I have, ma'am. I told you I will pay the rest of it as soon as I can."

Dr. Harris was looking on silently.

"That just won't do, young man," said Hazel Callahan. "Hospital policy says payment in full right now."

There was deep frustration on Dane's face.

Dr. Harris laid a hand on the boy's shoulder. "Dane, I admire you for what you're trying to do. You're a special young man. It's all right; I'll take care of the bill for Tharyn." He pulled out his wallet and extracted twelve dollars.

Dane looked up at him, eyes wide.

To the cashier, Harris said firmly, "Give him back his two dollars, ma'am." He laid the money in front of her.

The woman handed Dane his money, then looked up at the doctor. "It doesn't matter to me who pays, just so the bill gets paid in full."

Harris nodded.

She marked the bill Paid, and handed it to him.

"Thank you, ma'am," the physician said, the corners of his eyes crinkling as he smiled at her. "I hope your day gets better as it goes along."

Her mouth fell open, but she said nothing.

The doctor and the boy walked away toward the corridor that would lead them to room 123, smiles gracing both their faces.

As they headed down the hall, Dane said, "Dr. Harris, I know you're not wallowing in money." He pulled out the two one-dollar bills. "Take these. I'll pay you back the other ten as soon as I can."

"I'll be fine, son. You keep that money. You need it far worse than I do."

"But —"

"No buts, Dane. I'll be fine. Put that money back in your pocket."

Shaking his head as he stuffed the bills back in his pocket, he said, "I've never met anyone like you, Dr. Harris."

The doctor chuckled. "Well, one like me in your lifetime is enough, don't you think?"

They were drawing up to Tharyn's room. "This world would be a lot better off if there were *millions* like you, sir."

When they stepped into the room, Nurse Donna Yetter had Tharyn dressed and ready to go.

When Tharyn, Dane, and the doctor were seated in the buggy, Dane turned to Tharyn. "Dr. Harris and I were talking on our way over here. Would you like to go by your old apartment and pick up some of your clothes? It's pretty warm now, but you know come fall and winter, New York will be cold and damp."

"That would be good, Dane. I'll need my clothes, even the summer ones."

"Just point me the way, children," said the doctor.

Traffic held them up some, but they pulled up in front of the apartment nearly forty-five minutes after they had left the hospital.

When Tharyn first looked at the spot where the team and wagon had hit her parents and Aunt Althea, a chill slithered down her backbone.

Dane was having his own thoughts about the incident as he helped Tharyn out of the buggy. Dr. Harris joined them as they headed toward the steps. Dane felt Tharyn tense up a bit and sensed her reluctance to enter the building. Tharyn was thinking that this had been her home since birth. She was struggling with the memories that were passing through her mind.

Dane took her hand.

As they entered the foyer, a door to one side opened, and a white-haired woman stepped out. "Hello, Tharyn, dear. I'm so terribly sorry about your parents. I was hoping you would come by. We had to rent out the apartment this morning. My husband and I packed up all of your family's things. Would you like to take them now?"

Tharyn quickly cast a questioning glance at Dane.

"Sure," he said to the landlady. "We're in Dr. Harris's buggy, and it isn't very large, but if there isn't too much, we can handle it."

"Well, we have all of it packed in boxes down here in the storeroom."

She led them to the storeroom and opened the door. "These boxes right here." She pointed. "Everything is there, including the bedding and a few knickknacks that your mother had, Tharyn."

There were not as many boxes as Dane or Dr. Harris had expected.

"We can get these in the buggy, all right," said Harris.

Tharyn said, "Dane, we won't want these boxes in the alley, will we?"

"We can take them, and you can sort out what you want to keep. If you don't want all of it, you might be able to sell some of it and pick up some money. It'll be up to you."

The doctor, Tharyn, and Dane began picking up the boxes, and before they moved out into the hall, Tharyn said, "Thank you, Mrs. Trimble." She was trying to hold back the tears that were threatening to surface.

"You're welcome, child," said the landlady and patted her arm.

Moments later, the boxes were in the buggy, and as Dr. Harris put the horse into motion, Tharyn turned on the seat for one last look at the place that was the only home she had ever known. Memories of so many happy times with her parents flooded her mind.

Tears were threatening once again. She turned around on the seat, bowed her head, and let them come.

Dane took hold of her hand. "I know exactly what you're feeling. Tomorrow will be a better day. I promise."

She raised her head, wiped the excess moisture from her eyes, and squeezed his hand. "Thank you. With you to help me, I'm sure it will be."

Dr. Lee Harris put soft eyes on both of them, smiled, and said in his heart, *Please make it so, Lord.*

# Chapter Eleven

As the buggy moved along the streets amid other horse-drawn vehicles, Dr. Lee Harris was speaking encouragingly to Tharyn Myers, who sat between Dane Weston and him. He could tell that she was nervous about taking up residence in the alley, even though Dane would be with her, and wanted to encourage her in this new and difficult phase of her life.

She looked up at him and smiled. "Thank you for your encouragement, Dr. Harris. I'm finding out why Dane thinks so much of you."

The doctor chuckled and looked at Dane. "Well, I've got him fooled, Tharyn."

Dane laughed. "Oh no, you don't. And am I going to miss you when you're gone."

"Dr. Harris," said Tharyn, "I heard you tell Dr. Lynch that you would be retiring within six months."

"That's the plan, yes."

"When you retire, are you going to move away?"

"He and Mrs. Harris and their daughter are going to move to Virginia," said Dane. "They have a son and his family who live in Roanoke."

Tharyn's brow furrowed. "You have a daughter who still lives with you, Dr. Harris?"

Dr. Harris explained to Tharyn that Lawanda was mentally handicapped, and instead of putting her in an institution, they had chosen to keep her in their home. He went on to explain about Lawanda's fear of people and that they would have to buy a covered wagon and travel to Virginia in the wagon. He added that it actually would be best, because this way they could carry their clothing and other valuables at the same time.

Dr. Harris turned onto Broadway and was heading toward the alley where Dane and his friends lived.

When they were two blocks from the alley, Dane's attention was drawn to a buggy that was parked at the curb, and the faces of a couple who were talking to four street waifs and two uniformed police officers.

"Hey, Dr. Harris," said Dane, "it's Mr. and Mrs. Brace from the Children's Aid Society! Looks like they're about to take some children with them."

The doctor pulled rein as he spotted the small group.

"Are you acquainted with Mr. and Mrs. Brace, Doctor?" asked Dane as the buggy came to a halt.

"I've never met them personally," replied Harris, "but I recognize them because their pictures have been in the newspapers many times. I admire their great work with the orphans and have long wanted to meet them. Now is as good a time as any. You've met them, have you?"

"No, sir. They were pointed out to me one day by one of the girls in the colony as they were taking some street urchins off the street to put them on an orphan train."

"I see," said the doctor, stepping out of the buggy. "You two wait here."

By this time, the four children were climbing into the Children's Aid Society buggy under the direction of the Braces, when one of the officers spotted Dr. Harris moving toward them. "Hello, Doc!"

"Hello, James! Nice to see you!"

The two men shook hands, then Dr. Harris said, "I have a boy in my buggy who recognized Mr. and Mrs. Brace and pointed them out to me. I've long wanted to meet them."

Officer James Thornton had been on the beat in the area for several years, and knew the physician well. Motioning for the other officer to come to them, he said, "Dr. Harris, I want you to meet Officer Fred Collins. He's my new partner. Fred, shake hands with one of New York's finest physicians, Dr. Lee Harris."

While Harris and Collins were shaking hands, the Braces moved close. Charles Loring Brace — who was a small, thin man of forty-five — said, "Officer Thornton, did I hear right? This gentleman is Dr. Lee Harris, and he said he has long wanted to meet us?"

"You heard right, sir," said Thornton.

Harris moved to the couple, smiling. "You sure did, young man. I so much appreciate your wonderful work, and am glad for the opportunity to tell you so."

Brace and Harris shook hands, then Letitia Brace, who was much smaller than her husband, offered her hand. The doctor took it gently in his gnarled hand and did a

235

slight bow. "This is such a pleasure, Mrs. Brace."

"Well, let me tell you something, Dr. Harris. My husband and I have heard much about you and your marvelous work over the years."

"We sure have," said Charles Loring Brace, smiling from ear to ear. "And we are happy to finally get to meet you!" He then looked toward the doctor's buggy. "I heard you say you have a boy in your buggy who recognized us."

Dane smiled at Brace.

"Yes," said Harris. "In fact he and that pretty girl next to him on the seat are orphans."

"Oh, really? Do they live on the streets?"

"Yes. Let me introduce you to them."

Charles and Letitia followed as the doctor led them up to his buggy. "Mr. and Mrs. Brace, this is Tharyn Myers and Dane Weston."

The Braces said they were glad to meet them, then Charles asked where on the streets they lived. Dane explained that Tharyn was just now going there with him for the first time, and pointed that direction, saying his colony's alley was two blocks away.

The officers had drawn close, and James

Thornton said, "You look familiar, son. I think I've seen you before."

Dane smiled. "I know I've seen you, sir. I work at Clarkson's Pharmacy, and walk this street six days a week, going to work."

Thornton's eyebrows arched. "A street waif with a job. That's pretty rare."

"It was Dr. Harris who got me the job, Officer."

Thornton smiled at the doctor. "Good for you, Doc."

Letitia set her kind gaze on the girl with the auburn hair. "So you are just coming to the alley to live, Dane said."

"Yes, ma'am."

"Let me explain," said Dr. Harris, then proceeded to tell both children's stories in brief.

When he finished, all four adults were deeply touched.

Charles Brace said, "I wish I could take every orphan on the streets of New York, put them on the orphan trains, and send them out West to find families who would take them in."

"Me, too," said Letitia.

Brace hunched his thin shoulders. "But such a wish is impossible. The number of orphans on the streets is rapidly growing. I'm thankful to the Lord that we can at least send some of them out West."

Once again, Dane thought about his planned career as a medical doctor and wondered if maybe someday he would be able to go out West where a family would take him in who could afford to send him through medical school.

Charles Brace smiled at the orphans. "I'm glad to have met both of you."

"Me, too," said his wife.

Brace glanced at Letitia, then set his kind eyes on Dane and Tharyn. "Quite often Mrs. Brace and I come into this area and pick up children to put on the orphan trains. Maybe someday we'll be able to do it for both of you."

Dane grinned. "That would be real nice, sir."

As the Braces were driving away with the four orphans, Dr. Harris told Officers James Thornton and Fred Collins of Dane's goal to become a medical doctor.

Both men smiled at the boy.

Officer Thornton said, "I hope you make it, Dane, but this situation of your living on the streets will have to change before it will be possible. You will have to have adoptive parents or legal guardians before you can enter public school to finish your education and you will need lots of money for medical college."

"I know this, sir," said Dane, then boldly added, "I've been praying to my heavenly Father that just such a thing will happen."

Dane was surprised by Thornton's reply. "If you could get Mr. Brace to put you on an orphan train and you could find some wealthy cattle rancher out West to adopt you, it no doubt would work out beautifully."

Dane thought on it. "Yes, sir. That would be something, wouldn't it?" He turned to look at Tharyn. "Of course, if the Lord would do such a thing for me, He would also have to see that my little sister went with me."

Both officers looked puzzled. "Your sister?" said Collins. "Nobody said anything about you being siblings."

Dane grinned. "We're not *really* brother and sister, sir, but we adopted each other shortly after her parents were killed."

Collins grinned. "Oh, I see. Well, Dr. Harris told us that you saved her life. So why not adopt her as your sister?"

"That's how I look at it, sir. Whatever happens, I'm going to do my best to see that Tharyn is taken care of."

"Good for you," said Collins.

"That's for sure," put in Thornton. "I

wish both of you the very best."

Collins nodded. "Well, Officer Thornton, we'd better move on."

As the policemen walked on down the street, Dr. Harris climbed back in his buggy and put the horse into motion. He drove the two blocks, and turned the buggy into the alley.

Tharyn drew a shaky breath and looked at Dane. "Okay, big brother, it's time for me to meet your friends."

Dane grinned. "I've told you that you'll love them. You'll see."

The other nine orphans were there, having just returned from their morning of begging on the nearest street corner. Dane noted that they were huddled together, counting their money. When they became aware of the approaching buggy, Russell Mims looked up. "Hey, guys and gals, it's Dane! And he's got Tharyn with him!"

All of them hurried to the side of the buggy, calling out greetings to Tharyn and Dane and Dr. Harris.

The warmth of the children toward her touched Tharyn deeply.

As she ran her gaze up and down the alley, she was appalled at the squalid sight before her. There were large metal trash receptacles behind the buildings on both sides of the alley. Some businesses also had garbage cans and wooden crates near their doors. Rubbish of every description was scattered around the receptacles, the garbage cans, and the crates.

At the precise spot where the children were gathered it was somewhat cleaner, which she figured was due to the efforts of the children in the colony. Large cardboard boxes were lined up against the back wall of a brick building. Its rear door was recessed and formed an alcove which Tharyn decided would provide shelter for the orphans in a rainstorm, even though they would have to crowd themselves in tightly to make it work.

Dane explained to the others that Tharyn had brought some boxes containing some bedding, clothing, and other things that had been in the apartment where she and her parents had lived. The boys helped Dane and Dr. Harris take the boxes from the buggy. They were placed beside the large cardboard boxes, which Dane explained were the beds they slept in.

Dr. Harris excused himself to the children, saying he must get back to his office. Tharyn thanked him once again for his kindness to her.

When Dr. Harris was gone, the children gathered around Tharyn, each expressing their sympathy for the loss of her parents and her aunt.

Dane then introduced Tharyn to the children, one by one, giving their names. Melinda Scott and Bessie Evans immediately took Tharyn under their wings and guided her to the cardboard boxes while the others followed. They showed her a new cardboard box, which they had placed between theirs. Two tattered blankets lay in the bottom of Tharyn's box.

Smiling at her new friends, she said, "Bessie, Melinda, I appreciate your looking after me even before I got here."

Bessie said, "Actually, it was Russell who went down to the alley this morning and found this box for you behind the furniture store."

Tharyn turned to Russell. "Thank you."

"Glad to do it, Tharyn," said Russell, warming her with a wide smile.

Dane could tell that Russell was quite taken with Tharyn — he could hardly keep his eyes off her.

He understood why. Tharyn was very pretty and had a captivating personality.

Tharyn looked back at her new cardboard bed, then set her gaze on Bessie and

Melinda. "The only times I have ever slept outside was on the fire escape outside the window at the back of our apartment. This was in the summer, when the nights were hot. My mother would make soft pallets for each of us, and she, Daddy, and I would sleep there. At least there was usually a breeze and it was a little cooler than it was inside the apartment. I remember lying out there, looking up at the stars, and watching the moon sail across the dark sky. I wasn't a bit afraid, since Mommy and Daddy were right there with me."

Tharyn paused, looking around at the cardboard boxes. "But I have to admit, being right here in the alley like this is a little scary. I guess in time, I'll get used to it. Right now, it's all so new to me."

"We understand completely, Tharyn," said Melinda. "It was hard at first for every one of us, but after a while, we got used to it."

Dane moved up beside Tharyn and put a comforting arm around her shoulders. "It's only natural to be scared, little sis. I was pretty frightened myself when I left our apartment and went to the streets to find a place to live."

Tharyn nodded. "I can imagine so. At least I already have you and these new friends to make me feel welcome." She glanced at her box. "I think I'll use a couple of my blankets from home. And if any of you can use the rest of the bedding I brought with me, you're welcome to it."

Ears perked up in the group. Tharyn took out all the blankets, and reserving two for herself, passed them around to eager hands.

At that point, Russell said, "Well, everybody, it's time to get back to our street corner and do some more begging. Are you going to go with us, Tharyn?"

She smiled thinly. "I'm a little scared about that too, but Dane has told me all about it. I might as well get started right now."

The sun was lowering in the western sky when the colony returned to their alley, sat in a circle, and counted the money they had garnered from begging that afternoon. Tharyn had taken in eighty cents, and everyone congratulated her. Dane explained that she did quite well for a half-day's begging, which pleased her.

At that point, Billy Johnson turned to Dane. "Doc, we'd better have our Bible reading real quick, before it gets dark."

Tharyn thought it was neat that all of

the children in the group called Dane "Doc." She watched as Dane hurried to his cardboard box, reached in, and took out his Bible. As he sat down beside her, he said, "I will explain all of this thoroughly later, little sis, but I came to know the Lord Jesus Christ as my Saviour a short time ago, and ever since then, I've been reading Scripture to my friends before dark every day. They have become interested in what the Bible has to say, and we always enjoy it."

Tharyn nodded. "Sounds interesting to me too, Dane. I don't know much about the Bible, but what I've heard about it has always made me want to learn more."

Dane's eyes lit up. "Swell!" As he opened the Bible, he said, "Tharyn, most of what I've been reading to them has come from the four Gospels, Matthew, Mark, Luke, and John, which tell us about the earthly life of Jesus and His purpose for coming from heaven to earth."

"I'd like to learn all about that. I know that Christmas is about His being born into the world, and I remember hearing about the angels telling shepherds in the fields that God's Son had been born."

"That's about all I knew from the Bible,

myself, until Dr. and Mrs. Harris helped me. Well, I'm going to read from the Gospel of John right now."

Tharyn listened intently as Dane read John 6 and learned things about Jesus she had never heard before.

After Dane finished reading the chapter — during which he had made comments — it was discussion time. Because Dane was so young in the Lord, questions were asked by the group that he could not answer. He told them he would ask Dr. Harris the same questions as soon as he could.

Dane put his Bible away and went with Russell to pick up food for supper that had already been promised by the people at the Blue Jay Café. Tharyn was pleased with the food, but dreaded the times she would have to eat from the garbage cans.

Soon it was bedtime, and as Melinda and Bessie were showing Tharyn how to position herself in the cardboard box for sleeping, Dane drew up. "I want to tell my little sister good night."

Bessie frowned. "How come you call her your little sister?"

Dane made a quick explanation to the girls of how he and Tharyn adopted each other as brother and sister. He then kissed

Tharyn on the forehead. "Good night, little sis."

The fear that had been held at bay all evening now crept back into Tharyn's heart and showed in her eyes. Dane was quick to notice it. "Tharyn, you don't need to be afraid. These kids are all your friends now, and we protect and take care of each other. I'll only be a few feet away in my box. If you need me, just call out."

"I will," she said in a tremulous voice. "Thank you, Dane. I can't even imagine what would happen to me without you."

"I'm glad the Lord made it so we could be together." He kissed her forehead again. "Good night."

Tharyn looked at him with admiring eyes. "Good night, big brother."

Dane headed for his own cardboard box, which was situated next to that of Russell Mims.

Russell was sitting up inside his box. "Dane, I heard you tell Melinda and Bessie about you and Tharyn adopting each other, and I saw those kisses you put on her forehead."

Dane grinned. "Yeah?"

"Uh-huh. Tell you what —"

"What?"

"Personally, I'd rather be Tharyn's boyfriend than her brother."

"Well, neither you nor Tharyn are old enough for that yet."

Russell disagreed in his mind, but kept it to himself.

Later, when it was quiet in the alley, and Dane lay in his cardboard box, he pondered Officer James Thornton's comment earlier: *"If you could get Mr. Brace to put you on an orphan train and you could find some wealthy cattle rancher out West to adopt you, it no doubt would work out beautifully."*

He prayed and asked the Lord to bring it about if it was His will, adding that he knew that one way or another, the Lord was going to make it possible for him to one day become a doctor.

The next morning, after a meager breakfast of water and day-old rolls purchased from the grocery store, Dane went to Tharyn and asked if she was going to be all right while he was at work. She assured him she would be fine especially since she had Melinda and Bessie. Russell overheard the conversation and assured Dane he would look out for Tharyn.

Dane went to work at the pharmacy.

At midmorning, while he was washing

windows outside the front of the building, he heard people passing by who were talking about two teenage gangs who had gotten into a knife fight last night at Longacre Square, which was located at Forty-second and Broadway in downtown Manhattan. He learned that seven of the gang members were dead and thirteen of them were in hospitals. Most of them were in critical condition. Worse yet, two of Manhattan's adult citizens were dead, and three were hospitalized in serious condition. These people were caught helplessly between the two gangs when the fight broke out.

At one point, two police officers who were walking their beat came down the sidewalk. They stopped in front of the pharmacy, spoke to Dane, then let their eyes take in the street from one end of the block to the other.

Dane listened as the officers also discussed the bloodshed at Longacre Square the night before. The officers agreed that Manhattan's streets were becoming more dangerous all the time. One of them said the mayor was going to have to crack down even harder on crime in the city.

When Dane went back inside the pharmacy, he found Bryce Clarkson and some customers talking about last night's incident.

When the customers had gone, Dane told his boss what he heard the police officers say about the gang fight. Bryce and Dane discussed the incident and talked about the increase of crime in all five boroughs. People were murdered almost every night in Manhattan alone.

After work, Dane went to the tenement where he and his family used to live and spent a few minutes with Mitchell and Sylvia Bendrick. The Bendricks were glad to see him and to learn of his job at the pharmacy.

Dane told them he would come and get his winter clothes sometime in the fall, and when he actually had a place to live, he would come for his medical books.

Before heading back to the alley, Dane also went to the Baxter apartment. Mona was the only one home. She welcomed him warmly, and since it was lunchtime, she prepared him some hot potato soup, which he devoured eagerly. Mona told him she was glad that his job was going well for him, and that he enjoyed it so much.

As he was preparing to leave, Dane asked Mona to greet the rest of the family for him — especially his best friend.

When Dane arrived back at the alley, Tharyn saw him first and ran to him. The others looked on.

As Dane and Tharyn moved toward the others, she said, "Dr. Harris came by this morning on his way to a house call. We were all out there on the corner, begging. He told me he had just stopped at police headquarters. They informed him that my parents and my aunt will be buried at the 116th Street Cemetery on Wednesday morning at ten o'clock. The city is going to cover the cost of the burial and the coffins."

"I'm glad the cost is taken care of, Tharyn," he said, taking hold of her hand.

"Me too."

They drew up to the group, who had heard Tharyn's words about the burial.

Russell said, "Dane, I told Dr. Harris I was sure Mr. Clarkson would give you time off from work so you could attend the burial service."

"Oh, sure. Of course he will."

"Dr. Harris will be here at nine-thirty, so he can go with us."

"Us?"

"Yes. All of us are planning to go to the service."

"We sure are," put in Melinda Scott. "We want to be with Tharyn in that difficult time."

Dane said, "Bless all of you for this."

"It means so much to me," said Tharyn. "It's wonderful to have such good friends."

It was a bright, sunny morning on Wednesday when the group of children, along with Dr. Lee Harris, stood in a half-circle beside the three yawning graves.

While a minister appointed by the city conducted the brief service, Dane kept an arm around Tharyn, who was trembling with grief and had tears streaming down her face.

Dane fought the tears that were welling up in his own eyes. With his free hand, he wiped at them as they began spilling down his cheeks. His heart went out to Tharyn as he recalled his own family's funeral only a few weeks ago in this very cemetery.

Dane leaned down and whispered in her ear. "It gets easier as time passes, little sis. Every day is a little less painful. We're all here for you. You can lean on us."

"I know," she whispered back. "Thank you."

When the short service was over, Dr. Harris embraced Tharyn and left the cemetery in his buggy, heading back to his office.

Dane told Tharyn he wanted to go to the graves of his parents and brother and sister before they headed back to the alley. The others followed the short distance to the four graves, and stood close by as Dane stood in silence looking down at them while Tharyn held his hand.

After a few minutes, Dane wiped away his tears. "All right. Let's head back."

Soon the group began to talk about death and the graveside service, and the conversation went to the things Dane had read to them from the Bible. They were concerned about their own eternal destiny and began asking more questions.

Dane said, "I know how I got saved, and I can show it to you in the Bible. But it would be best if I could get Dr. Harris to come help you. He is well experienced at this. I'll go to his office and ask him to come to the alley as soon as possible, so he can help you."

"Even if it had to be after dark this evening, Dane," said Russell, "we can borrow a lantern from Mr. Powell. He and his wife live in an apartment above the grocery store. I want to get this settled in my heart."

"Me too," said Billy Johnson.

Some of the others spoke up, saying they wanted to be saved. Though Tharyn did not voice it, Dane could see from the way she looked at him that she wanted to know more about salvation.

Dane smiled at the group. "All right. I'll tell Dr. Harris we need him, even if he can't come till after dark."

# Chapter Twelve

It was just after three o'clock in the afternoon when Dane Weston and Dr. Lee Harris drew up to the end of the alley in the doctor's buggy.

All ten of Dane's friends were on the street corner a half-block from the alley's entrance, begging.

One of the girls noticed the buggy and pointed that direction. Russell Mims was just thanking a woman for the silver dollar she had placed in his hand when he heard the girl say that Dr. Harris and Dane were there.

The group waved and ran toward them. Dr. Harris and Dane waved back, then Harris proceeded to guide the horse into the alley and pulled rein at the spot that the children had established as their dwelling place. Both of them got out of the buggy, turned to see the children round the corner of the building at the end of the alley, and waited for them. When they drew up, they all noticed that Dr. Harris had his Bible in hand.

Dane said, "Dr. Harris cancelled a couple of his patients' appointments and rescheduled them for tomorrow so he could come and talk to you about salvation."

"Thank you for coming, Dr. Harris," said Russell.

Harris cracked a smile. "My pleasure. How about all of you sitting down over here on these wooden crates?"

When the colony was comfortably seated before him, Dr. Harris opened his Bible and went over the gospel message very carefully. He read the crucifixion story in the book of Matthew — including Jesus' blood-shedding death, burial, and glorious resurrection. From there, he took them to many other Scriptures on the subject of salvation, making God's salvation plan very clear for their young minds.

He then asked if they had questions, and some did. He answered each question with Scripture. Dane was glad he had brought Dr. Harris to them. Many of the questions he would have been unable to answer.

When there were no more questions, Dr. Harris dealt with them individually. Every one of them — except Nettie Olson — opened their hearts to Jesus Christ and received Him as their personal Saviour. It was evident to Dr. Harris that Nettie was still a bit young to understand. He then showed the new converts from the Scriptures that their next step of obedience was to be baptized as a public testimony of their salvation. Every one of them agreed, demonstrating that they were eager to obey their Lord.

By this time, Dane was standing beside Dr. Harris, his face beaming with joy.

"Boys and girls, I will go talk to my pastor on my way back to the office and see if the church can provide a special carriage to transport all of you to church for Sunday morning services. I feel confident that he will see that this is done. I'll come by tomorrow and let you know."

They thanked Dr. Harris for showing them how to be saved, and the doctor shook his head. "Don't thank me. If you want to thank someone, praise Jesus for answering your need."

The next afternoon, Dr. Harris went to the alley and gathered the small colony around him. He looked into their eager eyes. "Good news! Pastor Alan Wheeler has arranged a special carriage for you, not only for this coming Sunday so you can be baptized, but every Sunday from now on so you can attend Sunday school and church services regularly."

Bessie and Melinda applauded. The rest of them joined in, their happy faces shining.

When the cheering subsided, Harris said, "The carriage will be here to pick you up at nine-thirty on Sunday morning." He then looked at the boy who was standing beside Tharyn. "Dane, I want to commend you for reading your Bible to these children every day since you were saved. You are responsible for them coming to the Lord."

There was applause for Dane.

That night at bedtime, Dane headed for Tharyn as usual. She was sitting up in her cardboard box, and talking to Melinda and Bessie. Melinda saw Dane coming. "Here comes your big brother, Tharyn. It's time for that good-night kiss."

No one noticed that Russell was observing from his box with a watchful eye.

Bessie giggled. "Yeah. Melinda and I are
jealous."

Tharyn matched the giggle. "Sorry, girls,
only one big brother per girl in this
colony."

Bessie and Melinda laughed.

Drawing up, Dane frowned. "What's so
funny?"

Bessie giggled again. "We'll never tell!"

Dane shook his head, smiling, then
leaned down to Tharyn and kissed her
forehead. "Good night, little sis."

The redhead reached up and gave him a
sisterly hug. "I want to thank you for being
the one responsible for bringing me to
Jesus. It's wonderful to know that I'm
going to heaven."

Dane grinned at her in the dim light.
"I'm glad the Lord allowed me to be the
one. See you in the morning."

As time passed, life went on as usual in
the alley occupied by the little colony.
Dane gladly used the larger part of his
wages to help feed the group. What little
he kept for himself was put aside in his
pockets to help provide for his education

when needed. The others begged on the customary street corner in the mornings six days a week, and Dane joined them in the afternoons. Their begging schedule was interrupted, however, when it rained. When people hurried along the sidewalks in the falling rain — some carrying umbrellas — they made no effort to stop for beggars.

The children thoroughly enjoyed Sunday school and church services each week and the Bible readings with Dane every evening — especially since the church had supplied each one of the new converts with their own Bible. Some did not read too well, but Dane also helped them with this.

Dane eagerly went to work each weekday morning at the pharmacy and enjoyed being even this close to the medical world. Mr. Clarkson often took time to instruct him on the various kinds of medicine, and the use of each one. Dane was grateful for the information. He tucked it into his eager memory bank, longing for the time when he would become a doctor.

One day in mid-September, just after Dane had returned to the alley after his morning's work, the children were sitting together while eating their meager lunch.

They were talking about Pastor Wheeler's sermon on the love of Jesus and discussing how much Jesus loved all of them when Russell's attention was drawn to a pair of police officers as they turned into the alley off the sidewalk and headed toward them.

Russell squinted at the uniformed men. "Something's wrong," he said to the others. "It's Officers Thornton and Collins, and they're mad about something."

Everyone focused on the oncoming officers.

Dane swallowed the stale bread in his mouth. "I'd say so, Russell. They do look angry."

A hush fell over the little group as they watched the two policemen coming toward them. Living on the streets, they had learned that angry policemen meant trouble of some kind.

As the officers drew up, Dane started to stand.

Officer James Thornton reached down and gripped Dane's upper left arm tightly. "Come on, kid. You're going with us."

Alarm showed on the faces of the group.

Dane felt a twinge at the base of his stomach. His brow furrowed as he met the officer's hard eyes and looked at him curiously. "I don't understand, Officer Thornton. Where are you taking me?"

"To jail after some people take a look at you!" Thornton jerked him to his feet.

The words stung like wasps. "Wh-why? What have I done?" His mind was spinning.

"You know what you did, Dane!" rasped Officer Collins.

"I haven't done anything wrong. Please. Tell me what I'm supposed to have done. There has to be some kind of mistake. There *has* to be!"

Thornton took the pair of handcuffs from his belt. "Don't play innocent with me! You're under arrest. Turn around and put your hands behind your back!"

Dane's face was aflame with embarrassment as Thornton held one wrist and forced him to turn around.

The children looked on in stunned silence. They watched Officer Thornton handcuff him. All the while, Dane was shaking his head and strongly denying any wrongdoing.

Russell took a step closer to Thornton. "Please, sir. Why are you arresting him?"

Officer Collins scowled at him. "You just stay out of it."

As the policemen began ushering Dane

toward the end of the alley, Tharyn ran after them, darted into their path, and planted her feet, causing them to stop. "Please, officers," she said in a frightened voice, "won't you even tell Dane and us what you are arresting him for?"

"That, little lady, is none of your business. We have to deal with teen crime every living day in this city, and we don't have time to explain it to you or the others. Dane already knows. Now get back there with your friends."

Dane met her gaze and said shakily, "Tharyn, go on back with the others. It'll be all right. Somehow, we'll get this misunderstanding cleared up, and I'll be home soon."

Tharyn's vision blurred in an onset of tears. "But — but —"

Dane's voice steadied. "Please, little sis. You'll be safe with the others. I'll be all right once this business is cleared up."

Dane wasn't sure how he was able to speak in a steady voice at that moment, but he saw that it had a calming effect on Tharyn.

She swallowed hard and wiped tears from her eyes. "Okay. If you say so. But *please* hurry back. We all need you."

"I will. Now go on back with the others

so I can go with these officers and see what this is all about."

Tharyn stared at him for a moment, then moved past Dane and the officers and headed toward the group of stunned children, looking back over her shoulder.

When they reached the street, Dane saw two horses tied to a street lamp. "We're mounted police today," said Thornton.

While Collins was mounting one horse, Thornton lifted Dane into the saddle of the other, then swung up behind him. Reaching around the boy, he took hold of the reins. "Let's go, Fred."

As they rode down the street, Dane turned his head. "Now that we're away from my friends, will you tell me what I'm supposed to have done? What people are going to take a look at me?"

Thornton leaned close to him and spoke into his right ear. "Like I said, you already know. Less than an hour ago an eleven-year-old boy was stabbed to death in an alley three blocks from here. A man and two women who work in the business office of Denmar's Department Store heard an argument going on in the alley. They looked out the window just as an older boy plunged a knife into the eleven-year-old's chest. They got a good look at the assailant before he ran out of the alley with the knife in his hand.

"Officer Collins and I were riding these horses today instead of walking our beat. We were summoned by a man sent by the three witnesses, and when we reached the alley, we found the witnesses standing over the dead boy. Before he died, he told them his age, that he was an orphan, and that his name was Benny Jackson. The witnesses gave us a clear description of the killer: your height, your build, your jet-black hair, and even your facial features. They overestimated your age. They thought the killer was about seventeen years old."

Dane licked his lips. "Officer Thornton, it was not me! I didn't stab that boy. I would never do anything like that! I'm telling you, it wasn't me!"

"Mm-hmm. We'll see what the witnesses say when they see you. They were off a little on the age, but the minute they described the killer, Officer Collins and I both knew they were describing you."

"That's right," said Collins as the officers veered the horses around a bread wagon that was parked at an angle in the street in front of a grocery store.

Dane shook his head vehemently. "No! It was *not* me!"

Collins leaned from his saddle and looked Dane in the eye. "Where were you an hour ago?"

"I was on my way home from work."

"Oh yeah. I remember now. You're employed at the Clarkson Pharmacy. And, come to think of it, in order for you to get to your alley from the pharmacy, you have to walk right by the alley where the boy was killed."

"I don't know which alley you're talking about, but even if I have to walk by it to get home, that doesn't mean I did it. I'm telling you, sir, I didn't do it."

Even as Dane was speaking, they turned at the corner near Denmar's Department Store, rode to the alley, and stopped at the back door of the store.

Officer Thornton slid off the horse and helped the handcuffed Dane Weston from the saddle as Officer Collins dismounted. Dane was ushered by the officers through the back door, then into the business office.

The store manager was seated behind his desk, and two women and a man sat in chairs in front of the desk. All four rose to their feet as Thornton and Collins brought their prisoner in. The man and one woman were in their thirties; the other woman was past fifty.

"We have Dane Weston here," Thornton said flatly.

"That's him!" said the younger woman, pointing an accusing finger at Dane.

"Sure is!" said the man.

"Without a doubt," put in the older woman. "I'm glad you officers knew who he was. He won't be able to kill anyone else."

Tears welled up in Dane's eyes. "No! You're wrong! It wasn't me. You told the officers the killer looked to be seventeen. I'm only fifteen."

The man said, "We were wrong about your age, but we're not wrong that you're the one we saw kill that poor little boy."

"They won't execute you because of your age, Dane," said the older woman, "but you'll spend the rest of your life behind bars."

Dane's awareness of impending imprisonment was so harrowing that he was on the edge of blind panic. He felt as if a viscous fluid was seeping into his skull, compressing his brain. He bent his head, fought the handcuffs behind his back, and broke into sobs. "No! I didn't do it! I didn't do it!"

Officer Thornton laid a hand on his shoulder and pinched down tight. "Get a grip on yourself, Dane. None of this would be happening if you hadn't stabbed that boy to death."

Dane drew in a shuddering breath, swallowed with difficulty, and set his frightened gaze on his three accusers. "Wh-what was the killer wearing? Was he dressed like I am?"

The trio exchanged glances and both women slowly shook their heads.

The man looked at Dane. "We can't be definite about the clothing. We were too busy memorizing the killer's build, hair color, and facial features."

"That's right," said the younger woman.

The older woman glared at Dane. "You're the killer, all right, and I'll swear to it in court!"

"All three of us will."

Officer Thornton nodded. "No mistake, here. We'll take him to the city prison."

Tears shone on Dane's cheeks. He had been confident during the ride to the department store that once the three witnesses saw him, they would know he was not the person they saw stab the little boy. Now he stood dumbfounded. "Please! Take a real good look at me! I don't have an identical twin brother! Whoever the killer is, he can't possibly look exactly like me! You're mistaken! I'm innocent!"

All three fixed their eyes on Dane again, studying him closely.

"He's lying," said the man. "He's the killer, all right."

Both the women asserted their agreement.

"Come on, Fred," said Thornton. "We're wasting our time. Let's get him behind bars."

"Right," said Collins. "The sooner the better."

Each officer took hold of an upper arm and guided a weeping Dane Weston out of the room while the witnesses and the store manager looked on.

When they stepped into the alley, Dane sniffed and murmured, "I feel like I'm in a horrible nightmare and I can't wake up."

"The nightmare is what happened to Benny Jackson here in the alley," Thornton said.

Once again, Dane was lifted into the saddle, and Officer Thornton swung up behind him. Officer Fred Collins was already mounted.

As they reached the street and headed in the direction of the city prison, Dane knew they would take him to the Hall of Detention and Justice on Centre Street. He had seen it many times.

Dane had learned in school that the building was constructed back in 1838, and that it was fashioned after a drawing of an Egyptian tomb that caught the fancy of Manhattan's Common Council. Within the same building was the city prison which was now called "The Tombs" by the people of New York City.

A cold shiver slithered down his spine.

When they arrived at the Hall of Detention and Justice, the officers took Dane inside the building and entered the office of Officer Shamus O'Malley where they sat him in a chair in front of O'Malley's desk.

The officers gave O'Malley their prisoner's name and age, explaining that he was a street waif in their district, then filled him in on the details of his arrest and the corroboration of the eye witnesses that he was indeed the one they saw stab Benny Jackson to death.

O'Malley put it all down on paper, and while he was booking Dane for the crime, Dane looked at him with fearful eyes. "Mr. O'Malley, those witnesses were wrong. It wasn't me. I didn't stab Benny Jackson. This is a case of mistaken identity. Please believe me."

O'Malley paused in his writing and

looked up at Dane. "Well, sonny, you have the right to get a lawyer to defend you."

Dane stared at the man as if he had lost his senses. "Oh, sure I can. How would I pay a lawyer? Up till today, even though I'm a street orphan, I've had a job at Clarkson Pharmacy. Most of my wages go to help feed the other kids in my colony. My whole family was murdered by a street gang, sir. Do you really think I would turn around and do this to someone else?" A lump caught in his throat, causing him to choke up.

Officer O'Malley had been at the booking desk for a good many years, and he knew that nearly everyone who sat before him claimed that they were innocent. But to O'Malley, there was something different about this boy.

He set his bright Irish eyes on him. "If you're not guilty, the court will examine your case and pronounce you innocent. Try to be patient and let the justice system do its job."

O'Malley's kind words were the first that Dane had encountered since the two policemen had nabbed him in the alley. He felt tears burn the back of his eyes and blinked to keep them in check.

He fixed his gaze on the redheaded officer. "Thank you, sir. If justice is done, I will indeed be pronounced innocent."

When Officer O'Malley had finished booking Dane for the murder of Benny Jackson, a guard was summoned to take him to his cell. While they were waiting for the guard to appear, O'Malley said, "Dane, you are set to go to trial next Tuesday, September 19."

Dane took the news silently.

The guard arrived, and O'Malley gave him the details as to why Dane had been arrested, including the testimonies of the three witnesses.

While Officer Thornton was removing the handcuffs so the guard could take Dane away, he said, "I'd like to believe that you're innocent, but the testimony of three respectable witnesses is hard to discount."

Dane could only look at him as Thornton hooked the cuffs on his belt.

With that, Thornton and Collins left the office and the guard led Dane toward the office door.

Shamus O'Malley bit his lower lip as Dane was ushered into the hall, his head bent down. When he and the guard passed from view, O'Malley whispered, "Somethin' inside of me tells me you're innocent. I hope justice indeed is served."

As the guard was leading his prisoner down the hall, Dane asked, "Sir, how can I let my employer know what has happened to me? He will be expecting me on the job in the morning."

"There is no way you can send a message out," said the guard. "If somebody comes to visit you, you can have them deliver the message to your employer for you."

Dane nodded silently. *Please, Lord. Speak to the hearts of my friends in the alley to contact Dr. Harris, so he will come and see me.*

"I'm putting you in a cell in the short-term jail section. You will stay here until your trial. If you are convicted, you will then be locked up in that part of the building known as The Tombs, which is the prison where the long-term prisoners are kept."

Dane felt sick all over. *Lord, how could this awful thing happen to me? You know I didn't kill that boy. Please help me.*

They entered the cell block and walked down a corridor between cells. Another guard joined them, holding a ring of keys in his hand. Men behind the bars stared at them as they moved along. Dane felt his flesh crawl.

It crawled even more when they drew up in front of a cell with four bunks inside and three tough-looking boys in their late teens staring at him. The guard with the key ring unlocked the cell and motioned for Dane to step inside. When he did, the barred door slammed shut, and the two guards walked away.

The three boys quickly showed Dane which bunk would be his, and asked him what he was in for. When Dane told his story, emphasizing his innocence, they laughed mockingly, saying he was innocent just like them. They pressed Dane to give them the details and tell them how it felt to plunge the knife into Benny Jackson's chest.

Dane told them again that he didn't do it. They didn't like the way he talked to them. They cursed him, knocked him to the floor of the cell, and began pounding on him with their fists. Guards came instantly, broke it up, and transferred Dane to a cell by himself, farther down the corridor.

He lay on the cot, nursing a bloody nose, and prayed for God's help.

Later that afternoon, the children in Dane's colony were on the street corner begging when Russell Mims spotted Officers James Thornton and Fred Collins on their horses at the other end of the block. They were in conversation with two men on the corner.

Russell pointed them out. "The rest of you stay here. I'm going to go talk to them about Dane. Maybe they'll tell me now what he's supposed to have done."

The children watched Russell run down the sidewalk, then turned their attention to people coming their way so they could beg for money.

Some twenty minutes later, the children saw Russell coming back on the run. At the moment, there was no one to beg from, so they all collected in a knot as Russell drew up.

Gasping for breath, Russell said, "They . . . they told me . . . what Dane has been accused of. Let . . . me catch my breath . . . and I'll . . . tell you."

When his breathing became more normal, Russell told his friends what Dane had been accused of and of the witnesses who said they had seen him do it.

Tharyn's face was a gray mask. "No! Those people are wrong! We all know Dane wouldn't do a thing like that. Just think of what he's done for all of us. He's a wonderful Christian and would never kill anyone."

Everyone in the group spoke their agreement.

"Anyway," said Tharyn, "what reason would he have for killing that eleven-year-old boy? It's ridiculous."

Everyone agreed again.

Billy Johnson turned to Russell. "Is there anything we can do to help Dane?"

Russell nodded. "Yes. We've got to let Dr. Harris know about this. If anybody can help Dane, it'll be him. I know he will do anything and everything he can."

Tharyn had tears in her eyes. "Oh, Russell, please go tell Dr. Harris right now!"

"I will. See you later."

Maude Harris and her husband looked at Russell incredulously as they stood in the office and heard the story.

"This is totally ridiculous," said the doctor. "That boy is not a killer. Those people who identified him are grossly mistaken."

"This whole thing is preposterous!" said Maude.

Dr. Harris had just finished with his last scheduled patient for the day. As he went quickly to the washstand and soaped up his hands, he said to Maude, "Honey, if any patients come in while I'm gone, schedule them for tomorrow if you can; and if not, tell them I'll make a house call this evening. Right now, I have an emergency. Dane needs me and I'm going to him."

Maude smiled. "Of course, dear. I'll handle things here. You go to that sweet boy. Our precious Jesus is the Chief Justice and our Supreme Advocate. He can do *all* things."

The doctor dried his hands, hung up the towel, and kissed Maude's wrinkled cheek. "While Russell and I are going to the jail, please lift that boy to the Throne. I don't know what all of this means, but I do know that nothing gets to the sheep without getting past the Shepherd first. I'll be back as soon as I can."

When Dr. Harris and Russell Mims arrived at the jail, they were told that only one person could visit a prisoner at a time. Russell stayed in the waiting area while the doctor was taken by a guard to the visiting room after being searched for any kind of weapon.

When the guard ushered him in, Dane

had already been brought from his cell and was sitting in the adjacent room behind a barred window. His battered face brightened when he saw his friend.

As Dr. Harris sat down, he said, "I know the whole story. Russell got it out of Officers Thornton and Collins and came to me with it. Russell's in the waiting room right now. They wouldn't let both of us come in." He tipped his face down and eyed the boy over his half-moon spectacles. "What happened to you, son?"

"I was put in a cell with three older teenage boys. They didn't like it because I wouldn't admit to killing that boy, so they beat up on me."

"You've got iodine on your cut lip, I notice."

"Yes, sir. The prison doctor took care of me."

Dr. Harris looked him straight in the eye. "Dane, Maude and I both know you're innocent of this charge. God knows it, too. I see some despair in your eyes, and I understand. But the Lord has a reason for allowing this to happen. His timing is different than ours, but don't despair. He will take care of you."

Dane blinked at the excess moisture in his eyes and nodded.

Dr. Harris reached through the bars and gripped Dane's hand. "Let's pray."

Dane took hold of the doctor's hand and bowed his head.

Dr. Harris began to pray, imploring their Saviour to give Dane peace and grace beyond measure in the horrible situation. He told the Lord that he knew Dane was innocent of the killing, but that he also knew He had a reason for allowing this mistaken identity to happen. He asked when Dane was cleared of the crime that God would get the glory.

When he finished praying, Dr. Harris felt the tension leave the boy's hands. He looked into Dane's eyes and saw that God was already blessing him with immeasurable grace.

Dane formed a smile on his lips. "Thank you, Doctor. I feel better already."

"Praise the Lord. Maude and I will be holding you up in prayer all the way through this, son. Don't you despair. It'll turn out all right."

Dane nodded. "Dr. Harris, would you do me a favor?"

"Name it."

"Would you go to the pharmacy and tell Mr. Clarkson what has happened?"

"Certainly. I'll go immediately. He's not

going to believe these ridiculous charges, either."

"I hope not. And, Doctor, thank you for not believing them. And please thank Mrs. Harris for her confidence in me too."

"I will. You're no killer, Dane. You're not only a born-again child of God, but you're a soul winner. I'll be back to see you tomorrow."

Dane reached through the bars in the window and gripped the doctor's hand. "I'll look forward to it. Thanks, again, for believing in me and for coming to see me."

When Dr. Harris was gone, one of the guards stepped into the room. "Okay, kid. Let's go."

Upon entering his cell, Dane heard the barred door clank shut behind him as he headed for his bunk. The guard's footsteps faded away. He sat down on the bunk, bowed his head and asked the Lord to bless the Harrises, and to bless Russell for taking the story to them. He prayed earnestly, asking the Lord to get him out of the jail quickly and to take care of Tharyn and the others in his colony.

# Chapter Thirteen

Shortly after noon the next day, Dane Weston was sitting on his bunk in the cell, reading his Bible, which Dr. Lee Harris had brought him early that morning. He could hear the low rumble of the prisoners talking as usual in their cells.

His head came up when he heard the handle clank on the big steel door a short distance down the corridor. He could see the door from his bunk. The door swung open, and his heart thumped in his chest when he saw Tharyn Myers enter the cell block, sided by a big burly guard. The guard picked up a wooden chair that stood against the wall next to the door.

Dane closed the Bible, laid it on his pillow, and hurried to the cell door, gripping the bars as he watched Tharyn coming toward him. The huge guard dwarfed the little redhead, and Dane could tell she was a bit intimidated by him.

Tharyn's own heart was pounding her rib cage when the guard led her into the corridor, and it pounded harder when she saw Dane standing at his cell door, gripping the bars. In her heart, she was determined to put on a brave face and be a help to this young man who had done so much for her.

As they drew up to the cell, the guard said, "Somebody here to see you, kid. You've got ten minutes." As he spoke, he placed the chair on the floor in front of the cell door. Then he walked away.

Dane and Tharyn stood gazing into each other's eyes, then he reached through the bars, arms open.

As she moved into his arms, pressing against the bars, he said, "I'm so glad to see you, little sis."

Other prisoners were looking on curiously as Tharyn patted his cheek. "I'm so sorry that this horrible thing has happened."

Dane released her, then took hold of her hand. "Thank you for coming. You didn't walk all the way over here alone, did you?"

"No. Russell came with me. He's down in the waiting room by the office. He didn't want me on the streets by myself."

"Bless him. I don't want you on those streets alone, either." He let go of her hand. "Please sit down."

As Tharyn eased onto the chair, Dane said, "I'm surprised they let you come here into the cell block."

"Well, the visiting room for this section of the jail is full right now. It took some tall talking, but I explained to the chief guard in the office that Russell and I are street orphans and need to get back to our corner to beg for money. I told him you were my adopted brother, and that it was very important that I see you. This got to him, so he called for that guard and told him to bring me right to your cell." She flashed Dane a smile.

He shook his head at her audacity. "You're quite the little sister, Tharyn. Oh, it's so good to see you!"

She took a shaky breath. "It's good to see you, too. I —" She put a hand to her mouth and her brow furrowed.

"What?"

"This awful place. I feel so bad for you. It's — so dingy. It's worse than the alley. At least there we can see the sky and breathe fresh air."

Dane nodded grimly. "Yeah."

Tharyn's eyes strayed past Dane to the bunk where his Bible lay on the pillow. "I see Dr. Harris got here early, like he had planned."

Dane turned his head and followed her line of sight. "Oh. My Bible. Dr. Harris said he asked Russell to give it to him when he was at the alley checking on all of you this morning. He figured since the church gave each of you a Bible the day you were baptized, I should have mine here in the cell with me. I'm glad he brought it. I was planning to ask him when he came to see me today, if he would bring it next time he comes."

"Dr. Harris said when he was here this morning, he was going to try to find out when your trial will be."

Dane shook his head and rubbed the back of his neck. "I was told by the officer who booked me for the crime that the trial is set for next Tuesday. With all the emotion that I was experiencing yesterday, I completely forgot to tell Dr. Harris. He stopped by the office before he came to see me this morning and asked about it. They told him it was set for ten o'clock next

Tuesday morning." He paused and took a deep breath. "Dr. Harris said he wished he had the money to hire a good lawyer to defend me. But he just doesn't have it. He said the court is going to appoint a lawyer for me."

She nodded. "Well, I can tell you right now that the whole colony is coming to the trial. We all agreed. We'll walk all the way from the alley together."

Tharyn could tell by the look in Dane's eyes that this pleased him.

"This means more to me than I can ever say, Tharyn. I sure wish somebody could bring all of you in a carriage or a wagon, though."

"We'll be fine. And we don't mind walking. We just want to be here for you. Dr. Harris told us he was going to go by the parsonage after leaving the alley and tell Pastor Wheeler about you being in jail."

"He did. Pastor Wheeler was here to see me a couple of hours ago."

"I'm sure he was a help to you."

"Yes. I asked him why God would let this awful thing happen to me. He read a verse to me from the book of Romans. It was a real help."

"What does it say?"

"I'll show it to you."

Dane hurried to the bunk and picked up the Bible. While flipping pages, he said, "It's in Romans 8:28." He extended it to her through the bars. "Read it out loud."

Tharyn took the Bible, found the verse, and put her thumb next to it. " 'And we know that all things work together for good to them that love God, to them who are the called according to his purpose.' "

"That's talking about saved people, Tharyn. It's talking about *us.*"

She nodded, her eyes still fixed on the page.

"Pastor Wheeler told me that based on this verse, God has a purpose for this happening to me. He said when God is ready for me to be cleared of the crime and released from this place, He will see that it is done. And when it's all over, it will have worked out for my good."

Still looking at it, Tharyn said, "Sure enough. That's what it says. It doesn't say that all things that happen to us are good, but all things will *work together* for our good."

Dane grinned. "That is exactly how Pastor Wheeler put it."

At that instant, they heard heavy footsteps, and looked up to see the guard.

"Time's up. Let's go, little lady."

Tharyn stood up, handed Dane the Bible, and embraced him through the bars. "See you next Tuesday, big brother."

"Sure enough," said Dane, and pressing his face to the bars, kissed her forehead. "That will have to do until I get out and am back in the alley to kiss my little sister good night."

She struggled to keep her composure. "I'm looking forward to it."

The guard picked up the chair.

Tharyn smiled at Dane, then followed the guard down the corridor with prisoners in their cells looking on. She continued her brave front until she reached the big steel door and turned for one last look at Dane.

The guard set the chair down, jerked on the door handle, and pulled it open.

Tharyn's heart seemed to turn over inside her chest, and unbidden tears dimmed her blue eyes. She waved to Dane, then squared her shoulders and moved through the door, her back straight but her heart aching.

Dane stood there for a long moment, his eyes fixed on the last spot where he saw her, then turned and sat back down on the bunk. He opened his Bible and read Romans 8:28 again. And again.

"Lord," he whispered, "I'm such a young Christian. I really need You to help me to hold onto this. I know it's true because it's Your Word. Please help me not to have doubts."

The handle of the door clanked again and it swung open. Dane looked that direction, and saw the guard enter the corridor with a man in a business suit. He looked back at his Bible and read the verse again. He heard the footsteps of the two men coming his direction and looked up again.

The guard said, "Someone else to see you, kid. Take all the time you want, Mr. Watson."

The guard walked away, and the middle-aged man moved up to the bars, peering between them. "Dane Weston?"

Dane laid the Bible down, left the bunk, and drew up close to the cell door. "Yes, sir?"

"My name is George Watson. I'm the attorney the court appointed to represent you at your trial."

"Oh. Glad to meet you, sir."

"I need to talk to you."

"Yes, sir?"

"I want you to be honest with me, okay?"

Dane nodded.

"Tell me the truth about the murder of Benny Jackson."

"I did not murder Benny Jackson," Dane said levelly.

Watson sighed. "It'll go a lot better for you if you will admit your guilt."

"*What* guilt? I told you, sir, I did not murder that boy."

"The state has three credible witnesses who have identified you as the person they saw stab Benny Jackson. When they testify to this in court, the jury is going to believe them."

"The witnesses are mistaken, Mr. Watson. I swear to you, I didn't do it."

"But according to what the police told me, all three witnesses gave them a perfect description of you, even before you were brought in."

Dane shook his head. "Not a perfect description, sir. They said the killer was seventeen years old. I'm fifteen."

"That's a minor point. The physical description they gave of the killer *was* perfect. I talked to Officers Thornton and Collins. They said the instant they heard the three witnesses give the description of the killer, they knew it was you. So they arrested you and took you before the witnesses. All three said you were the one they saw stab Benny Jackson. That's all the jury will need to convict you. Now, if you will admit it, maybe I can get the judge to go easier on you. Instead of a life sentence, it may only be twenty or twenty-five years."

Dane shook his head stubbornly. "Mr. Watson, I am not going to admit to something I didn't do."

Watson sighed. "Okay, kid. Have it your own way." With that, he wheeled and headed down the corridor.

Dane went back to the bunk, sat down, and bowed his head, asking God to clear him of the murder charge.

That Monday night seemed an eternity to Dane as he lay on his hard bunk and stared unseeingly at the bottom of the bunk above him. He had not slept a wink when dawn came and the guards rolled carts along the corridor, handing out breakfast.

A guard stopped in front of Dane's cell and placed a tray of food on the floor, sliding it through the six-inch space beneath the door. "Breakfast, kid," he said, looking through the bars. "Just leave the tray right here after you eat so we can pick it up later."

As the guard wheeled the cart away, Dane left the bunk, leaned over, and slid the tray into the cell. One look at the grease floating on top of the thin gruel caused his stomach to wrench. He made a face and shoved it back under the door. "Oh, dear Lord, help me."

He went back to the bunk and lay down. His eyes were closed and his arm lay over his forehead an hour later when the guard came to pick up the tray. He heard the guard grumble something about the prisoners being unappreciative of the food as he pushed the cart on down the corridor.

It was almost 9:45 when two guards came to the cell. Dane was sitting up on the bunk, reading his Bible.

"Time to go to court, kid."

They moved into the cell, and one of them handcuffed Dane with his wrists behind his back. His insides were churning, and his steps slow and measured as the guards led him through the huge Hall of Justice building to the courtroom. Still unable to believe the horrible events of the last few days, his spirits were lifted when he set his red-rimmed eyes on all his friends from the alley, and the four adults who sat just behind them. Pastor and Mrs. Alan Wheeler sat between Dr. Lee Harris and Bryce Clarkson. They were all watching him closely, and a reassuring smile was on every face.

Dane smiled thinly in their direction, then the smile faded as he saw the three witnesses sitting on the front row. His stomach soured at the sight of them. All three were looking at him with accusing eyes.

The guards led him to a table that faced the judge's bench. One of them removed the handcuffs, and the other one shoved him down on a hard wooden chair. Both moved away a few steps, then stood looking at him sternly.

At that moment, George Watson appeared and sat down beside him. He leaned close and whispered, "If you plead guilty and show remorse for your crime, the judge will go easier on you, especially because of your age. Are you listening to what I am telling you?"

"I told you I'm innocent, Mr. Watson. I'm not going to plead guilty to a crime I did not commit."

There was a stirring among the children of the colony, who had heard Dane's words.

Twelve men came in from a side door and walked single file to the jury box. They sat down quietly, and when they were settled, the bailiff said, "All rise."

Everyone in the courtroom rose to their feet, including George Watson and his client. As the judge came from a rear door and approached his bench, the bailiff said, "The honorable Judge Hector B. Rigby, presiding."

Rigby sat down behind his bench, picked up the gavel, and banged it on the desk. "Court is in session. Please be seated."

When all but the bailiff and the two guards had sat down, the bailiff read the charge against Dane Weston, and the trial began.

The witnesses gave their testimonies under oath one by one, and each pointed the defendant out as the person they saw stab Benny Jackson to death.

When the testimonies had been given, Judge Rigby spoke to the court-appointed attorney. "Mr. Watson, how does your client plead?"

Watson rose to his feet, gave Dane a fleeting glance, and said, "My client pleads not guilty, your honor."

The jury was sent out and returned in less than fifteen minutes.

A deep feeling of dread assailed Dane as the men of the jury were filing in, their faces grim. He knew in his sore, hurting heart what the verdict would be.

When the jurors were seated, the judge looked at the man closest to him. "Mr. Chairman, has the jury reached a verdict?"

The chairman stood up. "We have, your honor."

Rigby looked at Dane. "The defendant will please rise."

Dane stood up, and George Watson stood beside him.

The judge looked at the chairman. "And what is your verdict?"

"We, the jury, unanimously find Mr. Dane Weston guilty as charged."

George Watson turned and looked at his client. There was blank dismay in the boy's eyes as he stared straight ahead. Then, he lowered his head, his chin nearly resting on his chest. A silent plea went heavenward: *Why, God? Why are You letting this happen to me?*

Judge Rigby set steady eyes on Dane. "Mr. Weston, you have been found guilty of murder in the first degree in this court of law. Do you have anything to say?"

Dane's features were like stone. He met the judge's steady gaze and took a sharp breath. "I am innocent, sir. I did not kill Benny Jackson."

Rigby nodded. "Notwithstanding your testimony, this court of law has found you guilty of murder in the first degree. I hereby sentence you to life imprisonment without possibility of parole. If you were not a minor, I would have sentenced you to be hanged for your crime."

Dane licked his dry lips.

"This trial is over." The judge banged the gavel on the desk. "Court dismissed."

The two guards moved up to Dane. One of them told him to put his hands behind his back, and while he was putting the handcuffs on him, the street orphans and the adults gathered in a circle.

"Dane," said Russell Mims, "we know you're innocent."

Dr. Harris spoke his agreement, and Bryce Clarkson moved up to face him. "Dane, I have no doubt of your innocence. Somewhere out there, the guilty party is on the loose. Because he strongly resembles you, he has the fortune of getting away with his crime. I'm — I'm sorry, son."

Dane nodded. "Thank you for believing me, sir."

"You understand that with this sentence, I must hire someone to take your place."

"Of course."

Clarkson laid a hand on his shoulder. "I'm sorry, Dane."

The boy blinked at the tears that were surfacing.

The pharmacist stepped back, and allowed Pastor and Mrs. Wheeler to step up. Mrs. Wheeler embraced Dane, spoke words of comfort, then allowed her husband to embrace him. The pastor held onto Dane's upper arms and said, "I'll come and visit you often. I assure you that the entire church will be in prayer. We're going to ask God to see that the guilty person is caught. You hold on to Romans 8:28."

Dane thanked him, saying he would, then Dr. Harris moved up and hugged him. "Don't give up, Dane. God knows you're innocent. I'll visit you as often as I can."

One by one, the children moved up to speak their words of encouragement while the guards looked on impatiently.

Tharyn purposely waited to be the last. With tears forming in her eyes, she hugged him and said, "You'll always be my big brother, Dane. I'll come and see you as often as possible."

Dane leaned close and kissed her forehead. "I'll look forward to each visit. I love you, little sis."

"I love you, too." She stepped back.

The tears were spilling down her cheeks as the guards led Dane away and out of the courtroom.

His mind numb, Dane followed one guard while the other stayed close behind him.

He was taken into the prison section of the huge building, where the guard behind him stopped at a desk and said something to another guard. He caught up quickly, as the other guard was ushering Dane down a long hallway. In his heart, Dane said, *Lord, I told Pastor Wheeler I would hold onto Romans 8:28. Help me to do that, and help me to trust You as I should.*

At the end of the hallway, the guards guided Dane through a heavy steel door into a corridor much like the one in the jail section. They moved him and finally drew up to a cell where one young man was sitting on a lower bunk. Each cell, like in the jail section, had four bunks.

While one guard was unlocking the cell, he said to the man on the bunk, "Got a cell mate for you, Jubal."

When the other guard removed Dane's handcuffs, Dane asked him if he would bring his Bible to him from the other cell. The guard told him he already had another guard going after it.

Dane stepped into the cell, the door clanked shut, and the two guards moved away.

Dane's cell mate — whom he judged to be in his early twenties — rose from his bunk, smiled, and extended his hand. "My name's Jubal Packer."

Dane met his grip. "I'm Dane Weston."

"How old are you?" queried Packer. "You can't be more than fifteen or sixteen."

"I'm fifteen."

"What are you in for?"

"They convicted me of murdering an eleven-year-old boy in an alley, but I'm innocent."

Packer chuckled. "That's what nearly every man in here says, kid."

"Well, I'm not lying. It was a case of mistaken identity."

Packer grinned. "You mean you have an identical twin nobody knows about? Your twin murdered the boy?"

Dane bristled. "No, I don't have an identical twin. The people who saw the boy get stabbed to death identified me as the killer. But I didn't do it. So there has to be a guy out there who looks a whole lot like me."

"Mm-hmm. So what do your parents believe about that?"

"I . . . I don't have any parents. They were murdered by a street gang back in April, along with my little brother and sister. I'm a street orphan."

"Mmm. I see."

At that instant, a guard drew up to the cell door with the Bible in his hand. Extending it between the bars, he said, "Here you go, kid."

Dane took the Bible. "Thanks."

"You're welcome."

The guard walked away.

Jubal Packer looked at the Bible and grinned. "Oh, so you got religion when they locked you up in jail, eh?"

Dane shook his head. "No. I don't have religion. I have salvation in Jesus Christ. I was saved before this case of mistaken identity ever happened to me. Before I was saved, I was headed for hell. But now I am headed for heaven."

Packer laughed mockingly. "Well your Jesus Christ couldn't even keep you out of prison. How could He keep you out of hell?"

Dane countered, "Jesus *could* have kept me out of prison, but He had a purpose for letting this thing happen to me."

Packer looked confused. "I don't get it."

Dane opened the Bible. "Here, let me

show you." When he had come to the proper page, he put his finger next to Romans 8:28. "See what it says right here?"

While Jubal looked at the verse, Dane read it to him.

"See that? I'm one of those people who love God, so I know that all things are working together for my good. Even being falsely convicted of murder. And see that word *purpose?*"

"Yeah."

"God has a purpose for me being here in this prison. I don't know what it is yet, but that's what it says right here."

Dane's own words were mysteriously adding strength to him.

Jubal was still looking dumbfounded as Dane asked, "What crime are *you* in here for?"

Jubal's head dipped. "Murder. I . . . I killed a man in anger after we had an argument in a barroom. I left the barroom so angry, all I wanted to do was kill him. It was night. I waited for him in the darkness. When he came out a little while later, I stunned him with a blow to the jaw, then dragged him into the alley and strangled him. Just as he died, two police officers came into the alley. There I was, with my hands still locked on his throat. Someone on the street had seen me knock him down and drag him into the alley. They alerted the officers, who were nearby."

Dane nodded. "So you don't claim to be innocent?"

Jubal shrugged his shoulders. "Can't claim that. I was caught red-handed. You see . . . I — I —"

"What?"

Jubal's features had turned pale. "I'm . . . I'm going to be executed on Saturday morning at sunrise. The judge sentenced me to be hanged. I have less than four days to live."

Dane's brow furrowed. "Jubal, you need to be saved. Jesus died on the cross for the whole world. He loves you and wants to save you so you'll go to heaven when you die."

Jubal Packer shook his head. "God can't forgive me for what I did, Dane. He can't save my soul. I'm going to die at the end of that rope Saturday morning and go to hell."

"God *can* forgive you. Let me read you some salvation verses from my Bible. I'll show you the ones that were shown to me and brought me to Jesus."

They sat down on Jubal's bunk, and

Dane took him to every verse Dr. Harris had shown him.

Jubal shook his head. "Those verses are for normal sinners, but not for a man like me, who took another man's life."

Dane found himself wishing he knew his Bible better so he could convince Jubal differently.

On Wednesday afternoon at 1:30, a guard came to the cell and told Dane he had a visitor. Jubal watched as his young cell mate was led down the corridor.

When Dane was led into the prison's visiting room, he was glad to see Pastor Alan Wheeler sitting behind one of the small barred windows.

He had his Bible with him.

As Dane sat down, the pastor asked, "How are you doing?"

"Well, better than I expected. I'm hanging onto Romans 8:28, and the Lord is using it to strengthen and help me."

"Good."

"Pastor, I'm really glad you came to see me. It helps a lot. I need you to do something for me."

"What's that?"

Dane told Wheeler about Jubal Packer, his upcoming execution, and how he had shown him the same salvation verses Dr. Harris had used to lead him to Jesus. He then told the pastor what Jubal said about God not being able to forgive him because he was a murderer.

"Pastor, would you talk to Jubal and show him from the Bible that the Lord can and will forgive him and save him if he will let Him?"

Wheeler pulled out his pocket watch and looked at it. "Dane, I have a funeral to preach over in Queens at three o'clock. I came by here to see you on my way to Queens. I have to leave right away, or I'll be late. Let me write some verses down for you, and you show them to Jubal. You have your Bible in your cell, don't you?"

"Yes, sir."

Taking out a pencil, the pastor took a slip of paper from inside his Bible and began writing the locations of the verses. "Dane, some of these are to show him that Jesus will save any sinner who will repent of his sin and come to Him. They will convince him that he is not beyond salvation and forgiveness if he will believe them. I'll put down some on hell too, so he will get a good dose of what's ahead of him if he doesn't turn to Jesus. I'll come back to-morrow, and if he still isn't saved, I'll try to lead him to the Lord then."

When the final Scripture reference had been written, Wheeler handed the paper to Dane through the bars and said, "Make him read every one of these verses if you can. You know what you did to be saved, Dane, so if he is willing to turn to Jesus after he sees these, just have him do what *you* did."

"All right, Pastor. See you tomorrow."

As Wheeler rose from the chair and slipped the pencil back in his pocket, he said, "I'll be praying that the Lord will give you the wisdom and power to lead Jubal to Jesus. See you tomorrow."

The pastor hurried away, and a moment later, a guard came and led Dane toward his cell. Hope arose in Dane's heart as he clutched the paper and went to his cell.

# Chapter Fourteen

Jubal Packer was lying on his bunk when Dane Weston and the guard drew up to the cell door. The guard turned the key in the lock and swung the door open without a word. Dane stepped in, the door clanked shut, and the guard walked away.

Jubal looked up at Dane. "So who was your visitor?"

"My pastor. I told him about you, Jubal. He wanted to see you, but he has a funeral to conduct over in Queens and had to get going." Dane lifted the slip of paper into view. "Pastor Wheeler wrote some additional verses down for me to show you in the Bible."

Jubal shook his head. "It won't do any good. Forget it."

"But these are Scriptures that will help you to see —"

"Weston," came the voice of another guard, "you've got a visitor."

Dane turned and looked at him. "Oh? My pastor was just here. You mean there's someone else?"

"Yeah," said the guard, inserting the key in the lock. "You can refuse to see anybody who comes if you want. This is a little lady. She said something about being your adopted sister."

Dane's eyes brightened. "Oh! Of course I want to see her."

As he stepped out of the cell, Dane looked over his shoulder. "We'll talk more about this when I come back, Jubal."

Packer's features had a stony look. He did not reply.

Moments later, when Dane stepped into the visiting room and saw Tharyn smiling at him through one of the barred windows, a huge grin spread across his face. She put her hands through the bars. Dane quickly sat down and grasped them. "Hello, little sis."

"Hello, big brother. How are you doing?"

Dane felt a slight trembling in Tharyn's hands, and noted that her eyes seemed dull and her skin seemed wan. "I'm all right, considering the circumstances — but you don't look like you feel well. What is it, little sis? Are you sick?"

"No. I . . . I'm not what you would call sick. I just — well —"

"Hey, I'm your big brother. You can tell me anything. I need to know what's going on in your life. Being in this prison, I may not be able to take care of you like I want, but God hears the prayers of His children no matter where they are. I have plenty of time for praying in here. Now, c'mon. Level with me. Why are you trembling and looking so pale?"

Tharyn felt that Dane had more than his share of problems already. She didn't want to worry him, but neither would she lie to him. She looked down at their joined hands and drew in a deep breath. "Well . . ."

"I know what it is. You're hungry, aren't you? The food's been scarce."

Tharyn raised her downcast eyes and nodded slowly.

"Oh, I'm so sorry. I'm in this awful place for something I didn't do, and I can't work at the pharmacy and bring in money for you and the others so you can have enough to eat."

She squeezed his hands. "Please, Dane, don't concern yourself over us. You've got more than enough to bear, just being in this place. We're God's children. He will take care of us. We're a bit low on food right now because the begging has produced very little money of late. The people at the café haven't had much in the way of leftovers to give us, and even their garbage cans have not had much in them. But we're not starving. The Lord won't let that happen. We've been taking the problem to the Lord and asking Him to provide more food one way or another."

"I know God has told us to cast all of our care on Him, and you're right to take the problem to Him. But —"

She cocked her head and looked deep into his eyes. "But what?"

Dane avoided her gaze by looking down at the floor. "Well, I just feel guilty. I know that the colony is suffering because I'm not there to provide money from my job."

"Dane, look at me."

He raised his eyes to meet hers once again.

"Nobody in the colony blames you for anything. We all know you are innocent of this crime they are accusing you of. Now please, don't worry about us. You have enough to contend with, being in this filthy place. Remember, Jesus loves the little children. He will take care of us."

A tiny smile crinkled the corners of his mouth. "I'll say this for you — you're a fast learner. Are you still reading your Bible every day?"

"Of course. We all are. We're trying hard to carry on just as you would want us to."

Dane's smile grew larger. "Good. Now, I have something I want you and the others to pray about."

"Sure. We'll be glad to. It will give us something to concentrate on besides ourselves. What is it?"

Dane told her about Jubal Packer, of his upcoming execution on Saturday, and his mistaken assumption that the Lord could not forgive him and save him because he was a murderer. He explained that he showed Jubal the verses Dr. Harris had used to lead him to the Lord, but they didn't seem to faze him. He went on to tell her about the verses Pastor Wheeler had written down for him to show Jubal, and that Pastor Wheeler would be back tomorrow to talk to Jubal.

"Tharyn," Dane said with emotion in his voice, "I'm going to show Jubal the verses Pastor Wheeler wrote down. I want you and the others to pray that I will be able to lead him to the Lord today, or that Pastor Wheeler will be able to lead him to the Lord tomorrow — or at least before Saturday."

Tharyn nodded. "Yes, of course. I'll tell the others in the colony, and we'll be praying."

At that instant, the guard who had brought Tharyn into the visiting room came in. "Okay, little lady. Time's up."

Tharyn turned and looked up at him. "Yes, sir."

Tears misted her eyes as she looked back at Dane and squeezed his hands. "I'll come back again as soon as I can, big brother. Remember, we're all praying for you. You know what?"

"Hmm?"

"I just thought of something."

"Yes?"

"Maybe the Lord arranged your arrest and all of this so you could give the gospel to Jubal and lead him to Jesus."

A tiny sparkle lit up Dane's dark brown eyes. "Yes. That might just be it. Thank you."

"You're welcome. I'll see you soon."

When Dane returned to the cell, he sat down on his bunk facing Jubal, who was now in a sitting position on his own bunk. Jubal said, "Your adopted sister, eh? You told me your little brother and sister were killed by the street gang at the same time they killed your parents."

"Those were my *real* brother and sister. The girl who just came to see me lives in the street colony that I'm from. Long story . . . but we sort of adopted each other as brother and sister."

"Oh."

"Jubal, will you let me show you those Scriptures that my pastor wrote down for you?"

"It ain't gonna do any good."

"Maybe you're wrong about that. Can I show them to you?"

Jubal shrugged. "If it'll make you feel better."

Dane picked up his Bible, carried it and the slip of paper across the narrow cell, and sat down beside Jubal. "Let's just take a look."

The first passage Pastor Wheeler had written down was Romans 5:6–8. Praying in his heart for wisdom from God, Dane turned to it, and read the verses silently to himself. "Okay, read verses six, seven, and eight to me, Jubal."

Jubal frowned. "If you say so. 'For when

we were yet without strength, in due time Christ died for the ungodly. For scarcely for a righteous man will one die: yet peradventure for a good man some would even dare to die. But God commendeth his love toward us, in that, while we were yet sinners, Christ died for us.' "

"Jubal?"

"Hmm?"

"Does it say that Christ died for certain kinds of sinners, but not for other kinds? You know, that He only died for those sinners who never murdered anyone? Or does it just say that He died for sinners?"

"It says He died for sinners."

"That would be *any* sinners then, wouldn't it?"

Jubal shrugged, but did not reply.

"It also says He died for the ungodly. Are murderers ungodly?"

"Yeah."

"Then that would include you, wouldn't it?"

Jubal did not answer.

"You're smart enough to know the answer to that. Let me show you another one."

This time, Dane turned to Proverbs 28:13, read it silently, then said, "Okay. Read verse thirteen to me."

Jubal licked his lips nervously. " 'He that covereth his sins shall not prosper: but whoso confesseth and forsaketh them shall have mercy.' "

"All right. Does it say that people who confess their sins and forsake them shall have mercy, *except* for murderers?"

"I guess not."

"What do you mean you guess not?"

Jubal drew a deep breath and let it out through his nostrils. "It just ain't gonna work for me, kid. God doesn't want anything to do with me."

Dane frowned. "What makes you think so?"

"I just know it."

"Let's look at another one."

Dane turned to Titus 2:13–14 and read it silently. "Here. Read verses thirteen and fourteen to me."

Jubal licked his lips again. " 'Looking for that blessed hope, and the glorious appearing of the great God and our Saviour Jesus Christ; Who gave himself for us, that he might redeem us from all iniquity, and purify unto himself a peculiar people, zealous of good works.' "

"Okay. This part." Dane put his finger below eight words in verse 14, and read them aloud: " 'That he might redeem us from all iniquity.' Jubal, is murder iniquity?"

Jubal nodded. "Yeah."

"Well, doesn't it say that Jesus gave Himself for us that He might redeem us from *all* iniquity?"

"Yeah. It says that."

"Then wouldn't that include murder?"

Jubal put his head down and rubbed the back of his neck. "I don't know, kid. Like I said, God doesn't want anything to do with me."

"That's not true. Let's read some more verses."

Pastor Wheeler had written down four more passages that dealt with sin and God's forgiveness. Dane saw that the next subject was hell, so he proceeded to have Jubal read the four passages to him. Still Jubal would not concede that any of these Scriptures applied to him and his sin of murder.

Still praying in his heart for wisdom, Dane had him read four passages that centered on hell and its horrors. When they had covered the fourth one, Jubal said, "That's all, kid. I don't want to read any more."

"All right. We've read all of them that Pastor Wheeler gave me to show you. Jubal, the passages I gave you yesterday that spoke of repentance and salvation leave no doubt that if a sinner repents and receives Jesus into his heart as personal Saviour, that he will be saved. These Scriptures that we have just read also leave no doubt that God is willing to forgive *all* sins if the sinner will call on Him in repentance and ask for forgiveness and salvation. The ones we read about hell make it clear that hell is eternal fire; that people who go there will burn forever with no opportunity of escape. You told me when we talked yesterday that you're going to die at the end of that rope Saturday and go to hell. After what we've just read, do you really want to go to hell?"

Jubal rose to his feet, rubbing a palm over his face. "I — I don't want to talk about it anymore. I just don't believe God can forgive me."

Dane's heart was heavy. His only hope was that tomorrow Pastor Wheeler would be able to handle Jubal better and convince him to open his heart to Jesus.

That night in the darkness of the cell, Dane lay on his bunk and prayed silently that the Lord would drive His Word deep into Jubal's heart so Pastor Wheeler could lead him to Jesus. Jubal had two days left.

On Thursday morning, a guard came

and told Dane he had a visitor.

When Dane arrived at the visiting room, he was glad to see his pastor. When Wheeler inquired how it had gone with Jubal and Dane told him, Wheeler turned and asked a guard if he could have some time with Jubal Packer.

The guard said he would take Dane back to the cell and tell Packer that the preacher wanted to see him.

The guard returned shortly, and informed Wheeler that Packer had refused to see him. His own heart heavy, Wheeler asked if he could have a few more minutes with Dane.

When Dane returned, the pastor told him since Jubal refused to see him, it would be up to Dane to keep trying. Disappointed that Jubal would not talk to the pastor, Dane assured him he would keep trying and asked that Pastor Wheeler pray for him. He would need special help from the Lord. Wheeler assured him he would and reminded him that God was not willing that any should perish, but that all should come to repentance. They prayed together with the pastor leading.

Just as Pastor Wheeler was leaving, a guard brought in Dr. Lee Harris, saying he wanted to see Dane too. The pastor and the doctor shook hands, and the pastor left.

When Dr. Harris sat down and looked at Dane through the barred window, Dane told him the whole story about Jubal, and how he had dealt with him from the Scripture about being saved, but Jubal had turned a deaf ear. He explained that Jubal had also refused to see Pastor Wheeler just now.

Dr. Harris asked if Dane thought he might talk to him, since he was not a preacher. Dane told him it was worth a try, and asked the guard in charge of the visiting room if he would take him back to the cell so he could see if Jubal would let Dr. Harris talk to him.

The doctor waited while Dane and the guard were gone, and a few minutes later, they returned with Dane telling him that Jubal also refused to see him.

Dr. Harris told him that he and Maude would be praying that the Lord would work in Jubal's heart in such a manner that he would see that there indeed was forgiveness and salvation for him, as well as for all sinners, and draw him unto Himself.

That evening Dane tried to talk to Jubal again, but met the same resistance. Dane warned him solemnly about the never-ending torment in the flames of the lake of fire, but still Jubal refused to open his heart to Jesus.

Once again, lying on his bunk in the darkness, Dane silently prayed for his cell mate. He asked the Lord to let Jubal have no rest tonight, and to make the Scriptures burn in his heart like He had when Dr. Harris had dealt with him.

As Dane was getting drowsy, he was aware that Jubal was tossing and turning on his bunk. This went on for some time, then Dane finally fell asleep praying.

When Friday morning came, Dane awakened just after dawn. He could tell by looking at Jubal as they were dressing that he had hardly slept, if at all.

"You don't look like you got any sleep," Dane said, setting his concerned gaze on Jubal. "You were awfully restless last night. You were still tossing and turning when I finally dropped off."

Jubal ran his fingers through his thick mop of sand-colored hair, sighed, and set his bloodshot eyes on his friend. He gave a little self-conscious shiver, and his face went deathly white.

"I'll be honest with you, Dane. I didn't sleep at all. I — I couldn't get all those Scriptures you showed me out of my mind.

I thought about those horrible things the Bible says about hell. And those verses about sin and forgiveness that you tried to get me to admit that made it clear that even a murderer can be forgiven and saved if he will repent and receive God's Son as his Saviour.

"I kept picturing Jesus hanging on the cross and dying for me, then some fearful picture of hell would flash into my mind, followed by another glimpse of Jesus shedding His blood and dying on the cross."

Dane nodded. *Thank You, Lord!*

Jubal drew a shuddering breath, his face still pale. "Dane, you remember I said God doesn't want anything to do with me?"

"Yes. More than once."

"Yeah. Well, to be honest, I didn't want anything to do with God. I've been so wrong, Dane. God gave his Son to die for me on the cross, and I've been rebellious and ungrateful toward Him."

Dane's face was beaming.

Tears welled up in Jubal's eyes. "Dane, I can't face the gallows tomorrow morning in my lost condition. Will you show me how to call on Jesus and be saved?"

Dane's heart was pounding with joy. "I sure will!" He picked up his Bible. "Let's sit down."

They sat down together on Jubal's bunk, and opening the Bible, Dane went over the gospel with him once more to make sure he understood. By this time, Jubal's eyes were spilling tears, and Dane had the joy of leading his cell mate to Jesus.

When Jubal finished his prayer of faith and repentance, he wrapped his arms around Dane, and with tears still flowing, he thanked him for caring enough about him to share the gospel with him. Jubal was so ecstatic about his salvation, it was all he could do to keep from shouting. He repeatedly thanked Dane for caring about his lost soul and rejoiced in the peace that was flooding his heart.

Prisoners in the cell block were gawking toward Jubal's cell.

Gripping Dane's upper arms, Jubal said, "Will you please tell Pastor Wheeler and your doctor friend that I apologize for not letting them talk to me?"

"Sure. They'll just be glad to hear that you've been saved. So will my little adopted sister. She and the whole colony have been praying that you would come to Jesus."

"Thank them for me, will you?"

"I sure will."

They heard the big steel door open and

knew the guards had come to escort the prisoners to the mess hall for breakfast; a luxury the prisoners in the jail section did not enjoy.

When all the prisoners on that floor had been escorted to the mess hall, gone through the food line, and been seated, some of the convicts who had heard Jubal's jubilant words in the cell block began to mock him about his new religion.

Those at the same table whose cells were adjacent to that of Jubal and Dane ridiculed both of them, calling them religious fanatics.

Dane smiled at them. "We have salvation, gentlemen. Not religion."

"Right," said Jubal. "You guys can call Dane and me what you want, but let me tell you something. I'm going to hang tomorrow morning for my crime, but I know — based on the Bible — that I've been forgiven by Almighty God for the murder I committed and for all my other sins because I received Jesus Christ as my Saviour this morning. And I know I'll already be in heaven when they take my body down from the gallows. How about you guys? Can you tell me that you know you'll go to heaven when you die?"

They looked at him for a few seconds,

then went back to their meals in silence.

That afternoon Dane was visited by Tharyn again. She rejoiced when Dane told her of Jubal's salvation and his strong testimony to the convicts who were making fun of him at breakfast. Tharyn told him everyone in the colony would be thrilled. She also told him that Russell was going to come on his own and see him tomorrow afternoon. At the moment, he was in the waiting room, and they needed to get to the street corner to do some more begging right away.

Dane told her to tell Russell he would look forward to seeing him tomorrow.

That night in the cell when the lanterns in the cell block had been doused, Dane and Jubal knelt beside Dane's bunk and prayed together. Dane was amazed at the peace his friend displayed.

When they had finished praying, and rose from their knees, Jubal reached out in the dark and laid a hand on Dane's shoulder.

"Dane, remember when you showed me Romans 8:28 and said the Lord had a purpose for you being falsely accused of the murder of Benny Jackson so you could be locked up in this prison?"

"Yes, and I know what you're going to say. Tharyn — my little adopted sister — suggested the same thing when she was here Wednesday. God's purpose for me being locked up in this prison and placed into this cell with you was to bring you to the Lord."

"That is exactly right. If you hadn't become my cell mate, I would have died lost and gone to hell. I'm sure, Dane, that the Lord will clear you of the crime so you can go on to pursue your career as a doctor."

Encouraged by this, Dane said, "I know it will happen when it's God's time for me to be released. Do you think you'll be able to sleep tonight?"

"I believe so. The Lord has given me such peace inside."

"Good. We'd better turn in, then."

The next morning at dawn, both Jubal and Dane were awake. As they were dressing, Dane said, "Jubal, there is one other Scripture verse I want to show you before — before the guards come to take you."

"All right."

Dane picked up his Bible and opened it to the Psalm 23. "Pastor Wheeler preached on this not long ago, and I'd like to share it with you."

"Sure."

At that moment, they heard the big steel door come open down the corridor. Both looked to see two guards coming toward the cell.

Jubal's heart quickened pace.

Both of them knew the names of the guards. As they drew up, Dane said to guard Hank Overton, "Mr. Overton, could I have just a couple of minutes to show Jubal something in the Bible before you take him?"

"Okay, but only a couple of minutes. The hangman is ready, and he's an impatient sort."

Dane nodded, then held the Bible in front of Jubal. "Look here at verse 4 in Psalm 23. David, a saved man, says to the Lord, 'Yea, though I walk through the valley of the shadow of death, I will fear no evil: for thou art with me; thy rod and thy staff they comfort me.' Will you take note, Jubal, that David does not call it the valley of death? He calls it the valley of the *shadow* of death. Pastor Wheeler pointed out in his sermon that for the lost person, it is indeed the valley of death. Total darkness. No light. But he showed us in Scripture that Jesus is the Light. And when a saved person dies, the Shepherd, Jesus Christ, is with him. So there is light. That's what it takes to make a shadow, isn't it? Light?"

Jubal nodded. "Yes. There can't be a shadow unless there is light."

"David said he would not fear because the Shepherd would be with him. David's Shepherd is also *your* Shepherd, Jubal. And he said he would be comforted when he died. You will too, my dear brother in Christ."

Tears filmed Jubal's eyes. "Yes. I know I will."

"Pastor Wheeler also pointed out something else here."

"Dane," said the other guard, "you said a couple of minutes. You're already past that."

"Just one more minute, please."

"All right. Hurry."

Dane pointed to verse 6 in the same psalm. "Look here, Jubal. David tells us where saved people go when they die. 'I will dwell in the house of the LORD forever.' That's heaven, Jubal. Heaven! That's where you will be in — well, just a little while."

Jubal nodded and wiped tears from his

cheeks. "And because you cared about me and showed me how to be saved, I'll meet you there someday."

"You sure will."

Jubal hugged Dane, then turned to the guards. "Okay. I'm ready. Let's go."

The man who was headed for the gallows walked away with the guards. When they reached the steel door, and the guards were opening it, Jubal looked back to see Dane with his face pressed to the barred door, looking at him. He waved and Dane waved back.

Dane was tense as he stood at the cell door for several minutes after Jubal had vanished from sight, then finally turned and sat down on his bunk.

He tried to imagine what was happening at the gallows that stood at the rear of the building.

He closed his eyes and took a deep breath. "Lord, please continue to give Jubal peace as he faces the noose."

# Chapter Fifteen

Dane Weston was still sitting on his bunk almost an hour later when he heard the door open and saw the normal group of guards enter, who would be escorting the prisoners on that floor to the mess hall for breakfast.

He rose from the bunk with a heavy heart over Jubal Packer's execution and moved slowly to the cell door. It was guard Hank Overton who moved up to his cell and unlocked the door.

"Breakfast time, Dane. Hungry?"

"Not exactly."

"The execution?"

"Yes."

"Well, let me tell you about Jubal. I've walked a lot of condemned men from their cells to the gallows. He showed absolutely no fear when he was being led up the gal-lows steps. Oh, I've seen some of them try to act tough when they were about to be hanged, but I could tell it was a facade. Even the toughest of them usually break down about the time the noose is being cinched tight on their necks."

"I can imagine."

"But not so with Jubal. He wasn't putting on a mask of toughness at all. There was just obvious serenity and peace of mind. I mean, even when the noose was looped over his head and tightened on his neck."

Dane sighed. "Oh, I'm so glad."

"It was like you had shown him from that verse in Psalm 23. God would comfort him at his time of death. Well, He did, Dane. It was quite evident that Jubal had comfort when he was facing death like no man I've ever seen."

Overton stepped into the corridor and Dane followed. As they headed for the big steel door with other guards and prisoners ahead of them, Dane said, "Thank you for telling me about Jubal. I'm so glad he finally believed what I showed him in the Bible about salvation and forgiveness of his sins and turned to Jesus before it was too late."

"Ah, Dane?"

"Yes, sir?"

"I . . . ah . . . I'd like to know about being saved too."

"Well, I'd love to show it to you."

"All right. I'll find time to come to your cell as soon as I can."

Dane smiled at him. "My time is your time, Mr. Overton."

Shortly after Dane had returned to his cell from breakfast, he was taken to the visiting room where Pastor Alan Wheeler was waiting to see him. Wheeler was glad to learn that Jubal Packer had indeed received Christ as his Saviour, and to hear what guard Hank Overton had told Dane about the peace Jubal had at his execution. He would tell the story to the church from the pulpit tomorrow morning.

Dane passed on Jubal's apology for having refused to see Pastor Wheeler when he had come to talk to him about salvation.

Later in the morning, Dane was called back to the visiting room, and was glad to see Dr. Lee Harris. The doctor was also happy to hear of Jubal's salvation and of the peace he had demonstrated when facing death at the gallows.

As with the pastor, Dane passed on Jubal's apology for his refusal to see the doctor when he had offered to talk to Jubal about salvation.

At midafternoon, a guard came to Dane's cell and told him he had another visitor. When he sat down at the barred window, he smiled at Russell Mims. "Sure is good to see you. I appreciate so much your walking Tharyn over here so she can see me. She said you'd be coming by yourself today."

Russell grinned. "Well, that's the way it was supposed to be, but guess who's down in the waiting room?"

Dane shook his head in amazement. "So she came, too?"

"Yes. She insisted I come up first, since it's been a while that you and I have seen each other."

"Some kind of girl, isn't she?"

Russell nodded. "I was so glad to hear from her when she visited you yesterday that Jubal had opened his heart to Jesus. How did it go this morning when the guards came to take him to the gallows?"

Dane told him of the peace that Jubal showed at the cell, then shared the story told him by Hank Overton about Jubal's peace demonstrated when the noose was cinched around his neck.

Russell smiled. "Everybody in the colony

will be glad to hear about this."

Dane told Russell about Romans 8:28 fitting with his being arrested and put in prison for the crime he did not commit, and how Jubal brought up that if he had not been his cell mate, he would have died lost.

"God really knows what He is doing, doesn't He, Dane?"

"That's for sure. I'm thinking that since Jubal got saved, the Lord may be going to clear me of the crime soon."

"Oh, I hope it will be *very* soon. That would make everybody in the colony happy."

Dane's brow furrowed. "Speaking of the colony, Russell, I'm really concerned about your lack of food. You look a little thin yourself."

"Well, I admit we miss the money you were putting in the kitty for our food. Tharyn said she told you the begging hasn't gone too good of late."

"Yes, and she told me about the café's garbage cans even being short of discarded food."

Russell nodded.

"I've been praying about that, Russell. The Lord has promised to take care of His own children, and I know He won't let you starve. But it seems He wants all of us to pray harder about it."

"And we are, Dane. We will also be praying hard about the Lord getting you out of here and back with us."

With that, Russell left the visiting room, and moments later, a guard brought Tharyn in. She was thrilled to hear how it had gone with Jubal, and she would pray that the Lord would soon deliver Dane from prison so he could be back with the colony.

The next morning, Dane was sitting on his bunk, thinking about the services that were going on at his church and wishing he could be there.

His attention was drawn to Hank Overton, who stepped up to the cell door. "Dane, I've got a little free time. Would you show me how to be saved?"

Thrilled to do so, Dane moved up to the cell door, Bible in hand.

Twenty minutes later, a happy Hank Overton walked away from the cell, a child of God. Dane wiped joyful tears from his face and sat down on the bunk. "Thank You, Lord. Mr. Overton was also in Your Romans 8:28 plan for my being put in this prison."

Time passed, and on Monday October

9, Dane was visited at separate times by Pastor Alan Wheeler and Tharyn Myers. Both had done their best to encourage him, saying they believed that with Hank Overton also being saved, it would be soon that the Lord would see that he was cleared of the murder charge and released.

On Tuesday afternoon, a guard escorted Dane to the visiting room. A smile lit up his face when he saw that his visitor was Dr. Lee Harris. As he drew up to the barred window, he was about to sit down when he noticed that Dr. Harris had his black medical bag with him.

"How come you brought your medical bag in here with you?"

The doctor let a grin curve his lips. "Well, my boy, I brought it because I want to give it to you."

Dane frowned. "I'd love to have it, sir, but don't you need it?"

"Not anymore. As of yesterday afternoon, I'm retired. I'm now a man of leisure!"

A sadness registered in Dane's brown eyes. "Y-you sold your practice?"

"Yes. To a fine young Christian physician. His name is Dr. Stanley Norris. He has agreed to look after the street children as I have — especially those in your colony."

"Oh, that's good. So you'll be moving to Virginia now?"

"That's right. I've already purchased a good-sized wagon, and at this moment, I'm having a canvas cover put on it. As I told you, this would be the only way we can transport Lawanda down to Roanoke."

Dane nodded. "Well, sir, I'm really happy for you. But I have to say I'm self-ishly sorry for me, my colony, and all the people you have so faithfully cared for." His eyes widened and he put a hand to his mouth. "Oh, I'm sorry, Dr. Harris. Please forgive me. It was unkind of me to say that. You and Mrs. Harris certainly deserve to live out the rest of your lives close to your family in Virginia. And you deserve to have time to enjoy the things that you have put aside for so many years to dedicate your life to healing and helping others. But — but I will most certainly miss you."

Dr. Harris looked at him kindly. "I'll miss you too, Dane. And believe me, I'll miss practicing medicine, and I'll miss all my friends. But, Dane, I'm so very tired, as is Mrs. Harris. We need to spend our re-maining years at a slower, less demanding pace."

"Of course, sir. I understand."

Harris lifted the medical bag. "I want you to have this as a keepsake to remember me by."

Dane smiled. "Dr. Harris, you have no idea how much I appreciate your giving the bag to me. Just having it to touch and hold will give me hope that someday I can use it as you did to heal and help people. Thank you, sir. Thank you with all of my heart. I will always treasure it." Tears clogged his throat. He swallowed hard. "And — and I will always treasure your friendship."

"That goes both ways, son. You have been such a blessing to both Mrs. Harris and me." He paused, looked at the bag, and said, "It's empty, so the guards will bring it to you."

"All right."

The doctor turned to the guard who had brought him in. "Will you see that this is given to Dane?"

The guard moved up, took the bag in hand, and opened it to make sure it was empty. "Yes, Doctor. I'll see that he gets it."

Dr. Harris thanked him, then turned back to the window. "Dane, I would be honored if you will use it when you become a doctor."

Dane started to speak, but before he could say a word, Harris said, "I am absolutely confident that the Lord will see to it that you are cleared of the murder of Benny Jackson. You are going to get out of prison, and the Lord is going to make sure that you get your education and become the physician and surgeon you've dreamed about."

"You are indeed a great encouragement, Dr. Harris. I promise you that when I become a doctor, I will use the bag. And sir, I want to thank you again for leading me to the Lord. I will never forget you."

"That also goes two ways, son," said the doctor, reaching into his shirt pocket. He took out a slip of paper and slid it through the small space beneath the barred window. "This is my son and daughter-in-law's address in Roanoke. I want you to write me when you get out, and let me know what happens next in your life. You can address your letter to me in care of my son."

"I'll do that for sure, sir."

"Well, Dane, I've got to keep moving. We're pulling out at dawn. Let's have prayer together."

Dr. Harris and his young friend prayed together, then as the doctor rose to his feet, he said, "Dane, you and I may never see each other again on this earth, but we'll meet in heaven."

Tears filmed Dane's eyes. "Yes, sir. I'll meet both you and Mrs. Harris in heaven."

Dane watched the doctor and the guard go out the door, and a moment later, the guard who was to escort him back to his cell came in and gave the bag to him.

The next evening as the sun was setting over Manhattan, the orphans in the alley had very little to eat for supper. Their breakfast had been very light, and they had not eaten lunch. Each one was definitely showing a loss of weight, and their faces were taking on the sallow look that was caused by malnutrition.

As the night chill began to settle over them, they stood in a circle around a metal trash can in which the boys had built a fire.

Tharyn rubbed her arms briskly. "I sure do miss Dane. I hope the Lord gets him out of that prison soon."

The others spoke their agreement.

Bessie Evans said, "Not only do we miss Dane, but we miss the money he always put in the kitty."

Nettie Olson looked at Russell. "Are we going to starve to death?"

Russell shook his head. "No, Nettie. The Lord is going to provide more food for us, but He wants us to pray harder, so we will do just that. Let's pray right now, even before we have Bible reading."

Russell and the older ones led in heartfelt prayer, asking God to provide the food they needed very soon. They also begged Him to let Dane be cleared of the crime so he could be released from prison and come back to them.

When they had finished praying, a chilly breeze whipped down the alley. They scattered to get their coats from their cardboard boxes.

When they returned to the fire, buttoning up their coats, they all noticed Tharyn standing there by herself.

She had no coat.

Russell slipped out of his coat. "Here, Tharyn. You can wear mine."

She shook her head. "No, Russell. You need your coat."

"I've got another one. Here, put this on."

When he had helped Tharyn into the coat, he returned to his cardboard box, took out an old tattered coat and was putting it on as he returned to the group.

Tharyn eyed the coat. "Russell, where did you get that?"

He grinned at her. "I found it in a trash receptacle last winter, and I've been keeping it in my box as a spare."

She frowned. "Then let me wear that one. You need this coat."

Russell shook his head vigorously. "You keep that one. I want you as warm as possible."

Tharyn's eyes showed her appreciation. "How can I thank you for being so good to me?"

"No need," said Russell. "Could we talk for just a minute?"

"Well, of course."

While the others watched with interest, Russell took Tharyn by the hand and led her a few steps away. He bent close, keeping his voice so only she could hear him. "Tharyn, I want you to know that I love you. I would do anything in the world for you."

There was enough light from the fire reaching them, that Russell could see Tharyn blush.

"Tharyn, someday you and I will be old enough to get serious about each other. And — and when we are, I want to marry you."

She gave him a strange look, but did not reply.

"I know you think a lot of Dane. So do I. But to you, he is your big brother. So even when he gets out of prison, he'll still be your big brother. But someday, I want to be your husband."

Tharyn said in a whisper, "I'm only thirteen, Russell. I'm too young to be in love. But — but maybe someday if we're still together when we're old enough to get serious, we might fall in love with each other. This will be up to God's plan for our lives."

This was enough to make Russell feel better. Later, when they had all gone to bed in their cardboard boxes, he prayed and asked the Lord to keep him and Tharyn close together as they grew into adulthood so they could fall in love and become husband and wife.

In Denver, Colorado, late in the afternoon on Thursday, October 19, attorney Mike Ross entered the post office to pick up the day's mail before going home.

Ross greeted a man and his wife who were on their way out, then moved up to the counter where postmaster Harvey Thompson said, "Howdy, Mike. How goes the lawyer business today?"

Ross chuckled. "Well, it's not as lucrative

as being in the post office business, but we're scraping by."

Thompson laughed. "Who do you think you're kidding?"

Ross noted a new face behind the counter. "And who's this?"

Griffin looked at the young man, then back at the attorney. "Mike Ross, meet Ed Griffin, my new clerk."

Mike reached over the counter and shook Griffin's hand. "Where are you from, Ed?"

"Colorado Springs. This job opened up here with Harvey, so I applied for it, and here I am."

"Well, good. I hope you'll like Denver."

"I already do."

"Ed's a Christian, Mike," said Thompson. "He'll be coming to our church on Sunday."

Mike smiled. "Hey, great! Ed, I'll look forward to seeing you at church. And I'll probably see you when I come in for the mail tomorrow."

Harvey turned and reached into one of the many cubbyholes behind him as Ed said to Ross, "If I ever need an attorney, you'll be my man, sir."

"Fine," said Mike.

Harvey turned back with a bundle of

mail in his hands. He gave Mike a sly grin, then looked at Ed. "I can recommend an attorney who's a lot less expensive."

Mike laughed. "You scalawag!"

Harvey laughed louder. "Here's your mail, Mr. Expensive Attorney."

Mike accepted the bundle. "Thank you, sir."

"How are Jerry, Theresa, and Mandy doing?" Then he chuckled. "After all, I haven't seen them since last night at church."

"Our children are doing fine, Harvey. And guess what?"

"What?"

"We're about to get another one."

"Really?"

"Mm-hmm. I'm expecting a letter any day from the Children's Aid Society."

Harvey's eyes widened. "Hey, come to think of it, I remember seeing a letter from them today when I put the mail in your box. It's in that bundle."

Mike unfolded the bundle and began sifting through the envelopes. He grinned. "Ah, here it is! I just have to go ahead and open it right now."

He laid the rest of the mail on the counter and tore the envelope open. The two men looked on as his eyes ran quickly across the lines and down the letter. The grin on his face spread from ear to ear. "Oh, I can hardly wait to get home and tell Julie and the kids the good news! They'll be so excited. Praise the Lord, another sweet child to raise for Him!"

"Tell me about it, Mike," said Harvey.

"Well, Mr. Brace says here that our next child is a blind girl whose name is Leanne Ladd. She's thirteen years old, and she'll be arriving on the orphan train that is leaving New York on November 6. It will arrive here in Denver on the tenth."

Ed Griffin had a puzzled look on his face.

Harvey nodded. "Well, I'm glad you and Julie are getting your fourth child. Are you still planning on adopting five?"

"Well, that's the plan for now, but who knows? Every child we take is so special in his or her own way. We feel so honored that God has chosen us for this most special mission. I have a feeling that if Charles Loring Brace has more unique children who need a loving home, we will take them into ours. Julie is so dedicated to the ones we have, and it is such a joy to watch her work with them.

"You know, Harvey, Jerry, Theresa, and Mandy have already come to know the

Lord. We're so glad Jerry has matured in his mind enough to understand about salvation."

"Oh yes. It was only a few months ago when he got saved, wasn't it?"

"Uh-huh. July. And he's learning better all the time. We thank the Lord for that. And now, according to this letter, the Lord is blessing us with another precious child. There is something so delightful about a houseful of happy children, and Julie and I wouldn't trade what we have for anything. If need be, we can always add another room onto the house and I can hire a lady to come in and help Julie."

Harvey shook his head in wonderment. "You two are so generous and kind. The world could use more like you."

Mike glanced at the clock on the wall behind the counter. "Whoops! Here I stand talking on and on. I've got to get home and tell Julie this very welcome news, and besides, we're having John and Breanna Brockman for supper tonight. Don't want to be late!"

Harvey laughed. "The chief U.S. marshal just might slap you in jail for tardiness!"

Mike laughed and hurried out the door, carrying the bundle of mail.

Ed Griffin looked at the postmaster, wide-eyed. "I've heard much about Chief U.S. Marshal John Brockman. Before he was a lawman, he was simply known as the Stranger, wasn't he?"

"That's right."

"He rode all over the West, helping people who were in trouble and bringing outlaws to justice."

"Oh, did he ever!"

"I'd sure like to meet him sometime, Mr. Thompson."

Harvey laid a hand on his shoulder. "You'll get to meet him Sunday at church. That is, unless he has some kind of emergency, which often happens in his business."

Ed's eyes grew wider yet. "You mean Marshal Brockman is a Christian?"

"He sure is, and a fine one, too. He is also a tremendous preacher. The pastor has him preach quite often."

"Well, I didn't know this. I've been told that Brockman is lightning fast on the draw."

"You never saw a faster one. Several outlaws have tried to outdraw him. Some of them are now six feet under. Others are behind bars. John tries not to kill them when they challenge him, but sometimes he just can't avoid it."

"Some kind of guy, I'll say. I've also heard that his wife is a nurse."

"Correct. Mrs. Brockman is a certified medical nurse. She works for Dr. Lyle Goodwin at the Goodwin Clinic. Dr. Goodwin also shares her with Mile High Hospital when her services are needed there."

Ed nodded. "Ah . . . are the Rosses' other two adopted children also handicapped? It sort of sounded like it."

"Yes, they are. You see, early in their marriage, Julie gave birth to a little boy who was severely retarded. Little Danny died on his second birthday. Julie had a hard time delivering Danny, and can't give birth to any more children. However, Danny so touched their lives in the short time they had him, that a few years later, Mike and Julie decided they wanted to adopt some handicapped orphan children so they could take care of them and give them a loving home."

"They sure are marvelous people."

At that moment, two customers came in, and after they had been taken care of and were gone, Ed said, "Tell me about the children the Rosses have right now."

"Well, Jerry was the first one they

adopted. He's eight years old. They got him when he was five. Theresa, the second orphan they adopted, was born with deformed legs. They got her when she was five, too. She just turned seven, and is confined to a wheelchair. But, praise the Lord, she is just now beginning to try to learn to walk with crutches. It's slow, but she's making headway. The third orphan, Mandy, was born deaf. She is ten years old. They have had her less than a year."

"I'll say it again. Those are marvelous people. So I assume they got each of these children from the orphan trains."

"Yes. They had heard about the Children's Aid Society and the orphan trains several years ago, but it wasn't until just a little over three years ago that they decided to contact Charles Loring Brace. Mike wrote to Brace, saying he understood that the Society sometimes took in handicapped orphans, but found it difficult to place them here in the West because most prospective foster parents didn't want a child who was handicapped in any way. In the letter, he told Brace about little Danny, and explained that he and Julie would like to adopt a handicapped child.

"Brace wrote back and said he would let him know next time they took in a handicapped child. Just a few weeks later, a letter came from Brace saying they had little Jerry, who was mentally slow. Mike immediately sent a telegram to Brace, saying they would take him. So, Jerry was put on the very next orphan train that was coming through Denver. It also worked this way with Theresa and Mandy. And as you heard, this next one is a blind girl they will take off the orphan train on November 10."

Ed smiled. "Well, I'll say it once more. They most certainly are marvelous people."

"I wholeheartedly agree. The average couple couldn't afford to take in these handicapped children, even if they wanted to, but the Lord has blessed Mike's law firm exceptionally well. And I believe this is one reason for it."

# Chapter Sixteen

When Mike Ross opened the front door of his large two-story red-brick home, the tantalizing aroma of baked chicken and dressing greeted him. As he closed the door behind him, he heard familiar voices at the rear of the house and headed down the hall toward the kitchen.

Happy chatter met his ears as he drew nearer the kitchen. "Thank You, Lord," he whispered, "for Your abundant blessings to Julie and me. That sweet sound coming from those precious children is heavenly music to my ears. And soon there'll be another one to add her own happy sounds to this household."

When he stepped into the kitchen, ten-year-old Mandy was first to see him. As

Mike was making hand signals to tell Mandy he loved her, she cried, "Papa!" and dashed to him, arms open wide.

Julie was at the stove, checking the contents of the oven, and turned to see her husband place the bundle of mail on a small table beside the kitchen door, then fold Mandy into his arms. She smiled while Mike was kissing the top of Mandy's head. "You're late, Mr. Ross, and we've got company coming for supper!"

Mike glanced at her, but was instantly jumped on by Jerry, who dashed in front of Theresa as she leaned forward in her wheelchair and spun the wheels to go to her father.

Letting go of Mandy, Mike leaned down and took Jerry up into his arms. "How's Papa's big boy?"

Jerry looked into his father's eyes. "I jus' fine, Papa. I been helpin' Mama fix subber."

"Good for you!" Mike put him back down.

He then bent over the seven-year-old in the wheelchair and kissed the top of her head. "Did you work with your crutches today, sweetie pie?"

While Theresa was nodding, Julie said, "She did well today, Papa. She walked all the way down the hall from the front door to the kitchen."

Mike smiled down at Theresa. "Really?"

"Uh-huh," said Theresa, smiling from ear to ear.

"Well, I'm proud of you."

Mike then moved over to Julie at the stove, folded her into his arms, and kissed her. "Sorry I'm late, sweetheart, but it just couldn't be helped. At least John and Breanna aren't here."

Julie looked up into the shining eyes of the man she loved. She gave him an impish grin. "And why are you late getting home, my dear?"

A smile that reached all the way from Mike's overflowing heart broke across his face. "Well, I've got some good news."

The children were looking on, and Theresa was using hand signals for Mandy to convey that their father had something good to tell them.

Mike reached into the inside pocket of his suit coat and chuckled as he pulled out the envelope containing the letter from Charles Loring Brace, making sure that Julie could only see the back of it. "I was late because of this letter."

"Well, what is it?"

He turned the envelope around to display the return address. When Julie saw it was from the Children's Aid Society, a hand went to her mouth. "Oh, darling, really? It's about our next child?"

"Mm-hmm. Sure is. I just had to open it at the post office, and when I read it, a curious Harvey Thompson wanted to know about the next orphan Charles Loring Brace is going to send to us. Took some time to tell him."

Julie's eyes were dancing. "I understand. Boy or girl?"

"Girl."

Mandy clapped her hands when Theresa signed her father's reply to her.

Jerry frowned. "Bud I wanded a brudder."

"Maybe next time, Jerry," said Mike, patting his head.

"How old is she, Papa?" asked Theresa.

"Thirteen."

"Oh. She can help me learn to walk on my crutches."

"Well, not exactly, honey. You see, she's blind."

"Oh."

"But you can be a lot of help to her!"

Theresa smiled. "Sure I can."

Jerry frowned again, looking puzzled.

As Theresa turned on the seat of the

wheelchair to sign for Mandy that their new sister was blind, Julie said, "This will be a challenge, darling, but I'm sure she will be a blessing to us."

"I have no doubt of that."

Theresa cocked her head to one side. "What's her name, Papa?"

"Leanne Ladd."

"*Leanne.* That's a pretty name, isn't it, Mama?"

"Sure is," said Julie. "I know we'll all love her. Honey, read the letter to me while I put the finishing touches on supper. The Brockmans will be here any minute."

Jerry and Theresa listened as Mike read the letter to Julie, and Theresa signed its contents for her deaf sister.

When Mike closed off the letter, Julie was placing the bowl of chicken gravy on the cupboard and covering it with its lid. She turned and looked at him with tears in her eyes. Putting the meal aside in her mind for the moment, she dashed to Mike and threw her arms around him, pressing her face against his chest. Mike held her tight, knowing she was overcome with joy, and was certain she was silently thanking her heavenly Father for answered prayer.

After a moment, Julie eased back in Mike's arms while noting the sheen of tears in his eyes. "Our Lord is so good to us, Mike," she said in a reverent voice. "He's going to give us another precious child to raise for Him."

He ran his fingers over her flushed face, smoothing away the tears. "Yes, my sweet. We are so very blessed."

The children looked on as their parents gazed into one another's eyes; each reading what the other was thinking; each thankful for this marvelous blessing.

"Oh my!" Julie said, easing out of Mike's grasp. "We've got company coming for supper. They may have to eat a burnt offering if I don't tend to my cooking! Excuse me, darling."

As she turned back to the stove, a contented smile glowed on her face.

While Julie was taking the baked chicken out of the oven, Mike said, "Another reason I'm late is because I stopped by the Western Union office on the way home and sent a telegram to Charles Loring Brace, telling him we definitely want Leanne and that we'll be waiting for the orphan train at the Denver depot at ten o'clock on the morning of Friday, November 10."

As she placed the pan of chicken on top of the stove, Julie looked over her shoulder.

"Good for you. Then it's all set."

"So Leanne will be here three weeks from tomorrow, won't she?" said Theresa.

Julie smiled at her. "She sure will, honey."

Theresa turned to Mandy and signed the message to her. Mandy clapped her hands again. "Three weeks. I can hardly wait!"

Mike looked down at Jerry. "Even though you want a brother, you'll love your new sister, won't you, son?"

Jerry smiled up at his father and said excitedly, "Yes, Papa. I gonna hab 'nother sidster! Bud she won' be able see me."

Just then a buggy passed the side window of the kitchen and hauled up at the back porch. Mike headed for the back door, looking back at the boy. "That's right, Jerry. Leanne is blind, so she won't be able to see you. But you'll love her anyway, won't you?"

In his dull, sweet way Jerry said, "Yes, Papa. I will lub her bery much."

The children looked toward the back door while Julie hurried up behind Mike as he opened the door. "Welcome to our humble home, folks!"

There was a definite nip in the fall evening air as John and Breanna Brockman moved up the porch steps, smiling. A stiff breeze was blowing.

Julie eased up beside her husband. "Come in! Come in! It has really turned cold this evening, hasn't it?"

"That it has," said Breanna.

"Makes me wonder if we're in for an early winter," commented John.

"Must have been a chilly ride from your place," said Mike, "with that cold breeze nipping at you."

As Mike spoke, both he and Julie stepped back to make room for them in the doorway.

"It was a bit chilly," said Breanna as they moved up and stepped through the door.

The chief U.S. marshal was in his midthirties. He was exceptionally tall, broad-shouldered, and quite handsome. Slung low on his right hip was a black gun belt and holster, which held his pearl-handled Colt .45 Peacemaker. As he removed his black hat, his full head of black hair was exposed, which was beginning to show a slight sprinkle of gray at the temples.

His lovely wife, who had recently turned thirty, was blond with bright blue eyes, and carried a winsome smile.

John sniffed the aroma of the hot chicken, dressing, and gravy. "If the food is even half as good as it smells, it will be well worth the chilly ride."

Julie hugged Breanna, then looked at John. Knowing his penchant for baked chicken, she said, "Oh, I think you'll find it palatable, John."

Breanna chuckled. "Without a doubt, Julie. You know John can eat his weight in your tasty cooking."

Noting the joy on the faces of the parents, John and Breanna immediately put their attention on the children, giving each of them a hug, and as they studied the excitement that showed in their eyes, John chuckled and looked at Mike and Julie. "I know you're all really excited to see us, but I get the strong feeling that we're not the real reason for the elation I see on your faces."

"We really do have some good news to share," Julie said. "But let's get everybody seated at the dining room table and I'll serve up the food. Then we can share the news."

Breanna turned to Julie. "I'll help you serve the food. The rest of you get in there and sit down."

Mike laughed. "Well, I guess we've been given our orders! Come on, John and children. Let's head for the dining room."

"Yes!" said John. "Let's get things going

here, so we can hear this good news."

"I'll hurry on ahead and get a fire going in the fireplace," said Mike.

"And I'll push my sweet Theresa's vehicle for her," put in John.

As John went behind Theresa's wheelchair, took hold of the handles, and began pushing her toward the hall door, all three children looked smugly at each other, delighted to be sharing such an important secret.

Fifteen minutes later, the Rosses' dining room was ready, with a cheery fire glowing in the fireplace and candle flames gleaming off the silver and china.

When the food had been set on the table, and everyone was in his or her place, Mike and Julie put appreciative eyes on their children. Each one sat up straight, hands folded, waiting politely. The Rosses were strong advocates of good manners and had taught their children proper etiquette. They were proud of how well they had learned. Even Jerry was doing well.

Mike asked John to pray over the meal.

When John had prayed and the plates were full, Breanna popped her hands together. "Okay, now. We've been patient just about as long as I can stand it. Let's hear the news before I explode from curiosity!"

Julie ran her gaze to her husband. "I'll let Mike tell you all about it."

"Go ahead and start eating," said Mike, "or your food will get cold."

Mike took a few bites, sipped coffee, then told the Brockmans about the letter they had received that day from Charles Loring Brace.

John and Breanna smiled at each other. Breanna said, "John, I had a feeling the good news was going to be that they were getting another child."

"I did too, sweetheart, but I thought it best to just keep it to myself and wait till it was confirmed." Then to Mike and Julie he said, "This will certainly be something different for you, to have a blind child."

"It will," said Julie, "but we're both excited about it. And so are Jerry, Theresa, and Mandy."

Jerry swallowed a mouthful of dressing and nodded. "Uh-huh. Gon' get 'nudder sidster. Bud she won' be able see me. Bud I will lub her bery much."

Breanna smiled, reached across the corner of the table, and patted Jerry's hand. "I'm sure you will, honey."

Theresa ran her gaze to John and

Breanna. "Mandy and I are really excited about Leanne coming."

"Well, congratulations to all of you," said Breanna. "This is wonderful." She ran her gaze between Mike and Julie. "I know that having a blind child in your home will be a real challenge. But knowing you two, I'm sure you're up to it. What a very fortunate young lady Leanne is to be coming into this home!"

"What do you know about Leanne's background?" asked John. "Are both of her parents dead?"

Mike set his cup in its saucer. "In telling you the contents of the letter, I haven't gotten to that part yet. Yes, both parents are dead. Mr. Brace explained that Leanne's father was pastor of a strong Bible-believing church on Staten Island, New York. He had taken Leanne's mother on a missionary trip to Mexico. While there, both of them were killed by bandits."

Breanna's eyes widened. "Oh my! What a blow it had to have been for that precious thirteen-year-old girl to lose her parents like that."

Mike nodded. "Then to make it worse, there were no family members to take Leanne and give her a home. Mr. Brace said no one in the church felt they could take on raising a blind child."

John shook his head in amazement. "But you two are willing to take on this responsibility. You are something very special. There aren't many people who would adopt one handicapped child, let alone four. The Lord most certainly has given you an unusual love for these special children, and He has given you the ability to cope with the challenge of raising them. Your love for them shines through in all that you do."

Mike looked at Julie, then back at John. "We're nothing special, John. We just saw a need because of our experience with little Danny, and the Lord led us into taking these wonderful children into our family. We wouldn't want our lives any different."

"We wouldn't either," spoke up Theresa. "Mandy and Jerry and I are so very happy here."

Julie smiled at her. "And your Papa and I are so very happy to have you, sweetheart."

"That's for sure," said Mike.

Julie looked back to the Brockmans. "With God's help, we will be able to handle Leanne's blindness and give her all the love and care she deserves. I was just thinking about what a joy it has been to be able to lead Jerry, Theresa, and Mandy to the Lord. We'll probably miss that with Leanne. With the kind of parents she had, no doubt she's already saved."

"I'm sure you're right about that," said John. "You both told us before that you felt the Lord wanted you to have five children. Are you still planning on taking in that fifth one?"

"Harvey Thompson asked me that same thing today," said Mike. "I told him that's the plan for now, but if Mr. Brace comes up with more unique children who need a loving home, we'll take them into ours." He glanced at Julie. "Well, as long as we can make room for them, anyway."

Julie smiled. "Right. I just can't see turning a needful child away as long as God provides for us both financially and in making space for them. These three precious ones each do their part to help me with the housework. If we take in more children than we're planning at the moment, and we need to hire someone to come in and help, we'll do that, too. Jerry, Theresa, and Mandy are such blessings to us. If the Lord leads us to go beyond five — well, you know the old adage: the more the merrier!"

Breanna took a sip of coffee and put her eyes on Mike and Julie. "I'm so very happy for the way the Lord has provided you a family." A definite glint touched her eyes. "John and I have something to tell you. It's really good news too!"

The Rosses exchanged glances, then waited in anxious silence to hear what the Brockmans had to tell them.

Breanna smiled at her husband. "Why don't you tell them, darling?"

John's features took on a gleam. "Well, we found out a few days ago that we are going to have an addition to our family."

Mike and Julie had attended John and Breanna's wedding back in June and both had known how much the Brockmans had wanted a child.

"Oh, wonderful!" exclaimed Julie, pushing her chair back. She rounded the table, leaned over and hugged Breanna's neck. "When's the baby due?"

"Well, I'm two months along, so the baby should be born in mid-May."

Mike popped his hands together. "That's great! So what do you want — a boy or a girl?"

"A boy!" spoke up Jerry in his thick-tongued manner. "Girls is good, bud you need a boy."

John laughed. "Tell you what, Jerry, I'll gladly take whichever the Lord gives me!"

Breanna giggled. "Guess you'll have to, won't you, darling?"

Mike, John, and Jerry helped carry the dishes to the kitchen, then went to the parlor. Julie, Breanna, Theresa, and Mandy teamed up to do the dishes, with Theresa employing a dish towel while sitting in her wheelchair.

The new Brockman baby was still the topic of conversation when at nine-thirty that evening, John and Breanna climbed into their buggy and headed for home.

The next morning in Manhattan, New York, Charles Loring Brace entered his office at the Children's Aid Society building to find his secretary, Myra Hinson, placing a telegram on his desk.

"Good morning, Myra," he said cheerfully, hanging hat and coat on pegs next to the door.

Myra turned, then picked the yellow envelope back up and handed it to him with a smile. "Good morning, Mr. Brace. This came in a few minutes ago. The Western Union deliveryman said it's from that couple in Denver — the Rosses."

"Oh yes! Concerning Leanne Ladd."

Eager to see if the Rosses wanted Leanne, Brace took a letter opener from the top of his desk and slit the envelope open. Taking out the telegram, he quickly read it.

A smile broke over his face. "Praise the Lord! The Rosses want Leanne. Will you go get her and bring her to me so I can tell her, please?"

"Of course," said Myra, heading for the door. "Be right back."

Ten minutes later, Brace looked up from his desk to see Myra come into his office, leading the pretty girl by the hand. Still the gentleman even though Leanne could not see him, Brace rose to his feet as they moved up to the desk. "Good morning, Leanne."

The thirteen-year-old was a little gangly, being at the stage in life when she was no longer a little child, but not quite a young lady. Her dark brown hair was shot through with reddish highlights and was worn in two long braids that hung over her slender shoulders.

Pointing her sightless brown eyes toward the sound of the voice, Leanne said, "Good morning, Mr. Brace. Mrs. Hinson said you wanted to see me."

"That I do, dear. I have good news for

you. Please be seated."

Myra took hold of the blind girl's shoulders and helped her to ease on to one of the chairs in front of the desk. She remained beside her and laid a hand on her shoulder.

Brace sat down, looked across the desk at her, and said, "Leanne, I have good news for you. I have been in correspondence with a fine Christian couple in Denver, Colorado, who have taken three other handicapped children from the Society in the past few years and given them a wonderful home. We have sent each one to this couple by the orphan trains."

Leanne's face brightened. "And they want me, sir?"

"They sure do. Their names are Mike and Julie Ross. They are in their midthirties, and are very active in one of Denver's fine Bible-believing churches. I sent them a letter several days ago. A telegram came from them this morning. Mr. Ross is a prominent attorney in Denver and makes a very good living. Both of them are kind and loving people."

Brace went on to tell Leanne about Jerry, Theresa, and Mandy, explaining their ages and their handicaps.

As he was describing the three children

already in the Ross home, a smile touched Leanne's lips. Even though she had no physical sight, she was picturing the Rosses and the other children in her mind's eye.

"So you see, honey," Brace concluded, "I'm happy to learn that the Rosses want you to come live with them."

"Ah, Mr. Brace," she said haltingly, "they — they do know I'm — I'm blind, don't they?"

"Yes, my dear. They know all about you. My letter explained about your parents and how the Lord took them home to heaven when they were in Mexico."

Leanne nodded.

"Let me explain something else, Leanne. The Rosses have gone beyond the foster stage with these children. They have adopted all three of them, and stated in the telegram that they will adopt you too. They also want one more child, so they will have a total of five adopted children — which they believe is the Lord's will for them."

Another smile curved the girl's lips.

"So you see, dear," said Brace, "you'll have a ready-made family, with two sisters and a brother. I know they will love you and that you will love them. This is a wonderful opportunity for you. I only wish I had more couples like the Rosses. So many orphaned, abandoned, and neglected children need loving homes." A deep sigh escaped his lips as he gazed at the sightless girl.

"That's for sure," put in Myra, her hand still on Leanne's shoulder.

Leanne turned and pointed her vacant eyes upward toward Myra. Her pretty features showed the joy she was feeling. "And just think, Mrs. Hinson, I'll be in a home where they love Jesus and serve Him."

"Yes, you will, sweetheart."

Leanne turned her face back toward the Society's director. "How soon will I be going to Colorado, Mr. Brace?"

"I told the Rosses in my letter that if they wanted you, we would put you on the orphan train that will leave Grand Central Station on Monday morning, November 6. Well, since they most certainly do want you, that's the train you'll be on."

This time, Leanne was smiling from ear to ear. "November 6 isn't far away. I'll look forward to riding the train. I've never been on one before. But most of all, I'll look forward to meeting the Rosses and my new brother and sisters."

"I want you to have a very happy life, dear," said Brace. "And I know you will."

Myra helped Leanne off the chair and

took her by the hand. "All right, honey, I'll take you back to your room, now."

As Myra was leading her out the office door, Leanne paused and turned toward Brace. "God bless you, sir, for caring about orphan children."

"Jesus cares about orphan children," said Brace, "so I do, too."

When Myra and Leanne moved through the door and passed from view into the outer office, Charles Loring Brace wiped tears from his eyes and dived into the paperwork that lay before him.

Less than half an hour had passed when Myra came in and said, "Mr. Brace, I'm sorry to interrupt you, but there's a police officer out here who wants to speak to you. His name is James Thornton."

Brace frowned. "I know Officer Thornton. Did he tell you what he wants to see me about?"

"No, sir. But he emphasized that it is very important."

Wondering what Thornton could want, Brace said, "Please bring him in, Myra."

# Chapter Seventeen

When Myra Hinson came into the office with Officer James Thornton on her heels, Charles Loring Brace rose to his feet behind the desk, and looked past Myra at the man in blue. "Good morning, Officer Thornton."

Thornton approached the desk and extended his hand. "Good morning, sir."

They shook hands, then Brace gestured toward the chairs in front of the desk. "Please sit down."

The man looked over his shoulder. "Thank you for getting me in to see him, Mrs. Hinson."

Myra smiled. "My pleasure, Officer."

As Myra closed the door behind her, both men sat down.

Brace met his gaze. "Now what is it you need to speak to me about?"

"Sir, you will recall that on several occasions I have expressed my appreciation to you for the marvelous work you are doing to take so many orphans off the streets and send them out West on the orphan trains."

Brace nodded. "You certainly have, and I appreciate your appreciation."

"Well, I'm here to tell you about a small colony of orphans on my beat who are about to starve. They live in an alley just off Broadway, and it's getting pretty bad for them."

Brace leaned forward, placing his elbows on the desktop. "Tell me more."

"Do you remember a few weeks ago when you and Mrs. Brace were picking up four street children on my beat, and Dr. Lee Harris approached you and your wife, wanting to meet you?"

"I remember it clearly."

"Do you also recall that Dr. Harris had two teenage orphans in his buggy at the time, and introduced you to them? Dane Weston and Tharyn Myers?"

Brace nodded, smiling. "Yes. I remember Dane and Tharyn. And I recall that Dane is employed at Clarkson's Pharmacy. I also remember their stories as told by Dr. Harris."

"Well, sir, Dane and Tharyn are from this same colony I just mentioned."

"I see."

"But I do have to tell you — and sadly — that Dane is no longer there, nor does he work at the pharmacy anymore."

Brace's brow furrowed. "What do you mean?"

"My partner and I had to arrest Dane for murdering a boy in a nearby alley."

"What? He — he seemed like such a nice boy."

"I know, sir, but three credible adult witnesses saw the incident and identified Dane as the killer. He stabbed an eleven-year-old boy named Benny Jackson to death in an alley not far from the one where this colony lives."

Charles Loring Brace looked stunned.

Officer Thornton went on. "When Dane went to trial, those same witnesses testified under oath that he was the killer. He was convicted of the crime, and the judge gave him a life sentence in the Tombs."

Brace moved his head back and forth slowly. "I'm sorry to hear this."

"Of course, Dane declares he is innocent." He chuckled. "But aren't all the criminals innocent, according to them?"

"Seems that's usually the case. But I'm really surprised about Dane. He very much struck me as being one fine boy."

Thornton sighed. "Well, sir, he had me fooled, too. The sad thing is that the colony — which still has ten children — was very dependent on the income Dane produced by working at the pharmacy. Without it, they're in real trouble." He paused. "Are you aware that Dr. Harris has retired and left New York?"

"No."

"Mm-hmm. A young doctor bought his practice. Dr. Stanley Norris. Dr. Norris has been keeping an eye on the street children as Dr. Harris did. It was Dr. Norris who alerted me just yesterday to the awful condition of the children in Dane's colony. I was just there earlier this morning to see for myself, and he's right.

"Those children are bringing in very little from begging of late, and they're eating what little they can scrounge from the garbage cans behind a nearby café."

Brace shook his head and sighed. "Poor kids."

Thornton cleared his throat gently. "I'm here to ask if it would be possible for you to put all ten of those children on an orphan train and send them out West to find foster homes."

Brace nodded. "It most certainly is possible. I have an orphan train scheduled to leave on November 6, and I still have room for a little more than ten children. Mrs. Brace and I were going to go out on the streets tomorrow to find some more orphans for that train. We'll just make those ten the greater part of that group. I'll take one of my staff men with me right now, pick them up, and bring them here. We'll get some square meals in their stomachs these next several days."

Relief was obvious on the officer's features. "Oh, marvelous! Thank you, Mr. Brace. Since you're going right away, I'll lead you to the alley."

"Fine. I appreciate that."

Brace then looked toward the door and called for Myra. When she came in, he said, "Will you tell E.P. I need him right now?"

"Certainly, sir."

Less than three minutes had passed when the door opened and a man stepped in. Brace introduced E. P. Smith to Officer Thornton, told him about the ten hungry children in the colony, and that they were going to go pick them up and keep them at the Society's headquarters until November 6, when they would be put on the orphan train.

Smith was glad to hear it. He hurried away to hitch up a team to one of the wagons, and Thornton went with him. Brace stopped at Myra's desk and explained what was happening. He asked her to advise his wife, so she could make sure there was enough food cooked for the noon meal to provide for the ten extra mouths, and plans could be made to accommodate five new girls and five new boys.

A cold wind was whipping down the alley, pushing debris in front of it. The ten children stood huddled around the fire in the metal trash can, their coat collars turned up.

It was Billy Johnson who first noticed movement at the nearest end of the alley and pointed. "Look! It's Officer Thornton. There's a wagon behind him."

Everyone in the group turned to see Officer James Thornton aboard his horse and looking straight at them. The team that pulled the wagon — as well as Thornton's horse — was sending billows of vapor into the wind from their nostrils.

Russell Mims greeted Thornton as he dismounted.

Bessie Evans's eyes widened as she ran her gaze from the unfamiliar face of the driver to the man in the seat beside him. "It's Mr. Brace!"

Other young eyes widened instantly.

As E. P. Smith drew rein, Officer Thornton stepped up close. "Hello, boys and girls. I've got some very good news for you. Seems you all know who Mr. Brace is."

"We sure do!" said Bessie.

"Well, he wants to talk to all of you."

By this time, Charles Loring Brace and E. P. Smith were out of the wagon. It was immediately obvious to them that the children were undernourished. They stepped up beside the officer, and Brace said, "Children, Officer Thornton came to my office this morning and told me about your lack of food. This gentleman with me is one of my staff members at the Children's Aid Society. His name is Mr. Smith. He and I are here to take you to the Society's headquarters, if you will go with us."

A wide grin spread over Russell's young face. "Sure we will, Mr. Brace! Right, kids?"

There was instant unanimous agreement.

Brace smiled. "I thought you'd all agree. This is the plan. We'll give you all the food you can eat, and nice clean beds to sleep in. We will also see that you all get new clothes. You will be cared for until November 6, when we will put you on an orphan train that will take you out West so all of you can be taken into foster homes."

"Yes! Yes!" exclaimed Bessie. "I was hoping this would happen someday!"

Tharyn Myers was standing next to Melinda Scott. As Melinda was speaking out to voice her agreement, Tharyn's mind was on Dane Weston. She welcomed the good news about the orphan train and a new home out West, but a cold hand seemed to squeeze her heart at the thought of going off and leaving her big brother in the prison.

Noting that Tharyn had not yet spoken out, Melinda turned and looked at her askance. "Tharyn? Aren't you excited about this?"

Tharyn forced a thin smile. "Yes. Oh yes. Just think! A home with a new family, plenty of food, and a house to live in!"

"Yeah!" blurted Nettie Olson. "That'll really be neat!"

"Okay," said Charles Loring Brace, "let's put the fire out, load up what few personal items you might have, and take you out of this alley forever."

Since Tharyn had already sold or given away what family items she had brought from her old apartment, there was nothing to take with her.

Soon what few items were to go had been placed in the wagon, and E. P. Smith called for all of them to climb aboard.

As the children were boarding the wagon, Brace stood close and offered his hand to the girls who moved past him.

When Tharyn drew up and he offered his hand, she took hold of it and looked up into his eyes. "Mr. Brace, do you remember me?"

"I sure do. You were with Dr. Harris that day he and I met. Your name is Tharyn Myers."

She smiled. "That's right. Do you remember the boy who was in Dr. Harris's buggy with me? Dane Weston?"

A somber look overtook his countenance. "Ah . . . yes. I remember Dane. Officer Thornton told me about his arrest and sentencing in court. I'm so sorry. I —"

"Dane is innocent, Mr. Brace. He didn't kill Benny Jackson. I know he didn't.

There is nothing I can do about his life sentence but pray. And I'm doing a lot of that."

"But Dane was identified as the killer by three responsible adults, Officer Thornton told me."

"I know, sir. I was in the courtroom. Dane still told the judge that he didn't do it, and I know he didn't. Dane is a fine Christian, Mr. Brace. He is the one who is responsible for me being saved. He wouldn't kill anyone."

Brace rubbed his chin. "Well, honey, the Lord knows all about it. Prayer is all you have, but keep it up."

"I will, sir. Would you do something for me?"

"Of course. What is it?"

"Would you take me to the prison before November 6 so I can let Dane know about our going west on the orphan train, and tell him good-bye?"

"Certainly. Mrs. Brace and I will take you in the next few days."

"Oh, thank you, sir."

"Glad to do it, honey," said Brace, and assisted her into the wagon.

The last to board was Russell Mims. Before climbing into the wagon, he stepped up to Officer James Thornton with gratitude showing in his eyes. "Thank you, sir, for going to Mr. Brace and telling him about us. I know we'll all have happy lives out West."

Thornton laid a hand on the boy's shoulder. "Happy to do it, Russell. It was Dr. Norris who alerted me to your lack of food. I couldn't stand to know you were going hungry."

It was just past noon when the wagon arrived at Children's Aid Society headquarters. As the ragtag group entered the large front door of the building, the indescribably wonderful aroma of beef stew greeted them and their mouths began to water.

Letitia Brace had been waiting for them and had a young woman standing close by. As her husband and E. P. Smith drew up to her, Charles said, "Here they are. And I'm sure they're plenty hungry."

Letitia smiled at him. "I'm so glad you've done this, dear."

Then she ran her gaze over the sallow-looking faces of the pitiful group. "Hello, children. We're very glad you're here. I'm Mrs. Brace. I know you are all extremely hungry, and we'll see that you're fed shortly. But first things first."

She turned to the young woman and said

so all could hear, "Millie, will you see to it that these boys and girls get their faces and hands washed thoroughly? Then they can eat lunch."

Millie nodded. "Yes, ma'am."

"I won't keep them waiting any longer, but once their tummies are full, I want each of them to have a bath and some clean clothes."

"Yes, ma'am."

Letitia set her gaze on E. P. Smith. "And E.P., will you see that these boys all get haircuts as soon as they bathe? They look pretty shaggy."

"I sure will," replied Smith.

"Thank you. Once they've all been bathed and given new clothes, we'll put them in the rooms we have chosen for them."

Some twenty minutes later, the ten orphans were led by Letitia into the dining hall. The other children were just finishing lunch, and were carrying their tin cups, plates, and eating utensils to a counter on one side of the room. They looked at the newcomers with curious eyes.

When the newcomers were all seated at a long table, steaming bowls of beef stew were placed before them, along with slices of dark bread slathered with butter, and cups of milk.

Letitia prayed over the food, then smiled. "All right, sweet ones, eat all you want. There's more if you need it."

For a few seconds the hungry group just sat and stared at the feast before them, savoring the delicious aroma.

When they picked up their spoons, ready to dig in, Letitia said, "I know you haven't had a meal like this in a long time, children, but please eat slowly. If you eat too fast, your stomachs might rebel. Just take your time and enjoy it. I promise — no one is going to come along and take it away from you, as it sometimes happens in the alleys."

Heeding her words of caution, the children ate slowly but steadily, smacking their lips with pleasure.

Letitia felt tears sting her eyes as she watched their enjoyment. Her heart was still heavy for all of the starving children still out there on the crowded, dirty streets of New York.

Later in the afternoon, baths were taken, the boys got their haircuts, the children were all dressed in clean clothing, and everyone was taken to their rooms.

Russell Mims, Billy Johnson, and the other three boys in their group were put in a dormitory room with three boys. Each boy had a cot of his own, and they looked forward to sleeping more comfortably than they had in the alley.

Tharyn Myers, Melinda Scott, Bessie Evans, Nettie Olson, and the other girl in their group were put in a room with four other girls. One of those girls was Leanne Ladd.

While the newcomers were getting acquainted with the others who had been at the Society's headquarters before them, the afternoon hours seemed to pass quickly. When the bell rang to call them to supper, they could hardly believe it.

On Sunday morning, October 22, after the Bible teaching service at Children's Aid Society headquarters, Tharyn Myers headed toward Mr. and Mrs. Brace with her heart hammering against her ribs.

She set her gaze on the Society director as she moved closer, then paused. *He has been so good to me. Maybe I'm wrong to ask any more of him. But he did say he would take me to the prison so I could see Dane for the last time.*

Gathering her courage around her like a

cloak, she moved forward again and timidly moved up to the Braces.

Charles was talking to one of his staff men, and though he noticed Tharyn's approach, he stayed in the conversation.

Letitia, however, picked up the fearful look in Tharyn's eyes immediately. She placed a hand on the girl's arm. "What is it, dear? Is there a problem?"

The gentle touch loosened Tharyn's tongue and she stammered, "Oh, n-no, m-ma'am. I — I just w-wanted to talk to Mr. B-Brace."

At that instant, the staff member walked away, and Charles heard Tharyn's words. "What is it, honey?"

She cleared her throat nervously. "Well, sir, I . . . ah . . . I just wondered if you'd forgotten about taking me to see my friend Dane Weston at the Tombs. It's — well, it's been almost two weeks, and I just thought maybe you had forgotten."

Brace shook his head. "No, honey, I haven't forgotten. Mrs. Brace and I were just talking about it last evening. Would Tuesday morning be all right? I have some business near there, and I could accomplish both at the same time."

Tharyn's face brightened. "Oh yes, sir. That would be fine. Thank you very much."

"All right, then. It's a date. Mrs. Brace and I will take you to see Dane Tuesday morning."

On Tuesday morning, October 24, Charles and Letitia Brace put Tharyn in their buggy right after breakfast and they drove through the busy streets of Manhattan toward the Hall of Justice building.

As the buggy carried her closer to the prison, Tharyn's emotions were running high. She was glad for the food and care she was getting at the Children's Aid Society headquarters, and for the new hope of a happy future somewhere out West. But there was also sadness squeezing at her heart because she knew this could very well be the last time she would ever see Dane in this world.

In his cell, Dane was talking to his new cell mate, Miles Coffer, about being saved. Miles had been put in the cell three days previously and Dane began to witness to him before the day was out.

On this day, Miles was showing interest, and as Dane was guiding him in reading salvation verses from his Bible, Hank Overton drew up to the cell door and heard what Dane was saying to Coffer.

Dane stopped what he was saying and looked up at Overton. "Yes, sir?"

Overton smiled. "That pretty little red-head with the big blue eyes is here to see you again, Dane."

Dane had wondered why Tharyn hadn't been to see him sooner. Eager to see her, he said, "Miles, this girl is like a little sister to me, and I really need to see her. I'll be back soon, and we'll pick up where we left off here, okay?"

"Sure."

"Please think over what I just showed you. If you have any questions, we'll discuss them when I get back."

"Fine," said Miles. "Take your time. I'll still be here."

When Dane entered the visiting room and looked at Tharyn, he could tell something was bothering her.

"Hello, little sis. I've missed seeing you. I know by the look in your eyes that something is wrong. What is it?"

Tears welled up in Tharyn's eyes as she told him about the colony being picked up by Charles Loring Brace and E. P. Smith. They were taken to the Children's Aid Society two weeks ago.

Dane nodded. "Oh, so that's why you haven't been in to see me. I'm glad for all of you, though. I'm sure you're eating well and sleeping a whole lot better."

"Yes, we sure are. You know, of course, that Mr. Brace always puts his orphans on the trains and sends them west to find them good homes."

Dane swallowed hard, closed his eyes, then opened them again.

"So when will you be leaving?"

"Our orphan train will leave on Monday, November 6. What's bothering me is that I'm afraid I will never see you again — at least not in this life."

Dane nodded.

Trying to control her quivering voice, Tharyn said, "I — I realize I've only known you for a few months, Dane, but you saved my life and then took care of me when I had nowhere to go. I — I feel such a strong bond between us. It's just so hard to face the fact that we may never see each other again here on earth."

Dane licked his lips, trying to come up with the right words.

Tharyn drew a sharp breath. "I'm very grateful for the opportunity to go west on the orphan train, and for the possibility of having a home and parents to care for me.

It — it is almost overwhelming. I just wish you could come too and start a new life with the rest of us."

"So do I, little sis. But God has put me in this place, and until He sees that I'm cleared and released, this is where I'll stay. I don't think He will leave me here, but right now this prison is where He wants me. I know He let me be falsely accused of Benny Jackson's murder and be locked up in here for two reasons. If I hadn't been in here, Jubal would have died lost. And I also had the joy of leading guard Hank Overton to Jesus. Hank probably would never have been saved if I hadn't been in here to be a witness to him."

"I'm so glad about both Jubal and the guard, Dane."

Dane nodded with a smile. "Tharyn, the Lord may have somebody else for me to reach. I'm witnessing to my new cell mate right now. Someday, I'll win the last one the Lord put me in here to reach, and He will see that I'm cleared and released. This is the only hope that gets me through each day. God has a different plan for you and your life, but if He wills it, we will be re-united at some time later in our lives."

Tears misted his eyes. He reached through the bars and took hold of her hand. "Tharyn, will you write to me here in the prison and let me know where you end up out West? That way we can stay in touch by mail. And when I do get out, we can see each other again. Once I step out into the fresh air of freedom, I will want to come wherever you are as soon as possible."

With a heavy heart, Tharyn nodded. "I most certainly will write you."

"Good. I'll look forward to hearing from you."

She looked into his eyes. "Dane, there is something else I would like to tell you before I have to leave."

"Uh-huh?"

"Your love of the medical world has rubbed off on me. I want to become a nurse someday."

"Wonderful! I hope you will hang on to that dream, and after you get out of high school, you will be able to find a good nurses' school and pursue it."

"That's my plan."

"Good."

Dane then told Tharyn about Dr. Lee Harris giving him his medical bag before he and his family left for Virginia. Tharyn commented that it was very nice of Dr. Harris to do that, and she was still praying that one day the Lord would allow him to become a doctor.

Tharyn told him about the girls in the colony and herself being put in a room with four other girls. She explained about Leanne Ladd, who was also a Christian and her age, and who was blind from birth. She said that the two of them had already become close friends.

Dane smiled. "It's just like you to take an interest in a blind girl and befriend her. I hope there will be a lasting friendship between the two of you that will go on."

"Well, Leanne has already been chosen by a Christian family in Denver, Colorado. At least this way, wherever I end up, I will know how to contact her in Denver."

"Good."

The guard who stood at the door on Tharyn's side stepped up. "Sorry, missy, but your time's up."

She looked up at him. "I know, sir. Could I have just a couple more minutes?"

"Okay." He returned to where he had been standing by the door.

Dane and Tharyn grasped each other's hands beneath the barred window. Tears filled their eyes, though they both were trying to put on a brave front.

Tharyn swallowed with difficulty. "Mr.

Brace is in the waiting room with his wife. He wants to see you after I leave."

"Oh. All right. I'd love to talk to him."

"Well, good-bye, big brother. Thank you for all you've done for me."

"That's what big brothers are for. Don't forget to write me."

"I won't. I'll write as soon as I have an address, so you can write me back. I'll be praying for you every day. You can count on that."

Dane sniffed, blinking at his tears. "Thank you."

Tears began spilling down Tharyn's cheeks. "I — I love you, Dane."

"I love you, too. Don't ever lose sight of your dream to become a nurse, and don't ever take your eyes off the Lord. In this life or the next, I will see you again. And that's a promise."

They looked longingly at each other.

Taking a deep breath, Dane said, "Go with God. Let Him be your constant guide."

Letting go of his hands, Tharyn rose from the chair with a hot lump in her throat. She turned and walked to the door, where the guard waited, holding it open. She looked over her shoulder, and her heart seemed to shatter in her chest as she saw the tears streaming down Dane's cheeks.

She waved and he waved back.

Tharyn faced forward, and with slow steps, passed through the door and out of sight.

Dane was still wiping tears when Charles Loring Brace was ushered in by a guard and sat down, facing him.

Brace asked to hear the story of Dane's arrest, conviction, and sentencing directly from him.

When Dane had told his story — including that he was innocent — Brace said he believed him. They agreed that it would take a miracle from the hand of God to clear Dane of the crime, and Brace assured him that he would be praying for that miracle.

They prayed together at that moment, then Dane thanked Brace for coming. He also thanked him for taking care of the children in his colony, especially Tharyn. He added that he was glad the children would be going west on the orphan train to find homes.

Brace said he was glad he could do it, and told Dane he would be back to see him periodically.

# Chapter Eighteen

On Monday morning, November 6, at the Children's Aid Society headquarters, sixty-four orphan children were gathered in the front center section of the auditorium — which had once been the auditorium of the Italian Opera House.

Tharyn Myers, Melinda Scott, Bessie Evans, Nettie Olson, and Leanne Ladd were sitting in the same row of seats. Leanne was sitting next to Tharyn, who was holding her hand and describing the auditorium to her. Leanne was listening intently. Nettie was sitting between Melinda and Bessie, excitement showing on her face.

Russell Mims and Billy Johnson were seated behind the girls, along with other boys from their dormitory room.

Several staff members were standing in the aisles talking to some of the children.

At precisely 7:45, Charles Loring Brace entered the auditorium from a side door. While he was mounting the platform, Tharyn leaned close to Leanne and said, "Mr. Brace is here, honey."

Leanne smiled. "It won't be long now, will it?"

"Sure won't. We'll be leaving for Grand Central Station shortly."

Brace moved to the center of the platform and ran his gaze over the faces of the nervous but excited children. "Boys and girls, your day has come. I'm so glad each and every one of you is here and I hope you will enjoy the trip west."

He then explained the basic rules that would be followed on the train during the trip, so they would understand what was expected of them.

"How many of you have ever traveled on a train? Raise your hands."

Only three of the sixty-four raised their hands.

"I see. Well, this is about how it is every time we send a new group of orphans out West. Very few have been on a train."

Brace then looked down near the

bottom of the stairs that led to the platform, where five adults had gathered while he had been laying out the rules for the young travelers. He motioned for the five to come to him.

As they were mounting the stairs, Tharyn fixed her eyes on the lady in the white uniform. She whispered, "There's a nurse among those people."

"Will she be going with us?" queried Leanne in a low whisper.

"I would say so. I think the other people are the escorts who will be traveling with us."

As the five people moved up beside the Society director, they smiled down at the children.

"Boys and girls," said Brace, "I want you to meet the four people who will be chaperoning you on your journey." He pointed to the couple who stood closest to him. "This is Mr. Mark Newton and his wife, Eva. Next to them are Mr. Colin Justman and his wife, Barbara. Mr. Newton and Mr. Justman will be riding in one coach with the boys, and their wives will be riding in another coach with the girls. The two coaches will be connected, with the girls' coach in front. The railroad companies always put the orphan coaches at the rear of the train, just in front of the caboose.

"Aboard the train during the entire trip, there will be Bible reading and prayer twice a day, just as it has been done here at the Society during the time you have been with us.

"Please let me emphasize that Mr. and Mrs. Newton and Mr. and Mrs. Justman are to be obeyed at all times."

Brace then looked to the lady in the white uniform at the end of the line. "I also want you to meet Miss Millie Voss. She is a certified medical nurse and will be aboard the train to care for any of you who become ill on the trip."

Millie flashed a winsome smile and waved at the children. Most of them waved back.

"Miss Voss will be riding in the girls' coach."

The Society director excused the five adults, who descended the steps and sat down in the front row.

Brace ran his gaze over the sixty-four faces once again. "I mentioned that the railroad companies always put the orphan coaches at the rear of the train. Ahead of them will be more coaches. These are for the train's regular passengers. From Grand

Central Station, your train will be stopping at Pittsburgh, Columbus, Indianapolis, Springfield, and Kansas City.

"At each stop from the Kansas-Missouri border on, there will be people waiting in the railroad stations, prepared to choose orphans to take into their homes as foster children.

"The first stop in Kansas will be at Topeka, which is the state capital. There will be several stops in towns across Kansas and some in eastern Colorado. You will stop at Denver, where there are usually many people waiting to choose foster children."

Leanne leaned close to Tharyn. "Denver!"

Tharyn squeezed the hand she was holding. "Yes, honey. Denver."

Brace went on. "After leaving Denver, the train will cross the Rocky Mountains and stop at Grand Junction, Colorado. Its final destination is Los Angeles, California, but there will be stops in southern Utah, southern Nevada, and eastern California before you reach Los Angeles."

Tharyn leaned toward Leanne. "It must be good to know already where you will be getting off."

Leanne smiled. "It sure is. I'm looking

forward to meeting Mr. and Mrs. Ross and their other adopted children. Oh, Tharyn, I wish you could be chosen by someone in Denver so we could always be close to each other."

Tharyn squeezed her hand again. "I wish that would happen. It sure would make me happy."

Charles Loring Brace smiled at the children once more. "Now listen to me, boys and girls. Don't become discouraged if you are passed over time and again. It usually takes the entire trip to see all of the orphans chosen by prospective foster parents. If any of you have not been chosen by the time the people in Los Angeles look you over, you will be brought back to New York. After some time passes, you will be put on another train west. The process will continue until every child is chosen. We've been running these orphan trains for over eighteen years — before any of you were born — and only very, very few have had to return to New York. And every one of them was chosen on the next trip."

Most of the young faces showed fear when the director had spoken of the possibility of them being brought back to New York, but they changed back to normal at his latter words.

Brace then led the group in prayer, asking God to give safety to the children, their chaperones, and their nurse on the trip.

When he finished praying, he asked the chaperones and Miss Voss to make their way to the front doors of the building. "All right, children, I want you to go outside now where you will be loaded into six wagons that are ready to take you to Grand Central Station. Everyone walk slowly. No running."

As the orphans were filing slowly out the doors to climb in the wagons, Charles Loring Brace hurried off the platform and moved up to the spot in line where Tharyn was guiding Leanne.

Tharyn said, "Leanne, Mr. Brace is here. I think he wants to talk to you."

"I sure do," said Brace, joining them in their slow walk.

The blind girl turned her face. "Yes, sir?"

"Honey, I know you are going to be very happy with the Ross family."

"I'm sure I will, sir."

"Will you please greet them for me?"

Leanne smiled. "Yes, of course."

Brace set tender eyes on the redhead. "Tharyn, I want to thank you for looking after Leanne as you have."

"I'm glad to do it, Mr. Brace. I love her very much."

"That's quite obvious. Every time I see you two together, you are doing something to help her."

Leanne patted her friend's arm. "I love Tharyn very much too, Mr. Brace. I'm praying that the Lord will let her be taken by a family in Denver. Or at least nearby, so we can be close together always."

"Well, you just keep praying, Leanne. We have a great big wonderful and powerful God. He can certainly do it."

"I will, sir. And thank you so much for guiding the Rosses and me together."

"It's been my joy, Leanne. God bless you."

"God bless you too, sir."

Brace moved on.

When it was time for Tharyn and Leanne to board a wagon, its driver stepped up and touched Leanne's arm. "Little lady, I'm the driver. Would you allow me to lift you up into the wagon?"

Leanne smiled. "Thank you, sir."

The driver looked at Tharyn. "You go ahead and get in. I'll put her on the seat next to you."

Tharyn climbed in. When Leanne was

placed gently beside her, Tharyn took hold of her hand.

About two minutes later, the caravan of wagons with *Children's Aid Society* lettered on their sides drove onto the street and headed in the direction of Grand Central Station.

As the wagons moved through the streets, Tharyn began giving Leanne word pictures of their surroundings. Quite often, Leanne commented that she knew about this building and that store.

"You know it pretty well, don't you, honey?" said Tharyn.

"You might say that. New York has been my home for all of my thirteen years. We lived here in Manhattan until my father —" she swallowed hard — "until my father finished his seminary work when I was eight and we moved to Staten Island. That's when he became pastor of the church there."

"I see."

"Even then, we came to Manhattan quite often, so I still have a pretty good picture of it in my mind." She paused. "I've never been outside the five boroughs, though."

"Me, neither. Kind of scary, isn't it?"

"Oh, is it! I've heard stories since I was

small about the Wild West."

"Me too," said Tharyn. "I learned a lot about it in school."

"Mm-hmm. I can remember shivering with fear as I heard tales about wild Indians out there, and the tough towns that are overrun by outlaws and saloons filled with drunken cowboys who are always fighting each other."

Tharyn nodded, though Leanne could not see her do it. "Yes, and gunfighters in the streets drawing against each other to see which one is the fastest." She snorted. "One of them always wasn't, and from what I've read, he always ends up six feet under at some Boot Hill."

Leanne giggled. "For sure. It sounds like a dangerous part of the country, doesn't it? I mean like a faraway place from which one never returns."

"Yes. You could say that."

"Of course, it's not that bad now. Before you kids came to the Society from your alley, Mr. Brace was talking to us about the West, and he said life is much calmer out there in the western states and territories than it was even ten years ago. He said it's still not as civilized as here in the East, but better than it used to be."

Tharyn said, "It's certainly going to be

different from what both of us have known up until now. But I'm really looking forward to living out there. Since living as a waif on the streets of New York, with all its dangers, as well as hunger and cold, I'm expecting a happy future."

Suddenly Dane Weston came to Tharyn's mind, and a lump formed in her throat. She pictured him there in the dismal, dirty Tombs, living in a cramped little cell. *O dear Lord, everything would be so good if only Dane was coming with me.*

Pain gripped her heart and moisture gathered in her eyes.

*Please, God, with Your mighty hand, clear him of the crime You know he didn't commit. Let us be together again one day soon. He said he would come and find me when he gets out. He's my big brother, Lord. I miss him, and I want him close to me.*

Tharyn sighed deeply and brushed the tears from her cheeks. In her heart, she vowed to make Dane proud of her in her chosen profession of nursing.

Hearing the sigh, Leanne turned. "Tharyn, are you all right?"

"Why do you ask?"

"You just made a sad sound."

"Oh. I did, didn't I? I was just thinking about Dane. I really miss him."

"From what you've told me, he's really been an excellent big brother to you. No wonder you miss him. Don't give up, honey. Like you've said over and over, the Lord knows he's innocent, and the Lord is going to set him free."

Tharyn sniffed and wiped away a tear. "I have to hold onto that."

"Just don't let go."

The city sounds surrounded them, punctuated by the clopping noise of the horses' hooves on the street.

Leanne squeezed the hand that still held hers. "Tharyn, could — could I ask you something?"

"Of course."

"I've never had a friend like you. Could we sort of adopt each other as sisters?"

Tharyn squeezed back. "We sure can. I'd love to be your sister."

The other children in the wagon smiled as they watched Leanne lean close and kiss Tharyn's cheek. "I love you, sis."

Tharyn turned and kissed Leanne's cheek. "I love you too, sis."

Soon the train of wagons filed into the parking lot at Grand Central Station and came to a halt.

The driver of the wagon bearing Leanne and Tharyn lifted Leanne from the seat and stood her on the ground. She thanked him, then took hold of Tharyn's arm as the five adults led the children inside the terminal. Since Leanne had never been to Grand Central Station before, Tharyn described as much as she could as they were being guided to the track where their train was waiting to be boarded.

Eva Newton, Barbara Justman, and Millie Voss ushered the girls toward their coach.

Russell Mims left the other boys long enough to slip up beside Tharyn. "You okay, Tharyn?"

She smiled at him. "Yes, Russell. I'm fine. A little nervous like everyone else in this group, but I'm fine."

Not attempting to lower his voice at all, he said, "I love you, Tharyn."

She smiled again, but did not voice the same sentiment.

Russell gave her a big grin. "I know. We're too young. But I love you, anyhow." With that, he hurried to catch up with Mark Newton, Colin Justman, and the other boys as they were starting to board the coach.

As Tharyn was helping Leanne climb

the steps of the small platform that led into the girls' coach, Leanne said, "You haven't told me about your romance with Russell."

Tharyn giggled. "I don't have a romance with Russell. We're both too young for that. Especially me. I'm only thirteen."

Leanne chuckled as they passed from the platform into the coach. "Sounds like Russell feels romantic toward *you.*"

"He's too young, Leanne. At fifteen, he can't possibly know what it is to be in love, yet."

Leanne shrugged. "Maybe not."

Eva and Barbara moved farther back in the coach, directing girls to various seats.

Millie paused at a seat about a third of the way into the coach, turned, and smiled at Tharyn. "How about this seat?"

"Looks fine to me, Miss Voss." Tharyn turned to Leanne. "There's room on each seat for two people. Do you want to sit by the window, or would you rather sit on the aisle?"

Leanne chuckled. "You sit by the window, honey, so you can see out when we're traveling."

Tharyn's features flushed. "Oh. Sure. Okay."

"You can describe it to me all the way to Denver."

"Unless she is chosen by a foster family before you get to Denver, dear," said Millie.

Leanne pressed a smile on her lips. "I'm praying hard that the Lord will keep Tharyn from being chosen before we get to Denver, ma'am. I want her chosen there too, so we can be close to each other. I really believe the Lord is going to do it."

Millie patted the blind girl's arm. "What's your name, dear?"

"Leanne."

"Well, Leanne, God says without faith it is impossible to please Him. I sincerely hope He does it for you."

"Thank you, Miss Voss."

Tharyn sat down, then took Leanne's hand and guided her onto the seat. Millie moved to another pair of girls.

Tharyn leaned close to the window. "I see lots of people out there, sis. Most of them are boarding the other coaches ahead of us. Some are telling others good-bye. No doubt family members and friends."

Leanne's mind went back to the day she stood at New York Harbor with people from their church and told her parents good-bye just before they boarded a ship that would take them south around the tip of Florida, then west to Tampico, Mexico.

A hot lump rose in her throat. *Little did I know,* she thought, *that I would never see them again in this life.*

Tharyn continued to describe the scene on the depot platform until the engine's whistle blew and the bell began to clang. As the train chugged out of the station, she described what she saw as it picked up speed and rolled westward across the trestle spanning the Hudson River toward New Jersey.

She grew quiet as she watched the familiar scenery slip away. Memory suddenly carried her back to the warm, loving home she had known until her parents were killed that awful day in front of their apartment building.

Hot tears welled up in her eyes. The home she grew up in was a loving place. The Myers family had been poor by many people's standards, but they were rich in love and in taking care of each other.

Leanne noted her friend's silence, but thought possibly Tharyn was having a hard time leaving the only place she had ever known as home and decided not to disturb her.

Tharyn pressed her forehead against the cold window pane and softly whispered, "Good-bye, Mama. Good-bye, Papa. I will never forget you. I will always love you."

As she let the tears fall freely for a few minutes, the pain in her heart began to ease. She closed her eyes, trying to picture what lay ahead for her in the wide open spaces of the West.

After a little more time, Tharyn began describing for Leanne what she saw out the window as the train rolled westward across New Jersey in a beeline for Pennsylvania.

When lunchtime came, Mark Newton and Colin Justman went to the dining car near the front of the train and were given two carts loaded with hot food. They pushed them back to the girls' coach, and began to hand out the lunches as they moved slowly down the aisle.

When Mark and Colin drew up to the seat where Tharyn and Leanne were sitting, they found a problem. How was the blind girl going to hold her soup bowl, plate of bread, and cup of lemonade while she ate?

As they discussed it, Tharyn said, "It's really not a problem, gentlemen. Just hold my meal on one of the carts and bring it back to me later. I'll help Leanne eat right now."

Colin frowned. "But, honey, your soup

will grow cold if we wait very long."

"I don't really care. The main thing is that Leanne gets to eat her soup while it's hot."

"But that isn't fair to you, sis," spoke up Leanne.

Tharyn patted her hand. "It's all right. Really."

The two men smiled at each other, then Colin said to Tharyn, "You are truly one sweet girl. We know you came from the streets and have been undernourished for quite some time. Mr. Brace pointed you out to us this morning after the meeting. He said you were taking care of this little girl and told us about your life on the streets of late. Yet, here you are, willing to delay your own meal so your friend can have her soup while it's hot."

"You're to be commended," said Mark. "I believe Mr. Brace said your name is Tharyn."

"Yes, sir."

Leanne pointed her blank eyes at the voices. "I haven't known Tharyn very long, gentlemen, but she is the best friend I've ever had."

Colin nodded. "I believe it."

"Me too," said Mark.

Tharyn noted a tea towel draped over

the handle of Mark's cart. "Mr. Newton, could I borrow that towel, please? It will help with the situation."

"Of course."

Mark handed her the tea towel, told her that one of them would be back later with her lunch, and moved on.

Tharyn tied the towel around Leanne's neck so that anything she might spill would fall on it, rather than on her clean, starched dress.

"With this towel, I can probably feed myself," said Leanne. "I've been blind all my life, and have lots of practice feeding myself. Why don't you catch up with the men and tell them to give you your lunch right now?"

"Honey, what about the sway of the train? You're liable to have a problem, don't you think?"

Leanne shook her head and smiled. "Oh yes. The sway of the train. I hadn't thought of that. Okay, you'd better help me."

Newton and Justman pushed their carts on through the girls' coach, handing out meals to their wives and the orphans, then pushed them out onto the platform of the boys' coach.

By the time the boys had been served, almost half an hour had passed since they started handing out lunches. They turned the carts around and went back into the girls' coach with one lunch left on Colin's cart.

When they came to Tharyn and Leanne, Millie Voss was entering the coach from its front door.

Leanne was just finishing her lunch with Tharyn's help. She drained her cup of lemonade. "That was really good."

While Mark took Leanne's empty bowl, bread plate, and cup, Colin handed Tharyn the bowl of lukewarm soup, along with her cup of lemonade and piece of bread. "I wish the soup was still hot, honey."

Millie paused and frowned. "Why is Tharyn just now getting her lunch?"

Mark quickly explained it to her.

Millie set admiring eyes on the redhead. "That was a very unselfish thing to do, sweetie."

Tharyn looked up at her. "Oh, it's no problem, ma'am. I'm just getting practice for what I plan to do when I grow up."

"And just what might that be?"

"Well, ma'am, I plan to be a nurse just like you, and I figure helping people will be a big part of it. So I might as well start now. Besides, it just plain makes me feel good to lend a hand when it's needed."

Millie looked at her with obvious admiration. "With that positive attitude, Tharyn, you will make a very good nurse. Just hold on to that dream."

Tharyn's mind flashed back to the last time she saw Dane, and he said essentially the same thing. "Yes, ma'am. I will. I've been given that advice before. I'll never let go of that dream."

Millie patted Tharyn's shoulder and moved on down the aisle. Mark and Colin both commended Tharyn for her nursing ambition, and moved on out of the coach with their carts.

Tharyn began eating her lunch. The fact that the soup was cold made no difference to her. It was an absolute feast after what she had been existing on the past few months. She savored every morsel, thanking God in her heart for supplying it.

When Tharyn was finished with her lunch, she left Leanne long enough to return her bowl, plate, and cup to the dining car, then as she returned to the girls' coach and sat down, she saw that Leanne's head was bobbing.

"Leanne, the seat is wide enough. Just lie down here with your head on my lap and take a nap."

"Thank you. I am pretty sleepy."

When Tharyn had made sure Leanne was comfortable, she watched her relax totally. The rhythmic click of the wheels and the steady sway of the coach soon lulled her to sleep.

While the train rolled across Pennsylvania toward Pittsburgh, Tharyn let her mind go once again to her parents and how much she missed them.

Her thoughts then drifted to her future, and she let her imagination take her out West where she invented her own foster parents and formed a mental image of what they were like, and the kind of house they would have.

It wasn't long until the rhythmic click of the wheels and the steady sway of the coach took their toll on Tharyn. Soon she was fast asleep.

# Chapter Nineteen

Tharyn Myers was running across a field of grass and colorful wildflowers near a jagged range of mountains. The sun was lowering slowly behind the majestic peaks.

A soft breeze was blowing and her long auburn hair danced in the breeze.

Earth and sky were bathed in the hue of sunset. There was a dense forest just ahead of her, and she marveled at the beauty of a swift-moving stream as it wended its way across the land toward the forest, reflecting the glorious light of the setting sun.

The mountains were a dark purple mass framed in sunset gold. Tharyn was in awe as she took in the all-embracing immensity of the mountains, magnified by the golden fringe of God's sunlight.

As she neared the stream, she saw a young man sitting on its bank, gazing into the water. When she drew up close, the back of the young man's head looked familiar.

Hearing her footsteps on the lush grass, he turned and looked at her.

*It was Dane Weston!*

He stood up, smiling, and opened his arms to her.

"Oh, Dane!" she gasped and dashed into his arms. "Dane! How did you get out of prison? Did they find the real killer?"

Dane did not answer her question, but kissed her forehead. "I love you, little sis."

Suddenly Tharyn was awake. The dream vanished, and the clicking sound of the steel wheels beneath the swaying coach met her ears.

Blinking her eyes, she gasped for breath. Her heart was pounding.

*The dream was so real!*

While her heartbeat was slowing down, Tharyn's thoughts ran to Dane there in that horrible prison. She looked down at the sleeping Leanne Ladd with her head in her lap, then closed her eyes and said in a low whisper, "Dear Lord, please do whatever has to be done to show the law in New York that Dane didn't murder that boy. I'm glad that Dane has been able to lead souls to You in the Tombs, but he shouldn't have to go on living behind bars in that awful place for something he didn't do."

She paused, took a deep breath, and went on. "Lord, I beg You: Please don't make him have to spend the rest of his life in there. Set him free. And, Lord, please bring him out West and let us be together again. He risked his life to save me from death. He — he's the best friend I have in this world. And he's my big brother. Please let us live near each other for the rest of our lives. I — I may be asking a whole lot, Lord, but it's the way I feel. I love my big brother, and I want to be close to him."

On Tuesday morning, November 7, the train pulled into the Pittsburgh railroad station. The orphans were allowed to leave their coaches so they could stretch their legs and release some of their pent-up energy.

They walked through the depot, escorted by their chaperones and nurse Millie Voss. Tharyn held Leanne's hand and described the interior of the depot to her as well as the milling people all about them.

After an hour of walking around, orphans, chaperones, and the nurse boarded their coaches once again, and soon the train chugged out of the station.

Moments later, the train was running at top speed over the Pennsylvania hills, headed toward Ohio.

In the girls' coach, Eva Newton stood at the front. "Girls, I want to tell you a little bit about where you're going. You've heard people talk about the wide open spaces out West. And that description is quite accurate. Out there, you can go hundreds of miles sometimes from one town to the next. Ever since the Children's Aid Society started the orphan train system, most of the orphans have been chosen by farmers and ranchers. Out there in farm and ranch country, the rolling land seems to stretch on forever. Depending on where they are, sometimes there are ranges of towering mountains with peaks that reach fourteen thousand feet or more above sea level. Those peaks are capped with snow in the wintertime, and on some of them, their snow never even melts off in the summertime."

The girls were surprised to hear this and looked at each other in amazement.

"Now many of the orphans have been

chosen by people who live in the rural towns. Those children learn quickly that living in the western towns is vastly different than living in New York City. Out there, it is a country atmosphere and the air is always clean and refreshing."

Eva ran her gaze over their excited faces and smiled. "How does this sound to you?"

Answers came back from all through the coach. The girls were very excited to see what lay ahead of them.

As the voices began to grow quiet, Leanne raised her hand.

Eva smiled. "Yes, Leanne?"

"Mrs. Newton, I won't be able to see the wide open spaces around Denver, and I won't be able to see the Rocky Mountains that I'm told are just west of there, but I'm going to love it anyhow!"

The other girls applauded and cheered her.

"And Mrs. Newton, I'm glad you mentioned about the air out West always being clean and refreshing. I can't see like the rest of you can, but there's nothing wrong with my sense of smell. We all know about the disgusting odors we so often have in New York City's air. I'm looking forward to the clean, refreshing air where I'm going to live!"

Eva nodded and said, "Girls, how many of you like music?"

Every girl lifted a hand.

"Good! Recently, one of the women sponsors at the Society composed a little song about the comparison of New York City's atmosphere to that of the wide-open spaces of the West. I would like to teach it to you. How many of you like to sing?"

Again, every girl lifted a hand.

"Wonderful! I'll teach it to you, then we'll all sing it together."

The girls listened intently as Eva sang the song:

> From city's gloom to country's bloom,
> Where fragrant breezes sigh;
> From city's blight to greenwood bright
> Like the birds of summer fly.
> O children, dear children,
> So blessed are you and I!

The orphan girls loved the song, which had a catchy tune as well as a message of hope to them, and Eva had them sing it over and over several times. She noticed that Leanne sang along with everyone else, a radiant smile on her lips.

Sitting on a front seat, Barbara and

Millie sang along with the girls, enjoying the happy enthusiasm they displayed.

Once the girls were singing the song well, Eva said, "Okay! All of you learned the song pretty fast. I'm going to the boys' coach now to teach it to them."

As Eva left the coach, the girls were singing it on their own.

When Eva entered the boys' coach, Mark left Colin's side on the front seat, and moved up beside her at the front of the coach.

Her entrance already had every boy's attention.

Mark said, "Boys, listen up. Mrs. Newton wants to talk to you."

Eva made the same speech as she did in the girl's coach, then taught the song to the boys. They sang it with her over and over again, showing that they loved the song as much as the girls did.

At the Tombs in the Hall of Justice, Dane Weston sat on his bunk, thinking about Miles Coffer, who had been transferred to a cell on another floor yesterday. He smiled as he thought of how Miles hugged him when the guards came to take him to his new cell and thanked him for caring about his soul, and for giving him the gospel.

He would never forget Miles's words as the guards closed and locked the cell door. As he looked back over his shoulder, he said, "Dane, my body will be locked up in this place for another twenty years, but my soul is free! I'll see you out in the prison yard one of these days."

"Sure will!" called Dane, his face pressed against the bars.

Dane shifted his position on the bunk and thought about Tharyn on the orphan train. "Lord, take care of her. She's such a sweet girl."

Now that Dr. Lee Harris had retired and moved away and Tharyn was gone, the only person that visited him regularly was Pastor Alan Wheeler. The pastor had been there two times since Dane had last seen Tharyn, and had been given permission by the guards to have a brief Bible study each time with Dane on the other side of a barred window in the visiting room.

These visits had been a real encouragement to Dane, and a source of inspiration for him to keep up his witness to prisoners and guards alike. Dane was becoming a serious student of the Bible, and between visits, he often jotted down questions to present to Pastor Wheeler the next time he came.

Charles Loring Brace had been there that very morning and promised he would be back as often as possible. Dane had told him that he understood he had a very busy schedule, but he would welcome his visit any time he could come.

The next morning, about an hour before noon, a guard drew up to the cell door and said, "Dane, you've got a visitor."

Dane smiled as he rose from the bunk and stuffed the slip of paper with his latest Bible questions in his shirt pocket.

Moments later, when the guard ushered him into the visiting room and told him which window to occupy, he was pleased to see that his visitor was his previous landlord, Mitchell Bendrick.

Sitting down with a smile that spread from ear to ear, Dane reached through the bars and said, "Mr. Bendrick! What a nice surprise!"

They shook hands, and Bendrick said, "It's good to see you, son."

"How did you know I was in here, sir?"

Bendrick grinned, his eyes twinkling. "Well, my boy, you know what the neighborhood grapevine is like. Slow, maybe, but always sure. The word about your arrest and trial finally got around to Mrs. Bendrick and me. I came as quickly as I could."

"Thank you, sir. It sure is good to see someone from the old neighborhood. So — so — you know why I'm in here."

"I know you were convicted of stabbing an eleven-year-old boy to death and sentenced to life in pr—"

"Mr. Bendrick, I didn't do it!" cut in Dane. "I swear I didn't do it. The killer looks like me, but I'm innocent!"

Bendrick shook his head. His voice was thick with confidence. "Son, I never believed for one moment that you committed that crime. I know you better than that. There's a mistake of some kind, here."

Tears moistened Dane's eyes. "Thank you, sir. It means a lot to me that you don't believe it."

Bendrick let a thin smile curve his mouth. "Maybe one of these days something will happen just the right way, and the guilty party will make a mistake and get himself caught by the law. Then you'll go free."

"I'm sure praying that way, sir."

Bendrick nodded. "Would you like for me to bring your medical books to you?"

"I sure would appreciate it, sir. I would love to have them so I could keep studying them. That way, when this 'something' happens and I get out of here, I can keep working toward my goal of being a doctor. I'm especially eager to read that new book my parents bought me for my birthday."

"Good. I'll bring them to you to-morrow."

"Ah, Mr. Bendrick?"

"Yes?"

"I was told a couple of days ago that I will soon be allowed to go out into the prison yard so I can walk around and get some exercise."

"Mm-hmm."

"I'll need my winter clothes that I left with you."

"Sure. I'll bring them, too."

"All right. Thank you. Ah, I'm curious, sir."

"About what?"

"Have you rented our apartment yet?"

"Yes. I rented it to a family named Atwood. They have a nine-year-old boy named Kenny. But, well, things aren't going too well with the Atwoods. I'm having some problems."

"What do you mean?"

"Leonard Atwood is a heavy drinker. He has a bad temper when he's sober, but boy, oh, boy, it's *really* bad when he's drunk."

Dane nodded. "I've seen men like that before."

"Me too, but Leonard's the worst I've ever seen. 'Nother thing. His wife, Vera, is not well. She has consumption. Vera's not completely bedridden yet, but she's moving in that direction. She still does the cooking, even though she has to spend most of the day lying down. Kenny does the housecleaning for her — you know, the sweeping, mopping, and dusting. He also helps her with the washing and ironing. One of these days she'll have to be put in a sanatorium. I don't know what will happen to poor little Kenny."

"That's too bad," said Dane, shaking his head slowly. "I sure hope this Mr. Atwood doesn't cause you and Mrs. Bendrick any trouble."

"Yeah, me too," said Bendrick, rising to his feet. "Well, Dane, I've got to be going. I'm not sure at this point what time I'll be here tomorrow, but I'll be here."

Dane reached through the bars and shook his hand. "I'll look forward to it, sir. And thank you for coming to see me. It's been real nice talking to you."

"Been my pleasure, son."

"Please tell Mrs. Bendrick hello for me."

"I'll do that. See you tomorrow."

Bendrick turned and walked toward the door behind him, and the guard who waited there opened it and let him through the corridor.

When the door clanked shut, a deep sadness invaded Dane's being. It was good to see his family's old landlord, but it evoked many memories of a time gone by and now lost forever.

The guard who had escorted him to the visiting room stepped up from behind. "Okay, kid. Let's go."

Mentally shaking himself, the young prisoner rose from the chair.

Moments later, Dane stepped into his empty, lonely cell. When the guard turned the key in the lock and walked away, Dane sat down on his bunk and sighed. As he thought back on his conversation with his old landlord, a small stirring of pleasure dispelled some of his sadness. *It's good to know that someone else believes I'm innocent. It'll be great to have my medical books with me. That way I can continue learning. Then when the Lord decides I've been in here long enough and sees that I'm cleared of the murder charge, I'll be even better prepared to get on with my education.*

He picked up Dr. Lee Harris's medical bag from the foot of the bunk, rubbed it lovingly, then lifted his eyes toward heaven.

"Thank You, Lord, for bringing me Mr. Bendrick for a visit. I *will* get out of here someday, and I *will* become a doctor. You knew exactly how to lift my spirits!"

When Mitchell Bendrick arrived at 218 Thirty-third Street and stepped into his apartment, he called out, "Sylvia, I'm home!"

Silence.

"Sylvia! Are you here?"

Silence.

Knowing his wife often visited neighbor women and women in their own apartment building, Mitchell was not concerned. He moved to the closet where Dane's medical books and his winter clothes were kept. "Guess I'd better put these out so I won't forget to keep my promise to that boy tomorrow."

He placed the books and the clothing on a chair nearby, then picked up the day's edition of the *New York Times* from a small table. A bit tired from his long walk to the Hall of Justice and emotionally drained from his visit with Dane Weston, he sat down in his favorite overstuffed chair and immersed himself in the paper.

Moments later, Mitchell heard the door open, and though he was engrossed in an article about crime on Manhattan's streets, he looked up at Sylvia. Having been married to her for many years, he was aware at once of the worried expression on her lovely face.

As she walked toward him, Mitchell folded the newspaper and laid it aside. "What's wrong, sweetheart? You look worried."

Sylvia sighed and sat down in her own favorite overstuffed chair. "I was just up in the Atwood apartment with Vera, darling. She's not doing well at all. About an hour ago, I was walking down the hall on the second floor, and as I was passing the apartment, I heard Vera sobbing. I knocked on the door. When she let me in, I found her with a large purple bruise on her face."

Mitchell's bushy eyebrows arched. "Oh no."

"Oh yes. Vera had been on the sofa, so I made her lie down again, and asked her to tell me about it. She told me that last night, Leonard came home quite late from work. He had stopped at his favorite barroom — as he often does — and was drunk when he entered the apartment. She was lying on the sofa, as usual. He asked why supper wasn't on the table.

"Vera told him that she and Kenny had eaten at the regular time. Since she had no idea when he would come home, she and Kenny did the dishes and cleaned up the kitchen. He told her to get up and cook him a meal. She told him she was too weak to cook another meal; that he would have to make himself a sandwich. He — he jerked her up off the sofa and slapped her face, demanding a hot meal."

Mitchell put a hand to his temple. "Oh no."

"It got rough, all right. Kenny was looking on and rushed to his weeping mother, screaming at his father to leave her alone. This made Leonard even madder, and he knocked Kenny across the room with his fist."

"That low-down —"

"Vera said that this morning, Kenny had a big purple bruise on his face, as well. At breakfast, Vera told Kenny he could stay home from school until the bruise was healed. She didn't want his teacher or anyone else at school to see him looking like that.

"She said at that point, Leonard looked like a madman. He told her Kenny wasn't going to miss school. He could tell anyone who asked about the bruise that he slipped and fell down the stairs here at the tenement. Kenny left for school, and ten minutes later, when Leonard was about to leave for work, Vera was standing beside the sofa, crying, and told him he shouldn't have struck Kenny when all he was trying to do was protect her."

"He's a beast."

"Yes, that he is. With his face beet red, Leonard told Vera Kenny had it coming. He should not have spoken to his father in that tone of voice. When Vera repeated that the boy was only trying to protect his mother, Leonard slapped her again, knocking her to the floor, and stormed out of the apartment."

Mitchell sighed. "It is just so sad that people have to live that way. I'll never understand why some people feel that alcohol will solve their problems, when in reality it creates more problems. I'm sure that when Vera married Leonard, he was a fine, hardworking man. From what I've been able to learn about him, he has just become so jaded and discouraged over the years with having to go from one job after the other to keep bread on the table and a roof over their heads."

Sylvia nodded sadly. "And the drinking just makes him meaner than ever."

Mitchell reached over and clasped both of her hands in his own calloused hands. "I know what you mean, sweetheart."

"I'm so thankful that you have always been such a loving husband and father. I can sympathize only to a point with Vera because I've never had to live with a man who was a drunkard and an abuser." Tears filled her eyes.

"There is nothing so strong as a gentle man."

Mitchell smiled at her, then the smile vanished. "If it were only Leonard, I'd put him out. But that poor sick mother and her child need a home. I know you want to do all you can to help them, honey, but please tread carefully. I don't want you in that man's way when he becomes violent."

"I'll be careful, dear. But I must lend a hand when it's needed."

"Okay, but let me go with you the next time you go up there to visit Vera. Just in case Leonard is home. I may be several years older than Leonard, but I'll protect you with my life."

"I know you would do that, sweetheart," Sylvia said softly, then rose to her feet, bent over, and placed a kiss on Mitchell's cheek.

It was then that Sylvia spotted the books

and clothing on the nearby chair. "Oh! Dane! I'm so overwrought about Vera and Kenny that I forgot where you've been. You got to see him, then?"

"Yes, I did. And I'm as sure as anything that he did not kill that Benny Jackson. Sit back down and let me tell you all about my visit with that precious boy."

# Chapter Twenty

That evening, Vera and Kenny Atwood sat down at the table and began eating the beef stew Vera had prepared for their supper.

Leonard was late, and they both knew it was because he had stopped at the bar to tip the bottle with his drinking pals.

Kenny looked across the table while chewing his food and set adoring eyes on his mother. It hurt him to see her so pale and thin, and it bothered him that the dark circles under her eyes were becoming more pronounced. Worse than that were the purple marks on her cheeks — the result of his father's brutality.

Vera felt Kenny's eyes studying her battered features. She forced a smile. "Honey, don't worry about me. These bruises will heal."

Anger suddenly showed in the nine-year-old's eyes, and it etched deep grooves in his forehead and around his mouth. "I'm sorry that Papa hit you again after I left for school this morning, Mama. If I was a man, I would beat him up real good for all the times he has slapped you around. I'd — I'd pound him so hard, they'd have to haul him off to the hospital."

Vera shook her head. "No, no, Kenny. You should never even think about such a thing. Even though your father is mean at times — especially when he has been drinking — you should never want to harm him."

"I can't stand it when he hurts you. He should never hurt you. If I was bigger, I would stop him, and I would fix him so he could never do it again. You know — like break his arms so he couldn't lift them."

Vera closed her eyes and shook her head vigorously. "No, Kenny, you mustn't think like that!"

"But Mama, you're already sick. He doesn't even care. He just beats on you, anyhow. If I was a man, I would —"

"No more, Kenny! I appreciate your concern for me, but no more talk about what you would do to your father if you were a man. Let's talk about something else."

The conversation went to what was happening at school, and Vera kept him occupied by asking questions about different schoolmates.

When they had finished eating, Vera pushed her chair back and rose weakly to her feet. "I'll keep the stew in the pot, and when your father comes home, he can heat it up himself."

Kenny knew his father would not like being told he had to heat the stew up, but he did not comment. Instead, he left his chair, rounded the table, and took her hand. "Come on, Mama. You're going to lie down on the sofa. I'll take care of the stew, and I'll wash and dry the dishes."

Vera looked down at him and ran fingers through his thick straw-colored hair. "All right, sweetheart. I'll let you."

When Kenny had led his mother to the sofa in the parlor and made sure she was comfortable, he returned to the kitchen.

Some thirty minutes later, he was just finishing his cleanup job when he heard his father enter the apartment. His body stiffened when he heard his father's whiskey-ridden voice thunder, "Get up from there,

Vera! I want my supper!"

Kenny left the kitchen, rage seething in him, and hurried into the parlor. His father was standing unsteadily over the sofa, glaring down at his mother, hands on his hips.

"I told you to get up, woman! I want my supper!"

As Kenny drew up beside the big, muscular man, Vera looked at her son and said, "Leonard, I had Kenny leave the beef stew on the stove in the pot. All you have to do is stoke up the fire in the stove so your stew and your coffee can heat up. The coffee is already in the pot."

Leonard's breathing became heavy. His fury charged the atmosphere in the apartment. "I want you to do it for me! It's your job! Get up and do it, right now!"

Fear was a cold worm in Kenny's stomach. He tensed up, his mouth going dry.

Vera's hands trembled as she sighed and struggled to get off the sofa. She fell to her knees on the floor. When Kenny started to help her, Leonard seized his arm and yanked him back. "Leave her alone! She can get up by herself!"

Kenny's fear intensified.

Vera grasped the edge of the sofa and

struggled to her feet. She staggered a few steps and fell again.

Leonard stood over her, his face bloated in drunken rage. "You ain't foolin' me, Vera! You're fakin' it." With that, he grabbed an arm, jerked her to her feet, and slapped her face.

Kenny's fear became blind wrath. He lunged at his father, pounding him with all his might. "Leave her alone! Stop hurting my mama!"

Leonard's wrath grew hotter. He let Vera fall to the floor, picked Kenny up, and threw him across the room. Kenny howled when his left leg slammed into a small table.

As he lay on the floor, wailing in agony and holding his leg, Leonard stomped to the spot, stood over him, and blared, "Stop that bawlin' and get up!"

Vera rose to her hands and knees, and looked at Kenny as the boy clutched his leg. Blood showed on his pants leg. He attempted to get up, but when he put his weight on his leg, he howled in agony and fell to the floor.

"I told you to get up!" roared Leonard.

Kenny wailed, "I can't, Papa! I can't!"

Vera was so weak; all she could do was crawl to her son. Drawing up to him, she raised her eyes to her husband. "Can't you see he's hurt? There's blood on his pants!"

Leonard watched as Vera told Kenny to let go of his leg so she could pull up his pants leg and look at it. Kenny obeyed and looked on as his mother carefully pulled up the leg of his pants. Her eyes widened when she saw the damage. "Oh, Leonard! We've got to get him to the hospital! His leg is badly broken. There are bone splinters poking through the skin."

The rheumy-eyed Leonard Atwood shook his head stubbornly. "He ain't goin' to no hospital!"

Vera broke into tears, pulled the pants leg down gently, then struggled to her feet. Looking at her husband through the tears, she said, "He's got to have a doctor."

"I said no!"

She staggered toward the door, wincing. "If you won't do it, Leonard, I'm going to tell Mr. Bendrick to find the policemen on this beat and have them take Kenny to the hospital."

Leonard scowled. "Vera, if the police get involved, they'll arrest me for what I did to Kenny. You are not to go out that door!"

Ignoring him, Vera opened the door.

Leonard swore and charged after her, but in his drunken state, he slipped on a throw rug and fell.

Vera stepped into the hall and saw a man and his wife who were occupants of an apartment four doors down. Jack and Lillian Dickson were just coming out of their apartment.

"Jack! Lillian!" cried Vera. "I need your help!"

"What is it, Vera?" called Jack.

"It's Kenny! He's hurt bad!"

The Dicksons hurried toward her.

Inside the Atwood apartment, Leonard was on his unsteady feet, and having heard Vera call to the neighbors, rushed to the open door. Vera was standing just outside the door. When he saw the Dicksons on their way toward Vera, he pushed his way past her, and hurried down the hall toward the rear of the building.

Vera turned and saw him rushing away. "Leonard, come back here!"

Leonard ignored her. When he reached the stairs, he stumbled his way down to the first floor, darted out the back door into the alley, and ran as fast as he could go.

By this time, Mitchell Bendrick had heard the loud voices in the hall on the second floor, and appeared at the top of the front staircase as other tenants were coming out of their apartments. He saw

Jack Dickson with Kenny in his arms, heading toward him with Vera and Lillian at his side.

Mitchell rushed up and met them, and looked at the boy, who was obviously in agony. "What happened?"

"Leonard threw Kenny across the parlor," Jack told him. "His leg is broken."

"Splinters of bone have broken through the skin," spoke up Vera. "We've got to get him to the hospital. Leonard ran away because he knows he'll be in trouble with the police for this."

Mitchell sighed and shook his head. "I'll go find the policemen on this beat and have them get a paddy wagon so we can take Kenny to the hospital. Just go down to the office and tell Sylvia what happened. I'll be back as soon as I can."

At Manhattan's Mercy Hospital, Vera Atwood and the Bendricks were in the waiting room while one of the surgeons and his assistants were examining Kenny in the surgical unit.

Vera was lying down on a couch while Mitchell and Sylvia were trying to comfort and encourage her.

Over an hour had passed since Kenny had been wheeled into the surgical unit on a gurney, when the surgeon, Dr. Robert Latimer, entered the waiting room, a serious look on his face.

Vera struggled to sit up and Mitchell hastily moved to help her. Sylvia placed a pillow at her back.

Dr. Latimer cleared his throat nervously. "Mrs. Atwood, I'm sorry, but the news is not good. Kenny's leg has been shattered from just below the knee, all the way to the ankle. We — we must amputate the leg from that spot down. We need your permission to go ahead with the surgery."

Vera felt like a spike had been driven through her heart. Face pinched, she said, "Doctor, are — are you sure the leg has to be amputated? Is there no other recourse?"

"I'm sorry, Mrs. Atwood, but there is no choice in the matter. In order to save his life, I must remove the leg. Gangrene will set in if I don't, and Kenny will die."

Vera's eyes filled with tears. "He's just a child. He will have to go through the rest of his life on crutches or in a wheelchair." She threw her hands up to her face. "Surely, I'll wake up from this terrible nightmare!"

Sylvia laid a hand on Vera's shoulder. "Honey, at least you will still have your son."

Vera sniffed, took hold of Sylvia's hand, and let the tears run unchecked down her bruised face. She set her wet gaze on the doctor and swallowed hard. "Dr. Latimer, you have my permission to amputate the leg. Could — could I see him before you do the surgery?"

"I'll be glad to take you in, but he is heavily sedated. He won't know you're there."

"I understand, but I still want to see him before — before you do the amputation."

The doctor took Vera's hand and helped her rise to a standing position. He looked at the Bendricks. "I'll bring her back shortly."

"We'll be here, Doctor," said Mitchell.

Dr. Latimer kept a strong arm around Vera as he guided her through the door and they moved slowly down the hall. "Mrs. Atwood, before I sedated Kenny, I could already tell that the amputation was going to be necessary. I told him what I would have to do. He shed some tears, but took it quite well. He told me he understood, and assured me he would learn to use crutches."

Vera nodded. "He's braver than his mother is about it."

They entered the surgical unit and Dr.

Latimer guided her to the operating room where Kenny lay on the table, deeply sedated.

Another surgeon was there, as well as two nurses. They observed in silence as Vera moved up to the operating table, steadied by Dr. Latimer, and looked down at her son. She was thankful that for the moment, he wasn't suffering.

Vera took Kenny's hand in both of her own and bit her lips. She feared what his life might be like, but steeled herself as she said, "Doctor, it's going to be hard to watch him have to adjust to being a cripple. But . . . but at least I'll have him with me."

"Right, ma'am. I can tell Kenny has real grit in him. He will be fine."

Vera kept her gaze on Kenny's motionless face. "Doctor, I don't have the money to pay for this. My husband may never come back. I have no idea how I'm going to —"

"Don't fret yourself about the money, Mrs. Atwood. Kenny's life is at stake. We need to get started right away."

Vera nodded, tenderly ran her fingers over her only child's face, then bent down and kissed each bruise, as if kisses would make then go away. "Mama will be here when you wake up, sweetheart. Be the brave boy you always have been. Mama is here for you. I love you, son, more than anything in this world."

Tears were streaming down her cheeks as the doctor guided her to the door, and when he opened it, Mitchell and Sylvia Bendrick were standing there in the hall.

"We'll take her back to the waiting room, Doctor," said Mitchell.

The doctor smiled. "Thank you."

The Bendricks walked the heartsick mother back down the hall to the waiting room. They settled her onto the couch, and Sylvia covered her shaking form with a blanket she had found in the closet.

Sylvia looked at her husband. "Honey, you stay with her. I'm going to see if I can round up some hot soup and coffee. I'll be right back."

Mitchell noticed the strained look on his wife's dear face. He knew she had to do something to keep herself occupied, and he knew that she believed that food was good medicine.

"I'll stay right here, sweetheart. You just go find this lady some comfort food."

Sylvia gave him a wan smile, under-standing that this man she married so many years ago knew her very well.

It was after midnight when Dr. Robert Latimer came into the waiting room. Vera was now sitting up on the couch with Sylvia beside her. An empty soup bowl and an empty coffee cup sat on the small table beside the couch. Mitchell sat on a chair, facing the women.

The doctor stood over Vera and managed a thin smile. "The amputation went fine, Mrs. Atwood. Kenny's doing fine. You need to understand that the recovery will be slow, but within a few weeks, Kenny will be able to begin learning to walk on crutches. We'll keep him here at the hospital for a couple of weeks and do some therapy as he grows stronger."

Vera nodded. "Thank you for taking such good care of my boy, Doctor. I just don't know how I'm going to pay for this."

"Like I said, don't fret the money. We'll talk about that later. Now let me say this. With Kenny's loss of the leg, it won't be an easy life, but there will be many things that fine boy will be able to accomplish. He's a strong boy, and with your loving care, he will make the necessary adjustments and do just fine."

"I'll give him all the loving care possible,

Doctor. Having his life spared is the greatest blessing. Thank you, again, for what you've done." She took a deep breath. "When will I be able to see Kenny?"

"He should be out from under the anesthetic in a couple of hours. He won't be very clear-minded, but he'll know you and be able to talk some. I assume you'll be back tomorrow."

"Of course."

"All right. Be sure to let me know when you're here. You can tell them at the receptionist desk in the lobby that I told you to find me. They'll see that we connect. Okay?"

"Yes, Doctor."

"You go home now and get some rest. I can tell that you are very tired."

Vera nodded. "Yes. That I am."

"May I ask if you have a physical problem, Mrs. Atwood?"

Vera closed her eyes, bent her head down, then looked back up at him. "Doctor, I have consumption."

"I thought it might be something like that. I'm sure it won't do me any good to tell you to go home right now."

"No. I want to see my boy and talk to him a little bit before I go home."

"I knew that's what you'd say. Well, you go home and get some rest after you talk to Kenny, and I'll see you tomorrow."

When the doctor was gone, Mitchell turned to Vera. "From what he said, I don't know what to think about the hospital bill and his bill. But Vera, Sylvia and I will give you a month's free rent. That's about all we can do."

"That will help a lot, believe me. Thank you both for your generosity."

Some two and a half hours had passed when a nurse came into the waiting room to find Vera wide awake. Mitchell was dozing, and Sylvia was talking to Vera.

Mitchell stirred on his chair when the nurse looked at Vera. "Mrs. Atwood, Kenny is awake now."

Sylvia helped the weary mother to her feet, and Mitchell stood up, rubbing his eyes. "Would it be all right if we come in with her, ma'am?"

"That'll be fine, sir."

Moments later, as the trio moved up beside the bed in the recovery room, Kenny looked up, a bit dull-eyed, but set his gaze on his mother. "Hello, Mama."

Vera bent down and kissed his forehead. "Hello, sweet boy. Dr. Latimer told us the surgery went well."

Kenny nodded.

Vera took hold of his hand. "Honey, do you see who else is here?"

Kenny focused on the two faces. "Oh, sure. Mr. and Mrs. Bendrick. Hi."

Both spoke to him, then Kenny looked around. "Mama, is Papa here?"

"No, honey. He's not here."

"Where is he?"

"I don't know. He ran away from the tenement when I was getting help, and I have no idea where he is."

Kenny squeezed his mother's hand. "I'm sorry for the way Papa treated you."

"It's not your fault, sweetheart. Thank you for trying to protect me. I'm just so sorry that this has happened to you."

He looked up at her tenderly. "I love you, Mama."

"I love you too, son. More than you will ever know."

Suddenly Vera's knees gave way. She made a tiny gasp and slumped to the floor.

Sylvia bent down over her as Mitchell headed for the door, saying he would get a nurse. When he stepped into the hall, there was a nurse just passing by. Mitchell said, "Ma'am, we have a lady in here who just passed out."

The nurse hurried through the door as Mitchell held it open.

It took the nurse only a few seconds to tell that there was something seriously wrong with the unconscious Vera Atwood. She hurried away to get a doctor.

Kenny watched with droopy eyes as the doctor came in, took one look at his mother, and called for two attendants to come with a gurney.

While they waited for the gurney, Mitchell and Sylvia filled the doctor in on the events of the day, and explained that Vera had a serious case of consumption.

The doctor thanked them for the information, and as the attendants hurried away to take Vera to an examining room, the doctor told the Bendricks to wait with Kenny. He would bring word about Mrs. Atwood as soon as he could. With that, he dashed through the door and was gone.

Mitchell and Sylvia sat down on wooden chairs next to Kenny's bed. As hard as the boy tried to stay awake, he finally slipped into a deep sleep, induced partially by the anesthetic that was still in his body.

Almost an hour had passed when the doctor came into the room, and noting that Kenny was asleep, he said, "I'm sorry to tell you folks this, but Mrs. Atwood just died. It was obvious that she was in the clutches of serious fatigue. That combined with the consumption was just too much for her."

Stunned, the Bendricks asked when Kenny would be told about his mother. The doctor assured them that it wouldn't be until the boy was feeling stronger.

"We would like to be here when he is told, Doctor. He'll need someone he knows to help comfort and strengthen him."

"Well, why don't you come back to-morrow afternoon? We'll see how he is by then."

The Bendricks agreed and headed for home. They were worn out from losing the night's sleep, plus the strain that they had suffered. Mitchell told Sylvia he would take the books and clothing to Dane Weston whenever he could after they got up tomorrow.

Late the next morning, the two police officers on the neighborhood beat who had helped Mitchell Bendrick obtain the paddy wagon, came to the tenement and told the Bendricks the police were searching, but had not found Leonard Atwood as yet. They assured him the search would go on.

The officers asked about Kenny and were sad to learn that he had to lose his leg. They were saddened even more when they were told that Vera had died.

Mitchell sighed wearily. "Sylvia and I would love to take Kenny into our home, but we just can't afford it."

One of the officers said, "With the amputation, Mr. Bendrick, Kenny is going to need special attention; something the orphanages wouldn't be able to do, even if they had room for him. All of them are already overcrowded."

Mitchell nodded sadly. "This is going to present a real problem. All I can do is talk to the directors of the orphanages and see if somehow one of them can take the boy in spite of his condition. I'll get on that after I visit a prisoner in the Tombs in the morning, and we go back to the hospital to be with Kenny in the afternoon. We want to be there when he is told about his mother's death."

# Chapter Twenty-one

Late the next morning, a weary Mitchell Bendrick stood at the desk of the chief guard at the Tombs and watched as the man searched through the medical books and the clothing. When he was finished, he looked up and said, "All right, Mr. Bendrick, I'll take these to the guard who will be bringing Dane Weston to see you in the visiting room. I'll send another guard to escort you there."

Some fifteen minutes later, Mitchell was escorted into the visiting room and saw Dane waving to him at window three.

As they were shaking hands through the bars, Dane said, "Thank you so much for bringing my medical books and my clothes, Mr. Bendrick."

"Glad to do it, son."

Dane's brow furrowed as he studied Mitchell's face. "You look tired, Mr. Bendrick. You all right?"

Mitchell nodded. "I am pretty worn out, Dane. Mrs. Bendrick is too. We both had a restless night."

"Some kind of problem at the tenement?"

"Well, yes, in a sense. You will recall that I told you about the Atwood family, who rented your old apartment."

"Yes, sir."

"I told you about Leonard Atwood's drinking problem, and that his wife, Vera, was sick with consumption."

"Yes, sir."

"And I told you they have a nine-year-old boy named Kenny."

"Mm-hmm."

"Well, something terrible happened. Let me tell you about it." Mitchell then told Dane the story. As he listened to the account of young Kenny being thrown across the room by his angry father and of having to have his left leg amputated from the knee down and finally heard of Kenny's mother dying at the hospital, he shook his head sadly.

"How awful, Mr. Bendrick. It's so sad

about Kenny's mother dying and Kenny losing his leg. That poor little boy. So what does his father have to say about all of this?"

"Leonard doesn't even know about Vera dying, nor of Kenny losing his leg. He ran away right after throwing Kenny across the room, knowing he was hurt badly, and hasn't been seen or heard from since. I seriously doubt that Leonard will ever come back. He's got to know the police are ready to charge him with assault and battery for what he did to Kenny."

"What's the poor little guy going to do? Where's he going to live?"

"Well, son, that's a good question. The city's orphanages are terribly overcrowded, and even if they had room for Kenny, I'm wondering if they would want him anyway, with his having so recently had his leg amputated. But I'm going to find out. As soon as I leave here, I'm going to start visiting the orphanages and see what I can do. I'm hoping I can find one orphanage director who will have sympathy about Kenny's plight and take him in spite of the amputation."

Dane's brow furrowed. "I know about the crowded orphanages, Mr. Bendrick, and I realize his being crippled might be a problem, but there's just got to be one orphanage director who will take the little guy in."

Mitchell sighed. "There's another problem too. Somebody's going to have to pay the hospital and surgeon's bills. The surgeon tried to keep Vera from worrying about these bills, but he didn't really offer any solution, either. He just wanted to get the surgery done on Kenny before gangrene set in and told her not to be concerned about the bills."

Dane rubbed his jaw. "I have an idea."

"Yes?"

"I am acquainted with Mr. Charles Loring Brace, the director of the Children's Aid Society."

Mitchell's eyebrows arched. "Oh? The people who send orphans out West and find them homes?"

"Mm-hmm. Even if Mr. Brace knows that nobody out West would take in a crippled child, he at least might keep Kenny at the Society headquarters. They have rooms they keep the children in while they're waiting to put them on the trains."

"Well, it would be worth a try."

"Mr. Bendrick, if anybody can help Kenny, it will be Mr. Brace. Would you go to the Society's headquarters and tell Mr.

Brace I need him to come and see me as soon as possible? I'll explain the whole situation to him and see what he says."

"I'll go there immediately. So, ah, Mr. Brace knows you're in here, I take it."

"Yes, sir. He has visited me. And he doesn't believe I'm guilty of killing Benny Jackson, either."

Mitchell rose to his feet. "Like I said, I'll go there right now and deliver your message to Mr. Brace, or if he's not there, I'll give the message to someone who can pass it on to him."

"Thanks, Mr. Bendrick. And thanks, too, for bringing my books and clothing."

"You're very welcome. Mrs. Bendrick and I are going to the hospital this afternoon. We want to be with Kenny when he is told about his mother's death. He's going to need comfort from someone he knows."

"Sure. I know you'll be able to help him a lot."

"I'll come back as soon as I can to see how it went with Mr. Brace."

Dane returned to his cell, sat down on his bunk, picked up *The History of Medicine*, and started reading where he had left off.

It was midafternoon when Dane was

taken to the visiting room by a guard and found Charles Loring Brace at a barred window, waiting for him.

When they had shaken hands, Dane said, "I assume you got Mr. Bendrick's message."

"Yes, I did. I was gone when he came to my office, but my secretary took the message from him. He didn't give her any details. He told her nothing more than that you were requesting that I come and see you as soon as possible because it was very important."

"That it is, sir. I have a story to tell you."

When Dane finished the Atwood story, Brace was deeply touched by the nine-year-old boy's heartrending situation. Looking at Dane, he said, "Mr. Bendrick is right, Dane. The orphanages are jam-packed. And they would shy away quickly from taking in a boy who had just had his leg amputated, even if they had room. But Kenny is going to be taken care of. There are many wealthy people who back the Children's Aid Society. I will contact a couple of the most generous ones, whom I feel sure will pay the hospital and doctor bills so Kenny can be released from the hospital.

"I will take Kenny into the Society's

headquarters, provide him a bed, food, and clothing, and I will see that he has the proper medical care."

Dane's pulse was skipping from the joy he was feeling. "Oh, thank you, Mr. Brace! I knew you would help Kenny!"

As Brace rose from the chair, he said, "I'll come back some time tomorrow and let you know about the money to pay the hospital and the doctor."

Late that afternoon, Dane was once again escorted to the visiting room and was pleased to see Mitchell Bendrick.

When they sat down, Mitchell told Dane about the graphic moment when the doctor informed Kenny of his mother's death in the Bendricks' presence. As was expected, Kenny took it very hard, but the Bendricks were able to comfort him, at least to a degree. The doctor administered a strong sedative to the boy, which soon put him to sleep, and assured the Bendricks that Kenny would sleep soundly until the next morning. Sylvia was going to be there early in the morning to be at Kenny's side.

Dane was glad to hear this and spoke his appreciation for the kindness the Bendricks were showing to the boy. He then told Mitchell of his visit with Charles Loring Brace, and what Brace had said about how he would raise the money to pay the hospital and doctor's bills, and about taking Kenny into the care of the Society.

Mitchell was very much relieved, and said he would go to the Society's headquarters in the morning and express his gratitude to Mr. Brace for what he was doing for Kenny.

When Charles Loring Brace arrived home that evening, he was late for supper. Being used to it, Letitia hugged him and said, "I put everything on the back burner, sweetheart. So what was it this time?"

While they ate, Brace told his wife Kenny Atwood's story.

They agreed that very, very few prospective foster parents out West would even look twice at a boy with only one leg, who was sitting in a wheelchair, or even standing in line on crutches with the other children.

Letitia sighed. "Even the best families out there on the frontier want a healthy child that can help around the place, and besides that, with Kenny there could be a lot of expense associated with his problem."

Charles nodded as he swallowed. "Right. The only answer to this boy's predicament is for us to keep him at the Society until the Lord does a miracle and provides a home for him."

"I guess that's the way it will have to be, honey."

It was still dark outside the next morning when Charles Loring Brace awakened at the sound of the grandfather clock chiming down the hall. Having lain awake a long time with his mind on little Kenny Atwood, he was still quite sleepy, but he lay there and counted the chimes.

It was five o'clock.

Suddenly, he sat bolt upright in the bed. "Thank You, Lord! Thank You!"

Letitia raised her head from the pillow, looked at him, and murmured sleepily, "Honey, what are you thanking the Lord for?"

"Sweetheart, the Lord just gave me the answer."

"The answer to what?"

"Kenny Atwood's predicament! I believe the Lord has His miracle ready!"

"Wha' you mean?"

"I'll tell you when you're wide awake," said Charles, getting out of the bed. "Go back to sleep. I'll tell you later."

"Okay." Letitia was soon asleep.

It was nearing midmorning that same day when Dane Weston sat down at a window in the visiting room and looked at the beaming features of Charles Loring Brace.

"Something tells me you have good news, sir," said Dane.

"I sure do! I went to the hospital first thing this morning and met Kenny. Mrs. Bendrick was there with him. Dane, he is a precious little boy. He has such a sweet way about him. Mrs. Bendrick has been a tremendous help to him in the loss of his mother. After spending about twenty minutes with Kenny, I went to the office and asked for the amount of the surgeon's bill and the hospital bill up to this point. They could only estimate what the total would be when Kenny is finally released, but when I had the figures, I went directly to the two wealthy friends I told you about, and they are going to cover both bills totally!"

"Wonderful!"

"On my way back to Society headquarters, I stopped by your old apartment and shared the news with Mr. Bendrick. He was elated."

Dane grinned, nodding.

"So, Dane," said Brace, "my wife and I will pick Kenny up when he is released from the hospital in some twelve or thirteen days and take him to the Society's headquarters. We'll keep him there until he is able to travel, then we'll put him on an orphan train."

Dane blinked and frowned. "But Mr. Brace, who in the world would take in a boy in Kenny's condition?"

"I gave this a great deal of prayer and thought before getting to sleep last night, and the Lord woke me up and gave me the answer at five o'clock this morning."

"Well, what is it?"

"There is a fine Christian couple in Denver, Colorado, named Mike and Julie Ross. He is a prominent attorney there and is quite well-off financially. They have devoted their lives and finances to adopting *only* handicapped children. They told me from the beginning that they felt the Lord would have them adopt five eventually. They already have three that we have sent them, and the fourth child — a thirteen-year-old blind girl — right now is on the most recent orphan train we sent that way.

"Kenny, if they agree to take him — and I feel certain they will — will make number five. It's perfect!"

"It sure sounds good to me, sir."

"Leanne Ladd is the blind girl's name. She will arrive in Denver on Friday, November 10. Kenny won't be able to travel until probably sometime in January. That will give the Rosses a couple of months to adjust to Leanne before Kenny would arrive. Like I said, it's perfect."

Dane frowned. "But, sir, what if the Rosses decide that taking in two handicapped children that close together is too much for them?"

"Well, son, I stopped at the telegraph office on my way over here and sent a wire to them. I expect a reply from them yet today. Unless I really miss my guess, Kenny Atwood has a brand new loving family and home waiting for him."

"I sure hope it works out, sir."

"I'm sure it will. I tell you, Dane, that little guy has already crept down into my heart. He is so young to face so many life-changing tragedies, and it just makes me glad to know kindhearted people like the Rosses. They will give Kenny the best care possible. He'll grow up in a solid Christian home, and I have no doubt that he will be successful in whatever he chooses to do with his life."

"This is encouraging, Mr. Brace. This kind of thing gives one hope, doesn't it?"

"Sure does."

"And we all need hope in order to carry on from day to day in our lives. I was reading my Bible this morning, and one verse jumped off the page at me. Psalm 146:5. I memorized it right then and there. 'Happy is he that hath the God of Jacob for his help, whose hope is in the LORD his God.' My every hope is in my Saviour, Mr. Brace, and in *His* time, I know I will be set free from this prison. But in the meantime, I'm so thankful that my soul has been set free from the bondage of sin because of my faith in the Lord Jesus Christ."

"Amen to that, son," said Brace, rising from the chair. "I must go now. I'll be back to let you know how it all goes here in the next several days."

"I'll look forward to it, sir. I sure hope that someday I will get to meet Kenny."

Brace smiled. "I'll do my best to see that it happens."

On Thursday morning, November 9, the orphan train pulled into Topeka, Kansas, the first stop where the orphans were lined up in the depot to be looked over by prospective foster parents.

While this was going on, nurse Millie Voss had Leanne Ladd standing with her nearby. Leanne listened closely to the conversations between prospective foster parents and orphans, and prayed silently that the Lord would not let anyone take Tharyn Myers before they got to Denver. She begged Him to see that someone in Denver chose Tharyn so they could be close to each other and grow up together.

Leanne sighed with relief when Millie told her that six children had been chosen. Tharyn's name was not among them. However, Tharyn's good friend Melinda Scott was one of the six. Leanne listened as Tharyn and Melinda shared a tearful good-bye.

The rest of the orphans boarded their coaches again, and as the train pulled out of Topeka, Tharyn was sitting with Leanne and had an arm around her. They prayed together once more that the Lord would cause a family in Denver to choose Tharyn.

The train stopped in Salina, Kansas, and three children were chosen there. The next stop was Hays, Kansas, and four more were chosen, including Nettie Olson. Tears filled Nettie's eyes as she told her friends good-bye.

At Oakley, Kansas, Millie Voss had Leanne beside her near the line and explained what was happening. A couple showed definite interest in Tharyn Myers and Bessie Evans.

Leanne was tense as she heard the couple explain to the girls that they could only take one of them into their home, and while they were trying to decide between Tharyn and Bessie, Leanne began to pray in a whisper. She was begging God to make them take Bessie.

Millie learned from what she was hearing that Tharyn and Leanne had been praying together that Tharyn would end up in Denver, too. Because of the blind girl's heartfelt plea to the Lord, Millie prayed silently, asking Him to grant the desires of the two girls.

At that moment the couple decided to take Bessie, and when Leanne heard the husband say this to one of the Society sponsors, she had to quickly clamp a hand over her mouth to keep from shouting for joy.

Millie put an arm around Leanne and said in a low voice, "Honey, I wish you could see the relief written all over Tharyn's face!"

Leanne clasped her hands together and

whispered, "Thank You, Lord Jesus! Thank You!"

The girls in the line wished Bessie their best, and tears were shed as they said their good-byes.

The next stop was in Burlington, Colorado, at sundown. Billy Johnson and one teenage girl were chosen. When the orphans were about to board the train again, Russell Mims came to Tharyn, saying he hoped they would both be chosen in the same town. He wanted to marry her someday.

Tharyn smiled. "Russell, if God wants us for each other, He will work it out."

It was dark in Limon, Colorado, when the train arrived there, where it would remain for the night. Prospective foster parents would be looking the orphans over in the morning before it pulled out for Denver.

In the girls' coach, Tharyn and Leanne made themselves as comfortable as possible for the night on their seat. Before going to sleep, they prayed together, asking the Lord once more to cause a family in Denver to choose Tharyn.

Tharyn had told Leanne all about Dane back in the Manhattan prison, and they prayed for him, asking God to clear him of the murder and set him free.

The girls were feeling the tension of the moment. Tomorrow, the train would stop in Denver and Leanne's new parents would be waiting to take her home. If the Lord should have reason to place Tharyn with some family down the line in spite of their prayers, they realized this would be their last night together.

They stayed awake, whispering long into the night. Finally, from sheer exhaustion, Leanne dropped off to sleep with her head in Tharyn's lap, and Tharyn fell asleep, her head leaning against the frosty window.

When Millie Voss came through the coach, checking on the girls, she stopped several times and pulled blankets up around their necks, attempting to keep them warm and comfortable. A low-burning lantern in the coach cast eerie shadows over the sleeping girls.

As Millie approached the seat where Tharyn and Leanne were sleeping, she carefully pulled Tharyn's head far enough away from the cold window to place a pillow under her head. She also tucked Tharyn's blanket firmly under her chin.

Tharyn stirred, but did not awaken.

Millie then leaned down to check on

Leanne. She saw that the girl's eyes were open. "What's the matter, Leanne? Can't you get to sleep?"

Leanne pointed her face up toward the nurse and whispered, "I guess I'm too excited to sleep, Miss Voss. Tomorrow will open a whole new world for me. I hope I'm not a disappointment to those good people who are planning to adopt me. It's — well, it's really kind of scary."

Millie patted her cheek. "I'm sure it is, but I really don't think you have anything to be worried about. From what Mr. Brace has told me about the Rosses, they are a very special, loving family. I'm sure you won't be a disappointment to them. They'll have room in their loving hearts for you, too."

"I'm sure you're right, ma'am. It's just that — well, it seems almost too good to be true, that someone would really want to take a blind girl into their home."

"It's not too good to be true, believe me. You'll see what I mean when you meet the Rosses."

"Thank you, Miss Voss," said Leanne, trying to stifle a yawn. "You've relieved me of some of my fears. I think I can sleep now."

"Good."

Millie tucked Leanne's blanket up close to her chin. She thought of suggesting that Leanne move to one of the empty seats vacated by the girls who had been chosen, but she refrained. She knew that Leanne found a certain comfort sleeping with her head on Tharyn's lap.

Millie started to say something else, but saw that Leanne's eyes were closed and she was breathing evenly. She stroked her hair. "Sleep well, little lamb. Your Shepherd is watching over you."

With that, the nurse turned and moved down the aisle. She found her own resting place at the rear of the coach and eased onto the seat. A satisfied smile played across her face as she rested her head on a pillow against the back of the seat and closed her tired eyes.

Chief U.S. Marshal John Brockman and his wife, Breanna, had a six-acre tract of land in the country some four miles southwest of Denver, and at the same time the orphan train was pulling into Limon that evening, the Brockmans and their neighbors, David and Kitty Tabor, were finishing a delicious supper that Breanna had prepared.

David and Kitty — who were in their

midforties — had talked to John and Breanna at church the past several Sundays about their plan to take a teenage orphan off the next orphan train. The Tabors had not been able to have children and wanted one so very much. They felt at their age, they should choose a child in his or her teens.

All along, John and Breanna had agreed that this was wise thinking. John had brought up some weeks back that since David had recently been promoted to vice-president of Denver's First National Bank, whatever child they chose would have a secure future financially.

As they left the table and went into the parlor, the Tabors talked about the orphan train that was to arrive tomorrow morning and how excited they were about the child they were going to take into their home and adopt in the near future.

Breanna brought up how excited Mike and Julie Ross were about the thirteen-year-old blind girl who would be on the train.

John smiled and said, "And bless their hearts, they plan yet to adopt a fifth handicapped child."

Everyone agreed that the Rosses were special people. Most couples who were looking to adopt a child would shy away from a handicapped one.

Breanna ran her gaze over the faces of David and Kitty. "I'm taking tomorrow off from the clinic so I can stay with the three Ross children while Mike and Julie go to Union Station to pick up Leanne Ladd."

Before the Tabors headed for their nearby home, the four of them had prayer together, asking the Lord to direct David and Kitty to the child He wanted them to adopt.

As the Tabors rode side by side in their buggy, heading home in the moonlight, David put his arm around Kitty and pulled her close to him. "Just think, honey, the Lord willing, this will be our last night alone in our big rambling house for many years to come."

"That's right, sweetheart. Won't it be wonderful to have a child to love and care for? I'm so excited I can hardly breathe!"

David chuckled. "Well, you'd better keep breathing, 'cause I don't want to raise a child by myself."

Kitty giggled. "Oh, don't you worry, dear husband. I'll be right here with you all the way."

As the train was pulling into Denver's

Union Station the next morning, the children in both coaches were singing the little song they called "Where Fragrant Breezes Sigh."

After the prospective foster parents had been cleared by the Children's Aid Society sponsors, the orphans lined up.

Mike and Julie Ross, who had already been cleared and approved by Charles Loring Brace, approached Mark Newton with the most recent letter from Brace.

Mark looked at the letter, smiled, and said, "I'm so happy to meet you folks! Come with me. Your new daughter is right down near the end of the line with our nurse."

Butterflies were flitting in Julie's stomach and Mike's heart was pounding a rapid tattoo against his ribs as they spotted the white uniform of the nurse and made their way toward the girl who stood at her side.

"Oh, Mike," whispered Julie, "she's so pretty!"

"That she is, honey. Pretty as a picture!"

"Isn't she precious? Even though her eyes can't see, she seems very much aware of all that's happening. The nurse is looking at us and telling her we're coming."

"Yes! And look at that smile! You would never know she was blind. The Lord has blessed us so marvelously."

Mark smiled and said, "Here they are, Leanne! Your new parents!"

Leanne's eyes were sparkling behind a dewy mist as she opened her arms and said with emotion tightening her throat, "Oh, Mama! Papa!"

They instantly stepped into a three-way embrace and clung to each other with tears moistening all three faces.

When Julie found a modicum of composure, she spoke with her voice full of joyful tears. "Oh, Leanne, we are so happy to have you as part of our family! Welcome, darling, welcome!"

Mike swallowed tears. "Yes, precious Leanne, welcome to the Ross family! We love you very much already!"

"Thank you, Mama and Papa!" said Leanne, almost squealing with delight. "I love you too, and I've been so excited to meet you!"

The trio stood close together while Mark and Millie stood looking on. After they had talked for a few minutes in an attempt to get acquainted, Leanne said, "Mama, Papa, before we go, I need to say good-bye to my best friend in all the world. She's an orphan too. Her name is Tharyn Myers."

Mark Newton spoke up. "Leanne,

Tharyn is being interviewed at the moment by prospective foster parents, but I'll lead the three of you there and interrupt the conversation long enough for you to tell her good-bye."

Leanne nodded. "All right, Mr. Newton. Thank you."

Mike and Julie looked at each other, smiling while Millie Voss hugged Leanne, telling her good-bye. Millie congratulated the Rosses, then hurried away.

Mike and Julie each put an arm around Leanne, and as Mark Newton led them down the line toward the spot where Tharyn was being interviewed, Mike said, "Julie and I know this couple who are talking to Tharyn. David and Kitty Tabor. They belong to the same church we do, and we are close friends."

Leanne's heart began pounding like a trip-hammer.

As they drew up, David Tabor smiled at Mark Newton. "Kitty and I were about to call for one of the sponsors. We want to take Tharyn home with us."

At these words, Leanne's heart lurched in her chest. It lurched again when she heard Tharyn say, "I want to live with Mr. and Mrs. Tabor, Mr. Newton."

"Oh, Tharyn!" squeaked Leanne. "God

answered our prayers!"

The two girls were instantly in each other's arms.

When their emotions had settled some, Tharyn told the adults how the two of them had prayed earnestly that the Lord would have a family in Denver choose her so they could grow up together.

Leanne leaned close to Tharyn. "Honey, my parents and yours go to the same church! We'll really be close."

Tharyn and Leanne embraced again, weeping happily while praising the Lord for answering their prayers so marvelously.

While the rejoicing was going on, Mike leaned down and whispered in Julie's ear, "And just think, sweetheart, in January, we'll have number five! Kenny Atwood will be here with us then!"

Julie's face beamed. "Yes, darling."

Russell Mims had been observing while in the line nearby. He stepped up to Tharyn and took hold of her hand. "I'm so glad for you and Leanne, both. Even though I'll be living somewhere else in this Wild West, I want to keep in touch with you . . . and you know why."

Tharyn smiled at him while holding Leanne's hand. "Yes, I know why, Russell." She turned to the Tabors and asked if they could write their address down on a piece of paper so she could give it to her friend, Russell, so he could write to her whenever he was chosen.

David wrote the address on a slip of paper and gave it to Russell. The boy asked Tharyn if he could give her a hug before she left, and she told him he could. Russell had tears in his eyes after he had hugged Tharyn and watched her walk out of the depot with her new parents, the Rosses, and Leanne.

In the parking lot, the Tabors and the Rosses climbed in separate buggies, saying they would see each other soon, and each drove its own direction.

In the Ross buggy, Leanne sat between her new parents. As they drove out of the depot and moved down the street, Julie described the surroundings as Tharyn had done on the trip. Leanne asked about the Rocky Mountains and Julie described their towering, snowcapped peaks as they touched the azure Colorado sky to the west.

Julie squeezed her hand. "Soon you'll be familiar with all of it, sweetheart, and any time you have a question about anything, there are enough Rosses around to give you an answer. I know Mr. Brace has already told you that you have a brother and two sisters at home."

"Yes, ma'am. It will be very nice living in a house with loving people. How can I ever thank you for taking me in?"

"No thanks are necessary, sweetie," said Mike. "You are a blessing from the Lord, and an answer to our prayers."

"That's very kind of you, Papa. I hope I'm *always* a blessing. Even though I'm blind, I can still do any number of things very well. I always want to do my part and never be a burden."

Mike patted her hand. "Neither you nor any of the other three children we have adopted will ever be a burden. We'll tell you more about it later, but there is a fifth one coming. His name is Kenny, and he'll be here sometime in January. Kenny recently had to have one of his legs amputated. He is nine years old."

Leanne's face pinched. "Oh."

Julie squeezed Leanne close. "Honey, God has blessed us with the marvelous privilege of bringing all five of you into our home. We're just so thankful for each one of you."

Leanne sat quietly thinking over what her new parents had just said, and a sweet sense of well-being wrapped its arms around her.

# Chapter Twenty-two

On Tuesday, November 14 it was a cold, cloudy day in New York City.

Officers James Thornton and Fred Collins were walking their beat as usual and were talking about an arrest they had made earlier that day, when they had caught a man who had put a gun on an elderly street vendor and had taken his money.

As they moved down the busy sidewalk, they spoke to people they met along the way.

There was a gap in the crowd ahead of them on the sidewalk for a moment, and as they were talking, the officers saw a dark-haired teenage boy coming toward them.

He was wearing a heavy coat with the collar turned up.

As they drew closer to the boy, Officer Thornton focused on his face. His eyes widened as he said, "Fred, that's Dane Weston. How did he get out of prison?"

"I don't know," replied Collins, fixing his gaze on the boy, "but if he'd been released, we'd know about it. Let's get him!"

Both officers darted toward the teenager, and when he saw them coming, he pivoted quickly and ran toward the nearest alley.

Both men drew their revolvers, and Thornton shouted, "Stop!"

The boy kept running, looking over his shoulder. Suddenly, as he drew up to the alley he pulled a revolver from his coat. Just before entering the alley, he fired off a shot at the officers.

The officers leaped aside and the bullet chewed into a light pole, scattering splinters. When Thornton and Collins had gained their balance, the boy had vanished.

"C'mon!" gusted Thornton. "Let's get him!"

When they rounded the corner of the building closest to them at the end of the alley, they saw the boy halfway down the alley, trying to get the back door of a building open.

"Stop right there!" Collins said.

The youth's head whipped around and he raised his gun, pointing it at the oncoming policemen.

Thornton took aim. "Freeze, Weston! Drop that gun!"

The boy fired at them again and the bullet hissed between them, striking a metal trash receptacle. Collins fired back. The slug struck the boy in the right shoulder. Thornton was just about to squeeze his trigger, but refrained when the boy went down, his gun falling from his grasp.

In spite of the bullet in his shoulder, the boy started to pick up his gun as the officers were running toward him. Thornton shouted, "Don't do it, Weston, or I'll have to shoot you! Get your hand away from the gun and put your head down!"

The boy was on his stomach. He pulled his shaky hand away from the gun and dropped his face low toward the ground.

Collins dropped to his knees, handcuffs in hand, pulled both hands behind his back and snapped on the cuffs while Thornton stood over him, holding his gun on him.

Blood was seeping through the bullet hole in the boy's coat.

"Okay, Weston!" said Collins, grasping

his other shoulder and turning him over. "You just about got yourself kill—"

The eyes of both officers widened as they focused on the wounded youth's face.

"Hey, you're not Dane Weston!" Collins said.

"But you sure look like him."

The officers looked at each other as Thornton picked up the boy's gun. Suddenly they both knew that this had to be the teenager who stabbed Benny Jackson to death. Dane had been telling the truth.

Collins hoisted the youth to his feet.

"Okay, kid," said Thornton. "What's your name?"

The boy was obviously in a great deal of pain, but still he jutted his jaw and gave Thornton a defiant glare. "I ain't tellin' you my name."

Thornton gave him an icy stare. "We'll see about that. Right now, we've got to get you to the hospital and get that wound taken care of."

They went to the street, hailed a paddy wagon that was passing by, and took the boy to Mercy Hospital. The slug was removed by the doctors and when the boy had come out from under the anesthetic, he was put in a private room, and cuffed to the iron bedstead even though he was still quite drowsy.

When Collins had snapped the cuffs in place while a nurse stood looking on, Thornton said, "You stay with him, Fred. I'm going to headquarters and get permission from the chief to bring the three witnesses who testified at Dane Weston's trial. I want them to look at this guy. He was carrying a gun illegally and no doubt has a criminal record."

"I'll wait right here, partner."

Nearly two hours had passed when Officer Fred Collins was still attempting to get the dark-haired youth to tell him his name. His mouth was clamped shut and a stubborn look was in his eyes.

The nurse came in, followed by Chief of Police William Yarrow, Officer James Thornton, and the man and two women who had testified at Dane Weston's trial, identifying him under oath as Benny Jackson's killer.

Collins stood up and shoved the chair to the side so the chief and the others could move up close to the wounded teenager.

Yarrow took one look at the boy and shook his head. He turned to the man and the women. "Take a look at him."

All three gasped in unison as they stepped up and focused on the face of the dark-haired boy.

"Oh my," said the tall, gray-haired man as he studied the boy through his thick spectacles. "Ladies, we have made a terrible mistake. This definitely is Benny Jackson's killer. It wasn't Dane Weston."

The older of the two said, "Oh, dear. We did make a mistake. This is indeed the young man we saw stab Benny."

The other woman nodded. "You're right. It is, indeed."

The wounded teenager glared at them, his lips pressed into a pencil-thin line.

"Are you absolutely sure?" Officer James Thornton said. "You were so certain before that it was Dane Weston you had seen stab Benny Jackson."

The gray-haired man cleared his throat nervously. "I know, and there are many similarities, as you can see. But I'm absolutely positive that this is Benny's killer."

The chief moved up close. "Then I'm going to make sure that justice is done speedily. Dane Weston was wrongfully convicted of a crime he didn't commit, just like he kept telling us." He looked the boy in the eye. "I want to know your name and where you live."

The stubborn look on the wounded teenager's face grew more defiant. "I ain't tellin' you."

"I'll eventually find out anyway, kid. If you don't tell me now, it'll go harder on you if I have to do it that way. I'll see that you're locked up in the Tombs until I learn who you are and if you have a criminal record."

"I said I ain't tellin' you."

Yarrow turned to Thornton. "I want a police photographer brought here right away. Once we have this kid's picture, we'll be able to identify him if he has a criminal record."

"I'll go get one right away, Chief."

Two days later, the low, dark clouds that had been threatening to deliver a storm finally lived up to their promise.

Dane Weston stood at the window in his cell and looked out at the fat snowflakes that were moving swiftly past him, driven by a stiff wind. The ground below was already covered with a white blanket. The clouds overhead looked as bleak as he felt.

Dane heard footsteps in the corridor and turned to see a guard draw up to his cell door. "Dane, Superintendent Thaxton wants to see you in his office."

"Oh?" said Dane, moving to the barred door as the guard turned his key in the lock and swung it open. "What's he want to see me about?"

"I don't know. I was just told to come and get you."

Dane looked puzzled. "Okay. Let's go."

Moments later, the guard ushered Dane into the office of Roger Thaxton, who sat behind his desk. Dane was stunned to see Police Chief William Yarrow, Officers James Thornton and Fred Collins, and the three witnesses who had identified him in court as Benny Jackson's killer. They were sitting on chairs in a semicircle.

Chief Yarrow stepped up to him. "Dane, I have a story to tell you. Come. Sit down."

Every eye was on the young man as he sat on a chair next to the police chief, looking puzzled.

Chief Yarrow told Dane of the incident two days previously when Officers Thornton and Collins were fired upon by a teenage boy whom they shot in the shoulder and took into custody.

Dane's heart was thumping in his chest. Had the Lord answered his prayer? Was this boy the one who had stabbed Benny Jackson?

Yarrow then reached into a brown envelope and took out a photograph. At first glance, Dane saw that it was taken in a hospital room. The dark-haired boy lay in bed.

Yarrow placed the photograph in Dane's hand. "This is the boy Officers Thornton and Collins shot. And these people who had identified you as Benny Jackon's killer all agree that it was not you. It was this boy in the photograph."

Dane's pulse throbbed and the expression on his face was a tangle of relief and excitement. He ran his gaze to the faces of the witnesses, then eyed the photograph closely. "He — he really does look a lot like me, doesn't he?"

"That he does," said the chief, "and I think you can see why these people thought you were him."

Dane nodded.

"The boy's name is Monte Smalz, Dane. He's sixteen. He was convicted of murdering a ten-year-old boy in the Bronx two years ago and was sentenced to life imprisonment at the New York State Prison known as Sing Sing at Ossining, New York. He managed to slip out of Sing Sing on a grocery delivery wagon about a month before he killed Benny Jackson. Benny was also from the Bronx and had done something to infuriate Monte before Monte was arrested and sent to Sing Sing. He tracked Benny down with the express purpose of killing him. We know this for sure now, because Monte broke down and confessed it all. He is going back to Sing Sing in a few more days."

Dane handed Yarrow the photograph, and saw that the chief had taken something else out of the brown envelope. It was an official-looking letter.

Yarrow placed the letter in Dane's hand. "This is a letter of apology for this miscarriage of justice. As you can see, it is signed by Judge Hector B. Rigby and me."

As Dane ran his eyes along the lines of the letter, which expressed the deep regret for the miscarriage of justice and a sincere apology, his heart pounded in his chest. In his heart, he was praising the Lord for answered prayer.

The three witnesses then spoke up one at a time and sincerely apologized for their error, asking his forgiveness.

Dane smiled at them. "You are forgiven. You were only doing what you thought was right."

Chief Yarrow laid a hand on the boy's shoulder. "Well, Dane, you're now free to go. No more prison cells for you."

Dane shook his head in wonderment. "I hear what you're saying, sir, but all of this is so sudden. I'm having a hard time grasping that this is really happening. I'm really free to go? No strings attached?"

Yarrow chuckled. "No strings attached."

"Yes, my boy," said the prison superintendent, rising to his feet behind the desk and moving around it. He extended his hand.

"You are free to go, no strings attached."

Dane stood up and clasped his hand. A smile as bright as sunshine on snow broke over his young face. *Thank You, Lord,* he said in his heart. *Thank You! In Your own time, justice was done!*

Officers Thornton and Collins moved up to Dane and apologized for being so rough with him the day they put him under arrest. Dane shook their hands, saying they were only doing their duty. After all, he had been identified by three credible witnesses as Benny Jackson's killer.

After thanking Chief Yarrow for seeing that he was cleared of the crime, Dane went back to the cell that had been his home for too long already. He gathered up his medical books and the medical bag given to him by Dr. Lee Harris, in which he stuffed what little clothing he had, then wearing his winter clothes and his coat, he was led by a guard to the door of the Tombs building.

Another guard was waiting outside to escort him across the prison yard to the main gate. Clutching his few belongings, Dane turned his face to the sky. Snowflakes landed on his cheeks and clung to his eyelashes.

When he stepped through the gate onto the street in front of the Hall of Justice, tears of relief and gratitude formed in his eyes. "Lord," he said, his gaze still pointed skyward, "even in my darkest hours, You were always with me, bringing me a ray of hope through Your precious Word. I memorized another wonderful Scripture just this morning. It means so much to me, Father. Psalm 9:9–10. 'The LORD also will be a refuge for the oppressed, a refuge in times of trouble. And they that know thy name will put their trust in thee: for thou, LORD, hast not forsaken them that seek thee.' Thank You, dear Lord, that You are ever faithful."

Since all of his friends in the alley were gone and he had nowhere to call home, Dane decided to go to the Children's Aid Society and ask Mr. Brace if he would put him on an orphan train so he could find a home out West where fragrant breezes sigh.

Drawing a hand across his face, Dane dried the lingering tears, squared his shoulders, and without a backward glance, walked down the street whistling a nameless happy tune that was coming straight from his heart.

At Children's Aid Society headquarters, Charles Loring Brace looked up as Myra Hinson opened his office door. "Sir, there is a young man out here who wants to see you. I believe you're going to be surprised but pleased when you see who it is. You've been telling me a lot about him the past several weeks."

Brace's brow furrowed. "A young man I've been telling you about?"

Myra smiled. "Mm-hmm."

Brace put a hand to his forehead. "I'm not sure who you're referring to."

Myra turned around and motioned to the person standing in the hall. "Come on in, young man."

Brace stood up behind his desk. When he saw Dane Weston, his jaw slacked and he stood transfixed, mouth agape and wide-eyed.

Dane smiled at the Society's director as

Myra gestured for him to go on in. "Hello, Mr. Brace. God did His miracle. The real killer was caught, and as you can see, I've been released."

A smile broke over Brace's slender features. He moved around the desk as Myra looked on and wrapped his arms around the boy. When he had hugged him, he gripped his upper arms and said, "Dane, this is wonderful!" He gestured toward a sofa that stood against one wall. "Sit down here and tell me about it. Myra, come over here and sit beside him and listen, too. I'll sit on this chair. Dane I've told Myra all about you, and I've kept her up with how it's been going for you."

"Yes, sir. She told me that when I came in." When all three were seated, Dane said, "I left my medical books and other things in Miss Hinson's office, but I brought this in with me so you could see it."

Brace and his secretary took note of the official-looking letter the boy held in his hand. Extending the letter to Brace, he said, "It's a letter of apology from the judge and the chief of police. Take a look at it."

Brace took the letter, read it, and smiling, handed it to his secretary. "Myra, I told you after I first visited this boy in the prison that I believed him when he told me he was innocent."

"You sure did, sir," she said, then began reading the brief letter. When she finished it, she handed it to Dane. "I'm so glad you were cleared of the crime."

Dane smiled. "Thank you, ma'am." Then to Brace he said, "Sir, I came here for two reasons. The first is to let you know that I am free, and the other, to ask if you would put me on an orphan train so I can find a home out West."

"Of course I will, son. I can put you on a train next week."

"Oh, that will be great, sir!"

Brace stood up. "Right now, I want you to meet that special little boy who knows what you did for him by contacting me about taking him in here at the Society."

Dane's face lit up. "Kenny! Oh yes! I want to meet him."

Myra said she would go get Kenny. Charles explained some things to Dane about the Society's sponsors who traveled with the children on the orphan trains and how the prospective foster parents were made aware when they would arrive in the railroad stations across the West.

Some ten minutes had passed when they heard Myra talking excitedly.

Dane's pulse quickened. He stood up from the sofa and fixed his gaze on the open door. When Myra came through the door pushing the wheelchair, Dane smiled at the little boy and hurried to him.

It was Kenny who spoke first. "Hi, Dane! Miss Hinson told me you got out of prison, and you came here to ride one of the trains." With that, he lifted up his arms toward the dark-haired teenager.

Dane smiled, bent over, and hugged the boy. "I told Mr. Brace I wanted to meet you, Kenny. And the Lord made it possible!"

When they released each other, Kenny looked up into Dane's eyes. "Thank you for sending Mr. Brace to me. Did he tell you that as soon as I get better he is going to send me to Denver, Colorado, to be adopted by a Christian family named Ross?"

"No, I didn't, Kenny," spoke up Brace. "I wanted to let you tell him. Kenny's father has never been located," he said to Dane.

Dane nodded. "So you already have a family in Denver who have agreed to take him?"

"Yes. Mike Ross is a successful attorney in Denver. He and his wife, Julie, have already taken four handicapped children from the Society, and have wanted one more. I wired the Rosses several days ago and told them about Kenny. They wired right back, saying they would take him."

Dane patted the boy's head. "Kenny, I'm so glad for you." He turned to Brace. "Do you have any idea when Kenny will be able to travel?"

"The Society's doctor has told me that Kenny should be ready to travel by January 1. So I have scheduled him on an orphan train that will be leaving Grand Central Station on Wednesday, January 3."

"I see. Sir, will Kenny still be in a wheelchair when it is time for him to travel?"

"Yes, he will. The doctor said he shouldn't try to begin using crutches until next spring."

"Will there be someone on the train to take care of him on the trip?"

"Well, there is always a Society nurse on board, but we will have to have one of the teenage boys look after him in the boys' coach."

Dane laid a hand on Kenny's shoulder. "Mr. Brace, if it's all right with you, I would like to delay my departure until Kenny is ready to travel. I'd like to be his companion."

Myra smiled and looked at Brace.

Brace laughed. "It doesn't surprise me. You're sure this is what you want to do, Dane? It'll mean that you'll be almost six weeks later leaving for the West."

Dane looked down at Kenny's adoring face. The little boy's eyes were fixed on him. "I'm absolutely sure, sir. God has been so good to me. I want to share my blessings with Kenny."

"That's fine with me, Dane. I'll make a place here for you to stay until your train leaves."

"Oh, thank you, sir. That way Kenny and I can get better acquainted, and I'll be very glad to do any work around here that you need done."

"Well, we will probably take you up on the offer, son. There always seems to be plenty of work to do around here."

"It will be my pleasure, Mr. Brace. You have no idea how happy I am to be here and out of that prison."

"I guess I'd have to experience it to really know, son, but I'm awfully happy for you, and I'm so glad we'll have you around here for a few weeks."

"Thank you. I was just thinking, if someone should choose me at one of the depots before we get to Denver, the sponsors will see that another teenage boy takes care of Kenny for the rest of his journey, won't they?"

"I'll see that they are prepared to do that, Dane, but I need to explain something about this particular trip. The train you and Kenny will be on doesn't go to Denver. It will arrive in Cheyenne, Wyoming, on Tuesday, January 9. The Rosses already know about this. They will take a train from Denver to Cheyenne to pick Kenny up. There will not be another orphan train into Denver until January 25. When I explained this to the Rosses in my wire, they replied back that they wanted Kenny as soon as possible, so they will go to Cheyenne to pick him up."

Kenny looked up at Dane. "Even if you get chosen before I get to Cheyenne, Dane, it will be really neat to have you for a good part of the trip!"

Dane patted his head. "Well, I'm going to pray that the Lord will let someone in or beyond Cheyenne choose me, so we can stay together all the way."

In Denver, Tharyn was superbly happy with David and Kitty Tabor. The Rosses and the Tabors allowed Tharyn and Leanne to spend a great deal of time together, which thrilled them no end. Both girls had been legally adopted into their respective families and knew they were loved. They both loved the church and were making new friends there.

Tharyn had come to love John and Breanna Brockman very much already. She stood in awe of the tall, broad-shouldered chief United States marshal, and having told Breanna that she wanted to become a nurse, had found Breanna willing and eager to begin teaching her about nursing and medicine immediately.

Because she was carrying her baby, Breanna worked fewer days at the clinic and the hospital, which gave her time to pick Tharyn up after school on some days and take her to the Brockman place out in the country. Breanna learned early about Dane Weston, his saving Tharyn's life at the risk of his own, his taking her to the alley and giving her a home, of Tharyn's closeness to him, and of his being convicted and put in prison with a life sentence for a crime he did not commit.

Breanna enjoyed Tharyn's enthusiasm about her medical career, and they enjoyed poring over Breanna's nursing manuals together. Each time they were together, they grew to love each other more.

Tharyn, of course, had told her new parents Dane's story, and had them praying — as were the Brockmans — that the Lord would clear Dane of the murder and free him from prison.

On the evening of November 24, Tharyn sat down and wrote a letter to Dane, as she had told him she would. She told him all about her new parents, that they were born-again Christians, and how happy she was with them. She told him about Leanne and how close the two of them were to each other.

She went on to say that her new parents were praying for him, as well as Christian friends and herself. She asked him to write back to her, then informed him that her name was now Tharyn Tabor, and gave him her address. As she closed the letter, she called him her big brother, and signed it: *Love, your little sis.*

On December 5 at the prison in the Hall of Detention and Justice in Manhattan, New York, the mail was delivered as usual. As Superintendent Roger Thaxton's male secretary sorted through the mail, he found an envelope addressed to Dane Weston from a Tharyn Tabor of Denver, Colorado. He shrugged his shoulders. "Well, little lady, it's too late. I have no idea where Weston is by now."

With that, he tossed Tharyn's letter in the wastebasket, unopened.

In the Children's Aid Society auditorium on Wednesday morning, January 3, 1872, Charles Loring Brace stood before the sixty-seven orphans who were going to board the train at Grand Central Station. He made the usual speech about the rules they would follow on the trip, then introduced the adults who would be their chaperones: Mr. Gifford Stanfield and his wife, Laura; Mr. Derek Conlan and his wife, Tabitha.

Brace also introduced Miss Rachel Wolford, who was in her white uniform. He explained that Miss Wolford was a certified medical nurse and would be aboard the train to care for any of them who became ill. Miss Wolford would be riding in the girls' coach.

Brace told them that the train would go through Chicago, Illinois; Des Moines, Iowa; and Omaha, Nebraska. He explained that when the train arrived in Kearney, Nebraska, they would meet prospective foster parents for the first time, and they would be at each depot from then on.

The train would stop next at North

Platte, Nebraska, then at Julesburg, Colorado. The next stop would be Cheyenne, Wyoming. After Cheyenne, there would be stops in western Wyoming, Utah, Nevada, and Sacramento, California, before the final stop in San Francisco.

The children were taken to Grand Central Station in wagons and put on the train.

In the boys' coach, Dane Weston kept Kenny Atwood on the seat with him, and when Kenny needed to be in his wheelchair, it was Dane who took care of it.

# Chapter Twenty-three

The days seemed to pass quickly for the orphans as the train rolled westward toward Illinois. The sponsors and the nurse kept them busy with Bible studies, games, and singing songs. They all loved the song about the fragrant breezes out West, and each time they sang it in the boys' coach, Dane Weston recalled his thoughts about the whispers he hoped to hear in the wind, welcoming him to the wide open spaces.

Dane stayed close to Kenny Atwood, and was always there to help him when needed.

On one occasion, as the train was rolling across western Pennsylvania, the pad of gauze that was tied over the stump where the boy's leg had been removed just below his knee, came loose. The pant leg had been folded upward at the knee on the back of his leg, and fastened with a safety pin.

Dane noticed his little friend carefully tugging at his pant leg in the seat beside him and asked what was wrong. When Kenny told him it felt like the gauze pad had come loose, Dane undid the safety pin, dropped the pant leg, then pushed it up above the knee. He found that the pad had indeed come loose, and quickly tied it again, exactly as the Society's doctor had done.

When the safety pin was once again holding the pant leg in place, Kenny looked up at Dane. "You really did good, Dane. You're gonna be a good doctor someday. Thank you for taking such good care of me."

Dane ruffled Kenny's hair. "Hey, sport, I want to spend my life taking care of people who are sick and disabled. You're just giving me good practice."

On Friday, January 5, the train pulled into Chicago's railroad station. It was extremely cold there, with a strong wind making it worse. The children in the orphan coaches were allowed to get off the train and walk around inside the part of the terminal that was enclosed and heated.

Dane was pushing Kenny through the terminal with Gifford Stanfield, Derek Conlan, and the other boys close by. When it was time to reboard the train, they headed through the double doors that led to the tracks and soon were moving beside their train toward the rear, where the orphan coaches stood ready.

Stanfield, Conlan, and the other boys were ahead of Dane and Kenny.

While pushing the wheelchair, Dane noticed two couples standing beside the second coach, talking. One of the men caught sight of Kenny and lifted a hand, signaling Dane to stop. The man appeared to be in his midforties.

"Hello, boys," he said with a warm smile. "Are you part of the orphan group?"

"Yes," replied Dane.

"I'm Dr. Jacob Logan from Cheyenne, Wyoming. What are your names?"

"I'm Dane Weston, sir. And this is my friend, Kenny Atwood."

Looking at Kenny, the doctor said, "I couldn't help but notice that part of your left leg is gone."

Kenny nodded. "Yes, sir."

"Did this happen recently?"

"It did," spoke up Dane. "As you can

probably tell, it had to be amputated just below the knee."

Logan rubbed his chin. "The orphan trains come through Cheyenne quite often, so I'm well acquainted with them. I know that each one has a nurse aboard. However, if Kenny should need my attention, my wife and I will be traveling here in the second coach behind the coal car."

"We'll sure call on you if we need you, Dr. Logan," said Dane. "Thank you for the offer."

The doctor gestured toward the lovely woman who had been standing nearest him. "I want you boys to meet my wife, Naomi. Honey, this lad in the wheelchair is Kenny Atwood, and his friend is Dane Weston. They're part of the orphan group on this train."

Naomi greeted the boys warmly, then the doctor said, "We've been at Northwestern University School of Medicine here in Chicago for several days. I've been giving a series of lectures to the students. We're heading home now."

Dane nodded. "It just so happens that Kenny already has a family in Denver, Colorado, who are going to take him into their home. They're going to take a train to Cheyenne from Denver and pick him up.

They didn't want to wait for the next orphan train to come to Denver because it won't be there till almost the end of January."

"I see," said Logan. "Well, Kenny, we'll be getting off at the same place then, won't we?"

"We sure will, sir."

Logan said, "Remember my offer, Dane. If Kenny should need me between here and Cheyenne, you tell the conductor or one of the Society sponsors to come and let me know."

"Sure will, Doctor."

All the orphans were on the train by the time Dane rolled the wheelchair up to the boys' coach. Gifford Stanfield was there waiting for them. While Gifford was carrying the wheelchair aboard and Dane was carrying Kenny, Gifford asked, "Who were the couple you were talking to?"

"That was Dr. Jacob Logan and his wife, sir. He has a practice in Cheyenne, Wyoming. He has been at the Northwestern University School of Medicine here in Chicago, lecturing to the students. He offered his services for Kenny if he was needed."

"Well, that was nice of him. I'm always glad to know it when we have a doctor on board. Miss Wolford is an excellent nurse, but sometimes things happen which require the attention of a doctor."

"I hope someday when I'm a doctor, I can give lectures like he does. And maybe I can have a wife as pretty as his!"

Gifford laughed. "Well, I hope both things work that way for you." As he spoke, he placed the wheelchair just inside the door of the boys' coach and sat down next to Derek Conlan, as Dane carried the boy toward their seat.

Kenny said, "Dane, I hope that whoever chooses you lives close to where I'm gonna live. What will I do without you to help me?"

"I don't know if that will happen, Kenny. But I promise you this. The people who are adopting you will love you and give you all the care you will ever need. From what Mr. Brace told me, they are a very special couple and their heart's desire is to help very special children such as yourself. You're going to be very happy with them, even if I'm not around."

"Really?"

"Really."

"Okay, if you say so." Kenny gave his friend a lopsided grin. "But I'd still like to have you around."

When the train had been out of Chicago

about an hour, Dr. Jacob Logan entered the girls' coach and introduced himself to Laura Stanfield, Tabitha Conlan, and Nurse Rachel Wolford. He told Rachel if anything should happen between here and Cheyenne where she needed his help, to please call on him. He and his wife were in coach number two. Rachel told him she was glad he was aboard and would most certainly call on him if he was needed.

Logan then went into the boys' coach to meet the male sponsors. Gifford Stanfield and Derek Conlan both welcomed him, saying they were glad to have him aboard. Gifford then informed him that Dane Weston had told him that he and Kenny Atwood had met the doctor and his wife just before reboarding the train.

Dr. Logan said, "I stopped in the girls' coach and met your wives and Miss Wolford. I wanted to let them know that I'm aboard, and if they should need me, I'm at their service, and I want you to know that too."

"We appreciate that," said Derek.

The doctor ran his gaze through the coach, smiling at all the boys, then set his eyes on Dane and Kenny. "Mind if I talk to my new young friends for a moment?"

"Go right ahead, Doctor," said Gifford.

Dane and Kenny both smiled brightly as Dr. Logan drew up to their seat. Dane had his arm around the little boy.

Dr. Logan said, "Dane, I want to commend you for the way you are taking care of your little friend. Looks to me like he's in good hands."

"Well, sir, it's good practice for me. You see, I'm planning to become a doctor when I grow up."

Logan's brows rose. "Oh, really?"

"Yes, sir. I'm praying that the Lord will give me foster parents who will back me as I finish high school, then go to medical school."

"Well, good for you. How old are you, Dane?"

"Almost sixteen, sir. I've wanted to be a physician and surgeon since I was younger than Kenny here. Let me show you something."

Dane bent down and picked up his medical bag and his medical books from under the seat in front of him. "See? Here are books that I've read, and still read."

Logan took them in hand, looking at one book after the other. "Well, you really are serious about this, aren't you?"

"Yes, sir. I sure am."

"And where did you get that medical bag?"

"From Dr. Lee Harris. I met him when I was living on the streets of Manhattan after my parents and little brother and sister were murdered by a street gang last April. He took care of lots of street children when they needed him. He's retired now and living in Virginia. Because of my interest in becoming a doctor, he gave me his medical bag."

"Well, that's really something, Dane. I'm proud of you for sticking with your dream, even though you've been orphaned. And something else. You said a moment ago that you're *praying* that the Lord will give you the right kind of foster parents."

"Yes, sir. I'm a born-again child of God, and I very much believe in prayer. God really answered prayer for me in a big way a few weeks ago, or I wouldn't be on this train right now."

"I'd like to hear about that some time. How long have you known the Lord?"

"Just a few months. It was Dr. Lee Harris who led me to Jesus."

"Wonderful! Well, I'm a born-again child of God, myself. So is my wife. We'll have to get together and talk some while we're on this trip."

"That'd be fine with me, Dr. Logan. I'd like to tell you about the medical care I gave to my friends in the alley under the direction of Dr. Harris."

"I'd love to hear it."

The next day, Dr. Logan asked permission from Gilbert Stanfield and Derek Conlan to take Dane to his coach so he and his wife could have some time with him. Permission was gladly granted, and during the three hours Dane sat with the Logans, he gave them more details on his family's murder, his life in the alley, and how he was led to the Lord by Dr. Harris in the Harris home. He then told him of his arrest for killing Benny Jackson and the ultimate clearing of his name, and showed them the letter of apology from the judge and the chief of police.

Before Dane returned to the boys' coach he asked if Dr. and Mrs. Logan would pray that the Lord would give him foster parents who would see his heartfelt desire to become a doctor, and would help him get his medical education once he had finished high school. They assured him that they would pray to that end.

The next day snow was falling heavily and was accompanied by a stiff breeze when the train pulled into Kearney, Nebraska, that afternoon. Since the weather was a problem, the orphans were taken inside the terminal building where the prospective foster parents could look them over. As many of the regular passengers looked on — including Dr. Jacob Logan and his wife — six children were chosen.

Kenny was happy that Dane was not one of them.

The next day, the train stopped in North Platte with two feet of snow on the ground, and four children were chosen. Another storm was approaching from the northwest.

When it was time to get back on the train, Dane pushed the wheelchair past a group of regular passengers. He and Kenny heard one of the men telling the other passengers about Indian trouble in western Nebraska, northeast Colorado, and southeast Wyoming. Dr. and Mrs. Logan were in the group.

Dane paused to listen, and at the same moment, Derek Conlan drew up and listened too. The man was telling the others that there was a Cheyenne chief named Black Thunder who was leading the warriors of his village in attacks on wagon trains, stagecoaches, and railroad trains that passed through that part of the country.

Dr. Logan spoke his agreement that Black Thunder and his warriors were especially vicious, adding that they had a burning hatred toward white people and had vowed to kill as many as they could.

The conductor called for everyone to board. As Derek carried the wheelchair into the boys' coach while Dane was carrying Kenny, he told both boys that he and the other Society sponsors had heard much about Black Thunder's attacks on trains, but so far no orphan train had been attacked. He went on to tell them that when Black Thunder and his warriors attack a train, they gallop up beside it while it is moving and fire their rifles through the windows of the coaches and the engine's cab.

"I really doubt they will do that now," said Derek, "with so much snow on the ground and more snow obviously on the way. Trying to gallop in deep snow is too dangerous for both horses and riders."

"I hope they don't," said Kenny. "I don't want no Indians shooting at us!"

The train pulled out of North Platte, heading northwest toward Julesburg, Colorado, which was seventy miles away. Word had spread throughout the train about the Cheyenne threat under the leadership of

Chief Black Thunder, and passengers were discussing it with fear-edged voices. Some of them stopped the conductor and asked him about it. He told them the weather would no doubt keep the Indians from attacking the train. Once they were in Cheyenne and beyond, they would be out of Black Thunder's territory.

Snow began to come down heavily, driven by a fierce north wind. The train stopped at Julesburg, and because of the near-blizzard conditions, few prospective foster parents were on hand.

Two children were chosen, and soon the train pulled out and headed toward Cheyenne, which was some ninety miles away.

After a half hour, the snow quit falling and only the wind was left. Within another hour, the sky was clear and the sun sent its pleasant light down on the snow-laden plains.

When they were within forty miles of Cheyenne, with almost three feet of snow on the ground and drifts piled ten feet high at some spots, the train began to slow down and finally came to a halt. Passengers, including orphans, pressed their faces to the windows of the coaches, wondering why the train had stopped.

Presently, the engineer and fireman entered the first coach and told the passengers the engine was approaching a trestle that spanned a deep gully, and they saw snow piled at least ten feet high on this end of the trestle. There was no way to tell just how far that depth of snow was on the trestle, and the engineer decided it was too dangerous to start across with the snow so deep. They had plenty of shovels in the caboose and would need the male passengers to help them remove the snow.

Every able-bodied man in the coach volunteered. It was the same in the next two coaches, and by the time the engineer and fireman reached the orphan coaches, the conductor had already advised the adults and the children of what had happened.

Conductor, fireman, and engineer went to the caboose and gathered what shovels they could carry and began distributing them in coach number three. They had a few left over, so they carried them into coach number two. Just as Dr. Logan was taking a shovel in hand, a woman in the coach pointed out a window. "Indians!"

Everyone dashed to the right side of the coach and saw a band of Cheyenne warriors slowly riding toward the train through the three-foot depth of snow.

Men dashed to the other coaches to

sound the warning. Some men had guns and were preparing to defend the train against the savages.

In the orphan coaches, frightened children peered over the bottom edge of the windows and looked on wide-eyed as the band of some twenty Cheyenne warriors approached the train. Each warrior was clad in a buffalo-skin coat with fur collar.

Terror was running rampant among the passengers in the other three coaches.

In coach number two, one of the armed passengers looked at the engineer and said, "Shouldn't we open the windows so we don't splatter glass when we start shooting?"

The engineer was about to reply when Dr. Logan spoke up. "Hey! Their leader is holding up his hand in a sign of peace. I can guarantee you, he isn't Black Thunder. I know what he looks like."

"Are you willing to go out there with me and talk to them, Doctor?" asked the engineer.

"Certainly. I really believe these are not hostiles. I know a lot about the Cheyenne. If they meant to kill us, they would be shooting, not making a sign of peace."

The engineer told the fireman to go tell the people in the next coach and the orphan coaches to sit tight. One of the male passengers volunteered to take the same message to those in coach number one. The engineer thanked him. "Let's go, Doctor."

Seconds later, everyone on the train was peering through the windows on the right sides of the coaches — including Dane Weston and Kenny Atwood. Dane's admiration for Dr. Jacob Logan took a big leap when he saw the doctor going out to talk to the Indians with the engineer at his side.

Outside, the engineer stayed close by Dr. Logan as he plodded through the deep snow and halted a few feet from the leader. "Do you speak English?"

Remaining on his pinto's back, the young leader nodded. "I do. My name Iron Hawk. We from nearby village led by Chief War Bonnet. We riding on high spot few minutes ago, see train stopped at bridge. See much snow piled on bridge. Think maybe you need help remove snow."

The engineer released his pent-up breath in a relieved sigh. He said to Dr. Logan, "We have enough shovels in the caboose if they want to help us."

Dr. Logan smiled. "Well, Iron Hawk, we really could use your help. We were afraid when first sighting you that you might be part of Black Thunder's warriors."

Iron Hawk shook his head. "No. We not. We at peace with whites. Do not want bloodshed. We against what Black Thunder and his warriors do to whites."

Dr. Logan smiled again. "I'm glad for that, but you are different than any Cheyenne I have encountered. I am Dr. Jacob Logan. I have a medical office in the town of Cheyenne."

"We have reason we not hostile toward whites, Dr. Logan. Do you know what 'born again' means?"

Logan's heart skipped a beat. "You mean as in the Bible?"

"Yes. Open heart to Jesus Christ and be born again."

"Am I hearing him right, Doctor?" said the engineer. "I used to hear a lot about being born again from my grandmother."

"We'll have to talk about it sometime," said Logan. Then he said to the Indian leader, "I am a born-again child of God myself, Iron Hawk."

Iron Hawk showed his teeth in a broad smile. "Then you my brother."

"Wonderful! Are these other braves with you born again too?"

Every one of them was nodding his head when Iron Hawk said, "Yes. People of our village, including Chief War Bonnet, have all become born-again Christians because of testimony of nurse from Denver name Breanna Brockman. She come to our village many moons ago when most of our village smitten with smallpox. She save many lives. Iron Hawk's squaw, Silver Moon, has become very close to Breanna Brockman. We visit Chief United States Marshal John Brockman and his wife, Breanna Brockman, in Denver quite often."

Logan said, "I have heard of both Chief Brockman and his wife. We welcome you and your braves, Iron Hawk. We have many shovels in the caboose for just such an occasion as this. Please dismount. We will get the shovels and let the passengers know that you are peaceful toward whites, and are going to help us clear the bridge. We have others that I know of who are born-again Christians on the train."

Moments later, the male passengers joined the Indians at the trestle and began shoveling snow. Inside the train, passengers in the coaches talked with relief that these Cheyenne were peaceful toward white people.

Dane Weston sat on his seat, thinking about what Dr. Logan had passed on to them. "God bless Breanna Brockman for the testimony she has for Jesus! When I meet her in heaven someday, I'm going to thank her for saving our lives."

Some two hours later, as the train chugged toward the trestle, Iron Hawk and his braves sat on their pintos and waved back at the people inside the train who were waving to them.

In coach number two, Dr. Logan and Naomi talked in low tones together for about twenty minutes, then the doctor said, "All right, sweetheart, I'll go get Dane so we can talk to him about it."

Less than five minutes had passed when Dr. Logan returned with Dane, who sat down in the empty seat ahead of them. "I'm ready to talk. What's this about?"

The doctor took hold of Naomi's hand, and Dane could tell that whatever was about to be discussed had both people very excited.

Dr. Logan took a deep breath. "Dane, Naomi and I have been talking and praying about something very important these past few days."

"Yes, sir?"

"The Lord has given you a special place in our hearts since we met you in Chicago, and — well, we want to take you into our home in Cheyenne and legally adopt you as our son."

Dane's heart thundered in his chest. His face was a sudden mask of pleasant shock. He said breathlessly, "You mean it? You really mean it?"

Naomi reached toward him and patted his cheek. "We really mean it, sweet boy."

The doctor tweaked Dane's ear. "We sure do." A sly grin was on his lips. "Well? What about it?"

"Yes! Oh yes!"

Other passengers heard Dane's outburst and turned to look at him. When they saw that he was smiling broadly, they went back to what they were doing.

"All right!" said the doctor. "Dane, we will see to it that you finish high school, and then we'll send you to Northwestern University Medical School in Chicago."

Overwhelmed, Dane felt tears fill his eyes. He raised his eyes heavenward as the Logans looked on. "Thank You, dear Lord, for Your wonderful guidance and for answered prayer!"

People were watching again as both the doctor and his wife stood up, bent over, and embraced Dane, telling him how happy they were that God had sent him into their lives.

Before sitting back down, Naomi kissed Dane's cheek. "I love you, son."

He grinned and wiped tears. "I love you too, Mama. And I love you too, Papa."

Dr. Logan chuckled happily. "And I love you, son."

When the train arrived in Cheyenne some three hours late, all the prospective foster parents were there — as were Mike and Julie Ross, who had come to pick up Kenny Atwood.

They all stood in a group while the sponsors came to question them before the children were brought off the train.

Mike Ross stepped up to Gifford and Derek as they drew up to the group. "Gentlemen, I'm Mike Ross and this is my wife, Julie."

Both stopped. "Oh, sure," said Gifford. "We were on the train when you took your first orphan."

"Right. I recognized both of you. It's been a while."

"Yes, it has," said Derek. "Tell you what, folks. I'll take you to the boys' coach and we'll get Kenny off for you right away."

"Sure!" said Julie. "The sooner the better."

When they drew up to the boys' coach

Derek said, "There's a teenage boy who's been taking care of Kenny since we left New York. His name's Dane Weston. I'll get the wheelchair off while Dane carries Kenny. Be right back."

Mike and Julie held hands while waiting. They noticed several boys looking at them through the windows of the coach.

A moment later, they saw a dark-haired boy lift a small boy off the seat, then caught a glimpse of Derek standing in the aisle talking to them.

Mike led Julie by the hand to the front platform of the coach, and at the same time, Dane came out with Kenny in his arms.

Since Derek had already told them the Rosses were waiting outside the coach for Kenny, Dane smiled at them. "There they are, Kenny!"

Kenny's eyes danced with glee as Dane carried him down the metal steps of the platform and the Rosses moved up.

Kenny looked at Mike, then set his eyes on Julie. The very instant Julie's eyes captured those of Kenny Atwood, she lost her heart to him.

"Hello, Kenny," Mike said with a warm smile. "I'm your new papa and this is your new mama."

Derek came down the steps with the wheelchair and set it on the platform.

Kenny reached for both of them, arms wide. "Papa! Mama!" Mike took him from Dane, and both the Rosses embraced the little boy, each kissing a cheek.

Tears misted Julie's eyes and love for Kenny filled her heart. "Welcome, son. We're so glad to have you!"

"We sure are!" said Mike. "We're so happy and blessed to have you as part of our family. Welcome home!"

All trepidation immediately left Kenny. He gave his new parents his lopsided grin. "Thank you. I'm glad to be home."

Dane pushed the wheelchair up close.

Mike saw it. "Well, Mama, we'd better let our boy sit in his wheelchair."

As Mike eased the boy into the wheelchair, Kenny looked up at Dane. "You were right, you know."

Dane smiled. "Right about what?"

"When you said that I would have a special caring family to take care of me. They're wonderful!"

Julie laughed. "We think *you're* wonderful, honey."

Kenny flashed her another lopsided grin. "This is my friend, Dane Weston. He took real good care of me all the way here."

Mike playfully clipped Dane's chin. "Good for you, Dane. Thank you."

"Yes, thank you," said Julie.

A serious look captured Kenny's face. "Dane, I'm gonna miss you." Then he said to his new parents: "Dane is being 'dopted by Dr. and Mrs. Logan. They live here in Cheyenne."

"It's already settled, Dane?" asked Julie.

"Yes, ma'am. We met them just before they got on the train in Chicago. During the rest of the trip, they decided they wanted to adopt me, so Cheyenne will be my new home."

"Papa?" said Kenny.

"Yes, son?"

"How far is it from here to Denver?"

"Almost exactly a hundred miles."

"That isn't real far, is it?"

"Not really. Why?"

" 'Cause I want to see Dane when I can."

"Well, that isn't beyond possibility, son."

"Of course not," said Julie.

"Good! Dane, will you come see me?"

"I can't say how often, little pal, but one way or another, we'll get together once in a while. But in the meantime, I'll write to you."

"Oh, boy!"

Dane turned to Mike. "Mr. Ross, would you have something you could write your address on for me?"

"Sure," said Mike, pulling a sales receipt from a shirt pocket. "I'll put it on here. Julie, you have a pencil in your purse, don't you?"

Julie produced the pencil, Mike wrote the address on the back of the receipt, and handed it to Dane. "There you go, Dane. And if you make it down to Denver, please come see us."

"I sure will."

"Stay in touch, and maybe we can bring Kenny here to see you sometime."

"Sure enough."

Kenny saw Dr. and Mrs. Logan coming toward them as all the other orphans began filing off the train to form their usual line. He raised his arms toward Dane, who bent over and embraced him tightly. "Bye for now, Kenny. I love you, little buddy."

"Bye. I love you too, big buddy."

Derek came out of the boys' coach again and handed Dane his medical bag and small stack of books. "Thought you might need these."

Dane smiled. "Thank you, Mr. Conlan. It's been nice knowing you."

When Derek was hurrying toward the spot where the line was forming, Dane put the medical bag down, laid the books on it, looked at his new parents, and introduced them to Mr. and Mrs. Ross. The adults chatted for a minute or so, then the Rosses excused themselves, saying they had to hurry and catch the next train for Denver.

Dane hugged his little friend one more time, and Kenny was still waving back at him when they passed from view.

Dane picked up his books and medical bag. "Guess we can go now."

Both Logans put their arms around their new son and Jacob said, "All right, Mama, let's take our boy home."

When they stepped outside at the front of the depot, a soft wind was blowing. Dr. Logan motioned to the driver of a hired buggy.

Soon Dane was sitting between his new parents on the buggy seat behind the driver, and as it moved out onto the street, the wind seemed to kiss Dane's face. He thought of the little song the orphans sang on the train — which was first read to him by Mona Baxter so many months ago.

As they moved along Cheyenne's main thoroughfare the soft whispers in the wind were saying in his ears, "Welcome, Dane. Welcome to the West! You will be very happy here!"

# Chapter Twenty-four

*Six years later*

It was the third week of May, 1878. At Mile High Hospital in Denver, Tharyn Myers Tabor — now twenty years of age — walked up to the door of the hospital's chief administrator, Dr. Matthew Carroll, in her white uniform and cap.

The door was standing open, and from behind his desk, Dr. Carroll spotted her, rose to his feet and said, "Come in, Tharyn."

A bit nervous as she approached the desk, the nurse smiled. "Breanna said you wanted to see me, Doctor."

Dr. Carroll nodded with a pleasant look

on his face. "Yes. Please sit down."

When she had eased onto one of the chairs in front of the desk, Carroll sat down, put his elbows on the desktop, and folded his hands. "Tharyn, since you graduated from the Denver School of Nursing and came to work here at the hospital two years ago, you have done a marvelous job for us. You are admired by everyone on the hospital staff."

Tharyn's face tinted slightly. "I'm glad, sir."

"You are aware that my sister-in-law is asking to work even fewer hours than she has been since her second child, Ginny, was born four years ago. That's when she quit working also for the Goodwin Clinic. She wants and needs more time at home with both Ginny and six-year-old Paul."

"Yes, sir. She told me about it just recently."

Tharyn knew that Dr. Carroll's wife, Dottie, was Breanna's sister, and because they all belonged to the same church, Tharyn had gotten to know the Carrolls and the Brockmans quite well. She was very fond of them. Especially Breanna, who had helped her and encouraged her in her pursuit of the nursing profession ever since she came to Denver and was adopted by David and Kitty Tabor.

Dr. Carroll proceeded. "You know Breanna, Tharyn, so you understand that even though she needs to be home with her children more, she still can't quite let go of her nursing career."

Tharyn smiled. "Yes, Doctor. And I can understand that."

"Well, since Breanna is cutting back her working hours even more, I want to give you a promotion which will put you in the spot she has held ever since the hospital opened, except that you will be full-time. Of course, along with the promotion will come a substantial raise in salary."

Overwhelmed by this unexpected turn of events, Tharyn's mind flashed back over the years — back to her childhood home with her mother and father in Manhattan. She thought of the horrible day when the team of startled horses pulling the wagon loaded with building supplies ran them down and took their lives, leaving her an orphan. She knew her parents would be proud of her for becoming a nurse.

She thought of Dane Weston, who had saved her life and helped her to survive as a homeless street urchin. Dane had been so glad when she told him through the prison bars that she was going to pursue a nurse's career.

Her mind then went to the long train ride from New York to Denver six years ago, and her best friend, Leanne, whom she still saw in church every Sunday, and quite often between Sundays. With these thoughts came the sweet memory of the eventful day when David and Kitty Tabor met her at the railroad station and chose her to be their daughter.

She reminisced of her days in nurse's training and how she reveled in every one of them, chomping at the bit to finish so she could put into practice what she had learned. Now this exceptional offer had come to her.

"Oh! Dr. Carroll, I'm sorry. I sort of got caught up in memories. Nothing would make me happier than to accept this position being vacated by Breanna."

Carroll's eyes brightened. "Wonderful! Then the job is yours."

"Thank you, Dr. Carroll. However, filling Breanna's shoes is a formidable undertaking, for sure! She's the best in the business. Why do I have the feeling that she had something to do with recommending me to replace her?"

"Well, she did strongly suggest that I

consider you, but I already had you in mind."

"I figured she had put in a word for me. Doctor, I — I'm humbly grateful that you've chosen me. There are several other nurses you could have chosen."

"I feel confident, Tharyn, that if anyone can fill Breanna's shoes, it is you. Just be yourself, let God guide you, and you will do fine."

"Yes, sir. I will."

"May I ask you a personal question?"

"Why, of course."

"Is there a young man in your life? I haven't seen you with one at church."

"There isn't, sir. I thought maybe things would work out with a Christian young man named Russell Mims, whom I met in New York when both of us lived on the streets. We even came west on the same orphan train in 1871, but after we exchanged a couple of letters, he wrote to tell me that he had fallen in love with a girl in his church in San Francisco and they were planning to get married."

Tharyn's mind went to Dane Weston again and how she had written to him at the prison in Manhattan several times, but never once received a reply. She had decided that the boy she called her big brother had elected not to keep contact with her since it seemed that he was going to spend the rest of his life in prison.

Carroll smiled. "Well, Tharyn, there are some nice young men in our church. Maybe one of these days something will click between you and one of them."

Tharyn bestowed her gentle smile on her boss. "I'm leaving that up to the Lord, Dr. Carroll. I'm sure He has a young man all picked out for me and *me* all picked out for him. When it is time, the Lord will bring the two of us together. In the meantime, you are looking at one happy girl who has realized her dream of becoming a nurse. And now, with this promotion, I'm even happier!"

In that same third week of May, 1878, at Northwestern University's Medical School, Dr. and Mrs. Jacob Logan were sitting in the auditorium on graduation night, proudly watching their adopted son, Dane, on the platform as he received three special honors for his scholastic achievements while studying medicine for the past four years.

As his long-awaited diploma was placed in his hand by the school's president and he was addressed as "Dr. Dane Logan,"

Dane looked down at his beaming parents and saw the tears glistening in their eyes and spilling down their cheeks.

When Dane stood with the graduates who had received their diplomas while the others were moving up one by one to receive theirs, his mind went back in time.

A sharp pang struck his heart as he thought of his biological parents and of his brother and sister who had been taken from him that tragic night on the streets of Manhattan. He also thought of the other orphans in his colony. *I wonder where each one is now. As far as I know, all of those who were old enough at the time got saved. I know my heavenly Father has watched over them, wherever they are.*

He thought of Dr. and Mrs. Lee Harris, who had been so good to him and who had brought him to Christ, and wondered if they were still on earth or had gone on to heaven.

And then almost as though it was happening again, he remembered that horrific day when he was arrested for the murder of Benny Jackson.

He thought back on how the Lord had protected him in the prison, and of the souls God had enabled him to lead to the Saviour. *I'm sure that's why God had me*

*in that prison — much like Paul of old —*
*to bring lost souls to Him.*

Dane rejoiced as he remembered the day he was informed that Benny Jackson's real killer had been caught and confessed his guilt, and he was told he was being released from the Tombs.

He set his gaze on his parents again and remembered the first time he saw them. Little did he know at that moment in the Chicago depot that before the train ride was over, they would tell him they wanted to adopt him.

And now, here he was, graduating from Northwestern with his medical degree, thanks to the Lord and Jacob and Naomi Logan.

His parents caught his eye and smiled at him from where they sat in the second row, directly in front of the platform. The pride they felt was shining in their eyes.

A verse of memorized Scripture pushed its way into his mind. Psalm 139:14. "I will praise thee; for I am fearfully and wonderfully made: marvellous are thy works; and that my soul knoweth right well."

Looking toward heaven, Dane whispered, "Thank You, Lord, for Your goodness to me, and for Your wonderful grace. 'Thanks be unto God for his unspeakable gift.' "

When the ceremonies were over and the graduates came off the platform to be greeted and congratulated by friends and loved ones, Dane's parents embraced him, and his mother kissed his cheek.

He took his parents to some of his friends and fellow graduates, and introduced them. There was much talk, and his friends told him how glad they were for him. They were already aware that Dane was set up at Memorial Hospital in Cheyenne to do his internship, and that after he fulfilled his two years of internship, his father was going to take him in as a partner in his medical practice.

One fellow graduate who was also a Christian, said, "Dane, the Lord has really watched over you. Just think! You will get to be part of your dad's practice! How many young doctors ever get a privilege like that?"

Dane grinned from ear to ear. "Not very many, Charlie. Not very many. The Lord has been so good to me and answered prayer after prayer all these years."

Dane's mind went to Tharyn Myers and he wondered why she never wrote to him after she had been chosen as a foster child — wherever she was.

But Dr. Dane Logan would not let this

dampen his spirits. He had never been happier in his whole life. His dream of becoming a physician and surgeon had been realized. His next big step would be to find the Christian girl God had chosen for him and marry her.

Dane's father laid a hand on his shoulder. "Well, son, let's go to your dormitory room and get you packed. Our train leaves for Cheyenne bright and early in the morning!"